CLOSER

Roderick Gordon & Brian Williams

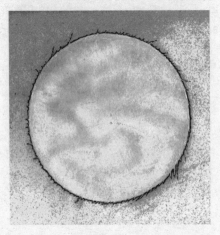

From The Chicken House

I love this underground world! But is the truth getting closer, or further away? Brilliant stuff. And I can't wait for the *Tunnels* movie, can you?

Barry Cunningham
Publisher

CLOSER

Roderick Gordon & Brian Williams

BOOK FOUR
OF
THE TUNNELS SERIES

2 Palmer Street, Frome, Somerset BA11 1DS

Text © Roderick Gordon 2010
www.tunnelsthebook.com
Cover illustration © David Wyatt
Inside illustrations and photographs © Roderick Gordon 2010

First published in Great Britain in 2010
The Chicken House
2 Palmer Street
Frome, Somerset BA11 1DS
United Kingdom
www.doublecluck.com

Cover design by Steve Wells
Designed and typeset by Dorchester Typesetting Group Ltd
Printed and bound by CPI Group (UK) Ltd, Croydon, CR0 4YY

The paper used in this Chicken House book is made from
wood grown in sustainable forests.

3 5 7 9 10 8 6 4

British Library Cataloguing in Publication data available

ISBN 978-1-906427-35-1

We dance around in a ring and suppose,
But the Secret sits in the middle and knows.

The Secret Sits, by Robert Frost

You've never seen me
You've never hoped, too fair to say
You just can't explain yourself
You can't explain yourself
I can't explain this pain ...

I Betray My Friends, by Orchestral Manoeuvres in the Dark

Am Tag aller Summierung, tragen Sie Ihren Körper vorwärts
auf dem Wrack Ihrer Tage. Für Sie seien nicht, was Sie waren,
aber was Sie anstrebten.

German Book of Catastrophes,
Author(s) unknown

PART ONE

Revelations

Chapter One

Waves of flame, red through white. Hair singes, skin contracts. The sound of a rushing, howling gale as all the oxygen is sucked from the place, then the splash of water as Rebecca Two throws herself into the pool, taking her sister with her. Stunned and barely conscious, Rebecca One's body is limp like a rag doll's, but even the chill water fails to shock her to her senses.

They sink below the surface. Beneath the intense heat.

Rebecca Two clasps a hand over her sister's mouth and nose, in an attempt to seal them. Then she forces herself to think. *Sixty seconds at the outside,* she tells herself as her lungs begin to strain. *What now?*

She glances at the raging inferno above, waves of crimson refracted by waves of water. Ignited by Elliott's charges, the bone-dry vegetation is feeding the firestorm, clogging the surface of the pool with thick black ash. And just to make matters worse, Elliott is still up there – *the half-breed bitch!* – watching and waiting and ready to pick them off the moment they show themselves. How does Rebecca Two know this? Because that's precisely what she'd do in the same situation.

No, there's no going back. Not if they want to make it through this.

Fumbling with her shirt pocket, she takes out a spare luminescent orb. More seconds wasted, but she needs to see where she's going.

Must decide soon . . . now . . . while I still can.

For want of any alternative, she decides to push deeper down into the murky half-light, tugging her sister after her. Rebecca Two can see that the girl is bleeding from her stomach wound, the trail of blood like wispy red ribbons swirling behind her.

Fifty seconds.

Light-headedness. The first sign of air deprivation.

Amongst the tumult of bubbles and the rush of water in her ears, Rebecca Two catches her sister's cries. The lack of air has brought the girl around, and her words are panicked and indistinct. She begins to struggle weakly, but Rebecca Two digs her fingers hard into her arm – she seems to understand and goes limp again, allowing herself to be borne down.

Forty seconds.

Fighting the compulsion to open her mouth and breathe, Rebecca Two continues to dive. The halo cast by her luminescent orb reveals a vertical weed-covered surface. A school of tiny fish darts away, their metallic blue scales iridescent in the light of the orb.

Thirty seconds.

Then Rebecca Two spots a shadowy opening. As she kicks out her legs and drives herself and her sister into it, her mind flashes back to a former life: to all those school swimming lessons up in Highfield.

Twenty seconds.

She finds that it's a channel. *Maybe*, she dares to let herself hope. *Maybe*. Her chest is burning – she can't hold on for much longer, but still she swims further into the channel, checking around her as she goes.

Ten seconds.

She's disorientated – no longer sure what's up or what's down. Then she notices the reflection. A few metres away, light from her orb ripples back from a shifting, mirror-like patch. With her remaining strength, she takes them both towards it.

Their heads break the surface of the water, bursting into a pocket of air trapped in the roof of the channel.

Rebecca Two fills her racked lungs, grateful that it's not methane or an accretion of some other harmful gas. Once her coughing and spluttering subsides, she checks her sister. Although the injured girl's head is clear of the water, it lolls forward.

'Come on! Wake up!' Rebecca Two cries, shaking her.

Nothing.

Then she slips her arms around the girl's ribcage and squeezes her hard several times.

Still nothing.

She pinches the girl's nose shut and gives her the kiss of life.

'That's it! Breathe!' Rebecca Two shouts, her voice booming in the enclosed space as her sister makes a small gurgling sound and water spews from her mouth. Then she inhales fully, but it only makes her choke up more water and she starts to thrash around in a blind panic. 'Easy, easy,' Rebecca Two tells her. 'We're okay now.'

After a while, Rebecca One becomes calm and her

breathing regular, if shallow. Clutching her stomach under the water, she's clearly in terrible pain from her wound. Her face is deadly white. 'You're not going to pass out again?' Rebecca Two asks, eying her with concern.

Rebecca One doesn't respond. The two girls look at each other, knowing they are safe – at least for the time being. Knowing they've survived.

'I'm going to check further along,' Rebecca Two says.

Rebecca One stares vacantly back. Then she makes a huge effort to speak, but only gets as far as forming a 'W' with her lips.

'Why?' Rebecca Two articulates the word for her. 'Look above you,' she says, prompting her sister to focus on what she's instinctively sought out as a handhold. Several snake-thick cables are fixed to the roof of the channel – old power lines coiled together with their casings broken away and their cores visible, crusted with slimy brown rust. 'We're in some sort of excavation. There could be another way out.'

Rebecca One nods slightly and closes her eyes, barely cling-ing to consciousness.

Chapter Two

After more than two days on the subterranean river, Chester steered the launch towards the long quayside.

'Use your light! See what's there!' he shouted at Martha over the roar of the outboard motor.

Martha lifted her luminescent orb, directing its beam at the shadowy structures to the rear of the quayside. As he eased off the throttle and the launch coasted along, Chester took in the buildings and dockside crane. This harbour was certainly much more substantial than any of the other, smaller ones along the route, where they'd stopped to refuel and catch an hour or two of rest. Chester's heart thumped with anticipation as he dared to let himself think that they'd finally reached the end of their journey.

The launch bumped against the side, and Chester cut the engine. Martha grabbed hold of one of the bollards, tying the mooring line up to it. Then she shone her light again, and Chester spied a large archway picked out in white paint. He remembered what Will had told him about the bricked-up entrance to the harbour, and how he'd said it was wide enough to drive a lorry through. It had to be the same one.

Although he was sopping wet and very cold, Chester was filled with elation. *I made it! I bloody made it!* he was shouting inwardly, but he didn't utter a word as they hauled themselves from the launch and onto dry land.

I'm back Topsoil again!

But despite the fact that he was almost home, the situation was far from ideal.

He shot a glance at Martha as she lumbered a few clumsy steps along the quayside. The rotund woman, in her many layers of filthy clothing, was making grunting noises like a wild boar about to charge. That was nothing new – her behaviour had always been rather erratic – but now he watched as she jerked her head round to the darkness and cursed as if someone was there. There wasn't.

Chester just wished Will had come back with him. Or one of the others. The way the cards had fallen, Chester had been stranded with this woman. She grunted again, even louder this time, then yawned so widely he caught a flash of her stained teeth. Chester knew she must be exhausted from the journey, and also that the full force of gravity probably wasn't helping. Even he felt it tugging down on his body, so he imagined it must be that much worse for Martha, who hadn't experienced anything like it in years.

And it also struck Chester how strange this moment must be for her. Raised in the Colony, Martha had never been to the surface before, and she was about to see the sun for the very first time. She certainly hadn't led the easiest of lives: she and her husband had been Banished by the Styx to the Deeps five miles below the Colony. Here they'd become part of the roving, lawless brigade of renegades, who were just as likely to kill each other as they were to succumb to the dangers of those darklands. Incredibly, she'd given birth to a son, Nathaniel, whilst in the Deeps, but her husband had later attempted to murder both of them by shoving them over the side of the Pore.

Although they'd survived the fall, Nathaniel had later died of a fever, leaving Martha to fend for herself. For more than two years she'd been totally cut off from any other living soul. Barricading herself in an old shack, she'd survived by trapping and eating the bizarre creatures which were in plentiful supply down there.

When Will, Chester and a badly injured Elliott had arrived on the scene, she had instantly formed attachments to the boys, as if they were substitutes for the beloved son she'd lost. In fact, these attachments had been so strong, she'd been quite prepared for Elliott to die so that the two boys weren't put at risk. She'd kept it from them that there was a supply of modern medicines in a submarine that had been sucked down another of the pores. But after Will had discovered the truth, she redeemed herself by taking him and Chester there, effectively saving Elliott's life. And the boys had forgiven her for her deception.

That had been then.

Right now Chester hadn't the faintest idea what he was going to do next. He had Martha to cope with, on top of the ever-present threat of the Styx, who would be after him wherever he went Topsoil. He had nowhere to go, and no one he could go to for help, except Drake. Drake was his only hope, his only lifeline.

Drake, please, please be here! Chester thought as he scoured the murky darkness of the quay, wishing the man would just appear. Chester wanted to scream out his name, but he didn't, because no doubt Martha would take it badly if she learnt he had tried to contact him. Chester knew how over-protective and possessive she was, and the last thing he needed now was for her to go into one of her protracted sulks. And Chester had no way of telling if Drake had received the message he'd left on the remote server for him. Or even if he was still alive.

Still without speaking, Chester and Martha followed Will's instructions and hauled the launch from the water. Labouring under the pull of gravity, in no time at all both of them were short of breath. However, with much groaning and cursing from Martha, they eventually lugged it over to one of the empty buildings, where they propped it up on its side.

As Chester leant with his hands on his knees to recover, he realised all he wanted to do was to go to London and see his parents again. Whatever the risk. Maybe his mother and father would be able to sort this terrible mess out. Maybe they could just hide him away somewhere. He didn't care – he had to see them and let them know he was all right.

Rebecca Two swam quickly back to her sister. She was relieved to find that she still had her fingers hooked around the electrical cables. The Styx girl had managed to hold herself above the water, but her strength was failing rapidly. Her head was slumped against her raised arm, and her eyes were firmly shut. It took Rebecca Two several seconds to rouse her. It was becoming imperative that she be moved somewhere dry and warm before shock set in.

'Take in as much air as you can. I'm going to get us out of here,' Rebecca Two said. 'There's a place up ahead.'

'What place?' Rebecca One mumbled listlessly.

'I followed some narrow-gauge railway tracks along the bottom of the tunnel,' Rebecca Two replied, flicking her eyes at the water just below their chins. 'I came up in a section that wasn't flooded. It was larger than just another air pock—'

'Let's do it,' Rebecca One cut her short. She took a deep breath and released the overhead cables.

Rebecca Two dragged her sister after her until they reached the place she'd described. As Rebecca One floated on her back, Rebecca Two pulled her along like a lifeguard.

Before long, the water was shallow enough to wade through, although Rebecca Two was forced to support her sister every step of the way. They stumbled and splashed along until they finally came to dry ground.

Rebecca Two noticed the tracks continued in the tunnel up ahead, but much as she wanted to find out where they led, she needed to deal with her sister first. She laid her down, then very gently peeled back her shirt to inspect the wound. There was a small puncture in the side of her midriff, just above her hip. Although the wound didn't appear to be that serious at first glance, an alarming amount of blood was welling out of it and leaving a translucent red film over the girl's wet stomach.

'How's it look?' Rebecca One asked.

'I'm going to roll you over onto your side,' Rebecca Two warned, then carefully lifted her sister to check her back. 'Thought so,' she said under her breath as she found a second wound where the bullet had exited.

'How's it look?' Rebecca One repeated through gritted teeth. 'Just tell me.'

'Could be worse. Bad news is you're losing a lot of blood. The good news is the bullet hit you in the side of your stomach, in the fleshy part—'

'What d'you mean, "fleshy part"? You saying I'm fat?' Rebecca One growled, indignant despite her weakened state.

'You always were the vain one, weren't you? Let me finish,' Rebecca Two said, lowering her sister onto her back again. 'The bullet's passed right through you, so at least I won't have to dig it out. But I've got to stop the bleeding. And you know what that means . . .'

'Yes,' Rebecca One murmured. She suddenly became insanely angry, clenching her slender fingers into fists. 'I can't believe that little runt did this to me. He actually shot me! Will shot me!' she fumed. 'How dare he!'

'Take it easy,' Rebecca Two said, as she took off her own shirt. She gnawed on the hem until she was able tear a strip from it, then tore several more.

Rebecca One was still ranting. 'His biggest mistake was he didn't finish me off. He should've finished the job when he had the chance, because I'm going back for him. And I'm going to make bloody sure he feels pain like this, but a million million times worse.'

'You better believe it,' Rebecca Two agreed, as she knotted two of the strips together, then folded the remaining ones so they formed pads.

'I want to cut and bleed the little pig, but slowly . . . so slowly . . . over days . . . *no* . . . weeks,' Rebecca One seethed in a semi-delirium. '*And* he took the Dominion virus from us. He's got to pay f—'

'We'll get the Dominion back. Now can you just shut up, please. You need to save your strength,' Rebecca Two said. 'I'm going to put patches on your wounds, then bind them really tight.'

Rebecca One tensed as her sister placed the pads of

18

material over both bullet holes. Then, as Rebecca Two passed the strip around her waist and pulled hard, the Styx girl's terrible screams of agony echoed down the darkened tunnel.

'Do hurry it up, love,' Martha pressed Chester as he tried to decide what he wanted to take with him. He didn't reply, but inwardly he was about ready to explode.

Oh, leave me alone, will you?

She really was like some annoying busybody of an aunt, always fussing over him and giving him cow-eyed looks of devotion. And she'd been sweating profusely since they hauled the launch out of the water, and Chester was sure he could smell a sour odour emanating from her.

'No point dilly-dallying round here, dearie,' she said in a sickly voice.

That was it. He couldn't take any more of her hovering behind him. She was always just that little bit too close, and it made him very uncomfortable. He snatched up a few items at random and stuffed them on top of the sleeping bag in his rucksack, which he then did up.

'Ready,' he announced, intentionally swinging the rucksack onto his shoulder so that it forced Martha to take a step back to avoid being bashed by it. Then he marched rapidly down the quay and away from her.

But within seconds she was behind him again, like some stray dog.

'Where is it then?' Martha demanded sharply, as Chester tried to recall Will's directions. He could hear her breathing was becoming louder, as if she was annoyed with him, or the situation she now found herself in.

While her behaviour was a general source of irritation for Chester, every so often another side to her would reveal itself. With very little warning, she would lose her temper and become thoroughly nasty. Chester found that he was really quite frightened on these occasions.

'I don't know,' he answered as civilly as he could manage, 'but if Will said it's here, then it's here somewhere.'

They were checking between the single-storey buildings, crude concrete structures, all of which lacked any glass in their windows. There was nothing to explain what the buildings had been used for – they were unmarked except for numbers stencilled on them in white paint. There was something about the buildings that made Chester shiver. He wondered if at some time in the past soldiers had been billeted in them, living down here in the dark and the isolation. But now the buildings were empty except for rubble and pieces of twisted metal.

As Martha began to breathe even more heavily, the prelude for another grumble, Chester's light fell on the opening he'd been searching for.

'Aha! This is it!' he announced quickly, hoping it would silence the woman. They both regarded the passage that Will had opened up by removing a number of breeze blocks.

'Yes,' Martha said, without emotion.

Chester got the sense she was disappointed. Raising her crossbow as if she expected trouble, she climbed through first. Chester didn't follow right away, shaking his head before going after her. On the other side, he found his feet were swilling through foul-smelling water, the stench becoming even more pronounced as their movement stirred it up.

'Meh!' he scowled, consoling himself that at least he wasn't able to smell Martha any longer. He caught sight of some half-submerged wooden planking, then several rusty oil drums. One of these drums was empty and floating on its side. As the water around it was disturbed, it was knocking against the wall and making a hollow metallic sound, like a bell being rung far out at sea.

But there was another sound – a steady *tap tap*. Chester spotted an empty Diet Coke can bumping against the oil drum. He stared at it, transfixed by its red and silver markings – so clean and clear and modern – and his spirits soared. The Coke can was unmistakably from the surface, and to him it represented something from his own world. Chester wondered if perhaps Will had discarded it here when he and Dr Burrows had come back to this underground harbour, just prior to making their return journey down to the fallout shelter. He liked the idea that it was a connection to his friend.

Martha noticed Chester had stopped to stare at the can, and grunted at him to get a move on. It meant nothing to her. They passed through a doorway and into the room beyond, which was lined with lockers. Exactly where Will had said it would be, they found the ladder in a small adjoining room that would allow them to climb the short distance to the surface. Martha tested a few of the treads set into the concrete wall, then, moving sluggishly, she began up it.

Am I really there? I can't believe it! Chester thought, as Martha led the way to the light. Although he was shielding his eyes, the brilliance of the sky was too much for him, and he tumbled blindly out of the hatch. He dropped on to all fours, crawling behind a clump of brambles where Martha had already installed herself. They both remained hidden there as, little by little, Chester's sight adjusted to the daylight.

Conditions weren't even that bright – it was late on a dreary afternoon, the sky crowded with clouds.

'Here we are then, my dearie,' Martha said conversationally.

If this was Chester's big moment, the moment he returned home from deep within the Earth, after more months than he cared to remember and after everything he'd had to endure, then it was a crashing anticlimax. To say the least.

'The land of evil Topsoilers,' Martha added in a disparaging tone. Chester watched as she wound a grimy scarf around her head, leaving only a slit for her eyes. As she tried to peer at him, Chester realised that it was going to take her a good while to get used to the light.

An idea sprang into his head.

I could ditch her!

Should he run away? While her vision was still impaired, she'd find it difficult to catch up with him. *Now's your chance,* he told himself, as she gave a full-bodied sniff. The snot in her nostrils rattled, and she lifted a section of her scarf and began to squeeze each of them in turn, exactly as if she was attempting to coax the last bit of toothpaste from the tube.

Chester recalled the moment when he, Will and Cal had first arrived at the Miners' Station in the Deeps, and he had done something similarly disgusting. Well, it had disgusted Will, anyway. It made him think again of his friend and all the times they'd had together – good and bad – and Chester realised he couldn't be angry with him any more. He had no idea if Will had survived the leap into the pore called Smoking Jean as he'd followed his father down it. Or indeed if Elliott had survived, as she'd chosen to go the same way.

Chester shuddered.

They'd all gone and perhaps they were dead and that was the last he would ever see of them.

Or perhaps they were continuing the great adventure that he and Will had embarked on that day in the basement of the Burrows' house, when they'd set off down a tunnel. Chester realised that he'd described it in his mind as an *adventure*, and felt a pang that he could be missing out right now.

He thought of the three of them doing extraordinary things . . . Will, Dr Burrows and Elliott . . . Elliott . . . *Elliott* . . . He visualised her with such clarity she could have been standing right in front of him . . . just as she'd been at the moment she'd drunk the fluid from the wolf's eyeball . . . he saw her mischievous, teasing smile as she'd turned to him and suggested he try it too. Chester had nothing but admiration for her – she'd kept them alive with her incredible skills. But, above all else, it was that smile which persisted in his mind's eye, filling him with such a feeling of loss and exclusion.

Chester sighed, reminding himself he had to be better off up here on the surface. He'd had more than enough brushes with death to last anyone for several lifetimes . . . it *had* to be safer up here.

At least that was what he tried to tell himself as Martha managed to coax a grey skein of snot from her nostril, wiping it on her already filthy coat.

Please, Chester thought.

Did it all boil down to this – had he made his choice between Elliott . . . and this revolting old woman?

'Yes, here we are,' he finally answered Martha, looking quickly away from her. 'We're Topsoil, all right.'

The light was failing rapidly as evening set in, making it

easier for Martha to see. From where they were hiding, they could glimpse various buildings, very square and functional in appearance.

So, after several hours and now under cover of darkness, they decided to emerge from behind the brambles. They carefully picked their way between the disused buildings of the former airfield. Will had told Chester it was in Norfolk, a good hundred miles from London.

They crossed what appeared to be the former parade ground, an eerie, echoing place with weeds growing through cracks in the asphalt surface. As he passed behind it, Chester inspected an open-backed lorry which, from its appearance, he guessed must belong to builders or some type of tradesman. He knew he was right about this when he noticed scaffolding around one of the buildings – events had obviously moved on since Will and Dr Burrows had last been here, and construction work was already well underway. Then, in the distance, he spotted a Portakabin. Its windows were illuminated and a Land Rover was parked beside it. Will had warned him about the security guards patrolling the airfield, and this had to be where they were based. Carried by the wind, Chester could hear the sound of their laughter and their raised voices.

'We could ask them for help,' he suggested.

'No,' Martha replied.

He didn't bother to argue with her, but when they were further away from the Portakabin, Martha suddenly seized hold of him.

'We do NOT go to the Heathen for help! Never!' she raved, shaking him. 'Topsoilers are evil!'

'Okay . . . yes . . . yes,' he gasped, completely taken aback by the ferocity of her reaction. Then, just as abruptly, her fury seemed to evaporate and a fawning smile dropped back into place on her chubby face. Chester wasn't sure which he preferred most. But he was going to be a damned sight more careful about what he said after that.

With the full weight of her sister on her back, Rebecca Two was grateful for the low gravity as she marched doggedly up the inclined tunnel. Although the injured girl had lost consciousness again, Rebecca Two was maintaining a one-way conversation with her.

'We'll figure something out – you see. You're going to be just fine,' she said. In truth, she was frantically worried about her sister's condition. The makeshift dressing seemed to have done the trick and slowed the bleeding, but Rebecca One had already lost far too much blood. It didn't look good.

However, Rebecca Two wasn't about to give up hope yet, lugging her human burden for kilometre after kilometre as she trod the dust between the corroded rails of the train track. Although she was passing the mouths of other passages, she kept to the track in the main tunnel, believing that it would eventually take her out of the mine.

And she was encouraged as she came across pieces of old machinery, further evidence of the civilisation that had been responsible for this underground working. She didn't stop to examine the equipment, which appeared to be pumps and generators. Although somewhat dated in their design, she assumed they were variations on Topsoil technology utilised in deep mining. From time to time she also spotted pickaxes, shovels and hard hats discarded along the way.

Her overriding priority was to get back out into the open,

not least because she herself was beginning to feel dizzy from lack of food and water. But she also wanted to replace her sister's temporary dressing with something more effective as soon as she could. Rebecca Two swore as she remembered the battle dressings in the jacket that she'd been forced to leave behind when Will and Elliott had ambushed them.

After several more kilometres with only the steady crunch of her boots to keep her company, she began to become aware of another noise.

'Do you hear that?' she asked, not expecting an answer from her sister. She stopped to listen. Although it was inter-mittent, it seemed to be a distant whining noise. She set off again and, as the railway track gradually took her around a corner, she felt a gust on her face. It was fresh air. Filled with hope, she picked up the pace.

The howling grew louder and the breeze stronger until she spotted a glow coming from up ahead.

'Daylight . . . I think this could be it,' she said. Then, as she followed the tracks up an even steeper section of tunnel, the source of illumination came into view.

The tracks continued, but along one side of the tunnel, where there should have been hewn rock, was a blinding light. As far as she could tell it wasn't artificial. But after so many hours in the darkness with only the green hue cast by her luminescent orb, it was difficult for her to look directly at it.

'I'm going to leave you here for a second,' she said, and carefully put her sister down.

Then, protecting her eyes with her arm, she advanced toward the light. The gusts of wind blew with such intensity that they pushed her back.

She told herself to be patient until her vision could cope

with the glare and, after a while, she was able to remove her arm. Through the jagged opening she could see white sky. Combined with the wind, the overall effect was that she was somewhere very high up, not far under the clouds if there'd been any.

'So . . . all this time . . . have I been climbing up the inside of a *mountain*?' she posed to herself.

Giving a shrug, she went nearer to the opening.

She cried out in wonder.

'You've got to see this! You'll love this!' Rebecca Two shouted to her unconscious sister.

Far down below her was a city with a river cutting through the middle of it. As she traced the route of the river, she saw that it ran into an area of water that stretched as far as the eye could see.

'An ocean?' she asked.

However it was the city that filled her with awe. Not only was it on an immense scale, but the buildings within it also seemed to be correspondingly large. Even at this great distance, it was possible to pick out with the naked eye what appeared to be a huge arch, not dissimilar to the Arc de Triomphe in Paris, with wide avenues radiating all around it. Although this arch was by far the most substantial structure, there were numerous other buildings, all of classical proportion, and all laid out in regular blocks. As Rebecca Two worked her way out from the centre of the city, there were extensive areas of smaller buildings, which she assumed were houses.

And this certainly wasn't some deserted ghost city.

If she looked really hard, what appeared to be vehicles were moving in the avenue and streets, smaller even than fleas at that distance.

She caught the steady beat of an engine and sought out a helicopter hovering over the city – it was unlike any type of helicopter she'd seen Topsoil, with rotors on either side of its fuselage rather than at each end. 'What is *that*?' she said.

She returned her attention to the ocean beyond the city. If she shielded her eyes, where the sun glinted off the surface of the water there seemed to be all manner of boats and ships.

But what made by far the biggest impression on her was the aura of order and power that emanated from this massive metropolis. She nodded approvingly to herself.

'My kinda place,' she said.

Chapter Three

Tired as they were, Chester and Martha travelled through the night, tramping through countless fields, and giving any inhabited buildings or roads a wide berth. Martha was adamant that she lead the way, although Chester knew she couldn't have the faintest idea where she was heading. He didn't either, but he resolved to go along with her for the time being – it wasn't as if he had any sort of alternative plan at that precise moment, not with her around his neck, anyway.

As he walked, Chester thought about Drake, deciding that he should try to leave another message for him. If nothing came of it, he would bite the bullet and ring his parents. But to make either call, Chester needed a phone, and he was prepared to bide his time until he came across one. He knew only too well that Martha would do all she could to stop him speaking to 'evil Topsoilers', so somehow he'd have to give her the slip. That decision sustained him as he went – he just wanted more than anything to be shot of the woman.

As the first signs of light mottled the sky, they stopped in a clearing in the middle of a small wooded area surrounded by fields. The dawn chorus was just beginning, and Chester couldn't believe how noisy and how numerous the birds were. There was chattering and activity everywhere. It was in such contrast to the subterranean environments Chester had grown accustomed to, where if an animal showed itself, it was either trying to eat you, or you might try to eat it.

And he'd certainly never witnessed such a profusion of birds in Highfield. *I'm a city boy,* Chester reflected, as he listened to the cacophony of birdsong, but then reconsidered this. His life in Highfield felt like such a long time ago, and he really didn't know *what* he was any longer.

Bustling around at the edge of the clearing, Martha was lopping off branches, which she was using to build a pair of lean-to shelters either side of a coppiced ash. The shelters were too close to each other for Chester's liking, but he had no say in the matter. Besides, he was utterly exhausted – he yearned to lie down and go to sleep. Both he and Martha had helped themselves to sleeping bags from the quartermaster's stores in the fallout shelter, and he was just pulling his from the bottom of his rucksack when he heard a hiss. 'Was that you?' he asked wearily, without bothering to look up.

'Quiet!' Martha ordered in a low voice.

'What did you say?' Chester replied.

Still on her haunches, she moved crablike towards him. He'd just turned to see what she was talking about when she knocked him to the ground. 'Quiet. Quiet. Quiet,' she was saying repeatedly as she fell on top of him, and tried to cup a hand over his mouth.

Caught in the beam from his luminescent orb, Martha's face was centimetres from his. Chester was treated to a close-up of the curly red whiskers growing on her chin.

'No!' he yelled, as he managed to push her off. Now they

were side by side on the ground, she still refused to let go of him. As he shouted at her, she kept trying to stifle him with her hands.

He was fending her away from his face, and they were both breathing heavily from the exertion as they cursed each other. Chester was surprised at just how strong she was. The struggle devolved into an exchange of slaps as they turned circles on the forest floor, ploughing up twigs and leaf debris in their wake.

'Just stop it!' he cried.

He'd drawn back his arm with his fist clenched, ready to punch her, when his panic cleared for a split second. His father's stern words came back to him.

You never hit a lady.

Chester hesitated.

'Lady?' he muttered, asking himself if Martha qualified for this description.

But he had to do something to stop this ridiculous struggle.

He swung at Martha, connecting with her jaw. The blow jerked her head to one side and she immediately released him. Chester couldn't get to his feet quickly enough, scrambling away from her.

'What the hell's wrong with you?' he yelled from the edge of the clearing, worried she was going to come at him again. He was short of breath and had difficulty getting his words out. 'Have you gone completely mad?'

She began to crawl towards him, but then got up on her knees. She didn't seem angry with him. Instead there was a look of terror in her eyes as she held her jaw, and peered up at the tops of trees around the edge of the clearing.

'Didn't you hear it?' she whispered urgently.

'Hear what?' Chester said, poised to run if she made a move towards him.

'That noise,' she replied.

Chester didn't answer right away. 'All I can hear is birds – millions of bloody birds,' he replied. 'That's all.'

'It was no bird,' she said, almost gabbling she was so frightened. She was still looking upwards, eyeing the grey sky between the trees. 'It was a Bright. I heard the beat of its wings. One of them's trailed us up here. They do that – I told you I had one of them after me in the Deeps. Once they fix on you, they don't give—'

'A Bright? That's totally hat stand!' Chester interrupted. 'You heard some pigeon or sparrow fly over us. There aren't any Brights here, you bloody idiot.'

He'd had enough of this nonsense. The Brights were huge moth-like predators with an unrivalled appetite for meat, particularly human meat. Although they might have been one of the worst threats in the levels deeper down in the Earth where Martha had been living, he just didn't accept that one could have pursued them all the way to the surface. 'You're losing the plot!' he shouted at her.

She was massaging her chin where he'd struck her. 'I was only trying to save you, Chester,' she said meekly. 'I was trying to protect you, so if it swooped, it would take me . . . not you.'

Chester didn't know what to think.

He felt bad about hitting her – if she'd really believed that a Bright had been about to attack, then he understood why she'd acted the way she had, and he should be grateful. *But how could it be a Bright?* Martha was obviously convinced she'd heard one, but then again she didn't look right. Her face was drawn and haunted, and, as Chester watched her, she was acting very strangely. Her eyes were continually darting from side to side, as if she was seeing things up in the trees.

Getting to her feet, she returned to the shelters to finish them, then began to prepare some food. When it was ready, Chester accepted it without a word – he was just too hungry and too tired to argue with her. As they ate in silence, Chester puzzled over the incident. Bright or no Bright, he decided he didn't want to be around her a moment longer than he had to. He had to make a break for it as soon as he could.

Rebecca Two staggered out into the sunlight. She didn't put her sister down right away, taking a moment to evaluate where she was. A narrow, rocky plateau stretched ahead of her, bordered on the left by a series of jagged peaks. The peaks were too steep to consider climbing them, although Rebecca Two's sense of direction told her the city she'd seen must lie on the other side.

Directly in front of her, the railway tracks continued for several hundred metres, then culminated in some sort of a low building. A dirt road appeared to lead beyond it. She wondered if this would prove to be the way down to the city.

As the wind got up and blew her long hair across her face, she turned to her right. 'I climbed a mountain, all right,' she muttered, looking out across the tops of the giant trees, which extended to the far horizon. 'We're on some kind of ridge above the jungle,' she told her unconscious sister as she held her in her arms.

Rebecca Two wasn't terribly surprised. She'd been climbing

continuously since the spectacular view of the metropolis, and even then she'd been at a considerable height.

'Follow the yellow brick road, I suppose,' she sighed, feeling the blistering heat on her skin as she kept to the railway track and walked down the slight incline to the building. The plateau was completely exposed to the sun, and there was absolutely no sign of any vegetation. 'Got to get you into the shade,' she said to her sister.

A weak moan came from Rebecca One.

The building was basic, fabricated from sun-bleached timber and pitted sheet metal. But at least it was a refuge from the heat. Once she'd put her sister down, Rebecca Two began to explore further. There were a number of railway trucks in one corner, and she went to the nearest of these and scooped up a handful of the material that still filled it. 'Mining,' she said, tipping pieces of rock from her palm. It was obvious that these trucks had once been used to bring out the spoils from the workings in the mountain.

She quickly searched the rest of the building, but there was nothing there of use to her. As she approached a door at the rear of the building, she knocked over some empty beer bottles with her foot. 'Just water would do me,' she murmured, as the bottles came to a rest on the concrete floor.

She passed through the door, finding she was out in the open again. There she discovered an old three-ton lorry, the rubber of its tyres perished away into dark piles around its wheel hubs. She touched the emblem on the battered radiator grille of the vehicle – although it had been damaged, there was an enamelled manufacturer's badge that resembled an old-fashioned space rocket, and underneath this was a name.

'BLIT—?' Rebecca Two read out loud, but the rest of the

letters were missing. Next to the lorry were four large fuel tanks – probably each capable of taking several hundred gallons. 'Petrol,' she decided as she sniffed at them.

Her eyes followed the dirt track until it turned a corner a little further ahead. 'So that's our way down,' she said. She'd been right – it was evidently the only means up or down the mountain, either for lorries or on foot.

Over the bluster of the wind, she heard her sister calling. They were both dehydrated and badly in need of water, but more pressing than this, Rebecca One required urgent medical attention. If she didn't receive it, then Rebecca Two was under no illusion; it would be touch and go whether the girl survived this ordeal.

Rebecca Two had just begun to turn back towards her sister when she spotted something from the corner of her eye. She held completely still.

A flare climbed above the trees on a vertical trajectory. It bisected the perfect white of the sky with a thin crimson line, much as a surgeon's scalpel when it makes the first incision into youthful skin.

It wasn't just that this was a sign of life – it wasn't any old flare – its colour was all-important to the Styx girl.

'Yes!' she said, her dry lips beginning to curl into a smile. 'Three . . . two . . .' she counted the seconds expectantly, hardly able to breathe she was so excited.

'ONE!' she yelled.

As the flare continued its trajectory, the line abruptly transformed from red to black. The purest black. Then, in a silent explosion, it blossomed momentarily into a spherical cloud. The cloud quickly dispersed, leaving no trace that it had ever been there.

'The red and black!' she exclaimed, clapping her hands together. 'Bless their SOPs.' She was referring to the Limiters' *Standard Operating Procedures*, for she had just spotted one of their call signs.

She was beaming widely now.

Somewhere out there in the jungle was likely to be at least one of her highly-trained and resourceful soldiers, and he was attempting to communicate with other Styx in the area. Limiters normally operated with zero profile, and would never dream of revealing their presence but in the most exceptional circumstances. And this was certainly an exceptional situation. Rebecca Two had little doubt in her mind that the sign was intended for her and her sister.

Somehow, she had to return the signal. She had to let them know her location. She cast about in desperation until her eyes fell on the fuel tanks. 'That's it,' she said, her determination making her voice husky.

It was worth a try. As she scanned the horizon, there were a couple of white columns of smoke rising above the jungle from the usual fires, but those were in the far distance. If she could light her own fire, it might just be enough to send a countersignal.

But then she realised she had nothing with her, only the clothes on her back. Even if there was enough fuel left in the tanks, how could she ignite it? 'Think, think, think!' she shouted. Glancing up at the sun, she was struck by an idea. 'Glass! The bottles!' she cried.

She tore into the building. 'You need to be somewhere safe,' she told her sister, as she hurriedly carried her back up the railway tracks to the entrance of the mine. She returned to the building alone and snatched up one of the beer bottles she'd knocked over. Taking it outside, she inspected the fuel tanks.

The only means she could find of getting at the fuel inside the tanks was the filling caps on top of each of them. Arming herself with a length of wood, she climbed onto the first tank, which creaked and only just supported her weight. The rust had eaten right through the metal and she was able to see inside it. All the fuel had long since evaporated, and that was no good to her. She swore.

She leapt the metre across to the next tank. It seemed to be in far better condition, resounding solidly as she landed on it. She tried to turn the filling cap, but it wouldn't move.

'Come on!' she shouted. Time was of the essence – she had to signal back as soon as she could. She struck at the cap with the piece of wood to loosen it, and then set about trying to open it again. With much heaving and straining, it finally began to turn. As she took the cap off, there was a hiss due to the higher pressure inside the tank, and the smell of the petrol fumes made her wrinkle up her nose.

'Perfect,' she said, and then thrust the piece of wood inside the tank and pulled it out. The wood was wet with fuel – she was relieved to find the tank was almost full. She repeatedly dunked the wood, allowing the petrol to spill around the opening, then quickly jumped down.

Back on the ground, she smashed the bottle against a rock and chose a piece of it – the concave circle from its base. She cleaned it by rubbing it on her shirt. Then she dropped on to her knees with the length of wood. She angled the circle of glass, focusing the sun's rays directly onto the wood, which was still saturated with petrol.

The sunlight was so powerful that, when concentrated by

the circle of glass, it ignited the petrol within seconds. She jumped to her feet and, making sure her makeshift torch was burning as well as it was going to, readied herself. She couldn't miss the top of the tank. She took aim, then swung the flaming torch at it. Then she wheeled around and ran with all her might.

She'd only managed to go twenty metres when the fuel went up with a loud popping sound. A millisecond later, there was a deafening explosion. The blast ripped off the entire top of the tank, which was propelled high into the sky, and she was thrown to the ground. She felt the searing heat on the back of her neck, but kept crawling. Two other adjoining tanks were set alight, both exploding almost simultaneously and sending a sheet of fire over the lorry and the building.

By the time she reached her sister in the entrance to the mine, the lorry and the building were engulfed in a mass of flames, and smoke was beginning to issue into the sky. A dense *black* smoke, which would set it apart from the jungle fires.

Rebecca One had been roused by the sound of the explosions.

'What's that?' she asked, trying to focus on the blaze.

'Reinforcements,' Rebecca Two replied.

'Huh?' her sister mumbled.

'Our people know we're here, and they've sent us help,' Rebecca Two told her, laughing. 'We've got Limiters!'

The Limiters who had climbed the tall jungle trees to act as spotters saw the smoke emanating from the distant mountain ridge. Like a dark bruise on the sky, it rose on the far horizon, and it was impossible for them to miss it with their high-powered binoculars. The three spotters didn't shout down to their comrades, but zeroed in on the source of the smoke, watching for several seconds to make sure. Although the range was too great to make out who was responsible for the fire, the volume of smoke seemed to be increasing, as if the blaze had only just been started.

The spotters signalled to each other and quickly slid down to the ground, where the rest of their squad were waiting. Not a word was spoken as Stalker attack dogs were untied from the trees at the edge of the clearing, and then the fifty-strong company of Limiters set off across the grasslands in the direction of the mountain.

Up to this point they'd had nothing to go on. They hadn't been able to locate the Rebecca twins' scent trail anywhere in the jungle. But now they'd seen the countersignal, they would keep going until they had reached the mountain and the source of the smoke. And beyond it, if it proved necessary.

Now nothing would deter them.

If anyone had been there to see them, they might have mistaken the men and dogs running at great speed across the grasslands for a thick shadow cast upon the ground.

The shadow of a very angry storm cloud.

Chapter Four

'Where's that damn city got to?' she grumbled.

Knowing she couldn't just hang on until help turned up, Rebecca Two had decided to head down the mountain. She estimated she'd gone at least five kilometres along the dirt track, which lay in the very bottom of a sheer-sided gulley. Its sides had long since obscured her view of the jungle and, more importantly, prevented her from seeing how far she had yet to descend, or how close she was to the city. And the combination of the unrelenting heat and the weight of her sister in her arms was beginning to sap the last of her strength.

She was just thinking how badly they needed water when she saw that the track before her levelled out and, if anything, was beginning to rise.

'Oh, give me a break!' she yelled.

This seemed to strike a chord with Rebecca One, who was drifting in and out of consciousness. 'Will,' she croaked. 'Gonna break his neck. Gonna kill him.'

'That's good – hang on to those positive thoughts,' Rebecca Two encouraged her. While the makeshift dressings had helped to slow the worst of her sister's bleeding, they hadn't stopped it altogether. 'Not far now. You're doing just great,' Rebecca Two lied to her, aware of the sticky dampness permeating her own shirt.

As the track swung through a series of hairpin bends, Rebecca Two was relieved beyond words that it had begun to descend again. Then, after a few minutes, it finally emerged from the gulley, allowing her a full view of the surrounding area.

She came to a sudden halt, blinking sweat from her eyes. 'Look at that!'

She'd made it down from the mountain, but this alone hadn't lifted her spirits.

Before her was a road – a real road. It ran beside an unfeasibly tall wall, on top of which was a tangle of barbed wire. And Rebecca Two had glimpsed something far more significant even than this. On the other side of the wall was a row of huge industrial chimneys, very square and regular. They stretched for some way into the distance. 'You've got to see this,' she urged her sister. 'We're on the home straight!'

Groaning, Rebecca One lifted her head from her sister's chest and tried her hardest to focus. 'Civilisation,' she whispered.

'Yeah. But which civilisation?' Rebecca Two asked, still marvelling at the scale of the chimneys.

'Don't care . . . hurry, please,' her sister begged her. 'Feel awful.'

'Sorry,' Rebecca Two said, as she moved onto the road. It wasn't made of tarmac, which would have become tacky or even melted under the never-ceasing sunlight, but of a light-coloured concrete. With the appearance of smooth chalk, it was perfectly level and precisely built. This may have been some minor service road by the side of an industrial estate, but someone had taken great pride in their work. Someone liked things to be just right.

Rebecca Two began to make out more chimneys in the distance, then, some twenty minutes later, she saw that a second industrial complex was looming. The sun glinted off bulbous stainless-steel structures, between which there were slimmer columns and a lattice of intricate pipe work, also of highly polished stainless steel. Small puffs of steam or white gas issued from multiple valves around the installation, hissing fiercely as if it was complaining to itself about having to work in the oppressive heat.

Now able to move more quickly on the solid surface, Rebecca noticed that the wall ended just before this new complex. As she reached the corner, she found that to her left was a much wider road. It was some kind of a dual carriageway, with palm trees growing in the central reservation.

The air immediately above the chalky surface of the road was so superheated, it had the appearance of shimmering pools of mercury. Rebecca Two strained her eyes but couldn't see any people, only the suggestion of a solitary vehicle parked a little distance down. She hurried towards it, noting the roadway was clean and free from debris, and that the central reservation was well tended. This, and the fact that the industrial plant seemed to be in operation, meant that she had to come across people before long. And people meant help for her sister.

'It's a car,' Rebecca Two said, as she came to it. 'But what type?'

Putting her sister gently down on the pavement, she began to inspect it. 'Looks a bit like a Beetle,' she reflected, although it was bigger and squatter than any Topsoil Volkswagen she'd ever seen, and the tyres far chunkier. It was painted silver and although there was no rust on the bodywork, it didn't appear to be very new. Holding up her hand to shield her brow, she peered through the tinted windows and tried to make out the interior. It was very unsophisticated, with a painted metal dashboard in which the usual dials and speedometer were mounted. She tried the driver's door but it was locked, and as she was passing around the front of the vehicle she stopped by the bonnet. 'It *is* a Volkswagen,' she said, studying the chrome emblem. 'But I've never seen this model before.'

Hearing a rumbling noise, she swung to the stretch of road ahead. Through the heat haze she caught a glimpse of a large vehicle, possibly a lorry, as it changed up a gear and accelerated across the carriageway at a crossroads.

'Come on, girl,' she said, as she picked up her sister, who murmured something unintelligible. Rebecca One's face was as white as a sheet except for the dark smudges below her eyes. 'Not far now. Just hang in there,' Rebecca Two told her, praying that help would be at hand when they reached the end of the road. And soon.

Chester slowly crawled a little way out of his sleeping bag. Although the sun was up, he had no idea what time of day it was. As he peered through the branches of his shelter, he thought he could make out Martha's slumbering form in her sleeping bag. In outline, she resembled a large pile of dirty laundry, which wasn't far from Chester's perception of her. For a few minutes he watched her carefully for any sign of movement.

The loopy cow's still out of it. Time to leg it, he finally told himself, remembering all too clearly how she'd set about him on the pretext that a Bright was about to attack. It really had been the last straw – and he wasn't going to stick around for more bouts of her deranged behaviour.

It's not as if I owe her anything, he decided and, trying his hardest not to make any noise, slid the rest of the way out of his sleeping bag. *She doesn't need me around. She can take care of herself.*

Chester checked Martha once again. His plan was simple. He was going to get himself back to his home in London, even if he had to walk the whole way. And as he didn't have any money, he had no alternative but to walk, unless he could hitch a lift. Or unless he handed himself into the authorities, which he knew he couldn't do because Will had warned him that the Styx had agents everywhere. The future looked rather bleak and uncertain, but anything was better than staying with mad Martha.

His joints felt stiff as he put on his rucksack and set off on all fours over the forest floor, grimacing as the dry leaves rustled under him.

He was some metres away from the shelters when he threw a last glance back at them to make sure she wasn't stirring.

'Sleep well?' Martha said cheerily.

As he wheeled around, his hands slid in the leaves and he nearly fell flat on his face.

She was in the shade of the low-hanging branches of an elder tree. On the ground beside her, feathers were wafting around in the light breeze, and the pink and plucked bodies of three small birds were laid out in a row. Like some obscenely overgrown toddler playing with its ghoulish doll, she was sitting with her legs splayed out in front of her as she worked on a fourth bird. From its size Chester guessed that it was a wood pigeon.

'Er, yes,' he gasped, watching as she tore the last feathers from its limp corpse.

'Easy pickings, these dumb Topsoil beasts,' she said matter-of-factly, putting the pigeon with the others. 'And I found a bumper crop of mushrooms,' she added, indicating the small pile beside the birds.

As she lit a fire, then began to cook the first of the birds over it, Chester could see she was having little trouble adjusting to this new environment. And he wondered if she realised that he'd been about to ditch her.

Rebecca Two continued through the industrial area until she came to an open gateway in yet another wall. It wasn't by any means the end of the dual carriageway she'd been following, which seemed to extend for some considerable distance. And, at the very end of it, Rebecca Two was sure she was again catching glimpses of the massive arch, despite the difficulty of seeing through the glassy and overheated air.

She entered the gateway.

There was a rumble of thunder as the rain started. She could hear it sizzling as it fell on the hot pavements, and her sister began to move her head. 'That's nice,' Rebecca One whispered as it splattered her face. She was repeatedly opening and closing her mouth as if trying to catch the drops.

But Rebecca Two was hardly noticing the rain as it turned into a heavy downpour. She stood in the middle of the gateway, held in thrall by what lay beyond.

Rows of houses.

Cars in the distance.

People.

'Good God,' she exhaled.

It could have been any European city – the architecture wasn't exactly modern, but the terraces of houses and shops either side of her were clean and in good repair. She carried her sister through the open gates, looking around her as she kept to the middle of the wide avenue. She heard strains of an opera playing from somewhere. It sounded thin and over-shrill, as if it was piped music, and Rebecca Two thought she could spot the source – an open window further down the way.

'No lights,' she said to herself, realising that street lamps were redundant in this world of permanent day.

She moved towards the nearest building. From its appear-ance she assumed it was some sort of office, with blinds pulled down inside all its windows. By the door was an engraved copper panel bearing a name and some writing. '*Schmidts*,' she read. '*Zahnärzte. Nach Verabredung.*'

'German . . . a dentist,' Rebecca One mumbled, squinting an eye open. 'To mend my broken teeth.'

Rebecca Two was about to reply when she turned to see someone. A woman had just emerged from the property next to the dentist's with two young boys in tow. She was descend-ing backwards down the small flight of steps to the pavement as she tried to keep the children covered by her umbrella. She was wearing a cream-coloured blouse and a calf-length skirt of grey, and on her head was a hat with a wide brim. She looked as if she had stepped from a newsreel of fifty years ago. *Hardly current fashion*, Rebecca Two noted. The boys were both no more than six or seven years old, and dressed identically in fawn-coloured jackets and short trousers of matching colour.

'Um . . . hello,' Rebecca Two said pleasantly. 'I really need your help.'

The woman wheeled around. There was a moment in which she stared in open-mouthed horror. Then she screamed and dropped her umbrella, which was caught by a sudden gust of wind and whisked off down the street. Seizing hold of the boys' hands, she almost yanked them off their feet as she fled. She was still screaming in alarm, but the boys were trying to look back, their eyes wide with wonder.

'I don't think we're dressed appropriately,' Rebecca Two said, noting that she and her sister must look quite disconcerting. Their faces were filthy and their clothes burnt, torn, and plastered with mud and blood.

'What's going on? Are you getting me some help?' Rebecca One asked weakly, as her sister sat her down on the bottom step in front of the building that the woman had just left.

'Be patient,' Rebecca Two replied. She made sure her sister was propped securely against the railings at the side of the steps, then moved to the kerbside. She glanced down at the gutter, where the rainwater was collecting and coursing into the drains. 'We won't have to wait long for some attention,' she added, pushing her sodden hair from her face.

And sure enough it was less than thirty seconds before sirens began to sound in the metropolis, a low howling that resonated between the buildings. A small crowd of people had collected on a far corner to watch the Rebeccas, but they were making sure they kept their distance.

A vehicle swished down the wet street and skidded to a

halt. It was an army lorry, and as the tailgate crashed open a squad of soldiers disembarked, their rifles at the ready. Rebecca Two estimated there were around twenty of them. Another soldier jumped from the cab of the lorry, approaching with his handgun pointed directly at her.

'*Wer sind Sie?*' the young soldier barked at Rebecca Two.

'He wants to know who we are,' Rebecca One mumbled. 'Sounds nervous.'

'Yes, I know – I speak German just like you,' Rebecca Two replied briskly.

'*Wer sind Sie?*' the soldier demanded again, this time emphasising each word with a motion of his sidearm.

Rebecca turned to face the soldier, who she assumed must be the senior officer. She took in his sand-coloured uniform, which was turning a shade darker as he was drenched by the downpour. '*Meine Schwester braucht einen Arzt!*' she enunciated flawlessly.

'Yes . . . need a doctor,' Rebecca One murmured.

The soldier seemed surprised at Rebecca Two's request, and didn't respond. Instead he issued a command and his squad lined up behind him, their rifles trained on the girls. Then, as he led them, they began to move slowly forward in formation.

There was a blinding flash of lightning, followed by more thunder.

Then, all of a sudden, the soldiers halted.

Rebecca Two realised that she couldn't hear the tinny opera music from down the street any longer.

And if the soldier had seemed anxious before, she could now clearly see the fear etched on his face. On the faces of all the soldiers.

Real, unbridled fear.

'Einen Arzt,' she repeated, wondering what was having such an effect on them. She heard a low growl and spun to the street behind her. As they advanced, it was almost as if the men were materialising from the heavy rain. Their dun-brown camouflage blended perfectly with the deluge of water, making them appear like shifting human shadows.

'Impeccable timing,' Rebecca Two said, as the brigade of Limiters came to a halt at precisely the same moment. There were forty of them positioned across the full width of the street, their rifles aimed at the German soldiers. At regular intervals along their line the dog handlers struggled to keep their stalkers under control. These attack dogs were making unearthly noises; low whining sounds vibrated in their throats, as their lips, drawn back to reveal their ferocious fangs, twitched in anticipation.

But the young soldier and his men weren't looking at the dogs. They were transfixed by the Limiters' deaths-head faces, whose eyes were so black it was if they had been drilled out.

There was no movement from either of the opposing sides. Except for the rain pelting down, it was as if the scene had somehow been frozen.

Rebecca Two strolled into the middle of the road and stopped between the two lines. *'Offizier?'* she asked the German soldier. She was as confident and relaxed as she would have been if she'd been asking a Topsoil policeman for directions.

He tore his gaze from the Limiters and, focusing on the slim girl in her ragged clothes, nodded mutely.

'Ich—' she began.

'I speak English perfectly,' he interrupted with a trace of an accent.

'Good, then I need—' she continued.

'Tell these troops to stand down,' he cut her short.

Rebecca Two didn't answer him, crossing her arms as she stood square on to the officer. 'Not going to happen,' she said firmly. 'You have no idea what you're up against here. These soldiers are Limiters. They'll do whatever I ask of them. And although you might not be able to see them, there's a sniper detachment positioned on the rooftops. If you or your men as much as *think* about firing . . .'

She didn't bother to finish the sentence, aware of the slight tremor in his arm as he kept the pistol pointed at her chest. 'I'm going to bring two men up,' she said. 'One's a medic for my sister. She's dying from a stomach wound. This is not an act of aggression, so tell your squad to hold their fire.'

He hesitated, throwing a glance at Rebecca One, slumped against the railing where her sister had left her. The German officer looked the picture of health, with blond hair and clear blue eyes, and the skin of his face and his forearms below his rolled-up sleeves was tanned. 'Okay,' he agreed, then addressed his men, ordering them to hold their fire.

'Thank you,' Rebecca Two said graciously, and with a few words in the Styx language, she raised her hand.

Two Limiters broke from the line. The first went straight for Rebecca One and lifted her from the steps so he could begin to work on her. The second stopped a few paces beside Rebecca Two, where he waited. He was a general, the oldest and most senior of the Limiters present, with a vivid white S-shaped scar across his cheek and streaks of grey at his temples.

Rebecca didn't look at him as she spoke to the German officer again. 'Tell me – what do you call this city?'

'New Germania,' he answered, sliding his eyes over the Limiter General.

'And what year did you come down here?' she asked.

He frowned before replying. 'The last of us settled here in . . . in . . . *neunzehn* . . . *ähm* . . . *vierzig* . . .' he trailed off as he groped for the right words.

One of the soldiers in his squad helped him out. '1944,' he volunteered.

'Before the end of the war. I guessed as much,' Rebecca Two said. 'We know all about those Third Reich expeditions to the Poles to investigate the Hollow Earth theory. But we didn't know they'd paid off.'

'We are not the Third Reich,' the German officer said categorically, bristling despite the situation he found himself in.

Rebecca Two went on regardless. 'Well, whoever you are, I assume you've got a radio or some means of communication in your lorry. And if you and your men want to get out of this deadlock with your lives, go talk to your commanding officer. Ask him if he has any knowledge of . . .'

Only now did she defer to the Limiter General, who was standing easy with his rifle cradled in his arms. 'Supplement sixty-six of *Unternehmen Seelöwe* – Operation Sea Lion. It was the Nazi blueprint for the invasion of England, drawn up between 1938 and 1940.'

The German officer didn't respond, his gaze lingering on the Limiter General's long rifle with its night scope.

'Does the name Grand Admiral Erich Raeder mean anything to you?' the Limiter General asked him.

'Yes,' the German officer confirmed.

'And is there anyone in this city from his staff, or with access to records of his operations from that time?'

The German officer rubbed the rain from his face, as if to hide the fact that this was all becoming too much to take in.

'Listen carefully to me – this is important,' the Limiter General snapped, talking to the German officer as if he was addressing one of his own subordinates. 'You will consult with your superiors about supplement sixty-six of the invasion plan, in which references to "Mephistopheles" will be prominent.'

'That was us – Mephistopheles was the codename for my people, the Styx,' Rebecca Two put in. 'Styx Chapters in England and Germany were working with you – you see, we were Germany's allies then, and we're your allies now.'

The Limiter General thrust his gloved hand in the direction of the lorry. 'Come on, man, look sharp! Locate someone who has knowledge of Operation Sea Lion and the sixty-six supplement.'

'We need to resolve this situation, before you and your men die needlessly,' Rebecca Two said. She shot a glance at her sister, who was laid out on a blanket the Limiter medic had spread on the wet pavement. He'd already inserted a plasma drip into the injured girl's arm, but Rebecca Two knew she needed to be in a hospital. 'It's vital you make it quick. For my sister's sake.'

The German officer nodded sympathetically. He spoke to his men again before running back towards the lorry.

Rebecca Two smiled. 'It's always good to get together with old friends again, isn't it?' she said to the Limiter General.

Chester hadn't been asleep long when he was woken by violent stomach cramps. At first he just lay there, telling himself they would pass, but they didn't. The pain became progressively worse until he was forced to crawl out from under his shelter and run into the trees where he threw up. And he kept throwing up until there was nothing left in his stomach, but the dreadful retching continued, making his throat raw.

When he finally staggered back to his shelter, ashen-faced and sweating, Martha was waiting for him.

'Tummy troubles? Me too. Do you want something for it?' she said. Without waiting for him to answer she continued, 'I'll brew up some tea – that should help.'

As they sat around the fire, Chester was forcing himself to sip his tepid tea when the cramps flared up again. He rushed off, but this time it was chronic diarrhoea in addition to the vomiting.

Martha was still by the fire when he returned, almost without the energy to walk.

'I feel really grotty,' he said to her.

'Go and get some sleep – you've probably just caught a germule,' she replied. 'Lots of rest and warm fluids will do the trick.'

In the end it took Chester nearly two days to get over it. All thoughts of escaping were abandoned – in the state he was in he wouldn't get very far. As he flitted between feverish sleep and a waking deliriousness, he loathed being completely dependent on Martha, but he had no alternative. When he was finally able to keep solid food down and felt his strength beginning to return, they got ready to resume their aimless trek.

'Martha, we can't just keep trogging around like this. What are we going to do?' Chester said. 'And I've really had enough of eating those bloody birds you're trapping. In fact, I reckon that's what's making me so ill.'

'Beggars can't be choosers,' she retorted. 'And they made me ill too.'

Chester looked at her askance. Contrary to her claims that she'd been similarly afflicted, he had no recollection of her rushing off to the trees, or even once complaining that she'd had stomach pains. But then again, he hadn't been noticing very much lately.

As dusk fell, they went on their way again, but Chester was still weak and unable to walk for a full night. So, after entering another wood some hours before dawn, they set up camp. And he just couldn't believe it when, less than half an hour after they'd eaten, his stomach began to gurgle and the cramps returned. This time it was even worse, and Martha had to help him away from the campfire and to a clump of trees where he had some privacy while he was violently ill yet again.

Over the ensuing days she was even forced to spoon-feed him because his hands were so shaky he couldn't manage it himself. He lost track of time, growing lethargic from his lack of nutrition, until Martha woke him one night. She was in a flap, jabbering something about how they had to move on. He attempted to ask her the reason for this, but she offered none. He wondered perhaps if she'd heard her imaginary Bright again.

However, he found he'd recovered sufficiently to walk for a couple of hours. In the drizzling rain they made their way around the edges of field after field, until they came upon a ramshackle barn. Although there were tiles missing from the roof and the interior was heaped with rusty agricultural equipment, Martha cleared one of the corners for them. At least it meant they were protected from the elements and had an opportunity to dry themselves out.

Aside from his persistent illness, Chester had had enough of being permanently damp – his legs were chafing against his trousers, and the skin between his toes had turned a rather alarming white colour and peeled off in chunks when he picked at it. Both he and Martha were badly in need of a change of clean clothes and a proper wash – Chester realised that in recent days Martha didn't seem to be quite so smelly, probably because his own body odour was masking hers.

As they sat huddled up in their sleeping bags in the corner of the barn, Chester was at the end of his tether.

'I've had all I can take,' he said to her, his eyes vacant as he gripped the sleeping bag around his neck with his filthy hands. 'I've never felt this ill, and I'm terrified it's going to get worse. Martha, I can't take much more.' He stopped to swallow back his tears – he was telling the truth when he said he couldn't continue like this. 'What if something's really wrong with me, and I need a doctor? Would you let me see one? And we're going nowhere, aren't we? We don't have any sort of a plan.' Indeed, Chester harboured a strong suspicion they'd been travelling in circles, but he had no way of proving it.

She was silent for a moment, then nodded. As she peered up at the dilapidated roof, the tic in her eye was going hell for leather. 'Tomorrow,' she said. 'We'll see to it tomorrow.'

Chester had no idea what she meant by this, but after spending the day in the barn, they set off at the start of a mild evening. For once it wasn't raining, which lifted Chester's spirits. He became convinced they must be nearing the coast;

there was a definite tang to the air and the occasional squawking gull wheeled overhead. It reminded him so strongly of his family holidays at the seaside, and this made him think all the more about how he needed to detach himself from Martha and get back to his parents.

The night sky was crystal clear as they walked. Chester was just peering up at the top of a hill, and at the thousands of stars that hung like some glistening and magnificent tapestry above it, when he blundered straight into a hedge. He'd lost sight of Martha until a hand shot out and grabbed his arm, yanking him straight through the hedge.

As he staggered a few steps and regained his balance, the contrast hit him right away. All he'd known for weeks were the endless fields of crops and rough grassland, but now he was standing on a manicured lawn. It felt so perfect under his feet, and the moonlight made it appear a little like a carpet of dark felt. He scanned around, noticing the borders of flowers and cultivated plants. Martha hissed at him to follow her and they crept around the edge of the garden, passing a greenhouse and then a large shed, in front of which were wooden chairs and a table. Martha changed course for the middle of the garden, and Chester found they were between two colonnades of conifers, at the end of which was a small gate. As Chester went through it, stooping to pass under the branches of a Weeping Willow, his eyes fell on the dark outline of a building.

'It's a cottage,' he whispered as he came to a standstill on the other side of the willow. It looked well kept, but showed no signs of being occupied. There weren't any lights on inside, and the curtains were wide open in all the windows. As they walked around the side of the cottage to the front, there was a small portico above the door with a climbing rose growing over it, and a gravel drive with no vehicles parked on it.

Chester didn't try to dissuade Martha when she said she was going to break in. The cottage was isolated and there was no evidence of a burglar alarm of any type on the premises. They returned to the rear of the cottage where Martha smashed a pane in one of the sash windows and, opening the catch, slid it up. As he climbed in after her, Chester felt a little uneasy about what they were doing, but he'd had enough of the outdoor life to last him for a very long time. And whether either of them realised it or not, the effects of normal Earth gravity were still taking their toll on them – particularly on Martha. They needed a place where they could have a proper rest.

Discovering there was a well-stocked larder and fridge in the kitchen, Chester declined Martha's offer to prepare some food for him. Instead he helped himself to a can of baked beans, which he ate cold. Having looked longingly at the made-up beds with their crisp white sheets in the rooms upstairs, he grabbed a quick shower after he'd managed to turn the boiler on.

He couldn't believe how much it hurt as the water washed away the grime of many months. Then, as his skin grew used to being clean again and settled down, he remained under the torrent of water, luxuriating in its warmth. He began to relax, feeling as though not just the dirt was being washed away, but his problems with it. Once he'd dried himself, he raided a wardrobe in one of the bedrooms, helping himself to a pair of jeans and a T-shirt, which weren't a bad fit. He caught himself staring into a drawer in the base of the wardrobe.

'Socks. They're only socks,' he said to himself with a chuckle. However, as he sat on the bed to put a clean pair on, then replaced his boots, he was wriggling his toes with a wide smile on his face. He felt so much better. He felt ready to face anything. 'Yes! Dry socks!' he proclaimed, as he stood up.

He returned downstairs, trying to find Martha to tell her he was intending to take a nap in one of the beds, when he wandered into the sitting room. He stopped abruptly as he noticed a telephone on the side.

This was it. The opportunity he'd been hoping for.

He could call Drake again, or even his mother and father. He thought about his parents. He had to let them know he was alive and well – he hadn't spoken to them for months, not since he and Will had gone into the tunnel beneath the Burrows' house on that fateful night.

With bated breath, Chester picked up the receiver and listened to the dialling tone. He could barely contain his excitement as he began to dial his home number. He couldn't wait to speak to his mother and father. 'Hi Dad, hi Mum,' he rehearsed quietly, praying that they wouldn't be out or, worse than that, hadn't moved house.

No! he reprimanded himself.

Be positive.

He'd only managed to dial a few digits when the phone fell from his hand, and he was knocked out cold by a blow to the back of the head.

Chapter Five

Drake's eyes flicked open, and in an instant he'd rolled off the bed and was on his feet.

He was in a darkened room – it was completely unfamiliar. Much as he was accustomed to waking up somewhere new each morning, he couldn't for the life of him work out how he'd come to be there. The atmosphere in the room was clean and cool, and he picked up the rumble of air conditioning.

As his cranium throbbed with pain, he clutched his hand to his forehead and staggered back towards the bed. It was at this point that he realised that although he was still fully dressed, he wasn't wearing any socks or shoes. And under the soles of his feet there was something that felt like luxuriously thick carpet.

'Jesus – where am I?'

It was a far cry from any of the vacant properties or lock ups he usually slept in.

Groping blindly beside the bed, he collided with a side table and knocked a lamp to the floor. He knelt down to locate the lamp and fumbled for the switch to turn it on. As the light caught his face, he groaned and blinked.

Will and Elliott would have been astonished by his appearance – this wasn't the man they would have recognised. With a week's worth of beard, his face was puffy and there were dark bruises under his tired eyes. And his usually short-trimmed hair had been allowed to grow, and was flattened on one side of his head where he'd slept on it.

With the lamp still in his hand, he found the edge of the bed and slumped onto it. He ran his tongue around the inside of his dry mouth, tasting a sour residue of alcohol.

'Vodka?' he croaked, almost gagging. 'What did I do?' he answered himself with another question, as he tried to piece together the previous evening. He had a vague recollection of walking into a bar, possibly in Soho, with a mission to drink the place dry. That made sense. His head felt fit to explode.

But the pain his hangover was causing him was nothing compared to the emptiness that filled him, the emptiness that was his life.

For the first time in a very long time, he was completely at a loss. He had no direction, no plan he should be working on. Years ago he had been recruited by a clandestine organisation, the purpose of which was to fight a race called the Styx who lurked below London in a subterranean city called the Colony. But the Styx's influence spread much further than the Colony, their evil intent pervading Topsoil society as if the tendrils of a pernicious fungus were growing up through the soil. For centuries the Styx had been plotting to overturn order in the Topsoil world, to weaken it sufficiently so that they could one day take over the reins.

And Drake's last initiative against them had ended in crashing and utter defeat. By pretending that he had the only phial of their lethal Dominion virus, the idea had been to lure one of the most important Styx out into the open and grab him. The handover of the virus was to take place on Highfield Common with Will's mother, Mrs Burrows, fronting it up to give it credibility. But far from being taken in by the scheme, the Styx had been one step ahead, and had incapacitated Drake, his right-hand man, Leatherman, and the rest of his hired guns with some sort of subsonic device.

Drake sincerely doubted if Leatherman or any of the others had made it through – the Styx were brutal and unforgiving when dealing with those that would dare to oppose them. And Mrs Burrows had also been lost in the operation – Drake could only presume that she was dead, too. As far as he knew, he was the only survivor, saved by help from a most unexpected quarter.

'Drink . . . need a drink,' he mumbled, trying to push these thoughts from his mind. He didn't feel he deserved to be alive. The terrible loss of all these people, for which he and he alone felt responsible, was too much for him. Smacking his lips, he put the lamp on the bed and shambled towards the window in the unknown room.

'What the hell?' he exclaimed as he threw open the blinds. He screwed up his eyes, his headache exacerbated by the daylight flooding the room. He was completely flummoxed as he took in the view. From a height of three or four storeys, he was peering straight down on a stretch of the Thames, while in the distance the sun hung brightly over Canary Wharf.

He spun around to inspect the room. It was spacious, the scarlet walls adorned with ornate, gilded frames in which there were old military prints, mostly of soldiers from the Crimean War. And in addition to the double bed there was a desk and a wardrobe, all of a dark wood, which could have been mahogany. It suggested to him a room in a hotel, and an expensive one at that.

'I've died and gone to Hilton,' he muttered to himself, wondering if there was a mini bar tucked away somewhere in the corner of the room. He needed a drink to anaesthetise himself, to stop the perpetual self-recriminations that he'd let so many people down. He glanced at the closed door but didn't make a move towards it, instead turning back to the window and propping his forehead against the cool glass. Sighing heavily, his bloodshot eyes traced the progress of a police launch as it headed upriver, towards where he knew Tower Bridge would be.

There was a knock at the door.

Drake straightened up.

The door opened and his rescuer from Highfield Common entered the room, a glass in his hand. He'd told Drake he was a former Limiter, one of the soldiers from the elite Styx regiment, which had a reputation for unadulterated ruthlessness.

It was strange to see one of these sinew-thin and savage killers completely out of context, and dressed in a grey-check sports jacket, flannel trousers and brown brogues. Despite his condition, Drake managed a smile. 'Ah, my very own personal Styx,' he said, then waved his hand to indicate the room. 'Cool place you've got here.'

The Limiter's voice was nasal, and the way he spoke was rather clipped and old-fashioned. 'Yes, I have several homes around London, but I prefer to spend my days here.'

Drake swivelled towards the window again. 'Bet the others don't have views like this.' He fell silent for a second, then turned back to the Limiter. 'So that's how I got here. You pulled me out of that bar last night. Do you think you're my

Guardian Angel or something?' The Limiter didn't reply as he passed the glass to Drake, who sniffed at it. 'Neat orange juice?' he said, with a fleeting look of disappointment, then took a slug of it. 'But it's good, just the same,' he exhaled as the liquid hit his jaded taste buds.

'It's fresh,' the Limiter said.

Kneading the bridge of his nose, Drake tried to order his thoughts. 'I know you feel you owe me because I looked out for Elliott, but – really – we're quits now. You saved my hide back there on the Common. You've done your bit, and we're all square.'

The Limiter nodded. 'Yes, I'm grateful for the help you gave my daughter. She wouldn't have lasted long on her own. The Deeps are a dangerous place – I know that only too well from my tours down there,' he said, as he sat on the end of the bed. 'But . . .' he tailed off.

'But what?' Drake rumbled, his patience growing thin as his headache continued to thump inside his cranium.

'If you don't pull yourself together, Drake, my people will get to you. They *will* neutralise you,' the Limiter said dispassionately, switching off the lamp that Drake had left on the bed, as if to emphasise the point.

Drake cleared his throat uncomfortably. 'I don't make a habit of getting smashed like that . . . like last night. It was a one-off.'

'Seems as though you've been having quite a few one-offs recently,' the Limiter said under his breath. 'You know that after the barman refused to serve you, you were abusive to him. You were shouting at him, calling him a Styx. Everyone in that place heard you.'

Drake grimaced at this, but then became defensive. 'What

I choose to do with my time is my business. If I want to . . .' he said, then stopped, wondering why he was making the effort to explain himself to this man. 'Anyway, what's it to you? I don't get it.'

'Because of Elliott. You said she's somewhere down in the Pore. I need your help to get her back and make sure she's safe. In return, I'll help you. And right now I think you could do with some help.'

Drake scanned the man's hollow-cheeked face, meeting his piercingly black pupils. It was the face of the enemy against which he'd fought tooth and nail for so many years, and at this very moment he was standing a few metres away from one of them, sipping his freshly-squeezed orange juice. What's more, the man was asking for *his* help. That was one for the books.

Drake laughed drily. 'And why the hell should I trust you? For all I know this is another of your clever-clever Styx double crosses. I'll end up being used, then chewed up once you and your scheming people have got all you want from me.' Drake shook his head. 'Been there, done that.'

'No, I told you, I'm not part of what they're doing any more. I faked my death to extricate myself from it,' the Limiter replied.

'Well, bully for you. May you rest in peace,' Drake replied sarcastically. 'So you went AWOL from a pack of homicidal megalomaniacs. I'm sorry but even if you're telling me the truth, what does that prove? That you're a traitor and not to be trusted?'

'Elliott proves everything,' the Limiter answered, a coldness to his voice which meant Drake had angered him. 'The moment I had a child with a Colonist, I was marked. I was a dead man in the eyes of my people.'

'How so?'

'As far back as the history books go, we have been a race apart. Even before the time of the Roman Empire, we were insinuating ourselves into the ruling classes and influencing events in our favour,' the Limiter said, slipping his hands into his jacket pockets. He may once have been a member of the Styx killer elite, but there was something vaguely professorial about him – he had the air of an academic discussing his latest research.

'You might not be aware of it, but we haven't always hidden ourselves away in places like the Colony. At various times, we've been spread across the continents, never coming together in numbers that would have made us obvious – never in ghettoes – because then we might have been singled out and persecuted. But while we've hidden in plain sight, the law is that we never interbreed – we *never* have children with outsiders. As the Book of Catastrophes decrees, 'Purity is sanctity'.'

'Your point being?' Drake interjected.

'Interbreeding results in what we call Dilution – it means that the edges become blurred. And that's precisely what I did. I broke one of our most sacred laws. If Molly – that's Elliott's mother – and I had been found out, we'd have just as likely been killed by a Colonist lynch mob as by the Styx. And, naturally, the same goes for Elliott too, because she's a half-breed. Molly had to feign illness to cover up her pregnancy, and her family took Elliott in after she was born. But as she grew older, it was becoming too obvious that she was different.'

Drake nodded, and the Limiter went on. 'The reality is, if Elliott hadn't fled to the Deeps, it was only a matter of time before she'd have been spotted for what she was. Styx blood flows in her veins.'

The Limiter's eyes were on the window, watching a jet creep above the city skyline. 'She had to get out. Down the years there've been a number of cases of children between my people and Colonists. They call them *Drain Babies*, you know.'

'Why Drain Babies?' Drake asked. 'I've never heard that one before.'

'Because all too often they're abandoned in the sluice pipes below the South Cavern. So what do you say?' The Limiter was now looking at Drake, waiting for an answer. 'Are we going to cooperate . . . work together?'

'I have to tell you, Mr Limiter, I'm out of all this now,' Drake replied in a strained voice. His shoulders sagged, and all of a sudden he appeared exhausted. 'Everything I've attempted has been shot down in flames by your lot. And you're wasting your breath if you're trying to hook me into one of your elaborate White-Neck games.'

'That all depends on *which* game you're talking about,' the Styx said. 'Ask yourself what you might be able to accomplish with a Limiter beside you. Someone who knows all the Styx's secrets, someone from the inside.'

A small smile played on Drake's face, as if he was taking none of this seriously. 'So you're telling me that you'd join the fight against your own race?' he suggested. 'You'd help me destroy them?'

The Limiter rose from the bed and made a small movement on the thick carpet with his foot. 'No, just because I disagree with the direction they've chosen, it doesn't mean I want my people to come to any harm. I won't countenance lethal action against the Styx. And neither will I allow any Colonists to be harmed in the process – Molly included.'

'No, of course not,' Drake growled under his breath. 'What kind of man do you take me for?'

The Limiter carried on regardless. 'I don't have to tell you that those at the very top of the Styx hierarchy, including the twins you call Rebecca, have brought the agenda forward, but we believe it's a heavy-handed and unnecessary approach.'

'We?' Drake asked.

'I am one of a number of Styx who don't agree with the more extreme initiatives against Topsoilers, such as the release of a biological reagent like the Dominion virus. We believe Topsoilers will bring about their own demise, without any intervention from us. Then the way will be clear for us to step in.'

'So you reckon we're all going to kill ourselves without your help?' Drake said. 'And if you disagree so deeply with the Styx top brass, why don't you just speak out against them?'

The Limiter's expression said it all as he regarded Drake.

'No, bad idea,' Drake muttered.

The Limiter brought his arm up and clenched his fingers into a fist. 'Both of us want to see these initiatives stopped, so strangely enough our objectives are aligned. We could work together to derail them.'

As he mulled over the Limiter's proposal, the light gradually returned to Drake's lacklustre eyes. He ran his hand over his hair, trying to make it lie flat, then looked across at the Limiter and gave him a slow nod. 'Okay,' he decided, 'I'd be lying if I said I wasn't interested. Tell me more.'

'Get yourself cleaned up first. It will be easier if I just show you,' the Limiter said, as he began for the door.

Now alone in the room, Drake went into the adjoining bathroom, where he washed and shaved. He gulped down several glasses of water, catching himself in the mirror as he replaced the tumbler on the basin. He stared at his reflection for several seconds. 'Enough is enough . . . time to get back in the saddle again,' he said, then returned to the bedroom to find his boots. When he was ready, he went through the door and down a short stretch of corridor to a much larger room. From a massive skylight in the centre of the ceiling sunlight filtered down onto what, at first glance, appeared to be a billiard table. But in place of the level surface of green baize Drake would have expected to find there, the entire tabletop was occupied by a scale model of a valley, peppered with armies of small soldiers arranged in intricate formation. The Limiter had been adjusting the position of some of the soldiers at one end, but now stood back from it.

Drake's eyes flicked rapidly around the scene as he surveyed the various armies, their brightly coloured uniforms so vivid against the verdant green of the landscape. 'Yes . . . so we've got the British and the Dutch over there on the Mont St Jean escarpment,' he said, taking sideways steps along the edge of the table, 'and here we come to the Prussians.' He moved further around the table, then stopped. 'And on the slopes here . . . these foot soldiers in the blue coats must be the French forces. So this is the eve of the Battle of Waterloo, in March 1815, isn't it?'

If the Limiter was impressed at how quickly Drake had identified which campaign it was, he didn't show it. 'That's correct,' he merely replied.

Drake was still taking in the scene. 'You really know your stuff, don't you? But why would a Styx have any interest in something that happened up here on the surface almost two hundred years ago?'

'Part of our training at the Citadel was to familiarise ourselves with Topsoil military tactics throughout the centuries,' the Limiter replied. 'And the Battle of Waterloo was always a personal favourite of mine.'

Drake nodded. 'Mine too, because the outcome was dependant on so many moving parts – so many factors had to come together in order that Napoleon, the greatest military mind of his generation, finally met his match. It was as if the hand of fate was finally moving against him.'

'The hand of fate?' the Limiter repeated, then shook his head. 'I take issue with that. Wellington's masterstroke was in gaining the support of the Dutch and Prussian forces when he staged his attack – that was what won the day. Luck – or fate, as you call it – had nothing to do with it. Wellington was a military genius – he completely outmanoeuvred Napoleon.'

Drake stared back at him. 'Then was the Seventh Coalition's victory down to Wellington's skills as a general . . . or as a politician?'

'What's the difference?' the Limiter answered.

Drake frowned as something in the battle scene didn't make sense to him. 'I can see Napoleon over there,' he said, pointing at the figure flanked by his generals. 'But where's Wellington?' Stepping around the table, Drake began to examine the British Forces more closely. 'Can't see him anywhere.'

'That's because I'm taking another look at him,' the Limiter said, going over to a rolltop desk by the wall where he picked up a single figure. 'I'm not completely happy with him yet.'

'May I?' Drake asked, holding out his hand.

'Certainly.' The Limiter passed the figure to him.

'The Iron Duke,' Drake said as he studied the figure, which appeared to be writing on a map. He lifted the figure up to the light, taking in its blue long coat and the red sash tied around its waist. 'You say that you're not happy with him . . . but this detail is quite breathtaking,' he complimented the Limiter, then glanced at the desk where the figure had been. On it were many small pots of paint, brushes in a mug, a large magnifying glass and a number of unfinished soldiers. 'Don't tell me you paint the figures yourself? You've done *all* the figures in the scene?'

'It passes the time,' the Limiter replied.

'No, it's much more than that . . . it's a labour of love,' Drake declared. 'Do you mind if I . . .?' he asked, leaning over the table where the British army was positioned.

'Be my guest,' the Limiter answered.

'That's better. He's where he should be, now,' Drake said, as he carefully placed Wellington in front of a small campaign tent with the other British generals.

Drake then gazed around the rest of the room. There were shelves of books and a row of glass-fronted display cabinets in which there were English army helmets from Waterloo, the Crimean War and other nineteenth-century battles, with polished brass badges and plume-like hackles. As Drake looked away from these, he caught the Styx scrutinising him, and met his impenetrable eyes.

'Something on your mind?' the Styx divined.

There were a thousand questions Drake wanted to ask this man, but he resolved not to bombard him with them all at once. 'Yes, there is something. You know my name, but what do I call you? I'm aware the Styx don't have names . . . well, not ones that any Topsoiler can pronounce,' Drake said a little awkwardly.

The Limiter considered this for a moment. 'The beneficiary on the lease for this warehouse is Edward James Green,' he answered. 'I have other identities such as—'

'No, that'll do,' Drake cut him short. 'Edward . . . James . . . Green.' He rubbed his forehead as he thought. 'Then I shall call you . . . Eddie . . . Eddie the Styx.' The notion of addressing one of these savage soldiers – albeit a retired one – by such an everyday Topsoiler moniker was so absurd that Drake couldn't suppress a chuckle.

'As you please,' the newly-christened Eddie replied, nonplussed that Drake seemed to be so amused.

They moved to the far end of the room, to a bank of CCTV monitors, which displayed scenes of the street outside and several other views that Drake didn't recognise immediately – they looked as though they were of the insides of brick tunnels. Eddie noticed Drake's interest. 'The sewers under this building. It's a precautionary measure – one can't be too careful,' he said.

'No, one can't, not with the Styx,' Drake agreed.

At the end of a small hallway was a heavy steel door. They passed through it and were descending a wrought-iron staircase when Drake drew to a halt. 'What *is* this place?' he asked. The contrast with the lavish apartment he'd just left couldn't have been more marked.

From his elevated viewpoint, he was looking out over what appeared to be a warehouse, an area approaching a hundred metres from end to end, and half that in width. The tall windows were filthy and barely any light made it through, but what little there was revealed the floor space was dotted about with chunks of machinery. As Drake descended the remaining distance and could see the machines closer at hand, their condition suggested that they'd been unused for decades.

'This was a Victorian bottling factory, a family-owned business,' Eddie said. 'When their competitors stole their market share, they just shut up shop. They simply mothballed all the plant, and sealed the factory doors. They left it all to rot.'

'And you took the lease on, then built living quarters in the roof space,' Drake said, glancing at the floor above. As he brushed a rubber conveyor belt with his fingertips, pieces of it crumbled away at his touch.

Eddie led them down an aisle, either side of which were machines draped with rotting tarpaulins.

'What's that over there?' Drake asked, straining to see what lay in the shadows by the far wall. 'Motorbikes?'

'Yes – I use them to get around,' Eddie said. 'But what I want to show you is this way.'

Near the corner of the warehouse, he stopped before an old lathe covered in a powdery orange rust. 'First step in the de-arming,' he told Drake as he pressed a grimy red button on its control panel.

Then he continued behind the lathe to a small structure in the very corner of the building. It was built of scaffolding and covered with thick polythene sheets. He lifted aside the sheets to reveal a metal door in the floor, set into a concrete surround.

It was obvious to Drake that this was a recent addition to the building, as the surface of the door was without any sign of corrosion, and the concrete around it was not yet stained by the damp. Eddie bent down and flicked open a cover on a keypad at the side of the door. He began to enter a sequence, pausing to speak when he was halfway through. 'If you don't follow this exactly, the whole place is rigged to blow.'

'A man after my own heart,' Drake said, as Eddie entered the final digits and the thick door clunked open a fraction. Then he pulled it fully up, and Drake followed closely behind him as they descended a short flight of steps.

'I think you're going to like this,' the thin man said.

Chapter Six

'I'm telling you, it *was* an aircraft,' Dr Burrows insisted.

'Well, I didn't hear anything,' Will replied, edging further out from the cover of the huge trees to peer at the bright white sky above. 'Did you?' he asked Elliott, who had joined him in scrutinising the stretch of sky. She shook her head.

'Well, it's no use looking for it now,' Dr Burrows grumbled. 'It flew off in an easterly direction.'

Will turned to his father. 'And you think it was a *what*?'

'I told you – a Stuka – a German bomber from the Second World War.'

Will frowned. 'Are you sure?'

'Of course I'm sure,' Dr Burrows retorted.

'Dad, maybe you nodded off on the side of the pyramid and dreamt the whole thing? I mean, you've been out in the sun for quite a—'

'Don't patronise me, Will!' Dr Burrows barked. 'I'm not tired, and nor am I suffering from heat stroke. I know my limits, and I know what I saw. I saw a Stuka, clear as day, flying about half a mile away.'

Will shrugged. Where they were, in this 'world within a world' in the middle of the planet, complete with its own ever-burning sun, there wasn't much that could surprise him.

Aside from the fact that the lower gravity meant that he, Elliott and Dr Burrows had almost superhuman powers, and were able to jump unfeasible distances and lift phenomenal weights, he was quite ready to believe just about anything. Much of the land of this apparently virgin world was either covered in Amazonian rainforest, with trees as high as skyscrapers, or grasslands on which free-ranging herds of animals roamed. Will had spotted quaggas, rather quaint half-horse, half-zebra creatures extinct for over a hundred years back in the outer world, and only a few days ago he and his father had stumbled upon a herd of the largest cattle he'd ever seen. 'Aurochs!' Dr Burrows had proclaimed, then proceeded to tell him how the last of these magnificent creatures had died out in Poland in the thirteenth century. But, even more amazing than this, there were also sabre-tooth tigers, if Elliott's sighting was to be believed.

However, these prehistoric animals were all a long way from what Dr Burrows was now adamant he'd seen. Will drew in a breath and scratched his head. 'But, Dad, a *Stuka*? Are you sure? What did it look like? Did it have markings on it or any sort of camouflage?' he asked.

'It was too far away to make out that sort of detail,' Dr Burrows replied. 'One can only wonder how it got into this world, and what it's still doing here. And you have to consider the full implications – this aircraft is just the tip of a very curious iceberg.'

'Iceberg?' Elliott asked. Her whole life had been spent underground and the word had no meaning to her.

'Yes, iceberg,' Dr Burrows repeated, not stopping to explain it to her. 'There must be a strip for the plane to take off and to land, fuel to power it, and engineers to service it and keep it airworthy. That's a whole bunch of people in addition to the pilot.'

'Engineers?' Will mumbled.

'Of course, Will. The Stuka is a type of aircraft that's over sixty years old! Any aircraft needs regular maintenance, particularly one of that age.'

'So it's from the Second World War,' Will said, a little dazed as he attempted to deal with what he was hearing. 'From the German army.'

'Yes, the Luftwaffe used them as short-range bombers, and . . .' Dr Burrows said, but didn't finish the sentence. His face was suddenly clouded as different explanations began to occur to him.

'Doesn't sound too good,' Will said, shivering despite the tropical warmth of their surroundings.

'No, it doesn't,' Dr Burrows mumbled.

'So what do we do?' Will asked. 'Do we move on somewhere else? Get away from here?'

Elliott cleared her throat and both Will and Dr Burrows looked at her. 'Why would we do that?' she said. 'I'm familiar with this part of the jungle now, and besides, our shelter is here.' She glanced over her shoulder at the structure she'd built in the lower branches of one of the giant trees.

Will opened his mouth to disagree, but she continued. 'We already know we might not be the only people here. What about the three skulls we found on stakes near the pyramid? They were old, but not that old. And how about that shed we blew up, Will, when we dealt with the Rebecca twins and the

76

Limiter? Somebody made that.'

Will nodded slowly, recalling the shed fabricated from corrugated metal, nothing of which remained after Elliott's explosions and the ensuing fire devastated the area.

Elliott gave Will and then Dr Burrows measured looks. 'If there *are* other people down here, chances are it's only a matter of time before we bump into them.'

'Yes,' Dr Burrows conceded.

'And what's the alternative?' Elliott posed. 'Bury ourselves deeper in the jungle?'

'No, there's too much left to do here,' Dr Burrows said firmly, turning towards the pyramid. 'I've barely even scratched the surface.'

Elliott wasn't finished. 'Or do we travel back through the crystal belt again, then try to climb up Smoking Jean to the Deeps so we can get to your outer world? What are the chances of us making it all the way Topsoil? And what would be waiting for us there even if we managed it?'

'Styx,' Will whispered.

Dr Burrows folded his arms and raised his chin aggressively. Nobody needed to ask him what he thought – he wasn't about to leave.

'So we stay put,' Elliott resolved, lifting her eyebrows in a what's-all-the-fuss-then gesture. 'But we have to take precautions: we don't go crashing into any unexplored jungle, and we have to keep our guard up. We might even have to start taking turns to do sentry duty if we pick up signs that someone else is close, and we should also be careful about lighting any fires.' She frowned as if something had occurred to her. 'In case the worst comes to the worst and we're forced to hide ourselves away, maybe I could find us a safe place somewhere else, and stockpile some food th—'

'That's an excellent idea,' Dr Burrows broke in. Will knew from the tone of his voice that his father was all too ready to let Elliott do whatever she wanted, as long as it left him free to carry on with his work.

Bartleby appeared, walking stiffly as if he'd just woken up. Will noticed one of his ears was turned inside out and he had leaves stuck to his bald skin – he'd clearly found himself a comfortable spot to nap on the jungle floor and their raised voices must have roused him. He came to a stop next to Elliott, shook his head to straighten his ear, then sniffed the air twice, as if trying to divine why the humans were sounding so serious. Because of the huge size of the cat, Elliott didn't need to bend to reach his hairless pate, which she began to rub absently. 'And I'll keep patrolling the surrounding areas with Bartleby. That way, if any hostiles come near we'll have advance warning.'

'Hostiles,' Will repeated quietly. 'I suppose that's right. I mean, if we're really careful, how can they possibly find us?'

***

As Eddie closed the door behind them, Drake had gone on ahead. At the bottom of the steps was a large basement, which appeared to run the full length and width of the factory above. And all around him in the walls were vaulted arches built of dirty yellow brick. He squinted in an effort to see the far end of the basement, where there was an illuminated area. As he and Eddie made their way towards it, he could make out a number of lockers and benches. But before they reached it, Drake's eyes had settled on something else.

In one of the alcoves at the side of the basement stood a

table. Stars, emitting a dim green light, were mounted on brass columns at each of its four corners. The light was similar to that of the luminescent orbs found everywhere in the Colony, but far more refined. Drake had seen these stars before; they were used by the Styx in their churches and shrines. Without reference to Eddie, Drake stepped towards the table, intrigued to see what lay on its surface.

The title of the leather-bound volume was picked out in gold letters. Drake didn't need to read this to tell what it was. He already knew too well. 'The Book of Catastrophes,' he muttered under his breath, shaking his head with contempt.

Eddie was silent.

To Drake it symbolised all that was rotten about the Styx and their demagogic regime. For this book spelt out a doctrine that had committed the Colonists to centuries of what amounted to incarceration and a life of servitude in their underground city, with the promise that one day in the future the surface would be theirs again. The huge majority of these repressed people followed the teachings of the book without question, believing unreservedly that the Styx were their spiritual guardians. The reality was that the religious dogma so closely adhered to by the Colonists was simply a means to keep them in check. A mechanism to ensure their total and unquestioning obedience.

When Drake finally spoke, it was with such vehemence that it was difficult to tell whether he was actually asking a question. 'You've rejected the ways of the Styx, but you still keep this around? This chalice of poison.'

'I keep it because it was given to me by the person you Topsoilers would call my father. He was a Limiter, like me, but as is the way with our society, I hardly knew him. He spent his whole life enforcing the book's laws.'

'The book's *lies*,' Drake spat.

'That depends on your interpretation of the Book,' Eddie countered. 'If you believe that Topsoilers will one day bring about their own demise, and that we and the Colonists will be there to pick up the pieces and repopulate the Earth, then we will be the saviours of this planet, and of mankind.'

'The Styx . . . saviours?' Drake said, shaking his head.

Eddie sighed. 'I didn't bring you here for a debate over my convictions. Before you judge me, why don't you take a look at what I'm offering you?'

Drake followed him to the far end of the cellar. The first thing he laid eyes on was a row of uniforms hanging from pegs. He recognised the distinctive grey and green combats which soldiers from the Styx Division wore, and next to them a couple of the Limiters' brown-striped coats. 'Rogues' gallery,' Drake commented, then he spotted gas masks and even a whole Coprolite dust suit. 'What's that doing here? A souvenir?' he asked, but his attention had already been drawn by something else on one of the benches.

'A Dark Light!' Drake exclaimed, stepping over to it. It resembled an archaic desk lamp, with a dark purple bulb in a shade on the end of a flexible stalk. As he touched the small box with dials connected to the base of the lamp, he nodded to himself. The Styx used these Dark Lights to interrogate and brainwash their captives, and Drake was filled with excitement at the prospect of opening one of them up to see how it worked.

Then, on the floor beside the bench, he noticed a rectangular object the size of a washing machine, but on four wheels. 'Is this . . .?' he began to ask, guessing it was a larger version of the subsonic device the Styx had used on him and his men on Highfield Common.

'An early prototype,' Eddie replied. 'As you saw for yourself, it's less compact than the current model.'

Drake squatted down beside it. The one on the Common had initially been disguised by panels of dun-coloured fabric and, in any case, he'd been too far away from it to make out any detail. The example before him had no such cover, and shiny silver concave areas were visible in its otherwise dull faces. 'So it's some sort of high-power sound generator?' he guessed.

Eddie nodded.

'And it emits very low frequencies tuned to disrupt brain patterns?' Drake ventured.

'Put very simply, yes,' Eddie confirmed. 'It's an offshoot of the Dark Light technology, utilising only the aural element. It produces a basket of oscillating frequencies, tuned to render most living creatures insensible.'

'I'd really like to strip some of this equipment apart . . . and find out exactly what makes it tick,' Drake said, glancing up at the Dark Light.

'It's all yours,' Eddie replied.

'I'll need to fetch some of my test gear . . .' Drake tailed off as something else caught his eye. He rose to his feet and approached a rack on the wall. He was humming in appreciation as he took in the extensive range of modern Topsoil weaponry on it. Then his gaze alighted on something at the very end of the rack. 'Hey, that's a bit out of place here. A Styx rifle with one of my scopes!' he said, going to the long rifle, which had a bulbous looking scope of burnished brass mounted on it. 'You know your people abducted me to—'

'To work on our night sights,' Eddie finished for him.

'Yes. I coupled a luminescent orb to some intensifying electronics. It wasn't exactly rocket science,' Drake said, as he ran his fingers down the length of the scope. 'You know if I patented the design of the luminescent orb up here on the surface, either as an energy or a light source, I'd make a bloody fortune.'

'And you'd be dead the moment you set foot outside the patent office,' Eddie said flatly. 'But that's your expertise, isn't it? Electronics?'

'Yes, that was the area I specialised in – mainly optoelectronics – although it feels like it was a different lifetime now,' Drake replied distantly. 'A million years ago . . .'

Eddie's face was expressionless, but he inclined his head slightly, which Drake took for bemusement.

'That's what we wanted from you – your expertise,' Eddie said. 'But *you* also wanted to be abducted, didn't you?'

'That was the plan, yes. So that while I was held in the Colony, I could gather intelligence on how the Styx operated. You see, that was the problem – it's near impossible to infiltrate the Colony because it's a closed society, so any outsider stands out like a sore thumb. But while I was underground your bunch decimated my network, and I ended up in the Deeps,' Drake replied, then took a breath.

'So, enough about me. Eddie, tell me, how did all this kit come to be here?' Drake asked, not wanting to say any more. He had no idea yet if he could really trust this man, and didn't want to be drawn on how his network had functioned in the past. Everything the former Limiter was offering him seemed to be a little too good to be true, and Drake wasn't about to throw caution to the wind.

'They don't know any of this exists. After Topsoil ops, when I had the opportunity I didn't destroy it as I was meant to. Instead I salted it away here,' Eddie answered.

'For a rainy day,' Drake chuckled, as he scanned the impressive array of equipment. There was Styx technology he'd never laid eyes on before, and he couldn't wait to start a thorough investigation of it. Moving over to a nearby bench, he began to leaf through the plans spread open on its surface. He took an involuntary breath as he realised the subject of the top one. '*A schematic of the air circulation system in the South Cavern*,' he read, lifting a corner to see what lay beneath the plan. 'And here's a layout of the Laboratories, floor by floor,' he whispered, trying not to show his excitement. Frowning, he looked across at the Limiter. 'One thing – how do you pay for this place? The warehouse can't have come cheap, and you say you've got other properties?'

Eddie's heels clicked on the stone floor as he went straight to a tall cabinet and gently slid out the top drawer. Its contents were covered by a square of velvet, which he lifted aside.

As Drake moved closer he was greeted by the sight of hundreds of small, glittering stones.

'Diamonds,' he observed.

'A perk of my tours in the Deeps,' Eddie informed him.

'But these sparklies are a long way from the rough specimens you find down there,' Drake said.

'I have a man in Hatton Garden who cuts and polishes them for me, then sells them when I require funds – no questions asked. Help yourself if you want some. I have more than I'll ever need.' Eddie covered the gemstones with the velvet, but left the drawer open. 'I'm going to check the screens upstairs, but you can stay here, if you like.'

'You're prepared to do that?' Drake asked. 'To leave me by myself down here?'

Eddie didn't reply as he fished in a pocket and dropped a couple of keys on the bench. 'These are for the warehouse and the flat.' Then he took out a pen. 'You'll also need the code to let yourself out of here and back upstairs.' He began to write a sequence of numbers on the corner of the plan that had been of so much interest to Drake. 'But take care – if you get it wrong, the system will detonate and—'

'Don't bother. I memorised the sequence as you were inputting it,' Drake told him.

Eddie began to walk away. 'Thought as much,' he said, without turning his head.

Chapter Seven

On the vertical cliff face, Will was hauling himself up the vines behind Elliott. They'd already climbed a good distance and although their hands occasionally slipped as the leaves came away, they weren't overly concerned. Life in the lower-gravity environment had become second nature to them, and they both knew if they were to fall it wouldn't be as disastrous as it would have been on the surface.

'Here we are,' Elliott announced, then seemed to disappear into the vines themselves. Will went in after her, pushing through the thick wooded stems.

He peered around the space he found himself in, some ten metres in width and several times that in length. A green-tinged light filtered through the vines over the entrance, and the air felt cool. 'How on earth did you find this? It's a cave!' he exclaimed.

'There you go again – stating the obvious,' she said, with mock weariness.

Will sighed. 'With all the time you're spending round my dad, you're beginning to sound like him.'

She flashed him a smile and he smiled back, then he went

over to inspect a pile of fruit that he'd noticed at the rear of the cave. Elliott had obviously begun to stockpile food in case of an emergency. 'You've been busy,' he said. 'And you've laid in some meat, too.' He was regarding the hock she'd suspended from the roof.

'Yes, and I'm hoping the ants won't find it up there,' she said.

'Fat chance of that – they get everywhere,' Will remarked. His father called them Seafu or Safari ants, and they were a constant nuisance. Once they'd discovered where food was stored, they would form red convoys several centimetres thick, which were quite capable of stripping most of the flesh from the carcass of a young gazelle or a small mammal over a single night.

'All that's left is to make sure we've got enough water,' Elliott said, as Will came to the heap of animal skins and lengths of wood she'd brought into the cave. 'And put some sleeping cots together from that stuff,' she added.

'You can always ask me to help, you know,' Will offered, impressed at how much she'd already done.

She shook her head, focusing on the ground. 'No, don't worry. I know you have your work cut out with the Doc.'

There was the slightest hint of disappointment in her voice. Despite the fact that he found Elliott so difficult to read, Will picked up on it immediately.

There had been numerous occasions when he'd been torn between working with his father or spending time with Elliott, but the tyrannical Dr Burrows always won the day. And each time as Will watched Elliott walk away, leaving him to continue with his drawings of the carved inscriptions on the pyramid or scrubbing the dirt from some minor artefact,

he'd stare after her, yearning to go with her. These were oppor-
tunities, moments, days, which would never present
themselves again, and sometimes he felt as if all the impatience and frustration inside him would make him implode.
But, each time, he would say nothing and buckle down to the
tasks Dr Burrows had set him, furious with himself and
unhappy with his lot.

'Your father always has so much to do,' Elliott added as she
gave Will a passing glance.

'Yes,' he agreed, his voice downbeat. But then Will made
an effort to lighten the mood between them. There was no
way he was going to let his father spoil what little time they
did have together. 'And this place is a perfect hideaway if we
need one. You're just brilliant.'

Elliott picked up a roll of animal hide which had fallen
from the top of the heap and put it back where it belonged.
'Thanks. And just remember to use the same route in or out
of here. Otherwise you'll leave a scent trail.'

'I knew it – that was why you took us through the stream,'
Will said, lifting a foot and planting it back down on the rock
floor with a squelching noise. 'But don't we need to be further
away from the base camp than this?' he thought out loud, as
he went back to the entrance. Parting the vines to survey the
view below, he stared at the shallow stream at the base of the
cliff. 'We're a bit close here.' He frowned. 'And, anyway, didn't
you tell me we had a long walk ahead of us? We've hardly
come any distance.'

Elliott joined him at the cave mouth. 'It can't be too far
away in case we need to get here at short notice. And as for
your second question, we're not done yet.'

'We're not?' he said, glancing enquiringly at her.

'No,' she replied. 'I have something to ask you, Will.'

He turned to face her. 'You do? What's that?'

'After we took care of the Rebecca twins, didn't anything occur to you?' Elliott put to him.

Will was silent for a while. 'To tell you the truth, I've been trying to forget the whole thing. It was just so horrible,' he replied eventually. He began to fidget with the Sten gun slung over his shoulder, a troubled look in his eyes.

'That's okay,' she said, placing her hand momentarily on his arm to still its movement. 'I'm not talking about *what* we did – you don't have to think about that. But have you never once asked yourself how the three Styx actually got here? I mean, what are the chances of them leaping off that submarine and floating across, just like we did?' She tapped the barrel of his Sten gun. 'And anyway, how would they have propelled themselves through the zero gravity belt? As far as we know they didn't have any firearms with them.'

Will frowned. 'Well, I'll be damned – you're absolutely right. I never thought of that. So how *did* they make it across?'

'Saddle up,' she said, sounding remarkably like Drake as she spun nimbly around and clambered backwards out of the opening, then began to descend the vines.

Once he was down, Will waded through the stream to the bank. As he clambered out and retrieved the Bergen from the undergrowth where he'd left it, Bartleby's head suddenly popped up from a nearby bush. His cheeks were puffed out, like a trumpet player about to blow a full-bodied note on his instrument.

'Oh, no. There's a tail sticking out of his mouth,' Will spluttered. 'And it's twitching!'

'Caught himself a jungle rat,' Elliott said admiringly. 'He's a born hunter.'

Will raised an eyebrow. 'Yes, that's absolutely right – he *is* a Hunter. There you go stating—'

'Oh, shut up, Will,' she laughed, pushing gently against him with her shoulder before moving away. Will grinned to himself, enjoying the moment.

They kept to the stream for several kilometres, Elliott and the cat wading ahead of Will. When the water was up to their waists and Bartleby was only just managing to keep his nose above the surface, they made for the side. Once they were out, Elliott didn't take them back into the jungle, but instead led them along the bank, which was covered in a thick growth of gymnosperms. By now the stream had grown so much in size that Will decided it was more accurate to describe it as a river.

Elliott called a halt several times by holding her fist in the air. Crouching low, she used her rifle scope to check around them, particularly concentrating on the opposite bank. On one of these occasions Will crept over to her.

'What's wrong? Why do you keep stopping?'

'I've got this feeling,' she whispered, not shifting her gaze from the far bank. 'Like there's someone there.'

'I can't see anybody,' Will said.

'It's as though . . . as though the trees are watching us,' she replied, still keeping her voice low.

Will was nonplussed. 'The trees?'

Elliott nodded. 'I know it sounds crazy. I've had the same feeling before . . . in other parts of the jungle.'

They were both silent as they continued to scrutinise the opposite side of the river. The bank was lined with gymnosperms several metres in height, and then the jungle began with its giant trees. It was here, in between the trees, that Elliott was staring. And Will also noticed that she was throwing the occasional glance at Bartleby to check if he was sensing anything. However, the cat seemed entirely preoccupied by the swarms of iridescent green dragonflies, playfully trying to swipe them with his massive paws as they zipped past. This made Will more confident that there was no cause for alarm. But he'd also learnt that Elliott's instincts weren't to be ignored.

'Could it just be some animal watching us?' he suggested. 'Other than those old skulls at the pyramid and the aeroplane Dad claims he saw, I don't reckon there's anyone close to us. I mean, we haven't seen any signs of people in our bit of the jungle, have we?'

She didn't answer, her body tense as her senses strained. 'It's nothing,' she said finally, setting off again.

A little further on, Will heard a distant rumble. He kept checking the sky to see if one of the sudden and tumultuous rainstorms was about to descend on them. But although the sky was its usual transparent white and there wasn't a cloud in sight, the sound grew louder. And it was continuous, telling Will that it couldn't be peals of thunder, as he'd first assumed. The sound was only explained when they rounded a bend in the river and a high escarpment came into view, torrents of white water tumbling over it and plummeting into a foam-topped lagoon below.

'Now that's what I call a *real* waterfall,' Will said, peering up to the top of the two- or three-hundred-metre escarpment. He noted that two rivers branched off from the lagoon: the one that had brought them there, and a second that led off on the far side.

As Will and Elliott advanced towards the lagoon, they emerged from the thick copse of gymnosperms and onto a stretch of trampled mud. Will realised that the ground must be so churned up because the lagoon was a watering hole for the local wildlife. He began to search for interesting tracks, but Elliott kept up the pace, leading them straight towards the side of the waterfall. Will couldn't work out where she was going until he saw her step up onto a rocky ledge that seemed to extend behind the waterfall itself. They trod carefully along this ledge, the sheet of water to one side of them, and a vertical rock face to the other. Within seconds they had entered a large cavern completely hidden behind the waterfall, where the profuse spray misted the air.

'This is so cool!' Will yelled, spellbound by the endless cascade of water. Sunlight intermittently penetrated the waterfall, dappling him in ever-shifting patterns. If it hadn't been for the thunderous noise, the effect would have been hypnotic. 'How do you find these places?' Will shouted as he mopped the spray from his face. Moving his gaze from the waterfall, he saw Elliott was at the far end of the cavern, where she was poised at the start of a flight of steps hewn out of the rock.

Seized with curiosity, he went over to her. As his sight adjusted to the gloom, he made out the arch above the steps. Then he saw that carved into the keystone at the apex of the arch was a symbol of three bars radiating slightly outwards. It was the same symbol as the one on the pendant Uncle Tam had given him, and which was around his neck at that very moment. And this symbol was the mark left by the Ancients, as his father referred to them, the people who had first made a pilgrimage from the Deeps to this inner world.

Filled with excitement, he slid off his Bergen and extricated his Styx lantern. As he and Elliott mounted the steps and went into the passage beyond, he shone the lantern around them, inspecting the rock, which showed unmistakable signs that it had been worked by hand. As they progressed further down the passage, the noise of the water diminished so that they were able to talk without raising their voices. 'Then the Rebeccas came this way?' Will asked.

Elliott nodded. 'They must have located the other end of this tunnel after they left the submarine. It brought them here without all that—' She interrupted herself to wave her arms in the air. 'Without all that floatey floatey stuff we had to do.'

'*Floatey* stuff?' Will repeated, but his mind was racing with the implications of her discovery. 'So this is the way home,' he said. 'But how did you find it? We're miles from the pyramid.'

'I followed the Styx's tracks back here after we ambushed them. I wouldn't have been doing my job if I hadn't checked where they'd come from.'

Will was still frowning. 'So you've known about this for weeks, but you didn't mention it to me?'

Her voice was barely audible as she swung about and began to retrace her steps to the arch. 'I was scared,' she said.

'What did you say? You were *scared*?' Will asked as he went after her. 'Why?'

She came to a halt. 'I thought if I told you and your father, you might decide to go home. And I don't want to leave this world – I don't have anywhere else to go. Besides, I love it here with . . .' Her voice petered out as the beam of Will's lantern flicked over the ground beside her feet.

'Back here! Shine it back here!' she ordered him urgently as she squatted down on her thighs. 'Hurry up!' she snapped, panic evident in her voice.

She pointed at three pieces of rock. They were lying in a row.

Will was immediately concerned. 'What is it?'

She snatched the lantern from him, and tore back through the arch and down the short flight of steps. In a second she'd found what she'd been looking for on the rocky ledge behind the waterfall. Another three pieces of stone had been placed at the base of the wall. 'I knew it! Look!' she cried.

'So what?' Will asked.

Elliott shook her head. 'It's Limiter procedure. That's how they mark the trail for other soldiers. Textbook stuff.'

'But surely the Rebeccas and first Limiter could have left th—' Will tried to suggest.

'No way! I went over every inch of this place when I first found it. I searched it thoroughly, and also the surrounding area. I wouldn't have missed something like this.' She swung her rifle from her shoulder and cocked it. 'Will, you know what this means, don't you?'

He really didn't want to hear what she was about to say.

'It means that we've got more Limiters with us in this world. It's not over yet.'

Carrying a tray, Eddie approached the end of the basement where Drake was working. Perched on a stool, Drake had the parts of the Dark Light he'd taken apart carefully arranged on the bench in front of him. After spending the morning evaluating the items that Eddie had collected together in the basement, Drake had concentrated all his efforts on the Styx interrogation device. He'd gone off to fetch his test equipment and had used it to examine each component as he extracted it. So far the exercise had taken him most of the afternoon.

'Thought you might be hungry,' Eddie said as he placed the tray on the bench.

'Yeah . . . thanks,' Drake mumbled.

'Making progress?' Eddie asked.

'Slowly but surely,' Drake replied, wiping his forehead. 'This is a very clever piece of kit. I've never seen the likes of some of these components before.' He reached across the bench to pick up a small metal cylinder with rounded ends. 'There are four of these in the base of the Dark Light. Have you any idea what they do?'

'No. My job was to use the Dark Light on subjects – nothing more,' Eddie said. 'Were you ever Darklit?'

But Drake didn't reply, completely absorbed by the cylinders to the exclusion of all else. 'When I pass a charge through them, these ionising tubes emit different wavelengths. The spectrum for each tube is incredibly narrow, incredibly specific. When all the tubes are in full swing, the combination of the four spectra is unique, and I reckon I might be able to rig something up to detect them.'

'To what end?' Eddie asked.

'As long as it's above ground, I should be able to tell when and where Dark Lights are being used.' He put the metal tube down and straightened up, stretching his arms.

Eddie didn't show any signs of leaving as he hovered on the other side of the bench. Drake shot a glance at him. 'You look like you want to ask me something?'

'Yes, about Elliott. You said there's a route down to the area beneath the Deeps, and I want to know more about it, and how we're going to proceed.'

'Sure. Let's talk about it later,' Drake said dismissively. Sliding from the stool, he crossed to an adjacent bench. 'Eddie, tell me about these. I found a box of them.' He held up a fistful of phials by their cords. They were identical to the pair Will had been given by the Rebecca twin, although the silver stoppers on these hadn't been painted.

'They're receptacles for viral agents,' Eddie answered. 'The clear liquid you see in them is a compound manufactured by the Scientists. They call it a *static* – it keeps a virus alive, even though it's outside the body of the host.'

'Yes, I had some of it assayed when we couldn't figure out how they'd managed that,' Drake said, moving rapidly on to some items he'd put at the end of the bench. 'And these?' he asked, indicating a group of bottles several centimetres in length, with sealed tops. Inside each was a small object suspended in yellow fluid. 'I'm no zoologist, but these look suspiciously like snails. What's their significance?' Drake asked.

'They are snails – *Plague Snails*. Their natural habitat is the vegetation around the perimeter of the Eternal City. I often went into the city with patrols from the Division. And on a couple of occasions, we were there on handholding duty, looking after parties of Scientists. You see, they collect the snails, for the viral strains they harbour.'

'You're telling me these are the original source of the Dominion virus? These are the vector?' Drake asked eagerly.

'Not *these* snails specifically, because they've been dead for too long. But, yes, fresh specimens carry many different viruses, and the Scientists harvest them for the deadlier strains. Once they've isolated these viruses, they're modified into more effective infectious agents in the Laboratories.'

Drake nodded. 'Neatly packaged and ready to unleash on us Topsoilers . . . I can only guess?'

'That's correct,' Eddie confirmed. 'The Scientists convert them into weapon-grade pathogens.'

Drake was studying the specimen bottle in his hand with evident excitement. 'So these little blighters . . . these Plague Snails . . . are to blame.' His eyes lit up as he had an idea. 'And if we were to wipe them out, every last one of these snails, the Styx would lose their source of pathogens.'

Eddie nodded sceptically. 'But the Eternal City is a pretty big place. It would be an impossible task to eradicate all of them.'

'Not impossible, no,' Drake replied. 'Not if you happen to know a top-notch biochemist with a thing for pesticides.'

⁕

Making pitiful groans, Chester tensed against the cords around his wrists, stretching his fingers in an attempt to get the blood flowing in his hands. And his legs were cramping up yet again because his ankles were bound so tightly together. He was silent for a while, unsure whether he wanted to cry or to resume his tirade at Martha. He chose the latter – at least it made him feel marginally better.

'YOU STUPID MAD *STUPID* OLD COW!' he screamed at full volume. 'YOU'VE KEPT ME IN HERE FOR BLOODY WEEKS! LET ME OUT!'

In the confined space, his shout made his ears ring.

He waited to see if there was a response, but there was only silence.

'Oh, God,' he whimpered, looking at the light seeping in from cracks around the door of the otherwise completely dark and narrow under-stairs cupboard in which Martha had locked him. 'Harry Potter, I know just what you went through,' he said.

The memory of how his life had been not so long ago . . . spending time with his mother and father . . . immersing himself in his favourite books . . . enjoying his wonderful home . . . playing games on his PlayStation . . . all without fear and nice and predictable – it all flooded back to him.

In the last year he'd travelled such a long way, completing a journey of many hundreds, if not thousands, of kilometres into the deepest recesses of the Earth, only to return to the surface for this to happen. He thought back to when he and Martha had set off in the launch from the fallout shelter. Despite his misgivings about her, he'd been filled with such hope and optimism.

Why had it all gone so horribly wrong?

He longed to wake from this nightmare.

Why? Why? Why?

But it was no nightmare.

What did I do to deserve this?

It was real.

Won't someone save me?

He wailed with frustration.

The moment that Dr Burrows, Will and Elliott had leapt down Smoking Jean, he should have foreseen how it was going to turn out. There was a marked change in Martha's behaviour. Almost straight away, she'd begun to act very strangely, following him around like some bloated balloon, and fussing over him and nagging at him to eat the food she prepared in her less-than-hygienic fashion. And worst of all, she was constantly trying to touch him in a sort of monstrously overdone maternal way.

'Warped psycho granny,' Chester muttered to himself, shivering as he thought about it now. He heard a vague shuffling sound from the other side of the door, knowing only too well she was lurking there.

After she'd caught him trying to use the phone and knocked him out cold, he'd regained consciousness in the under-stairs cupboard. And that's where she'd imprisoned him, for how many weeks he didn't know, only allowing him out for a short time each day to get some exercise. Even then it was at knifepoint, with his hands still bound.

To begin with he'd tried to reason with Martha, pleading with her to untie him. She merely shook her head in response. 'It's for your own good,' was all she'd say, over and over again. The nervous twitch in her left eye had also grown progressively worse, as if she was forever winking at him over some private joke. Only there was nothing remotely funny about the situation he found himself in. Quite frankly, he was petrified by the woman, believing she was eminently capable of sticking the knife into him, no doubt 'for his own good', too.

Now as he lay in the cramped cupboard, he was listening to every little noise. He heard another movement on the other side of the door. No question then that she was there, most likely sitting on the floor with her legs splayed out as she always did. He could picture her, her crossbow resting in her lap as she fidgeted with her large knife, like some mad aunt from an old horror movie. But this was no movie, and it was so unfair. He just wanted to go home. All his feelings welled up inside him again until he could stand it no longer, and he began to shout at the top of his voice. Still shouting, he rolled over so that he could bang his head against the door, thumping it with such force he was hurting himself.

'HEY, LOONEY TUNES, I KNOW YOU'RE THERE! BLOODY LET ME OUT!'

Suddenly, with a click, the door swung open, and he was staring at a pair of stocky ankles. He looked up – there she stood, a rather overweight lady with flame-red frizzy hair, and swathed in the usual thick layers of filthy clothing.

'Now, now, my darlin', don't go getting yourself all worked up,' she said, the muscles around her eye going wild in their very own St Vitus's Dance.

But Chester was so angry he didn't care about the consequences any more. As she squatted down beside him, he began to shout again and tried to head-butt her knee.

'I WANT TO SEE MY MUM AND DAD,' he shrieked. 'LET ME GO HOME! THIS IS JUST SO WRONG!'

'Silly boy. No need for all that ballyhoo – *I'm* your family now,' she said calmly, and grabbed his head, pushing it down against the floor inside the cupboard. 'Martha's the one who cares for you now, not foul Topsoilers.'

With that, she whipped out a yellow duster and shoved it against his mouth.

At first he thought she was trying to smother him, and he struggled with even more urgency. But there wasn't much he could do – his bound limbs and the restrictive space inside the cupboard hindered him. And she was deceptively strong.

''OO 'ITCH!' he yelled through the cloth, jerking his head in an attempt to shake her off.

Without any warning she slapped him viciously across the side of the face. He screamed, not from the pain, but from the shock of what she'd done. He felt so vulnerable.

'Silly, silly boy,' she said breathlessly, still holding the duster over his mouth to muffle him. 'There's nobody around to hear you, and you mustn't get yourself all in a tizzy like this.' She sounded as though she was disciplining a badly behaved puppy.

The fight had gone out of Chester, and he stopped struggling and trying to shout. In the ensuing calm she took away the duster. He watched her with mounting horror as she drew out her knife and waggled it in front of him. 'And if you insist on using such language, I'll be forced to cut out your tongue. Do you really want me to do that?'

Chester clamped his mouth tight shut and shook his head, making a frantic 'Mmmm' noise to show he would obey her. For an instant she narrowed her eyes and her expression went blank, as if she was waiting for instructions from someone. Except there was no one there but the two of them. Then she became animated again and spoke. 'If you know what's good for you, you'll just do what old Martha tells you.'

Rigid with fright, he continued to stare up at her, tears running down his cheeks. She brushed the hair from his forehead and then stroked the side of his face with her short, grubby fingers. He didn't dare do anything to resist her touch.

Inclining her head towards him, she smiled as if nothing had happened, but that eye was twitching as though it was going to leap clean out of its socket.

'Martha's going to look after you. Martha will always be there for you . . . always and for ever,' she said, dabbing away his tears with her thumb.

Chapter Eight

The doctor was humming to himself and it was the only sound in the room other than the ticking of the grandfather clock in the corner. He leant over Mrs Burrows as he shone a light – a tiny luminescent orb set into a chromed tube – directly into one of her eyes. The doctor's demeanour said it all – he didn't look hopeful. But for one moment, as he continued to move the light from side to side in front of her face, he ceased his humming and appeared to become more optimistic. 'Ah, yes . . . was that . . .?' he whispered, but after he'd continued the examination for several more seconds he shook his head.

'I thought I saw a flicker . . . a reaction, but I must have been mistaken,' he finally decided, and released Mrs Burrows' eyelid, which flipped down again. Then he produced a pin and took Mrs Burrows' arm by the wrist. Turning her hand over, he stuck the needle several times into the palm. He moved on to the fingertips where he did the same, each jab drawing little spots of blood. All the time he was scrutinising Mrs Burrows' face, trying to discern whether there was any response to the stimuli. 'Nothing,' he muttered, and finished the exercise by sticking the needle deep into the back of her hand, where he left it. It seemed a little unnecessary to the Second Officer, who opened his mouth to say something, but then thought better of it.

Taking a step back the doctor grimaced. 'No, it's as I expected – there's no sign of any improvement.'

A wizened old man with a grey beard, the doctor wore a black frock coat over a waistcoat that was almost the same colour as his beard. And his clothing had various splatter marks on it, which might very well have been dried blood. He began to make tutting noises as he returned his light, a ther-mometer and a set of reflex hammers to his valise. It was clear the examination was over.

Beside the doctor, the Second Officer rocked on the balls of his feet, the floorboards creaking under his not inconsider-able weight. He'd been observing the doctor perform the medical procedures without any comprehension, much as a dog watches a card trick. 'But isn't there anything more that can be done for her?' he ventured, staring at Mrs Burrows' motionless body. The room, formerly the sitting room, had been turned over for her care, and a bed had been installed in one corner. Mrs Burrows herself was propped up in a wicker bath chair, an ancient contraption on three wheels.

The regular ticking of the grandfather clock continued as the doctor took his time to coil up his stethoscope and replace it in his valise. Still he said nothing as he shut the valise, press-ing the catches each in turn. Once this was done, he tucked his hand into his coat pocket, and struck a pose as if he was about to address an audience of his peers.

'Is there anything more that can be done for the patient?' he intoned, as he turned towards Mrs Burrows. The saliva collecting behind her slightly protruding bottom lip chose that precise moment to overflow, and a long treacly string of it seeped from her mouth and extended towards her chest.

'Well, we can make sure the patient is comfortable, and continue to administer the Pinkham's twice a day,' the doctor said, watching as the saliva pooled on Mrs Burrows' front, spreading through the weave of the cotton blouse which was far too big for her. The doctor drew in a breath as he swivelled his head to the Second Officer. 'If you need more Pinkham's from the apothecary, I can write you a script.'

'No, we have a few bottles left,' the Second Officer replied.

'Very good. And here's the bill for my services. Pay it when you can,' the doctor said, as he whisked a folded slip of paper from his waistcoat pocket and handed it to the Second Officer.

The Second Officer had been about to look at the bill, but a forced cough made him half turn to the hallway, where his mother and sister had been listening to the proceedings. Out of sight of the doctor, they both started to gesticulate wildly, prompting the Second Officer to broach the question he had been avoiding until then. He cleared his throat. 'Doctor, she's survived this long, hasn't she, against all odds? Don't you think that she might get a little better, with time?'

The doctor stroked his beard thoughtfully. 'It's a miracle that the patient's still with us, I grant you that,' he answered. 'But one cannot argue with the facts. While the patient is able to breathe for herself, there's not the remotest chance that she'll recover her cognitive functions. She demonstrates no reflex responses whatsoever – none at all – her pupils are completely non-reactive.' The doctor screwed one eye shut as if what he was about to say was difficult for him. 'I presume you thought that you were doing her an act of kindness bringing her here. But it might have been kinder to let her slip away peacefully after the interrogations.'

'I couldn't just leave her to die in the Hold,' the Second Officer said. 'There've been too many done that already.'

The doctor nodded grimly. 'But sometimes nature should be allowed to take its course. You told me that her ordeal was one of the most severe you've ever witnessed?'

'It was,' the Second Officer confirmed. 'They used as many as seven Dark Lights on her.'

'You are better placed than most to know what damage those contraptions can exact. The Dark Lights evidently took their toll on this woman. It's as though . . . how can I put it . . .?' The doctor faltered as he sought a suitable analogy, then stuck his index finger in the air. 'It's as though all the peas have been stripped from the pod.'

The Second Officer frowned through his confusion.

'Yes,' the doctor went on, rather pleased with himself. 'The patient has been well and truly shelled, and there's not much left . . . merely the husk. And peas don't grow back, do they? It doesn't matter how strong she was before, there's no return from where she is now.'

'No new peas,' the Second Officer said as he understood what he was being told, and looked at Mrs Burrows with his sad eyes. 'Yes, she had a strong will, all right. She put up one hell of a fight,' he said, then laid his hand on the doctor's arm. 'But, please, doctor, I need your help. I'm desperate. If you were in my shoes, what would you do now?'

'Give her back to the Styx,' the doctor replied abruptly, pulling his arm away. He seized his valise and trilby, and made towards the hallway with undue haste. He acknowledged the elderly lady and the younger woman with a nod. Then, placing the trilby on his head, he left the house as fast as his thin legs would carry him, still watched by the two women hovering in the hall.

'Well, 'e left like 'e thought the place was on fire. 'E couldn't get out quick enough,' the elderly woman observed, as she shut the front door behind him. ''E thinks the Topsoiler is a dead duck.'

The Second Officer had come out into the hallway. 'Ma, she . . .' he began to reply, but his mother's countenance was so unsympathetic, he turned to his sister for support. 'Eliza, I'm only doing—'

'Doing *what*?' his sister cut him short. 'He's been our family doctor since the year dot – he even delivered both of us – but now he just wants to wash his hands of us,' she said unequivocally. 'And can you blame him? We're an embarrassment, for Christ's sake! A bloody joke!'

Hearing his sister use profanities like that had the effect of a slap across the Second Officer's face. He gasped.

But Eliza was unrepentant. With her pale blue eyes and her wide face, and her almost white hair tied behind her head, she was typical of the women in the Colony. And the Second Officer, with his scalp sparsely covered by hoary bristles, his sloping face and thickset physique, was equally typical of the male contingent. Indeed, they were both immensely proud of their origins, descended as they were from the 'Faithful' – the loyal employees Sir Gabriel Martineau had invited to live in his new kingdom beneath the soil almost three hundred years ago.

The Second Officer and his family were highly respected members of the community, and obedient to the Styx.

Moreover, the Second Officer's work in the police station meant that he dealt with the Styx on an almost daily basis, doing their bidding however distasteful its nature. But now his erratic conduct in helping this Topsoiler had jeopardised his standing, and had alienated all three of them from the tight-knit community in which they lived. And all three of them knew it.

'Eliza, the doctor's a busy man,' the Second Officer said. 'Maybe he has something urgent to do – another house call to make.'

'Sure, and my best friend's a mushroom,' she snorted derisively.

'Got all of us in a real bind, 'aven't you, son?' the old lady burst out. She and Eliza advanced on the Second Officer, who did the only thing he could and retreated into the sitting room. 'Look at 'er. This Topsoiler's eatin' us out of 'ouse and 'ome, and she ain't never ever going to get better. At my age I can't be doing with all this moppin' up after 'er, and tryin' to force costly food we can ill afford down 'er greedy gullet. And now we've got to cough up for yet another bill. What *were* you thinkin' of, son?'

Eliza now joined in the attack. 'And tongues are wagging all right. People want to know what drove you to haul a half-dead Heathen into our family house, some evil *Above Grass* we don't know from Eve. I ask you!'

'Eliza—' the Second Officer tried, but his sister wasn't finished yet.

'At the shops yesterday, both Mrs Cayzer and Mrs Jempson ignored me completely. They crossed the road to avoid me, they did,' she said indignantly.

The Second Officer didn't have anywhere to go – the two

women had him backed right up to Mrs Burrows' bath chair. And they were going in for the kill, like hounds after a lame fox.

'Exactly who do you think we are? The patron saints of sick Topsoilers?' Eliza pressed him. 'Because what we are is . . . is the laughing stock of the South Cavern!'

Hemmed in, the Second Officer let out a small moan of anguish. He scratched the short stretch of neck that supported his broad head on his equally broad shoulders, but didn't attempt to offer any sort of explanation.

The old lady had noticed the dribble on Mrs Burrows' blouse and pushed past her son. Taking out her handkerchief, she began to dab roughly at it, her staccato words timed with each dab. 'There's also talk down the market that the Styx are takin' a special interest in us . . . because of what you've done,' she said. Then as she tossed her handkerchief on a side table, she raised her voice and shouted, 'You've brought them on us!'

There was a meow from the doorway.

'Colly,' Eliza said, turning around.

The cat had come to investigate what all the fuss was about. She was a Hunter, a giant cat unique to the Colony, bred for its rat-catching prowess. She cast her large copper eyes over the three humans, sniffed loudly in Mrs Burrows' direction, then slunk over to the hearth. Here, basking in the heat from the embers, she dug her claws into the rug and stretched luxuriously.

As the old lady saw the cat settling down for a nap, she thrust an arthritic finger at the door to the room. 'No, you don't, Colly! Out you go!'

'Leave her be, Ma,' Eliza said gently, as the grandfather clock began to chime, adding to the tension in the room.

'Even if we've been banished to the kitchen, why shouldn't she enjoy the fire, same as this slothful Topsoiler?'

Colly was slightly smaller than Bartleby, the Hunter currently in the centre of the Earth with Will and Elliott, but she differed from him in that her hairless skin was of the purest black.

Making herself comfortable at Mrs Burrows' side, she curled up with a contented yawn.

'Colly,' the old woman said again, but the cat continued not to pay the slightest attention to her.

The clock still chiming, the Second Officer took advantage of the diversion Colly had brought. 'Ma, let her stay here. Instead, why don't I make you a fresh cuppa,' he offered, slipping his arm around his mother's bowed shoulders as he began to steer her away. 'All this excitement's not good for your heart.'

Eliza hung back in the room, glaring at Mrs Burrows' comatose form. She couldn't understand what had got into her brother. These people were the enemy, and this one in particular had been hiding something from the Styx – hence the treatment she'd received at their hands. Eliza wasn't a bad woman by any means, but now her bitterness built to the point where she couldn't contain it.

She leant forward and struck Mrs Burrows across the face, a full-blown slap that left a red mark on the woman's wan skin. It was so loud that Colly leapt up in surprise. Then Eliza literally squeaked with her frustration, and stormed from the room.

As the raised voices continued in the kitchen down the hallway, the twelfth and final chime sounded and Mrs Burrows' eyes flicked open.

'The dead duck lives,' she said defiantly, then worked her jaw and touched her cheek where she'd been struck. 'Temper, temper, Eliza,' she quietly reprimanded the absent woman. As she wiped the spittle from her lips, she remembered the pin that was still stuck in the back of her hand. For a moment she chuckled, holding her hand before her and splaying her fingers as she examined the pin, which she made no effort to remove.

Then she felt the damp patch on her blouse. 'Did you catch my routine with the dribble, Colly?' she said, smiling at the cat, who was watching her attentively. 'I thought it was a nice touch.'

The interrogation with the Dark Lights had caused untold damage to Mrs Burrows' brain, and her body had all but shut down. It was only because her autonomic nervous system was still intact that she didn't die. Fortunately it kept her major organs functioning, so her heart continued to beat and her lungs to draw air. And although she'd been in a catatonic state and on the edge of death for several weeks, she'd been cared for by the Second Officer and his family. With the regular nourishment and the constant nursing, she'd been bought some extra time, and with that time something exceptional started to take place.

Week by week, the neural pathways in her brain, which had been so badly disrupted, had begun to reform and reconnect themselves, like a computer autorunning a recovery program. Some small corner of her frontal lobes – the seat of her memories and her conscious will – had embarked on the mammoth task of piecing the rest of her grey matter back together again.

But the neural pathways hadn't reconnected quite as they

had been before. She found her sight had been impaired to the extent that she could only just differentiate between light and dark. However, as if to compensate for this disability, there were some surprising benefits to the new, Mark II Mrs Burrows.

She found that she had virtual mastery over many aspects of her body, like she'd never had before. Although she'd felt each jab of the pin made by the doctor, she was able to isolate the pain and show no reaction to it. But this was only a fraction of what she was capable – she could reduce all her physiological processes, including her heart rate, to such a low level that she barely needed to draw breath. And in conjunction with this, she could raise or lower her body temperature, making herself break into a sweat or her breath come out as clouds of condensation. She told herself it was as though she'd exceeded the levels of control her Yoga master had said only the most advanced practitioners could hope to attain.

But there was yet more. There was something truly inexplicable. While her eyesight was so poor, in place of this she had another faculty. Whether it was because of a heightened olfactory sense, or whether some long-forgotten animal ability hidden deep in the recesses of the brain had been switched on, she didn't know. But she found she had something akin to an early warning system for people. She could literally *smell* them.

She was able to distinguish between people familiar to her and strangers, even if they were just walking past in the street outside the house. And she could tell what sort of mood they were in – angry, sad, bored, happy – it didn't matter – she could detect the whole gamut of human emotion. A biologist might have speculated that she'd developed the ability to read the pheromones that people emit – the airborne chemosignals that play such a central role in the lives of other animal species as they utilise them for communication and in their behavioural patterns. But Mrs Burrows wasn't a biologist and had no knowledge of this; she was just content to develop her new sense, which seemed to be growing more potent by the day. She was also certain that it would eventually help her escape from the Colony. And the way things were going in the Second Officer's home, that day might not be far off.

So now she didn't need to hear the argument going on in the kitchen in order to know that it was still in full flow. She could smell the exasperation and frustration radiating from the Second Officer's mother and sister – it was so strong it made her wince. And she could also sense the Second Officer's indignation and the slight emanation of fear from him as he made a valiant attempt to defend himself against the verbal onslaught.

Rising from her bath chair and stretching her limbs each in turn, Mrs Burrows sighed. 'Ah, that's better,' she said, adding, 'Come here, Colly.'

The Hunter instantly went to her side. Mrs Burrows had spent a great deal of time with this cat, and it was as if Colly recognised that this human's unique abilities matched and even surpassed her own – for her Hunter's sense of smell was also incredibly well developed. It might have been this, or something on a more bestial level, that had forged the bond between them, but the cat did exactly as Mrs Burrows told her.

Mrs Burrows extended a hand until she found the cat's large head. 'Let's take a stroll round the room. I need the exercise,' she said.

With Colly as her guide, Mrs Burrows followed beside her, avoiding the pieces of furniture and all the while talking to her. For it had been a lonely time for Mrs Burrows, forced to pretend she was still in a coma whenever Colonists were near.

And, of course, the cat could tell nobody about the startling changes that had come over the new woman in the house.

Chapter Nine

Chester shifted his position to ease his limbs. He was sure it had to be about time that Martha brought him some more food and water. He didn't know how long it was since she'd last opened the door to check on him – the hours crawled slowly by, with nothing to differentiate them other than his bouts of desperation and crying.

Except there had been something.

There'd been noises that he couldn't quite place – the scrunch of gravel outside as if a car had drawn up, then some banging. But the sounds had been so short-lived and so muffled through the door that they didn't give him much of an idea what was happening outside his diminutive prison. He assumed his monstrous captor was probably up to something that made sense in her twisted world. As he groaned from his hunger and thirst, he put the sounds from his mind and tried to go back to sleep.

Drake stormed into the warehouse flat and hurried through to his bedroom, returning a few seconds later with a kitbag and a

Bergen. Eddie had seen the urgency with which he was moving, and rose from his chair.

Drake upended both the kitbag and the Bergen, tipping all the equipment from them onto the floor, which he then began to sort through as he selected what he needed.

'Something happened?' Eddie asked.

'Yes, I've got to go to Norfolk. I just dialled in for messages on the remote server – it's accessed by a Topsoil number I gave Elliott, to contact me in an emergency,' he said.

'Is she in trouble?' Eddie asked quickly.

'No, the message is from Chester, and doesn't mention her,' Drake said, putting some of his gear back into the Bergen. 'It's not very clear but, from what I can make out, he may have resurfaced by now.' He shook his head, furious with himself. 'What a bloody fool! I haven't been checking the server on a regular basis – the message is from weeks ago.' He picked up a handgun and a couple of magazines, one of which he slotted into the weapon. As he cocked it and tucked it into his waistband in the small of his back, he paused to glance across at Eddie. 'I just hope that boy has the nous to hide out up there, and not try to go home. If he's gone back to Highfield, your buddies will have nabbed him.'

'But there's still a chance Elliott might be with him,' Eddie reasoned, putting his jacket on. 'In which case I'm coming with you.'

'I'm parked a couple of blocks away,' Drake said, glancing in the direction of his Range Rover, as he and Eddie stepped out of the warehouse.

'Let's use mine, instead,' Eddie suggested, striding off in the opposite direction.

For a moment Drake didn't make a move to follow him, adjusting the strap of his heavy Bergen so it sat more comfortably on his shoulder. Then, further down the street, he saw the indicators flash on a brand new Aston Martin as Eddie depressed his key fob.

'Classy wheels,' Drake said, as he approached the car, giving the gleaming black paintwork an appreciative look. Eddie opened the driver's door and waited for Drake, who seemed to be hesitant. 'A bit conspicuous though, isn't it?' Drake added. 'Unless you're James Bond. Perhaps it would be better to take the Range Rover?'

Eddie didn't reply.

Then Drake recapitulated. 'Okay, we'll use yours, but I'm driving,' he said.

It was late in the evening and the traffic didn't present a problem as Drake raced out of London, then tore up towards Norfolk. As the dual carriageway came to an end and the road narrowed to a single lane, Drake didn't ease up on the speed. For a while they listened to the news on the radio, but once this had finished neither spoke as the last light from the sun faded and they found themselves in a moonless nightscape. A strong wind had picked up, and every so often the headlamps caught the shining eyes of plump deer grazing on the verges.

Spotting a car coming in the opposite direction, Drake dipped his lights. As expected, the driver of the other car did likewise, but when he was almost level with Drake, he flipped them onto full beam again, hooting his horn like a maniac. An empty beer can struck the side of the Aston.

'Bloody idiot!' Drake exclaimed as the glaring lights blinded him.

Eddie lurched sideways in his seat as Drake executed a

perfect handbrake turn, slewing the car round so it was facing in the opposite direction. The V8 roared as he floored the accelerator, and he sped off in pursuit of the other vehicle.

'What are you doing?' Eddie asked quite calmly.

'Someone needs to teach that prat a lesson!' Drake said. Catching up and overtaking the car, he cut so sharply in front of it that it was forced to stop with one wheel on the grass verge.

'I don't think this is a good . . .' Eddie began, but Drake leapt from the car. The other driver had climbed out of his vehicle and was staring insolently at Drake as he leant against the open door and drew on his cigarette. He was in his twenties, with long hair and a sleeveless black T-shirt with a faded white pentagle printed on it. In the passenger seat his girlfriend was sipping a can of cider, giggling tipsily as she watched Drake approach.

'Think you're police or sumthing?' the driver drawled insolently as Drake stopped in front of him. 'What'ya going to do now?' He flicked his cigarette at Drake, who stepped to the side to avoid its trajectory. As it struck the road with a shower of tiny sparks, Drake extinguished it with his boot.

A further two men of approximately the same age as the driver were in the rear of the car and competing with each other as they provided non-stop, drunken banter. This was punctuated with coarse laughter, as if a pair of donkeys was braying at each other. Drake heard them saying, 'It's the Five-0,' and 'Buzz off, fuzz'.

Then, as the driver made out that the vehicle parked in front was the latest model Aston Martin, he straightened up sharply, a resentful sneer spreading across his face. 'You rich tosser!' he yelled. 'Get back to the city where you scum belong.' Still using his car door as a shield, he brandished his fist in Drake's face.

In less than the blink of an eye, Drake had covered the space between him and the driver, and had seized the man's arm, twisting it so that he was spun around and pushed up against his car. The driver tried to fight back with the elbow of his free arm, but Drake slammed his head hard against the roof of the vehicle. It made a satisfying thud, and the driver's girlfriend stopped giggling with a yelp, then gave a piercing squeal as she dropped the can of cider in her lap.

'Oi, mate! You can't do that!' the driver objected, still held in a lock by Drake. 'That's assault and batteries!'

He tried to use his free arm again, this time to punch out. Drake retaliated by slamming the man's head against the roof even harder than the first time. The other passengers were now completely silent and craning their necks to see. Drake put his mouth very close to the driver's ear and spoke in a threatening whisper. 'Want some more?'

'But what did I do?' the driver whined.

'You know what you did, and from now on I'll be watching you. If you step out of line again, so help me, I'll kill you,' Drake growled. The driver's already pale face turned even paler. 'Now get out of here,' Drake shouted, throwing the driver into his seat. He watched as the car crept off, moving at a very sober speed.

Drake returned to the Aston and slid behind the steering wheel, gripping it with such force one of his knuckles popped. As he stared straight ahead, he seemed to be transfixed by the scene through the windscreen. Illuminated by the headlamps, the branches of the trees were being whipped by the wind into a frenzied animation.

As they sat side by side in the car, Eddie couldn't help but notice that Drake was shaking with fury.

Eddie broke the silence by clearing his throat.

Drake remained staring straight ahead, his voice strained as he spoke. 'Come on – out with it, Eddie. Tell me I'm a bloody fool for doing that, and they might report it to the police. *Aston Martin involved in road rage incident*,' he said, as if reciting the title of a newspaper article.

Eddie shook his head. 'No, I'm not concerned about that. I was going to say we've more in common than you'd like to admit.'

'And if I said I didn't want to know, would it stop you from telling me why?' Drake responded brusquely.

Eddie went on regardless. 'We're both driven by the same thing – we're both incredibly angry. And that anger is always there, eating away at us.'

'I've never seen you lose it,' Drake interposed.

'We control it in our different ways. Or try to,' Eddie said. 'And the paradox is that as it destroys us, it also defines us – making us who we are.' He paused for a moment while he found the right words. 'It's as though we're perpetually on a knife edge, always on the move, always striving for something, but all the while that knife edge is cutting deeper into us.' He took a breath. 'You know about how I got to be this way, but you've told me next to nothing about yourself. What happened to make you like this?'

'You did,' Drake replied. 'You Styx.'

A fox gave an almost human cry from somewhere in the undergrowth close to them, but Drake remained staring straight ahead through the windscreen. 'A lifetime ago,' he began, then swallowed. 'I was an undergraduate at Imperial . . .

there were three of us: Fiona, Luke and me, and we didn't mix much with the other students. We didn't have time for them, while they called us the *Wunderkinder*,' he said, closing his eyes for a moment. 'We lived together in the same digs, but we spent virtually all our time at the university – the faculty gave us free rein . . . anything we asked for . . . the run of the labs. They didn't interfere with our various research projects, as the university would eventually benefit from what we were doing.'

'In optoelectronics?' Eddie asked.

'That was my field, yes. Luke was the mathematician and Fiona the software whiz kid, and we complemented each other perfectly. But out of the three of us, Fiona was the genius – she could generate code like no one else. And in the second year, she wrote a piece of software that assimilated news events, and employed unique algorithms to analyse them. Once the business community and the security services got wind of what she was up to, they all tried to headhunt her. They all wanted the program, at any cost. But she held out and kept working on the project. And once the program had absorbed sufficient data and hit critical mass, it worked better than she'd ever imagined. But she began to find something strange . . . something anomalous. It began to red-flag events that didn't quite seem to fit. Patterns of events that were inconsistent, even with random-walk theory.' Drake slid his hands lower on the steering wheel. 'And I expect you can guess why?'

'It was us – the Styx. These red-flags were our interventions?' Eddie said.

'You got it,' Drake answered. 'And in the final week before graduation, she said goodbye to Luke and me in the morning and – as she always did – pedalled off for the university lab. That was the last time we saw her – they never found her or her bicycle. And nobody could explain how all her work vanished along with her – her laptop, the back-up disks she kept in her room, and everything on the university network. Anything even vaguely related to the program simply disappeared, without trace.' Drake swallowed. 'Then my friend had a nervous breakdown.'

'You're talking about Lukey?' Eddie said.

'Yes, he was one of those incredibly bright but highly strung young things – he went to pieces after Fiona disappeared. Dropped out of university and went back to live with his mother. He'd drunk himself to death within a year.' Only now did Drake turn to face Eddie. 'For all I know, you were on the snatch squad. You might have been one of the Limiters who took Fiona.'

Eddie shook his head slowly; as usual his expression didn't give any clue as to what he was thinking. 'No, and I don't know what I can say. I can ask for forgiveness for the actions of my people, but that would be meaningless to you, wouldn't it?'

'Completely,' Drake muttered, turning the key in the ignition. Then he steered the car back around and onto its original course.

The door to my room is shut and my dressing gown hangs on the back – it's dark blue and so thick it feels rather like I'm wearing a piece of carpet, but it's really warm. Mum bought it for me before Christmas because my old one was getting too small. Chester moved his head slightly. *There, next to the door . . . the posters on my wall . . . yes, I can see them . . . all where they should be. I*

know them so well because sometimes when I can't sleep, I lie on my bed and just look at them. The forest scene with the pine trees is my favourite. Some of them are a bit crooked on the wall because I put them up when I was little – I've had most of them for as long as I can remember, and I've been thinking of getting some new ones. Chester turned his head a little more. *And, yes, there's the Anglepoise light that Dad gave me – it's painted orange – his dad gave it to him, but it was black then and very chipped, so Dad painted it orange when he was about my age. I can see where he put too much paint on the base and it ran a bit, but I don't care because it was my dad's and I like the way the springs make the light stay wherever you move it. Sometimes, when I half close my eyes, the shade looks like the Apollo space capsule – I watched a brilliant programme about the Apollo moon landings on a Sky channel once.* Chester put his head completely on its side, and smiled. *Ah, yes, there are my books. All the different colours of the spines. I love my books and I never lend them to anyone in case they mess up the covers. I've read most of them more than once. I always want to get the whole series and I always always make sure I keep them in the right ord—*

'Food for you, my darlin', Martha said in a sickly-sweet voice as she threw open the cupboard door. Chester was wrenched abruptly from his illusory world and back into the real one. To pass the long hours in the dark and escape from the horrible situation in which he was trapped, he was spending increasing amounts of time imagining he was back at his home in Highfield. He could conjure up the different parts of the house with such realism, remembering even the tiniest details. In addition to his room, he often walked around downstairs or in his sunny garden, where everything would be perfect and just as it should be.

'Do you want some food or not?' Martha pressed him as he failed to answer.

Still rather groggy, he mumbled a yes. She was silhouetted by a flickering light from behind her. Chester's first thought was that she must have found some candles, but there seemed to be far too much smoke for this to be the case – it was as if a bonfire was burning close by. He had to remind himself that they were in rather a smart cottage, as the shifting illumination and the clouds of smoke lent the place a primitive feel. Through the smoke he could also pick out the smell of burning meat.

'Martha, please can I come out for a while? Can't you untie me, just while I eat?' he asked meekly. 'My legs are really stiff. I promise I'll do everything you tell me to.'

She looked at him with a frozen grin on her lips, her deranged eye twitching in its socket. Chester held his breath as several seconds went by, then she snapped her head round to look behind her. 'Not right this moment . . . cleaning . . . got some cleaning up to do,' she mumbled, turning back to Chester. 'Have your food,' she ordered, her voice adopting a nasty tone.

'Yes, yes, I'm very hungry, yes,' Chester gabbled immediately, not wanting to provoke another of her insane outbursts. And he wasn't about to refuse something to eat, even if she'd prepared it with her insanitary methods.

She propped up his head as she spooned it into his mouth.

'Yum,' he said, gulping down the almost raw meat. 'Tastes great. Thank—' But he couldn't speak as she rammed another large chunk into his mouth.

'There,' she said, when he'd finished, and lowered his head to the floor. 'Good boy.' She simply chucked the plate and spoon on the floor beside her, wiped her hand on her skirt, and then grunted as she got to her feet.

Chester was thinking rapidly. He had to do something. He had to try to make contact with someone outside.

But how?

Then he had an idea.

'Martha,' he began.

The mad eye was fixed on him now, but he wasn't going to let this put him off.

'Martha, please may I have my rucksack?'

The mad eye narrowed a little as it regarded him with suspicion.

'Why?' she hissed, her lips barely moving. Then she repeated the word, stridently this time.

'Er . . . I'm so used to resting my head on it . . . and just lying on the floor like this is really uncomfortable,' Chester explained. As she gave no response, he girded himself for what he was about to say next. 'Mother . . . *Mummy*, please may I have it . . . please?' he begged.

This had an immediate effect on the woman.

'Why, yes, of course,' she said, her voice almost normal. 'You stay right there, my lovely boy, and I'll go and fetch it.' She lumbered off, and Chester tried to worm his way out of the cupboard just enough to see what was outside. He was sure he could glimpse a real fire in the sitting room – it wasn't in the fireplace, but in the middle of the floor. And there were also dark smears all over the fawn-coloured carpet in the hallway, as if something had been dragged along it. *Mud?* he asked himself.

He heard her returning and quickly retreated back inside his prison.

'Thank you so much, Mummy,' he said.

She slid his rucksack under his head, then stood up to look at him.

'Anything for you, my wonderful son,' she cooed, then slammed the cupboard door shut.

He waited until all was quiet, then very slowly rolled on to his side and brought his hands above his head so he could delve inside the rucksack. It was difficult because his wrists were lashed together, but after a while he found what he'd hoped would still be there.

'Got it!' he whispered, holding it in the meagre light that was seeping under the door. It was a small plastic box about the size of a pack of cards with a length of wire attached to one end, which acted as an aerial. He put the box in his mouth to grip it while he felt for the microswitch. Finding it, he turned it on. Then he quickly returned the box to the rucksack, pushing it all the way down to the bottom and making sure his dirty clothes were on top of it.

As he rolled on to his back and laid his head on his rucksack, he held his hands in front of him. 'Please, God, I haven't asked you for much before, but I'm asking now. Please let someone notice my signal,' he prayed in a tense whisper. *'Please!'*

<hr>

After they had passed through a village with a small combined shop and post office, Drake began to slow as he searched for somewhere to leave the car. He found a track leading into a wooded area, and came to a stop under the trees where the Aston Martin would be hidden from the road.

'We'll go on foot from here,' he said to Eddie, and then, in the silence of night, they sorted out the equipment they were going to take with them. Eddie opted for a pair of semi-automatic pistols, one silenced, as though he was expecting trouble. Drake had no idea why he considered this necessary, but didn't question him about it.

Instead he put on his headset, making sure the band was positioned correctly across his forehead. He flipped down the single lens over his right eye before activating the power unit in his belt. The scene through the lens flickered with orange snow, clearing within a second so that he had a view of the surroundings that wasn't far off daylight.

As Drake hoisted his Bergen onto his shoulders and they set off through the damp grass, he was thinking about what they might find when they arrived in the subterranean harbour below the airfield. The last time he'd been there was to see Will and Dr Burrows off as they'd left in the launch. It was a journey of many hundreds of kilometres down to the deep-level fallout shelter. And that was where Chester had been calling from when he left his message. Although the message was more than a fortnight old, it wasn't out of the question that the boy might still be hiding out somewhere close by in the airfield, or even waiting for him in the harbour itself.

As he and Eddie continued to parallel-track the small country lane, they stole along the side of a field of barley. Through his headset, this appeared to Drake as though it was the rippling surface of a large lake as the wind fanned it. But he hardly noticed this as he wondered who might have accompanied Chester in the launch. It was a two-person journey up the river – one to man the outboard engine, and the other to refuel it and act as pilot. Chester hadn't given any indication in the message, although he'd sounded pretty desperate.

A faint drizzle began to fall as Drake and Eddie crossed a narrow road and mounted the opposite verge.

'Norfolk,' Drake chuckled. 'Rain, always rain – it's always raining in this county.' Although Eddie didn't make any sort of response, Drake sensed disapproval from the man that he'd spoken out loud.

Within a short distance, they came to a gap in the perimeter fence of the airfield and squeezed through it, noting a Portakabin in the distance that was lit from within. Then they cut behind a group of 1960s houses arranged in a small close. Drake assumed these properties had originally been used by the enlisted men and their families. But now they were very much unoccupied, and in the process of being refurbished, judging from all the building materials lying around.

As he and Eddie headed towards one of the larger buildings, Drake found that he was continually checking to make sure the other man was still there. Although the former Limiter claimed it was years since he'd been active in the field, he moved in total and absolute silence. It was as though Drake's sense of hearing was defective – he could see Eddie treading on an area of dry bracken or pushing his way through patches of undergrowth as he followed, but the man didn't make the slightest sound. It had been just the same with his daughter, Elliott.

They penetrated a clump of brambles, and there Drake removed a few pieces of rotten timber laid over the hatch, revealing a concrete-lined shaft around two metres square. Lowering themselves into this, they used the rusting treads set into the side of the shaft to reach to the bottom. Then they were wading through a room filled with lockers and flooded with filthy brown water, deep enough to come in over their boots.

After Drake opened a door at the end of the room, they quickly passed down a corridor in which empty oil drums and some lengths of mildewed timber were floating. Then they were at the wall of breeze blocks that Will had broken through.

Eddie drew out one of his handguns as he and Drake climbed through the jagged opening. They both dropped into low crouches, listening and checking the harbour either side of them. No one was in evidence. With a hand signal, Drake directed Eddie to search one end of the quay while he took the other.

Drake came across the launch where it had been dragged from the water and, close to it, a military kitbag and two holdalls. He was working through the contents of one of these holdalls, finding cans of the aerosol he'd given Will to repel the monkey-spiders, some military food rations, and a bundle of flares, when he became aware of Eddie beside him.

'All clear,' the man said, then glanced over his shoulder at the rapidly flowing river in the darkness. 'So this is the way down to Elliott?'

Drake didn't answer the Limiter, instead raising the holdall so that he could see it. 'Whoever's come up from the fallout shelter, they've left a lot of kit behind. But where's Chester?' Drake posed.

'Somewhere he feels safe?' Eddie suggested. 'You thought he might go to London, so perhaps he's on his way there?'

'Maybe, but he'll know your mob will be waiting for him the moment he pops up. And he has no way of contacting me except for messages on the remote server.'

'Well, you know the boy,' Eddie put in.

'I do, but it also depends who's with him – if it's Will, then they might have chanced returning to Highfield together. Chester – by himself – would be far more cautious. No, I reckon he might have just dug himself in somewhere not too far from here.'

Eddie pointed one of his thin white fingers upwards. 'So we should canvass the buildings,' he suggested, 'and keep an eye out for any tracks.'

Drake nodded, his expression one of concern. 'But if he left here a week or two ago, then the weather will have removed all trace of them,' he said.

Chapter Ten

'Ah, there you are. Come and see this,' Dr Burrows shouted. Will had just emerged from the shade of the trees, and was ambling over to where his father was working at a makeshift trestle table by the base of the pyramid.

Glancing up from the skull in his hands, Dr Burrows only looked at his son when he was almost at the table. 'What happened to your hair?' he asked. 'Someone try to scalp you?'

'Elliott cut it for me,' Will replied indignantly. He scratched his rather short hair and a few tufts came away in his hand. 'Actually, it was rather painful because her knife isn't very sharp.' He glanced back at the trees. 'She's cutting hers now – must be something to do with this place or the sun or something, but her hair grows so much faster than mine. I swear it's as much as a centimetre a day. Maybe it's a Styx th—'

'This is fascinating,' Dr Burrows interrupted, as if he hadn't been listening to a word his son had been saying. He put the skull in a space he'd cleared on the cluttered tabletop. Will saw that there were three skulls in total, lined up in a row.

'Where did you get these?' Will asked.

Dr Burrows fanned his fingers so he could touch both the top of the skull he'd just been examining and the one next to it. 'This pair was in a small compartment towards the top of the pyramid. I dislodged a cover stone with an inscription on it, which translates roughly as *Origins*. They were both inside.'

'In a small compartment?' Will said. 'You didn't tell me. Where was I when you found them?'

'You were off with your hairdressing pal,' Dr Burrows replied caustically.

'Was I?' Will asked, frowning. He had a pretty good idea which day it must have been, but resented the fact that his father was trying to make him feel guilty. Will devoted nearly all his time to helping his father, and he felt he deserved a break every now and then.

'Yes, she was showing you her hidey-hole or something. You remember – it was the memorable occasion she claimed that the trees were watching her,' Dr Burrows replied disinterestedly, then his whole demeanour transformed as he lowered his hand onto the third skull. It was sun-bleached and very white. 'And this fellow is from the trio impaled on the stakes.'

'Dad! You shouldn't have moved it!' Will exclaimed. 'They were there for a reason. It doesn't feel right that you've messed around with them.'

'Don't you go getting all superstitious on me,' Dr Burrows retorted. Will could see his father's eyes were sparkling with excitement, and decided not to push the matter any further. It was obvious Dr Burrows thought he was on to something, and Will knew he wasn't going to have to wait long to find out what it was. He was right. 'There's no question that the skull from the stake is human. *Homo sapiens*, same as you and me,' Dr Burrows announced. 'And so is this other one, from the pair in the compartment.'

'It's a darker colour,' Will observed.

'That's not important – focus on the smaller skull next to it, which the Ancients thought was significant enough to preserve in the pyramid. Tell me what you see,' Dr Burrows instructed Will, snatching up the skull and pushing it into his son's hands.

'It's heavy. It's definitely a fossil,' Will observed, gauging its weight. 'And it looks different from a human sk—'

'I'll say it does,' Dr Burrows cut in. 'What about the overhanging brow, and the way the jaw protrudes much more than the others?'

'It isn't human?' Will asked.

'I only took a couple of courses in anthropology so I'm no expert. However, to my eye, it has features that are neither human, nor fully simian,' Dr Burrows gushed.

'Simian?' Will said. 'So it's not an ape or a monkey either?'

'No, not in my opinion, because—' Dr Burrows interrupted himself, waving his hands enthusiastically. 'Remember back in Highfield when you were young – I told you all about the missing links and Leakey Man?'

'Bedtime stories about Leakey Man,' Will recalled, allowing himself a chuckle. 'Yes, I remember . . . the skull that was dug up in a river in Africa.'

'Precisely! It was solid proof of one of man's distant ancestors. But while skulls from the *Homo erectus* stage and a number of other stages that came before it have been discovered, there's absolutely nothing to demonstrate the transitional steps from ape to man. Nothing at all. No fossil remains have been found yet for the so-called hominid gap, which was millions of years long. Don't you think that's odd?'

'Yeah – very,' Will answered.

'Of course it is. There's always been this unexplained mystery as to why there's a gaping hole in the human evolutionary record.'

'And?' Will urged his father.

Dr Burrows snatched the small skull back from his son and replaced it on the table. 'This may sound a bit off the wall . . . but what if they've never been found on the surface because . . .' He now stuck his finger in the air, urging Will to finish his assertion.

When Will didn't answer quickly enough, Dr Burrows continued impatiently. 'Because it all went on down here.'

'Ah,' Will put in, but his father was in full flow now.

'What if this inner world was the melting pot of human evolution, and possibly even the evolution of an ark-full of other animal species?' Dr Burrows threw his arms open at the jungle around them. 'I mean, all the plants and trees we can see before us are specially adapted to live without night – all the flora on the surface need darkness for photosynthesis and to trigger photoperiodic changes.'

'Photo – *what*?' Will asked.

Dr Burrows ignored his question, talking rapidly. 'So my theory is the 24/7 sunlight in this closed ecosystem actually promotes accelerated evolution. And it also promoted *our* accelerated evolution.'

'You're saying apes evolved into humans here in this inner world, and then somehow got back to the surface,' Will said.

'Precisely!' Dr Burrows exclaimed again. 'Which is amazing . . . and the Ancients, the people who lived here, were clued-up enough to be interested in it, too. From what's written on their pyramid, they were close to figuring it out.' He took a breath. 'And what this also means is that I've probably just made the single most important discovery of the century.'

'Another one?' Will murmured under his breath, shaking his head at the old skulls.

Drake glanced at his watch as he squatted by the launch on the quayside. 'Sun up is around six hundred hours,' he said. Although he could have used his headset to search the former airfield up above for any tracks Chester might have left there, he and Eddie had decided it would be better to wait until dawn. To pass the time, Drake was making an inventory of the rations in the holdalls. Buried under the packets, he found something that he took out very slowly.

It resembled a rather crude gun.

'Weapon?' Eddie asked, immediately interested.

Drake shook his head. 'No, it's a prototype low-frequency detector. It hasn't been properly trialled yet, but if we got the specs right, it should work as a tracking system – even over great distances underground.'

Eddie was intrigued. 'Through the Earth's crust?' he said.

Drake was examining the dial on top of the unit. 'Yes, through rock – no matter how thick the strata.'

'Useful,' Eddie said.

'Yep, and I gave Will a pair of these and a batch of radio beacons so he could find his . . .' Drake trailed off. He got to his feet and pressed the trigger on the device.

As he pointed it downriver, there was a very faint clicking and the needle gauge on the top of the device moved the smallest degree. 'That must be the fallout shelter, unless he marked one of the way stations.'

Then as he happened to turn around to where the river emerged from the other end of the harbour, the detector emitted a much louder burst of clicking and the needle went wild. 'That's funny,' he said. He homed in on the signal, finding it led him towards the opening in the breeze blocks. 'It's even stronger here,' he noted, a thoughtful look in his eyes. 'I wonder . . .'

Rebecca Two and the Limiter General were being driven in a large black limousine, with military vehicles in front and behind, and a pair of motorcycle outriders leading the way.

'What do they take me for?' Rebecca Two grumbled, as she looked down at the skirt of the pure white cotton dress she'd been given, decorated with cream ribbons. 'At least you don't look like the sugarplum fairy,' she muttered to the taciturn Limiter General beside her. She would have been far more comfortable in a version of the dark grey military uniform with which he'd been provided.

They had glimpses of the ocean as the motorcade skirted the docks area, and then cut in towards the centre of the metropolis. Through the tinted windows in the rear of the limousine, Rebecca Two gazed at the people on the streets and the different sights. As they passed a school, a crocodile of young children was leaving the gates, all of them wearing wide-brimmed hats to protect them from the sun. Rebecca Two was astounded at the scale of the city; endless terraces of houses flashed by, interspersed with boulevards of shops. These eventually gave way to buildings the size of hangars: imposing neoclassical structures constructed from granite or lighter chalk-like stone, with names on their facades such as *Institut der Geologie* and *Zentrum fuer Medizinische Forschung*.

Then the motorcade dipped into an underpass and came up again in a tree-lined avenue. Rebecca Two saw that beyond these trees and directly ahead was some kind of immense plaza. Across this huge open space, many intersecting roads buzzed with heavy traffic. But her eyes were drawn to the statues between the trees at the edge of the avenue – the proud figures of men standing on granite plinths. 'Frederick the Great,' she read on one of them.

'And in place of honour, Albert Speer,' the Limiter General said. Rebecca Two craned her neck to see the large besuited figure with a set of plans spread open in its hands. It was the final statue in the row and, unlike the other figures, its head wasn't facing its counterpart on the opposite side of the road, but was instead staring at the giant arch the limousine was fast approaching. There were also armoured vehicles stationed all around the plaza, and the Limiter General was particularly interested in a long rank of tanks, some painted neutral grey and others in a woodland camouflage. 'Panzers?' he asked himself, under his breath.

'Hey, I know this arch – I could see it from the mountains,' Rebecca Two said, realising why it was so familiar to her.

The motorcade drew up by one of the two monolithic legs of the arch, and the doors of the limousine were opened for her and the Limiter General. The soldiers from the military escort quickly disembarked and encircled them in a protective cordon. The arch was built on a large island in the middle of the plaza, around which traffic was passing, and the soldiers arranged themselves so that the curious faces in these vehicles could see very little of the two Styx.

As she stepped across the pavement, Rebecca Two recognised one of the soldiers in their escort – it was the young officer who'd been in command of the squad at the city gates. As the officer checked his detail was positioned correctly, he appeared far more at ease that he had done on that first occasion.

'We meet again,' Rebecca Two announced.

Giving her a fleeting smile, the officer nodded once in response. It was obvious that he wanted her to keep moving towards the arch, but she remained where she was.

'I want to thank you for standing your men down,' she said. 'It could have very easily gone all Wild West, but you kept your cool and saved your men's lives. And, most importantly, you helped save my sister's life. That's something I will *never* forget.'

He nodded again, then indicated that she and the Limiter General should go towards the entrance in the nearest leg of the arch. As she peered all the way up to the top of the massive structure, she could see row upon row of dark-tinted windows in its many storeys. She began to move towards it, then stopped.

'What is this place?' she asked the officer.

'*Das Kanzleramt* . . . I think in English you would call it the Chancellery,' he replied.

'Right,' she said.

Once Rebecca Two and the Limiter General had entered through a set of rotating doors made of glass and solid brass, they were ushered along a marble hall to a lift. Their military escort remained behind as the two Styx ascended some thirty floors by themselves. They were met at the top by a woman in a dark suit. Rebecca Two wrinkled her nose at the woman's overpowering perfume. Although she was young, her make-up was heavily applied, and her platinum blonde hair was so rigid it could have been varnished.

'Welcome,' the woman announced in a friendly voice, then wheeled towards Rebecca Two. 'And don't you look so pretty in that lovely dress?' she simpered. The manner of the woman was such that she could have been complimenting the daughter of some visiting dignitary. But she certainly didn't get the response she was expecting.

'It's gross,' Rebecca Two snarled, shifting her shoulders uncomfortably under the light cotton. 'First chance I get, I'm going to rip it to shreds and burn it.'

'Oh!' the woman exclaimed, her eyes widening. 'Th– . . . This way if you please,' she stuttered, and led them through another hallway, walking a little too quickly as her high heels clicked on the polished stone floor. She studiously avoided looking at Rebecca Two as she knocked on a pair of large wooden doors, then pushed them open.

'Do come in,' a voice called.

With the Limiter General several paces behind her, Rebecca Two walked into the room. Her gaze fell on a long table of highly lacquered dark wood, around which were numerous chairs. The centrepiece of the table was a large, fierce-looking eagle emerging from a shattered bronze globe, which on closer inspection Rebecca Two saw was meant to represent the world.

'Hello.' A man had risen from the far end of the table and now approached them. As Rebecca Two tried to avoid staring at his rather small moustache, she couldn't tell his age but estimated him to be in his late fifties. He was corpulent, and breathed heavily as he walked. His black hair was slicked back, and he wore a beige-coloured uniform with epaulettes striped with gold braid.

'I'm Herr Friedrich, Chancellor of New Germania,' he introduced himself. His voice was warm, and but for a slight accent, he spoke impeccable English. Extending a soft palm, he shook hands with Rebecca Two and the Limiter General, then gestured towards the end of the table where he'd been sitting. But Rebecca Two slowed as she came to a long window. From their elevated position, the view over the metropolis was breathtaking, and she and the Limiter General stopped to take it in.

'Quite something, isn't it?' the Chancellor said proudly. He pointed to a black-and-white photograph mounted on the wall beside the window. 'When we arrived in this new world a little over sixty years ago, that's all there was – a strip of land between the sea and the mountains, with only trees and a few ruins on it.' The photograph showed an area of the jungle in the process of being cleared – workgangs of men stripped to the waist were wielding axes and moving felled trucks, while around them many fires were burning. Rebecca spotted tents in the background, beside which were some of the unusual helicopters.

'Sixty years,' Rebecca Two repeated as she returned her gaze to the metropolis through the window.

'It all began in the thirties when Himmler sent expeditions to the far corners of the world, to Tibet and both Poles. He was in search of ancient knowledge that would assist the Nazi Party in its pursuit of power. Amongst other things, Himmler was a believer in the Hollow Earth theory. The fact we are standing here in a city with a population of nearly five hundred thousand is because Hitler wanted to ensure that the

Third Reich endured the thousand years he promised our nation. New Germania was to be his refuge, his last outpost, in case he lost the war.'

'But he never made it down here,' Rebecca Two said. 'He died in his bunker.'

The Chancellor was about to answer when a servant appeared from a small door in the corner of the room, and instead he grinned and clapped his hands together. 'I thought we should take some luncheon. As our meeting is such an auspicious event we're having Plesiosaurus,' he said, as he began towards the table, where three places had been laid.

'Plesiosaurus?' Rebecca Two asked with a frown. She realised as soon as she'd said the word why it was so familiar to her – Will and Dr Burrows would babble on interminably about fossil remains they dreamed of finding on their trips together. The plesiosaurus and ichthyosaurus were two of them. 'It's an extinct dinosaur, like a huge lizard with a long neck?'

'Very impressive and absolutely correct,' the Chancellor praised her, 'except for one thing. The creature is not extinct in our oceans, and the choicest cuts come from the rump. My chef is the finest in the city – he lightly sears each steak and serves it on a bed of mango rice.' The Chancellor licked his shiny lips. 'You're in for a rare treat, I promise you.'

They took their places, and the servant filled their glasses with chilled water from a silver jug. 'One quickly learns that in order to adapt to this world and its high temperatures, one has to drink enough fluids, and eat well,' the Chancellor announced, helping himself to a bread roll and breaking it open on his side plate. 'We are not used to entertaining visitors from the outer crust, but I trust you have been well looked after? I hope everything has been to your satisfaction?' he enquired. He'd evidently been briefed that this young girl was in charge, but perhaps didn't quite believe it, making sure he also addressed his questions to the Limiter General.

'Very satisfactory, thank you,' Rebecca Two answered politely. 'I have to say all the showers your medical officers insist that I take and the endless doses of iodine I've been gulping down do get a little tedious after a while.'

The Chancellor nodded in sympathy. 'Quite so. It is unfortunate that you reached our city through the uranium mines, but I'm informed your exposure to the radiation wasn't excessive. I'm afraid the showers and the iodine are precautionary measures, but very necessary. As I'm sure you've been told, we limit our time in those mountains and certain areas of the jungle due to the high radiation counts there.'

Rebecca Two nodded.

'And your sister? She is recovering well?' the Chancellor asked.

'Your doctors have done wonders,' Rebecca Two replied. 'She'd lost so much blood, it was touch and go at first whether she was going to make it through. But she did, and she's well on the mend now, and I'm very grateful to you for that. And she's also over the moon that a dentist was sent to fix her broken teeth.'

The Chancellor waved his hand dismissively. 'Such assistance is only to be expected between old allies like us,' he said. He glanced at a file on a bureau behind the Limiter General. 'So . . . Mephistopheles. I've been reading the files on you – they're stored photographically so they took a while to locate, but I'm up to speed now. And I apologise for not meeting with you before now, but I have been directly in touch with my staff all the time you've been our guests.'

'Guests?' Rebecca Two responded sharply just as the Chancellor was taking a mouthful of water.

There was a moment as the man swallowed loudly – he was unused to being spoken to like this. He put his glass down on the table with great precision, then leant back in his chair, waiting for Rebecca Two to continue.

'Guests, or *prisoners*? We've been confined to a compound, where we've been kept under armed guard. Other than this visit to you now, you haven't allowed us to go anywhere,' Rebecca Two levelled at him.

The Chancellor knitted his fingers together. 'The protection has been for your own good. We do not want to alarm the civilians in the city who are unused to the presence of outsiders. You are free to leave the city whenever you wish – but whilst within its walls we must insist that you remain under our supervision.'

'So you'd let us do that? You'd allow us to go? Aren't you afraid we might reveal your existence to the outer world when we return there?' Rebecca Two said.

'I don't believe you would,' the Chancellor replied without hesitation. 'It seems to me that the Styx value their privacy every bit as much as we do. In any case, the fissure in Antarctica through which we entered has been sealed with explosives by our engineers. While we don't know which route you used to enter our world, we could find it if we were so minded, and seal it too.'

'There's no need for that,' Rebecca Two confirmed. 'Your secret is safe with us.' Without pausing to take breath she continued, 'But I need some help from you.'

'That depends—' the Chancellor began.

'No, it doesn't *depend* on anything.' Rebecca Two interrupted. 'Prior to the invasion of Poland, we struck a deal with the German High Command. We furnished you with intel which was invaluable in achieving a number of military objectives throughout your European campaign. That intel didn't come cheap – Styx lives were lost in obtaining it. And the deal was – how can I put it? – a two-way street. We delivered on our side, and in return we were promised a place at the top table if you won the war. Although you didn't, I'm calling in that debt right now.'

The Chancellor tried to read her dark eyes as he spoke. 'You must forgive me, but this was all long before my time and, besides, none of the High Command made it to this world,' he countered.

The servant chose that moment to enter with a trolley of food, but the Chancellor waved him out of the room.

Rebecca Two was staring coldly at the Chancellor. 'Don't try to wheedle out of the deal. I'm not asking for much. I'm asking you to assist us in the search for something we want to recover . . . something that has been stolen from us. You owe the Styx. And when we collect on our favours, we do not expect to be disappointed. I'm not going to stoop to making threats, but you *really* don't want to cross us.'

The Chancellor's eyebrows had hiked up a little while Rebecca Two had been speaking, and now remained there.

'The generals with whom you struck your deal are, I fear, long gone,' the Chancellor said. 'They were killed at the end of the war or faced the Nuremberg trials. But while we carry on Prussian military tradition for maintenance of order in New Germania, we are a very different beast. We do not persecute those races we persecuted before. We are not warmongers. We are *not* Nazis.'

Rebecca Two nodded at the bronze eagle emerging from the ruptured globe in the centre of the table. 'So what's that then? Window dressing? You found a nice, cushy place to hide away when your country was defeated, and you've gone soft?' she said scornfully.

There was silence in the room, which lasted for several seconds.

'Yes, if you want to look at it like that,' the Chancellor conceded. 'We heard what happened to the mother country in the aftermath of the war, and we have no interest in what's going on back in the outer world. In the first months of this outpost, the Nazi party members who accompanied the helicopter convoys from Antarctica were – how do you say? – lost *en route*. The SS officers and all the technical people who were airlifted down here with their families wanted to forget the past and build new lives for themselves. Many had been at Stalingrad and on the Eastern Front, and after five years of pointless slaughter, they'd had their fill of death and destruction.'

'The lion that stopped roaring . . .' Rebecca Two smiled sourly. 'So that's it – you just ducked out and left your nation to it? You're weak and pathetic. You might as well call yourself New *Geraniums*.' She flicked her head insolently.

The Chancellor adjusted his position in his chair as if he had no idea how to respond to this.

'Well, we as a people, haven't given up. And if you don't honour your obligations to us, there will be serious consequences,' Rebecca Two continued.

The Limiter General spoke, his tone casual, almost conversational. 'Comply with our request, or several thousand

Limiters – just like me – will be sent down here to kill every single man, woman and child in this city.'

The Chancellor's eyebrows were now so high up his forehead they looked as though they would never come down again.

Rebecca formed a tight fist and lowered it slowly to the table, then she took a breath and fastened her jet-black pupils on the Chancellor. 'So you will provide us with men drawn from your very best regiment, and some transport. And once we have what we've come for, we will leave you in peace. Got that?'

There was a pause, then the Chancellor nodded.

The Styx girl and the Limiter General rose from the table at precisely the same moment.

'You're leaving? What about our luncheon?' the Chancellor asked quietly.

'We're going back to the compound. I eat with my men,' Rebecca Two said. She glanced at the trolley the servant had abandoned and smirked. 'But don't let us keep you from your lizard arse.'

Chapter Eleven

'Want me to shift some of that stuff over to the hide-away?' Elliott offered, as she tied up the Bergen ready to take with her. 'It might be safer there.'

In the base she'd built up in the tree, she was watching as Will rather aimlessly checked through his belongings. There was no real reason for him to be there – he just wanted to be with Elliott.

She stood up and came over to him as he failed to answer. 'You should keep a couple of weapons and some rounds here, but the rest is just cluttering up the place,' she said.

'Yes, sure, okay,' he replied. He began to pick out a few items, then stopped to look up at her. 'I didn't mention anything about the tunnel to Dad, you know,' he told her.

'No?' she asked.

While Dr Burrows hadn't shown any interest in the hide-away, Will knew that the tunnel behind the waterfall would be something he'd insist on seeing. As evidenced by the carving at its entrance, the Ancients had built it, and no doubt he'd want to explore it thoroughly.

'You should tell him,' she said, as she knelt down beside

Will and selected a few items to take with her, as if he was incapable of doing it himself. 'If it runs all the way back to Martha's level – which it very well might – then it's the way home for you. And that's important.'

Will nodded. 'Yeah, but, like you, I don't want to leave here. One day soon, Dad's going to go back and tell everyone about his discoveries. He wants to be recognised. He talks about it all the time.' Will's inner conflict was evident as he furrowed his brow. 'And he'll make me go with him, because he'll need help carrying all the skulls, stones and other arte-facts, to support his claims.'

'Maybe he'll want you to go with him so he can keep an eye on you, and make sure you're okay,' Elliott suggested.

Will was quick to answer this. 'No, you know that's not the way it is with him.' He rubbed his face and sighed. '*Some ideas are too big and too important to let people get in the way*,' he said, quoting what his father had declared just before he'd thrown himself down Smoking Jean, a leap of faith which had ultimately led them all to this secret world. Will looked point-edly at the girl beside him. 'No question his work comes first. Before me, even.'

Elliott nodded.

Will pretended to examine a broken fingernail. 'And I'm not leaving you here . . . not by yourself,' he said, his voice quavering.

'We'll see,' Elliott replied noncommittally. Gathering some of Will's belongings in her arms, she rose to her feet. 'Look on the bright side – maybe something will kill us before we have to make any decisions,' she said, returning to her Bergen.

Will was in turmoil. He'd tried to let Elliott know how he felt about her in the only way he knew how, without embarrassing either of them, but she hadn't responded how he'd hoped she would. In fact, Will felt that her response amounted to a rejection.

Maybe it boiled down to something very simple – maybe she didn't like him that much. Perhaps he wasn't *special* enough in her eyes. She could see him for what he was – it wasn't as if there was much mystery to him, because they both lived in such close proximity to each other. And it wasn't as if there was much he could do to impress her – she was the one equipped with all the incredible skills that enabled her to thrive in this environment. There was nothing he could do to impress her that she couldn't do ten times better.

They'd been thrown together in this unreal situation due to extraordinary circumstances, and maybe that was as far as it went. Given the opportunity, perhaps she'd rather be with someone else. 'Chester,' Will sighed under his breath.

And even if that wasn't the case, Will couldn't help but think that Dr Burrows might be spoiling everything for him with his selfish and single-minded pursuit of knowledge. Will turned his head in the direction of the pyramid. Through the leaf cover he could just see his father scuttling along one of the tiers, his scrawny limbs carrying him like some errant spider as he continued on his exhaustive study of the carved inscriptions. A spider weaving a web in which, whether Will liked it or not, he was ensnared.

As the first knell of the bell filled the South Cavern with its low, forlorn sound, Mrs Burrows began to emerge from the dark corner of her mind in which she spent her days. But although she was returning to her body, much as a hand slips into a glove, she didn't move a single muscle. Instead she listened to the commotion in the hallway where Eliza and her mother were putting their hats and coats on, and fussing over each other.

'She's all right,' Eliza reported brusquely to her mother as she poked her head around the door to check on Mrs Burrows. Then the two of them bustled from the house, clucking at each other like a pair of old hens.

It was the appointed hour for vespers – the religious service which took place without fail each and every evening all over the Colony – and it wasn't done to be late. That particular night the Second Officer was still at work in the Quarter and so wouldn't be accompanying his mother and sister, instead going to a service at a church closer to the police station. That was if he didn't have some poor wretch in the Hold to watch over.

As the bell sounded for the seventh and final time, someone with heavy feet ran down the pavement outside, then there was complete silence. Except for the infirm and those who were too ill to be moved, it was obligatory for anyone without official duties to attend vespers. These services provided the people of the Colony with religious instruction from the *Book of Catastrophes*, and also gave the Styx a perfect opportunity to monitor the congregation. It was said the pairs of Styx stationed at the entrances to all the churches knew exactly who should be present, and kept a particular watch on anyone they considered to be a potential troublemaker.

When the Second Officer had first brought Mrs Burrows home, Eliza insisted on doing her duty and wheeling her along to a service in the bath chair. But as Eliza had approached the church, a small crowd of resentful Colonists had been milling around the pavement, doing their damnedest to obstruct her way. Ignoring the grumbles of 'Foul Topsoiler' and 'Heathen', Eliza had given up trying to circumvent the human slalom, and moved from the pavement into the road. But when, finally, she reached the entrance, a hastily-formed cordon of Colonists steadfastly refused to let her enter. Looking the other way, the pair of Styx either side of the church doors had done nothing to help.

Although Mrs Burrows' brain was still badly scrambled by the Dark Light, and to any onlooker she appeared to be unconscious, she'd been sensitive to the waves of pure hatred emanating from the angry mob. Feeling as though her head was about to explode, she suddenly developed a nosebleed. Not just any nosebleed – there was so much blood spilling down her face and front it was as if an artery had been nicked.

As Eliza tried to stem the flow, the delighted mob had chanted 'Bleed, Topsoiler, bleed!' and 'Bleed the pig, bleed the pig!' Abandoning all hopes of attending the service, Eliza had finally pushed Mrs Burrows right back home again, the cheers of the crowds echoing down the street after her.

Following that incident, Mrs Burrows was relieved that Eliza left her unattended in the empty house. And in the days since then, Mrs Burrows' sensitivity to the emotions of those around her had become even more acute, and she really wasn't sure if she'd be able to stand the herd-like fury of all those ranting Colonists again. And that could spell disaster. Mrs Burrows knew if she let the pretence slip and showed any reaction – however small – the game would be up. She'd be back in the Hold in a flash, and in all likelihood the Styx would subject her to further rounds of interrogation with the Dark Light.

So now, in the empty house, where there was no one around to observe her, Mrs Burrows flicked her eyes open and sat up. She flung off the towel which had been draped across her chest to catch any trickles of saliva, and rose to her feet. 'That's better,' she said, stretching her arms wide in her voluminous dress, and yawning as if she had woken from a deep slumber.

She sank to the floor and did a quick yoga routine to loosen up her stiff limbs, then sprang to her feet again.

'Colly,' she called gently. 'Where are you?'

The Hunter scampered in, and Mrs Burrows stroked the smooth black skin of her head. 'Good girl,' she said, then went into the hall, the cat by her side.

Despite the fact that Mrs Burrows' sight was still severely impaired, she no longer relied on Colly to act as her guide. During the night hours when the rest of the house was asleep, she'd been honing and experimenting with her peculiar extra sense, testing its increasing limits. And with each new day it definitely seemed to be growing more powerful.

Mrs Burrows could see, but in a different way from other people.

She stepped to the front door and opened it to the deserted street. Then she unleashed her ability. It was as if she was sending out invisible tendrils, and those tendrils could bring information back to her, as surely as if she was seeing or touching anything they encountered. They went in all directions, to the houses opposite, to the ends of the street and beyond, always probing and sensing. There were no people close by – she could divine that – and it was only when she stretched a tendril way out that she came across the packed hall where vespers was underway. From the massed group of people inside came mixed emotions – ennui, fatigue and the frisson of fear – the Styx preacher must be giving his usual fire and brimstone sermon. But as she quickly recalled this tendril, it picked up something.

'No!' she exclaimed, stepping fully outside the house and moving swiftly down the garden path, her nose in the air. She couldn't help herself, drawn to the scent she'd discovered, like a moth to a flame. Colly meowed plaintively, as if she thought Mrs Burrows was mistaken to leave the house.

'It's okay,' Mrs Burrows assured the cat. 'Look – there's nobody around.'

Arriving at the end of the street, Mrs Burrows turned the corner, then passed down several more roads until she spotted the place she'd sensed. It was a house in the middle of a terrace. Sniffing to make sure it was the right one, she went up to the front door and pushed on it. It was locked, so she tried the windows on either side of the door, finding she could push one of the casements up.

Straddling the sill, she entered inside. She found she was in a sitting room where the remnants of a fire burnt in the hearth, and plates with half-eaten food had been left on the dining table. She ignored all this, raising her head to sample the air again. She went directly to the rear of the house. There, propped against the wall by the back door, was the object that had brought her here.

'Will,' she said, reaching out to touch her son's beloved spade. She couldn't comprehend how it had come to be there, but she had to have it. She snatched it up, running a hand over the stainless steel blade and remembering how much care Will had taken of it. At the end of each day after his digs in Highfield, he would never fail to clean and polish it before going to sleep.

But it wasn't the feel of the blade and the wooden shaft that had brought her here. Even after all these months in the Colony, the scent that still lingered on the spade conjured up a vivid picture of her son in her mind's eye. She smiled, but her smile was short-lived. As her brain had gradually healed and rewired itself, she realised she'd detached herself from the very reason why she'd ended up in the Colony in the first place. She'd been trying to help Will in his struggle against the Styx, and at this very moment she had no idea where he was, or even if he was still alive. The last time she'd seen him was at the Little Chef on the way to Norfolk, and she wondered how he'd fared deep in the bowels of the Earth on the quest that Drake had set him.

'I can't stay here much longer. I've got to leave the Colony,' she mumbled to the cat, who had followed her in and was watching her intently. 'But we've got to leave this house right now!' she said urgently, as one of her olfactory tendrils alerted her to a burst of activity from the church several streets away. Mrs Burrows tore back to the window and scrambled out into the street, dropping the spade in the process. 'Damn!' she swore as she retrieved it, then began to run.

'Keep up, Colly!' she hissed. She could sense the presence of people all around as they began to filter into the streets again. She wasn't far from the Second Officer's house when she realised that someone was approaching too rapidly from the opposite direction and would head her off. She sensed a pair of Colonists. She couldn't allow herself to be seen. Pulling the Hunter with her, she sheltered in an alleyway between two houses. Although her lack of sight didn't allow her to know for certain, she just hoped that she was out of the illumination shed by the orb street lights. The approaching Colonists were merely two young children – a boy and a girl – and they ran straight past, laughing and shouting.

As soon as they had gone, Mrs Burrows emerged from the alleyway and sprinted down the pavement to the house. Once inside, she hid the spade behind the sideboard in the room where she slept. Colly was prancing around, overexcited at the mad rush they'd made together. 'Quieten down now,' Mrs Burrows ordered the cat. 'Go to your basket.' The Hunter obediently slipped out of the room, and Mrs Burrows had taken her place in her bath chair when she heard the front door open. She remembered the towel that had been spread on her chest. *Oh no!* she thought. *You idiot!* Reaching over to retrieve it from the floor, she laid the towel on her chest and slumped back in the chair just in time for Eliza and her mother as they entered the room.

Dressed in their hats and coats, they regarded Mrs Burrows for several seconds, the disapproval radiating from both of them.

'Still 'ere then, you bloomin' deadweight?' the old woman said eventually, her voice dripping with resentment.

'Of course she is. She's never going anywhere,' Eliza said, then hesitated. 'But she doesn't look too clever, does she? Bit flushed, I'd say. Maybe she's coming down with a fever?' she added hopefully, going over Mrs Burrows and feeling her forehead.

Mrs Burrows immediately reduced her breathing and lowered her body temperature – she couldn't let them see that she was out of breath or hot from her recent exertions.

'No, she hasn't got a temperature,' Eliza decided, her disappointment evident.

The old woman lowered her voice. 'Perhaps we need to

give 'er a little nudge to 'elp 'er on her way,' she suggested. 'She's never going to be right again, so it'd be like snuffin' out a smoulderin' wick on a tallow.'

'We can't go on like this,' Eliza agreed.

'No, we can't, and *desperite* times call for *desperite* measures,' the old woman whispered, whipping off her hat. 'We could stop feedin' 'er or somethin'? Or lace 'er food with slug poison?'

There was no response from Eliza as she continued to stand in front of Mrs Burrows, but her very lack of response spoke volumes.

We'll see about that, Mrs Burrows thought to herself as she crept back into the dark recess of her brain, still cherishing the image of Will that the spade had conjured up. *Just you try anything, you old witches!*

Chapter Twelve

Eddie was at the wheel as they powered through the Norfolk countryside. With the detector in his hand Drake was tracking the signal from the radio beacon, at the same time as consulting the car's Sat Nav unit to find the most direct route.

'Hang a left,' he instructed Eddie, then as he scrolled through the roads on the Sat Nav, he added, 'No, scrub that – keep going and take the second left.' He glanced up at the road ahead and caught sight of a sign. '*Walsingham*,' he read. 'At this rate, we're going to end up on the coast.'

Within ten minutes, the signal was so strong that the clicking from the detector was almost continuous. Drake muted the sound. 'Right, this is close enough. Let's dump the car and recce the area on foot.'

Eddie found a place to park and they climbed out. After taking what they needed from the boot, Drake spent a moment to get a final fix on the direction of the signal before putting his headset on and firing it up. Then they crossed the road to a field of rapeseed, keeping to a footpath at the edge as they marched at a brisk pace.

Through the lens of his headset the rapeseed appeared to Drake as a sea of white gold, churning with slow breakers as the wind stroked it. Eddie came alongside him, moving soundlessly in long, easy strides. In his Limiter fatigues and with his Styx rifle in his hands, there was something timeless about the dark form of the soldier set against the backdrop of the golden sea. Like a heroic warrior from an epic tale. *Always to be best, and to be distinguished above the rest,* Drake thought to himself, recalling the line from Homer.

It occurred to Drake just how grateful he was for the Styx's company. He'd spent so much of his life isolated and alone in the seemingly impossible battle against his foe, and now at last he had an ally, and dare he even think it, a *friend*. This kinship with someone who'd been in the opposing camp was still strange to him, but Drake conceded that Eddie had been right about what he'd said in the car. The two of them were alike in so many ways.

Within another kilometre a small hillock came into view as they neared a hedge at the far end of a grassy meadow. Eddie held up his fist to tell Drake to stop. They both squatted down.

As he surveyed the hedge through his lens, trying to discern the reason for Eddie's concern, Drake saw that the Styx was more interested in the ground just in front of him. Drake took out his handgun and watched as Eddie picked away some fallen branches and tufts of dried grass. Drake couldn't understand what he was doing. Then he saw why. Eddie had cleared enough of the branches and grass to reveal that they were masking a panel of criss-crossed sticks, under which was a slit trench. Drake could see that in the bottom of the deep trench a row of stakes had been stuck in the newly dug earth. Stakes with sharpened tips.

He met Eddie's eyes. It was a *trap pit* – hardly what one would expect in rural Norfolk. Although they didn't speak, the question that occurred to both of them was whether the trap had been laid for an animal – and a relatively large one at that – or for a human being. Its size and position certainly suggested the latter.

Eddie gave the sign and they went around the trench, checking and double-checking every inch of the ground on the way to the hedge. Drake found a point in the hedge where the growth was less dense, and began to probe it with his hand. He came across a length of twine stretched tight at about shoulder height, and was careful not to disturb it. It might have been completely harmless, but he wasn't about to take the risk.

Keeping close to the hedge, they moved to their left, spotting the roof of a shed on the other side. As the hedge turned a right angle, the small hillock lay directly ahead of them. Eddie pointed at his rifle and then to the top of the hillock – Drake understood he was going to get himself to a high viewpoint where he could use his night scope.

Meanwhile Drake continued along the hedge, finding another place where he could ease himself through it. He emerged onto a flower bed and remained there for a moment, keeping low as he surveyed the garden. It all looked innocent enough – an arbour, some chairs and a bench, and a bird table – nothing out of the ordinary, and all rather twee. A city dwellers' idea of a country garden.

But whoever had dug that trap pit had wanted to discourage visitors, and didn't mind killing them into the bargain. It was unlikely to be the Styx – the trap was far too crude for them. Drake's mind raced with the alternatives. It suggested renegades to him, but that was only a wild guess. He was beginning to wonder if he'd even find Chester at the end of this trail – for all Drake knew someone might have helped themselves to one of the radio beacons and planted it here.

He edged forward, smelling something unpleasant. It grew stronger as he came closer to the garden shed. As he reached it, he waited for a moment, listening and making sure there wasn't any movement in the garden, then stuck a finger behind the door and gently pulled it open.

Angry flies buzzed at his intrusion and the stench was indescribable.

He gasped in horror.

He counted four bodies on the floor of the shed, in a state of semi-undress. A woman and three men, and from the dark blue trousers and light blue shirt, the uppermost and most recent of the corpses could have been a postman. It was one thing to see soldiers who had been recently killed in a combat situation – that was something he'd learnt to deal with – but these were civilians, and badly decomposed ones at that.

Then he noticed something else.

'Oh, Jesus,' he croaked.

He brought his hand up to his mouth and tried not to make any noise as he gagged.

It wasn't just the warm reek of decay in the shed and the spectacle of the slaughtered.

Pieces of the bodies were missing, flesh carved from the bones.

He quickly backed away, pulling the door to as he left, then headed for the avenue of trees just beyond the garden furniture. He might have been moving a little too hastily, but he couldn't take any more of that smell.

So now there was no question that he was dealing with someone completely beyond the pale, someone savage. At least Chester hadn't been one of those bodies, but who knew what sort of situation he was caught up in? If he was still alive, Drake had to get him out fast.

Drake controlled his breathing as he drew on all his senses. He could see the cottage clearly through his lens, but he didn't go down the avenue of trees – both it and the small garden gate at the end were an obvious location for an ambush or a booby trap.

Instead he moved across the lawn to his left, heading towards the side of the cottage. Once there, he stayed off the path, treading carefully in the soft earth of the border, and then climbed over a low picket fence. In the drive at the front of the cottage a car was parked carelessly, as if it had been left there in a hurry. And two suitcases lay on the ground under the rear of the vehicle. One of these had been opened and a few articles of clothes had spilled out. Drake didn't venture any closer – he didn't want the sound of his boots on the gravel to give him away.

Keeping low as he went, he stole over to the front of the cottage and squatted under a window, rising slowly so he could peer over the sill. There was the glow of a fire inside the room, but he couldn't see anyone moving around. Drake wished that he and Eddie were hooked up with communications units. He was torn between entering the house there and then, or going to fetch Eddie who was probably still up on the hillock and watching the area with his light-gathering scope. Although Drake was desperately concerned about Chester and his first impulse was to storm the cottage, he knew the right thing would be to involve Eddie. If there was to be an assault on the building, then better that they entered the front and back simultaneously to confuse the occupant or occupants. So he retraced his steps down the side of the cottage, heading towards the gap in the hedge.

He'd almost reached it when he caught a fleeting glimpse of something – it was a person, and a woman at that. She had wild, frizzy hair and her fleshy face glistened with sweat. And there was a weapon in her hands.

He heard a swish.

He had no time to react as a projectile struck the lens over his eye. It was enough to knock him back and he let himself go with it, rolling as he hit the ground and coming up a few metres away. He was poised with his handgun, but the view through the lens of his headset flared an intense orange, then flickered out. Pieces of shattered glass dropped down his face. Whatever the projectile had been, it had struck him with enough force to smash the lens.

And without his night vision, he had no hope of seeing the woman in the murky shadows.

In the bushes to his left he heard a click.

A crossbow?

Had he been hit with a bolt? He remembered what Will had told him about the former renegade who had taken Elliott and the boys under her wing. He was sure Will had said that she used a crossbow.

'Martha?' he called out.

A loud crack issued from the hill and he heard a woman's guttural voice as she swore. Then there was another crack as Eddie fired again, the report of the rifle shot echoing all around.

Drake ducked down behind a bush and remained hidden

for what seemed like an eternity, listening for any movement. Then he made a break for the cottage. He was running blind in the darkness and he wanted something solid behind him, to protect himself from an attack from the rear. As he reached the building, he flattened himself against it, still listening to every sound and watching. That was when he heard the panicked shrieks coming from inside. He found the back door to the cottage and tried the handle, but it was locked.

He heard more cries.

'Chester!' Drake said, recognising who it was.

He kicked the door open and found the boy lying in the hallway.

'STYX! HELP!' Chester was yelling as, still tied up, he bucked and squirmed on the carpet, like a maggot on a hotplate. He'd seen Eddie slip in through the front door.

'Tell him I'm a friend,' Eddie said.

'Chester, it's okay. He's on our side. And thank God you're all right,' Drake shouted.

Chester's startled eyes found Drake, then filled with tears of gratitude as he began to weep.

'You're safe now,' Drake said, slicing through the boy's bonds with his knife.

Chester wouldn't let go of Drake, clutching on to his arm. He was still crying and trying to speak, but not making any sense.

'The woman?' Drake asked Eddie.

'I winged her but couldn't get a killshot. She fled around the side of the house and towards the road. There was no sign of her when I got there, except this,' Eddie said. He held up her crossbow, which Drake noticed was covered in blood, then Eddie moved to the open front door to peer out at the drive. 'No question she's a renegade – I saw the bodies of those people in the shed she's been eating. I've come across canni-balism like that bef—'

'No – don't . . .!' Drake yelled, too late.

Chester went rigid as he took in what Eddie had been saying. He sought out the various dirty plates and spoons Martha had discarded on the hallway carpet – pieces of dried meat still clung to some of them. 'Bodies . . . people . . .?' he whimpered, and began to tremble. 'Not birds? It wasn't birds?' He knew then, knew exactly what Martha had been feeding him. He was violently and uncontrollably sick.

'Oh, Chester, I'm sorry,' Drake tried to console him.

'This is what I wanted to show you,' Dr Burrows said as Will leapt up the tiers to where his father had been waiting. At head height and overhung by a small ledge, there was a row of ten stones, all around five centimetres square and with symbols cut into their faces. They were slightly proud of the surface, and when Dr Burrows pushed on the nearest of them, it moved in.

'Wow!' Will exclaimed. 'Maybe there's something hidden behind it, like those skulls you found?'

'That was what I thought at first, but there's something keeping these in place.' Dr Burrows demonstrated to Will that the stone block would only travel a small distance out, then he pushed it back in again. 'And they're all like this.' He went to the next stone in the row and did the same again, moving it in and out.

'What's written on them?' Will asked, squinting at the glyph on the closest block to him. 'Letters?'

'Yes, each has a single letter on it, and if you read them from right to left, as with all the Ancients' records, the result is pure gobbledygook. I've even tried to mix up the letters, to see if it's an anagram, but the result is still the same,' Dr Burrows replied. 'Doesn't mean a dammed thing.' Stooping to retrieve his journal, he began to whistle through his teeth as he opened it at the page where he'd copied down the letters.

'You're going to need to get yourself a new one of those,' Will commented, noting how few pages his father had left.

'I'll worry about that when I need to,' Dr Burrows mumbled impatiently as he scrutinised the sequence of ten letters. 'No, I don't get it. Everything I've seen on this pyramid tells me that the Ancients were a highly intelligent and, above all else, *logical* race. What they've left behind is a précis of their erudition in the fields of philosophy, medicine and mathematics and, I can tell you, in these areas they were far in advance of even the Greeks, who came centuries after them.'

'What about that stuff on astronomy?' Will put in.

'Yes, that's highly significant because it shows that they'd been to the outer world, and for long enough to undertake a detailed survey of the night sky up there. And if they *could* get to the surface and back, then my guess is that they had a better means to travel there than our hit-or-miss jaunt past the crystal belt.'

Besieged by guilt, Will looked at his feet. He still hadn't told his father about the entrance to the tunnel that Elliott had discovered, and he felt terrible that he was holding back on information which could be vital to his father's research. Taking a breath, he was on the point of mentioning it when Dr Burrows suddenly raised his head to the white sky, his expression distant. 'Will, if you wanted to leave a record for posterity, something to tell future generations about yourself, how would you go about it?'

'What do you mean?' Will asked, relieved that his father had moved onto another topic, and that the need to reveal the tunnel didn't seem to be so pressing now. Spilling the beans would have felt like a betrayal of Elliott.

'Look on my works, ye mighty, and despair!' Dr Burrows declaimed in a dramatic voice, sweeping his hand in a stagy way in front of him.

'Huh?' Will said, wondering if his father had had too much sun.

'It's from a poem called *Ozymandias*,' Dr Burrows explained. What I'm talking about is the vanity of mighty races,' he added, now looking at his son, but not really seeing him. 'How do you leave a testament, a record, that can withstand the ravages of time? Paper's no good – with the odd exception like the Dead Sea Scrolls, it doesn't survive. Libraries burn. In fact, buildings don't last either, do they? They're destroyed by natural disasters or by looting. By time.'

Will shrugged. 'I dunno – what do you do?'

'We're standing on it, Will,' Dr Burrows said. 'You build an edifice so large, so substantial, that nothing can wipe it from the face of the Earth.' He shook his head, correcting himself. 'Or from the guts of the Inner Earth, in this case. Except for the effects of weathering, this pyramid will last for aeons, like the ones in Egypt which, chronologically speaking, are mere babes in comparison.'

Dr Burrows' expression suddenly changed to that of frustration. 'And I've only got a third of the picture here. I haven't even seen the other two pyramids yet, have I? Who knows what might be there, and whether there's a solution to this.' He inclined his head at the row of stones. 'Maybe it's a code of some sort, and the key is on the other—'

Will cut across him. 'But we can't go to the other pyramids – not now that Limiters could be in the area. Elliott said it would be—'

Dr Burrows turned on his son. 'Don't listen to what she says. I don't believe she just happened to chance across this Limiter sign of hers in the middle of the jungle. No, this is far more important. And, it's downright crazy that we haven't made the effort to explore the remaining pyramids yet.' He slammed his journal shut. 'In fact, there's no time like the present. Go and pack up what we need from the camp and we'll hit the road – right now!'

Will hesitated. It wasn't the reaction that Dr Burrows was after.

'Come on – the nearest one isn't far. The journey will be a doddle,' he said.

'Okay,' Will replied. Although he didn't feel like a long hike through the jungle, he knew that it was futile to argue. He was descending the side of the pyramid when Dr Burrows shouted after him.

'And don't forget my compass!'

'Yeah, yeah,' Will said to himself, dragging his heels as he made his way across the clearing to their base in the tree.

'Let's get you away from here,' Drake said, as he took Chester through the front door and across the drive to where the road lay.

Drake was appalled at the boy's appearance. As he had wiped the weeks of accumulated filth from Chester's face, he'd been alarmed at both how much weight he'd lost, and his eczema, which he had never seen look so red and inflamed.

'Slowly does it,' Drake coaxed him, helping him step by step. He'd taken a blanket from one of the bedrooms and put it around the boy, who was leaning heavily on him for support.

'It's cold,' Chester said through chattering teeth. He was very badly shaken and shivering as Drake talked gently to him, encouraging him to keep going. But Chester didn't seem to be taking any of it in. 'You know, before we came to this place, I was ill for weeks . . . really ill . . .' he said, resisting Drake's attempts to guide him towards the road by stopping for a moment to look back at the cottage. 'I thought about it a lot when I was in that cupboard, and I reckon she was poisoning me . . . with toadstools from the forest. Just so I couldn't run out on her.'

'Try not to think about it now,' Drake said, managing to get Chester moving again.

After they'd gone a little further, the boy put his head back and sniffed. 'Is that the sea? I can hear the waves.'

'Yes, it's just a little further,' Drake told him, as they began to mount the verge on the other side of the road.

'So you're working with a Styx now?' Chester asked as he tried to process everything that had just happened.

'He's a former Limiter,' Drake replied. 'And Elliott's father.'

'Really?' Chester mumbled, as they continued down on to a shingle bank. Although a fog was rolling in over the North Sea, the sun was nudging above the horizon and baking it off.

'This is far enough,' Drake said, and he and Chester sat down on the beach.

The boy stared at the waves, his face impassive. 'Sometimes I see things that remind me of how it used to be . . . of my old life, and I try to pretend nothing's changed,' he said. 'But it

166

has, and I've changed too, haven't I? All these things I've been through have made me like someone else. I'm . . .' He put his hand to his mouth and Drake could barely hear what he was saying through his fingers. '. . . some sort of freak that has eaten . . .' Chester tailed off as he let his head sag forward onto his knees.

'I've got her,' Eddie announced, making Chester start. He hadn't heard the Styx approaching, and now saw that the thin man was sighting up on something with his rifle. 'She's a long way down the beach, near the headland,' Eddie added.

'Let me see,' Chester demanded, throwing off the blanket as he heaved himself to his feet. Eddie passed him the rifle and he used the telescopic sight to locate the tiny figure in the distance.

'Yes, that's her all right . . . and she's moving like she's hurt,' Chester said, observing the figure as it swayed from side to side in a meandering gait. He set his jaw, and his voice became hard and uncompromising. 'She deserves to die. Do you think I can nail her from here?' he asked as he worked the bolt on the weapon to chamber a round.

'No, the range is too great,' Eddie said. 'The wind would make the shot drift.'

'I don't care. I'll take that risk,' Chester rasped. He was silent for a moment, then began to chuckle strangely.

'What is it, Chester?' Drake asked, concerned that the boy was becoming unhinged after his recent experiences.

'I don't believe it!' Chester replied, still chuckling. He'd caught sight of something above Martha, who was now running like a frightened rabbit in a zig-zag pattern. 'She wasn't completely nuts. A Bright *did* follow her up here.' He could see the huge moth-like creature making passes over her head, although it was moving far less rapidly than if it had been in its usual habitat. Chester knew this was because of the increased gravity up here on the surface.

As he watched, the Bright spread its wings wide, the scales on them catching the morning sun. They flashed with a dazzling whiteness, making the creature appear like a giant swan in flight. Then the Bright tucked them back along its body and tipped into a sheer dive, hurtling straight for Martha. She flung herself down on the beach, just managing to avoid it at the last moment. Picking herself up, she began to run again. 'She's got nothing to defend herself with. She hasn't got a chance,' Chester said, taking great delight in the spectacle as he saw the Bright make another dive. 'It's homed into her because she's bleeding. It knows the smell of her blood. It's going to get her.'

'If you want I can go down there and make sure the job's finished,' Eddie said, as casually as if he was offering Chester a cup of tea.

Chester lowered the rifle and turned to the Styx. 'Thank you,' he declined the man politely. There was a steeliness in the boy's eyes as he added, 'But she's more scared of Brights than anything in the world . . . and I don't want it to be quick. I want her to die really slowly.'

'Okay, Chester . . . why don't you give the rifle back to Eddie, and sit down again,' Drake urged him gently.

Chester looked from Drake to Eddie, then back to Drake again. 'I honestly don't know what's more upsetting – what that horrible old bag put me through . . . or the fact that you're best friends with a Styx . . . and he's called *Eddie*.'

Chapter Thirteen

W ill collected some water and supplies, and was just about to return to his father when Elliott appeared. She was carrying some firewood in her arms, with Bartleby scampering along behind her.

'Going somewhere?' she enquired, seeing the Bergen on Will's back and the Sten gun in his hand.

Will looked at her, the resignation in his eyes saying it all. 'I left you a note. Dad thinks he's got as far as he can with this pyramid, and he's set on seeing one of the others. You know what he's like – he's decided it has to be right now.'

Elliott clicked her tongue against her teeth. 'And after all I've tried to tell him.'

'Yeah, I know,' Will sighed.

She dropped the pieces of wood. 'Right, I'm coming along for the ride too.'

Will was delighted. 'Really?'

Dr Burrows was far from pleased when he saw Elliott was with Will. But he didn't say a word because he knew that he'd gone against her advice that they shouldn't stray far from the camp.

It was unusual for all three of them to be together on an outing. In fact, other than the odd foray to the ruins of the city in the jungle, Dr Burrows hadn't been anywhere for some time, instead concentrating all his energies on the pyramid by the base camp.

They were following a bearing he'd taken on the nearest of the two new pyramids, tramping through the jungle in an extended line. As expected, Dr Burrows had chosen to lead the party himself and was striding off ahead, with Will next, and Elliott and Bartleby bringing up the rear. It reminded Will so much of the moment they'd entered this secret world for the very first time, without any idea what they'd find, or where they were going. It felt like an age ago to him now.

Other than the odd bird call or crack as a twig snapped underfoot, all was silent as they traversed the platform of leaf detritus on the jungle floor. The three of them were soon covered in sweat because of the high humidity; the huge weight of tree foliage above trapped a layer of air where they were walking, and there was very little in the way of a breeze.

Then they began to notice that the ground was becoming damper and that the giant trees were no longer affording them as much protection from the sun. They had entered a sparse forest of dumpy-looking Cypress trees, their lower trunks disproportionately large as if they were swollen. And everything up to a height of around four metres was stained with mud and draped with dried-out weed.

'Flood basin,' Dr Burrows proposed, as they broke off to gaze around.

'What's that over there?' Elliott said, pointing ahead to an area of disturbed water, its undulating surface bright green with algae.

'A swamp?' Will suggested.

'Let's find out,' Dr Burrows said, heading straight towards it.

'I just knew he was going to say that,' Will moaned.

They waded through the water, which came up to their thighs, keeping an eye out for snakes or crocodiles. However, the place seemed to be populated entirely by lizards, ranging in size from small geckos to one-metre-long iguanas, but nothing more threatening than that. The lizards' iridescent skins shone vivid blues, reds and greens as they basked in the sunlight. Hardly moving, they opened their mouths to make hissing sounds when Will or any of the others came too close, or to shoot out their long tongues at passing dragonflies. Bartleby seemed to be really quite unsettled by them, and stuck close to Elliott.

As Dr Burrows sloshed along, he had a dreamy look on his face. 'You can very easily imagine the beginning of all life in a swamp like this.' He waved his hand overhead. 'You've got ultraviolet light on tap all day long from the sun, and ample water, at just the right temperature. Think . . . maybe this very swamp was the primordial soup – the exact place where the first unicellular organism was born, and then evolved.'

'I would've evolved pretty damn quick if it meant I could get out of this place,' Will said, swatting a mosquito on the nape of his neck.

As they left the swamp and returned to solid ground, they found that they were in a forest of thorn-covered acacia trees. Between these was a tangle of thick undergrowth, which made the going much harder, until they finally crashed through to what appeared to be a track.

Wide enough to drive a vehicle down, the track was unnaturally straight. Will frowned as he surveyed the short grass covering it. 'This isn't man-made, is it? An old river bed?' he asked, warily looking around as Elliott caught up.

'I'd say . . . neither of those,' Dr Burrows replied.

Will still didn't like the look of it. He glanced at Elliott, but she seemed perfectly relaxed.

'Ah,' Dr Burrows exclaimed, as he spied something further down the track, and started towards it. As Will and Elliott joined him, they could see that it was a massive pile of animal dung, which appeared to be recent from the wisps of steam rising from it. 'This is evidently a main thoroughfare for the local fauna,' Dr Burrows decided. 'A well-used animal trail.'

'Yes. See the marks on that trunk,' Elliott pointed out, 'where the bark's been scraped away?'

Will and Dr Burrows switched their attention from the dung to the tree trunk. A diagonal abrasion went straight through to the white wood beneath, and sap had leaked down the bark and hardened into amber drips. But Dr Burrows was more interested in the monstrous pile of dung, to which he now returned.

'What could have left that?' Will asked, as his father crouched down and probed it with a stick. 'A very big cow? An Auroch?'

'Not a carnivore – I can see the stones from some kind of fruit, and cellulose . . . bits of undigested vegetation,' Dr Burrows replied. 'We need to investigate this further.'

'What, you mean look for more giant poohs?' Will asked facetiously.

Elliott barely managed to stifle a giggle.

'Don't be stupid. I meant that we should search for the animal *itself*,' Dr Burrows replied curtly. Standing up, he flicked open the top of his compass with undue force and checked the bearing. 'And as luck would have it, this is roughly the right direction for us,' he announced. Will and Elliott smiled at each other, as Dr Burrows deliberately avoided looking at either of them, then stalked off down the trail.

Bartleby was the first to spot the slow-moving beast some distance up ahead. With an apprehensive meow, he came to a halt, and flattened himself to the ground. Will, Dr Burrows and Elliott crept from the trail and hid themselves in the undergrowth.

There was a trumpeting sound and a large grey-skinned animal moved down the trail in their direction. With its heavy limbs and lumbering walk, Will immediately assumed it was some kind of elephant. And there were more of the same kind of animal following behind it in a procession.

Will and Dr Burrows exchanged amazed glances.

'Probably a family group,' Dr Burrows whispered. 'The ones behind it are younger.'

'But their ears look weird, and what's wrong with their trunks?' Will asked. 'They're half the length of a normal elephant's.'

'Nothing's wrong with them – they're meant to be like that. Can't you see the two pairs of tusks?' Dr Burrows said, breathless with excitement. 'Will, don't you have any idea what these creatures are, and how important this is? These creatures are either Gomphotheria or Palaeomastodons. Yes, I reckon they're Palaeomastodons – early ancestors of elephants from the early Oligocene period. Yet more living fossils!'

'But are they friendly?' Will asked, as the nearest Palaeo-mastodon, which also happened to be by far the largest, continued to approach them. As it did so, it raised its stubby trunk as if sampling the air.

'It can smell us,' Elliott whispered, raising her rifle.

The gigantic beast kept coming and then, some twenty metres away, it chose a tree stump to make a display of its strength. With a bellow, it whipped its head to one side, striking its more prominent upper tusks against the rotten stump, which toppled over with a dull thud.

Peering out from behind Elliott, Bartleby made a deep growling noise in the back of his throat.

'Shh!' she said.

Maybe it was because he was so alarmed by the sight of the animal, but the Hunter suddenly did the last thing any of them expected. He leapt out from the undergrowth and landed right in the middle of the trail. His back was arched and the muscles in his shoulders bunched as he hissed loudly at the Palaeomastodon.

'Bartleby!' Will cried.

There was moment in which Bartleby, although he was dwarfed by the larger animal, locked eyes with the Palaeo-mastodon. Then the Palaeomastodon let out a bellow and, moving more quickly than Will had seen it do before, reared its head around and began to tramp away.

'Preservation instinct,' Dr Burrows laughed. 'I bet the nearest thing it can compare Bartleby with is a jaguar or sabre-tooth tiger, and it doesn't want to tangle with him! It thinks he's too much of a threat.'

Will wasn't amused. 'Get back here, right now, you daft cat!' he chided the Hunter.

*

The remainder of the journey was uneventful. As they emerged from the trees and the pyramid loomed before them, they were all hot and exhausted. For a second, the three of them simply regarded the giant edifice, which appeared to be identical to the one by their base camp.

Will wiped the sweat from his forehead. 'So . . . pyramid number two. I thought you said the journey here would be a doddle,' he grumbled to his father.

But Dr Burrows wasn't going to allow his fatigue to affect him. He had that intense look in his eyes – he was only interested in one thing. He stormed towards the pyramid and, as he reached it, whipped out his journal and began to inspect the first tier.

'That's him happy,' Elliott said, as she and Will slumped onto the ground beside each other. She undid her rucksack. 'I've brought some food along if you're hungry.'

'Starving,' Will said.

Elliott produced a package, well wrapped in layers of cloth to conceal the smell from any over-inquisitive animals. 'This is an experiment of mine,' she said, removing the cloth to reveal several green bundles. 'I cooked the meat in palm leaves, and I think it's turned out quite well.' Will took one of the bundles from her and, just as he began to eagerly peel the leaves away, a shout echoed around the trees.

'Will! Here! I need you here!' his father demanded. 'Now!'

Will acted as if he hadn't heard, biting off a hunk of meat. 'Mmmm! This is delicious,' he said.

'Will! Will!' the shouts came again.

'It's antelope, isn't it? You've really outdone yourself this time,' Will complimented Elliott, chewing slowly as he savoured his mouthful.

'The Doc's calling you,' she said, amused by the way Will was completely ignoring the summons.

'Know something?' he muttered, shaking his head with a mock serious expression.

'What?' she replied, unable to keep a straight face because Dr Burrows was still yelling frantically, as if the world was about to end.

'In the old days in Highfield, all I wanted to do was go on digs with him. I didn't really think about anything else.'

'And?' she asked, as he stuffed his mouth with more antelope.

'Reckon I was a bit of a saddo then. No wonder I didn't have any friends.' He grunted as he got to his feet and, still munching on his food, stomped over to the pyramid. He saw his father was on one of the uppermost tiers, jumping up and down with excitement.

'What is it?' Will asked disinterestedly as he reached his father.

'See for yourself!' Dr Burrows gushed, sweeping his hand vigorously over the wall before him.

On the facing stones were the usual friezes and inscriptions, but there was something different about them. Will couldn't place what it was.

Dr Burrows jabbed his finger at a line of script carved at the base of the wall. '*To the garden of the second sun a warlike people came, with . . .*' He stumbled slightly at this point. 'I can't get that word, but it goes on to say '. . . *like birds that fly and . . .*' He hesitated again, then continued, '*carts – or wagons – that drive themselves. The people took the life from our lands and made fire and smoke in its place.*' Dr Burrows turned his head and fixed his eyes on Will. 'Look at it! Look at the carving!'

Picking a piece of the meat from between his teeth, Will shrugged. 'So your Ancients were running scared because someone, another tribe maybe, tried to move into their patch?'

'No, you dullard,' Dr Burrows barked. 'I said look at the *carving*! See how the stone is hardly weathered at all.'

Will still wasn't getting the significance. 'It's not old? This wasn't carved thousands of years ago?'

'No, decades ago, more like,' Dr Burrows said. 'We could be learning about the moment when the first aeroplanes and some other types of vehicles arrived.' He began to whistle atonally, then stopped as if he'd remembered something. 'There's more. Tell me what you make of this.' He rushed further along the tier and, finding the place, gestured at the wall.

Will contemplated the images, focusing on one in particular. 'No question that's meant to be an aeroplane,' he said.

'Yes – and it bears a remarkable resemblance to a Stuka,' Dr Burrows announced, in an 'I-told-you-so' voice.

Will had moved on to some of the other carvings – crude depictions of odd-looking aircraft with twin rotor blades. 'And helicopters?' he added.

'My thoughts entirely. And then look at the tier above us,' Dr Burrows directed him.

'Wow!' Will exclaimed. 'It's completely blank!'

Some of the facing stones were cracked and pitted from the centuries of heat and rain, but there was nothing carved on them at all.

'So we might assume that this pyramid is a work-in-progress, much like the empty pages in my journal that I have yet to fill,'

Dr Burrows hypothesised. 'Which means if these people were around to witness the appearance of Topsoil technology in their world . . . and document it on this pyramid . . . maybe they're still alive to this very day.'

'Wild!' Will said. 'But if that's true, where are they now? And more to the point, where's this other lot with their Stuka plane . . . and *helicopters*?'

Although she couldn't read the words that proclaimed 'Buttock & File', or appreciate what was on the sign above them – a rather curious caricature of a red-skinned devil grinning to itself in the cabin of a steam engine – Mrs Burrows was left in no doubt as to what the place was. The empty tavern reeked overpoweringly of stale ale and old urine, and the pavement in front of its black-painted windows was sticky as she hurried along it.

'Stay close, Colly,' she urged as the cat hung back to sniff at the doors of the establishment. 'We haven't got long.'

Since that very first time Mrs Burrows had stepped outside the Second Officer's house and flexed her olfactory supersense, she had only dared to venture into the streets of the Colony on a handful of occasions. But just out of reach of her new ability she sensed a place that puzzled her. And the picture she'd formed of this place as she'd probed it had horrified her. Although it was quite some distance from the house and she'd be cutting it fine to get there and back before vespers ended, she felt driven to investigate it.

It was large, that much she did know.

And it smelt like the pit of hell.

And now as she jogged down a succession of wide streets,

easily avoiding the puddles and ducking to the side as sporadic gushes of water fell from the cavern roof high above, she was nearing her destination.

She crossed the road, stopping before a tall wall – from the smell of the lime mortar, she could tell it was newly built. She began to explore the surface of the wall, using her sense of touch. 'Too high to climb,' she said, and began to follow it along. Coming to a stretch that hadn't been completed yet, she ducked under a wooden barrier and stepped across a slit trench dug for the foundations of the wall. She didn't stop there, moving into an area strewn with loose rubble until her feet encountered cobbles.

She held completely still as she unleashed her ability. The predominant smell was of ash – lots of it – from burnt beams and floorboards, and then there was charred stone. But in amongst this, there was the scent of death, and of immeasurable cruelty. As she concentrated, it was as if small voices were calling out to her from a great distance, demanding her attention. Her head switched this way and that as she located where they had perished, bones young and old just left where the bodies had fallen in the debris. Where people had been incinerated.

'Oh, God,' she gasped, overwhelmed by the sheer number of them. It was as though the place was one big tomb to those who had died in there, burnt alive. Her imagination was working overtime; she could almost hear the screams of panic from the victims, who had nowhere to go, no means of escape.

All of a sudden she knew precisely where she was.

Drake had mentioned an incident to her in passing. He hadn't been too forthcoming about it, as if it was still painful for him to recall what he'd seen. In any case, her time with Drake had been limited in the days leading up to the operation on Highfield Common when they'd planned to snatch the old Styx.

But Mrs Burrows knew that she now had to be in the district he'd referred to as the Rookeries; overcrowded slums, which housed the rougher elements of the Colony, those at the very bottom of the microcosmic society. And this was where Drake had witnessed their systematic slaughter.

'The Rookeries,' she whispered, as if the dead could hear her, and took a step forward. Her shoe knocked against something in the ash. She bent to pick up the object, which she explored with her fingers. It was the porcelain head of a small doll. The rest of the doll, its cloth body and dress hadn't survived the flames. As Mrs Burrows shook the dust from the head and held it to her nose, there was something retained in it – the tiniest suggestion of the generations of children who had played with it. These were poor people, and this toy had probably been handed down from parent to child through the centuries, only for its last owner to lose her life in this terrible carnage.

And in the religious services all over the Colony, those responsible for this crime were at that very moment preaching to the Colonists on how to lead their lives. The Styx.

Mrs Burrows gently placed the doll's head on a pile of broken masonry, and returned towards the opening in the wall.

After calling it a day at the new pyramid, they were returning to the base camp. But as they emerged on to the grassy track again, Dr Burrows was lagging behind Will and Elliott. Whistling through his teeth, he was trying to read his journal as he sauntered along. Will and Elliott watched as his foot went into a pothole and he staggered a few steps. But after he'd managed to regain his balance, he went straight back to his journal as if nothing had happened.

'Look at your father – he could walk smack bang into a sabre-tooth and not notice it was there,' Elliott observed disapprovingly. 'He's in a world of his own.'

'He is,' Will replied, turning to Elliott. 'But this is what he does best . . . he's at his happiest when he's picking away at a problem and trying to solve it.'

A flock of birds flew lazily past them and alighted in the trees by the side of the track.

'Yeuch!' Elliott said.

The bodies of the birds were chubby and flaccid – like extremely old men with protruding beer bellies. Their bald heads and necks only helped to emphasise this impression as they lacked feathers, their wrinkled skin covered instead with patchy down. Fixing their beady eyes on Will and Elliott, the assembled birds were silent except for the odd squawk, as if they weren't sure what to make of these human interlopers in their jungle, and were conferring amongst themselves.

'They're ugly. What are those things?' Elliott asked.

'Maybe some kind of vulture?' Will ventured.

As Bartleby crept into the open the birds began to flap their scrawny wings and squawk even more loudly, but they didn't fly away. It was obvious they were chary of the Hunter, whose jaw began to quiver as he prowled up and down, ogling them with his big amber eyes. He gave a low frustrated mew because the birds were too far up in the trees for him to reach them.

'Yes, they are really creepy looking,' Will said, putting the birds out of his mind as he and Elliott set off down the track again, chatting away to each other. Will realised that it wasn't only Dr Burrows who was happy – the weeks they'd spent in this inner world had been some of the best of his life. He glanced at Elliott. She too seemed to be totally in her element in the jungle, and content with her lot.

In the Deeps her expression had been permanently haunted, and her pale skin – which bore the scars from her time in that most savage of environments – had made her appear like some lost wraith as she'd flitted about the place. But with the exception of the gouge in her upper arm, the scars were barely noticeable now, and her tanned face and her sleek black hair made her look radiant and transformed. There and then it struck Will how incredibly beautiful she was, and how lucky he was to have her as his friend.

She'd been speaking to him about something, but he hadn't been listening. 'It's been just brilliant today,' he announced abruptly.

'Huh?' she said, surprised at his outburst.

'What I meant is that this has been great fun . . . at least if we both go on these expeditions with Dad, we get some time together, don't we?' Will was flustered as he tried to explain himself. 'You know, without him interrupting us every ten minutes,' he added, aware his face was colouring.

Will turned his head away from Elliott and grimaced, thoroughly frustrated with himself. He found he wasn't able to express what he really wanted to tell her – how he felt about her. His was the lexicon of a fifteen-year-old, and the words just weren't there. He clamped his jaw shut, lacking the confidence to say anything further to her in case his feelings weren't reciprocated. In case he was making a complete and utter fool of himself.

But Elliott nodded in response, then beamed at him. Will felt a crashing sense of relief as she'd seemed to understand what he really wanted to say. Their eyes stayed on each other, but the moment was short-lived as Dr Burrows interrupted them.

'Blast it!' he yelled. 'Filthy, bloody stuff!'

Will and Elliott spun around. Dr Burrows was hopping on one foot. He'd evidently stepped in a pile of animal dung. Will and Elliott couldn't help but laugh as he tried to clean his boot by rubbing it on the grass.

'Was it a good specimen of a Palaeomastodon pat?' Will chuckled as he made his way to his father, who had suddenly fallen silent as he became distracted again.

'I wonder,' he began, as he took his bulging journal from under his arm and opened it, flicking through to the back pages. 'Those stones . . . those stones . . .' he muttered.

Will had no idea what he talking about. 'Which stones, Dad?' he asked.

'I found another set of those stones that move – you know, like the row on our pyramid.'

'You didn't say anything about them to me,' Will complained.

'I did try, but – as ever – you were too tied up with your friend,' Dr Burrows said, then scratched his chin as he thought. 'This second series of stones is obviously more recent, and all the letters on them are different . . . and I'm trying to figure out if they can be combined with the first sequence to give some sort of meaning.'

'There might be even more on pyramid number three,' Will pointed out. 'When we get to see it, the answer might be there.'

'It might,' Dr Burrows repeated several times. He was poring over a page in his journal and, as he took a step to the side, he planted his foot in an even bigger heap of animal dung, which came halfway up his calf. Despite the squelching sound and the pungent smell, he seemed completely oblivious to this.

'Dad! *You're* not coming near the base tonight,' Will laughed. 'Elliott will make you . . .' He stalled in mid-sentence as it occurred to him that she hadn't joined them yet. He sought her out, finding that she'd remained exactly where he'd left her, training her rifle on the trees further down the track. 'She's seen something,' he whispered, quickly hurrying over.

She silenced him with a look as he came alongside her, and continued to scrutinise the trees with her rifle scope.

Dr Burrows had caught up with them by now and was peering at the undergrowth Elliott seemed to be so interested in. 'More of those nosy trees watching us?' he enquired mockingly.

'I don't understand . . . I've got this feeling . . . as though something's there,' she said slowly, frowning to herself. 'But I can't *see* anything . . . not a thing.'

'The only life forms round here are those loathsome scavengers,' Dr Burrows said, waving his hand at the vultures. 'And correct me if I'm wrong, but we're not carrion yet, so they don't pose any sort of threat to us.' He bent to pick up a stick and tossed it in the direction of the birds. It missed them by a mile, tumbling into the undergrowth below the branches.

Bartleby was the only one who noticed.

A pair of eyes flashed in alarm, and what appeared to be a small tree moved swiftly to the side to avoid the stick as it landed. But Bartleby didn't react, because it made absolutely no sense to him. While he'd seen the movement, there was no scent he could discern. Nothing that smelt even remotely like an animal – or a human – for that matter.

PART TWO

Contact

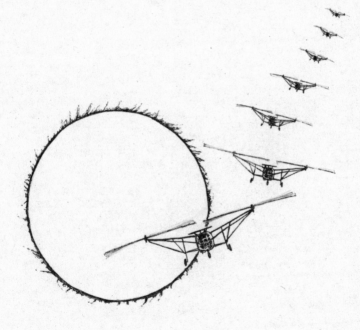

Chapter Fourteen

A low tent had been erected on the edge of the runway, where gusts of wind stirred up swirling dust devils. As a small convoy of angular coaches with blacked-out windows drew up, the doors flew open and the brigade of Limiters disembarked. Depositing their rucksacks and equipment at the entrance to the tent, they began to file inside. The dog handlers amongst them were restraining their growling stalkers, which clearly preferred the look of the wide open space after being cooped up for so long.

Without any direction from their superiors, the Limiters began to fill the seats on one side of the tent. The seats on the other side were already occupied by New Germanian troops. There was a terse silence under the flapping canvas as these youthful men with blond crew cuts and pristine combats eyed their opposite numbers. The grizzled Limiters, many of them veterans with the scars to prove it, exhibited no such interest, instead facing straight ahead as they waited for the briefing to start.

Outside the tent, a black limousine under military escort screeched to a halt. Dressed in combats, the Rebecca twins emerged from it. They were followed by the Limiter General, who hung back for a moment to take in the rank of helicopters parked on the runway. 'Fa 223s. Also known as the Drache Achgelis,' he said, as he looked at the nearest one, examining the peculiar arrangement of twin rotors mounted either side of what appeared to be little more than a standard aircraft fuselage.

The Limiter General then peered at the hangars beyond the helicopters, in which various aircraft were visible. Many he didn't recognise, but then his gaze fell on a pair of tan-coloured aeroplanes. 'ME 263s!' he exclaimed, as he realised what the stubby-looking aircraft with swept-back wings were.

Having just arrived in another limousine, the Chancellor happened to overhear the Styx. 'Yes, our fighter-interceptors. Jet powered,' he announced proudly. 'We continued their development after we arrived here. Fastest, most manoeuvrable aircraft in the skies,' he boasted.

'Maybe down here. Things have moved on back in the real world,' the Limiter General replied. Then he continued towards the tent, leaving the Chancellor looking most unhappy.

As the Limiter General took a seat next to his men in the first row, the Rebecca twins remained at the front of the tent, where a campaign table and an easel had been set up.

The Chancellor bumbled in. With a sideways glance at the massed Limiters, he stopped before the Styx girls. Not being able to tell which of the identical twins he'd met before, he hesitated, giving each of them a small nod. Then, so as not to look a complete idiot in front of the audience, he went for broke and made his choice, correctly picking Rebecca One. 'Very good to make your acquaintance, my young lady. And how are you feeling today?' he asked her with forced joviality.

She gave the slightest shake of her head to show she wasn't at all pleased with this form of address.

'I must say you've astounded my doctors,' the Chancellor added quickly, realising he'd said the wrong thing. 'You healed much more quickly than they ever expected – much faster than most people.'

Rebecca One gave a dry smile. 'I'm a Styx,' she said. 'We're not *most people.*'

'No, no, of course, not,' the Chancellor gabbled. It was evident that he was highly uncomfortable in the girls' presence and was going to extract himself from the situation at the first opportunity he could. 'I'd like to introduce—' he began to say.

All of a sudden there was a scuffling noise from the back of the tent, and four New Germanian soldiers appeared with a dark form between them. It had ropes tied around it, as if they had captured a wild animal.

'Oh, yes, a security patrol caught this . . . this . . .' the Chancellor floundered before going on. 'This *man*. He was skulking around the outskirts of the city, stealing food.'

As the soldiers tried to hold it back, the dark shape – swathed from head to foot in cloth – forged forwards, straining against the ropes. Then it stuck out a thin, twisted arm, and hooked aside an overhang of greasy material to reveal a badly deformed face, covered in grapefruit-sized growths, and with eyes like peeled eggs.

'He claims he knows you,' the Chancellor said.

'Coxy!' Rebecca One exclaimed. 'What the hell are you doing here?'

Tom Cox sniffed loudly and pushed his crooked lips together before he spoke. 'Ah, me friends – knew you were still alive. I was sent to protect you.'

'To protect us?' Rebecca Two repeated sceptically.

Rebecca One frowned. 'You came down the Pore and thousands of miles, voluntarily?'

''Course. Followed the Limiters, I did,' Cox said.

Rebecca Two was shaking her head, wholly unconvinced. 'And you made the journey all the way to this city, cross-country?'

'And you didn't melt in the sunlight?' her sister quipped.

'Yeh . . . and I don't like it. Don't like the sun,' Cox mumbled. 'It's like Topso—'

'So I take it you *do* know this person,' the Chancellor interjected, wiping his palms on his handkerchief as if the very sight of Cox made him feel unclean.

'Yes, in a way,' Rebecca Two confirmed. 'And he doesn't need the escort. Let him go.'

Yanking the ropes from his captors' hands, Cox suddenly surged forwards like a lively steer. Still trailing the ropes after him, he advanced up the aisle between the seated soldiers.

'New chums?' he said in his coarse voice as he flared his cankerous nostrils at the contingent of fresh-faced soldiers. Sidling up to the twins, he turned his unseeing eyes on the Chancellor, who was still regarding him with overt disgust. In a bid to get the proceedings back on track, the Chancellor was on the point of saying something to the Rebecca twins, when Cox croaked, ''Allo, big boy,' then blew a frothy kiss at him through his blackened lips.

'This . . . this . . . this is Colonel Bismarck,' the Chancellor stuttered. All heads turned to the man who had risen from the first row of seated New Germanians. With a fine example of moustache, he was tall and balding, and held himself with a very upright bearing. He bowed formally to the Rebecca twins with a click of his polished riding boots. 'I'll leave you in his capable hands,' the Chancellor gabbled, and jogged out of the tent as fast as his fat legs would carry him.

'I'm to be your military liaison,' Colonel Bismarck said, striding towards the easel. He waited as one of his soldiers unrolled and pinned a map on it. 'Before we talk about protocols and how our personnel will cooperate in the search operation, I want to review the terrain with you.' He tapped and held his finger on a feature on the map as he addressed the Rebecca twins. 'This is the former pit head – the entrance to the disused uranium mine where you were ambushed.' Sliding his finger across the map, he was about to continue when Rebecca Two spoke up.

'There in the jungle . . . what are those?' she said, indicating the three golden triangles.

'Those are large monuments, visible for some distance around,' he answered. 'They're ancient pyramids . . . but we don't—'

'Pyramids!' Rebecca Two exclaimed, exchanging glances with her sister. 'Is there anything else that big in the jungle?'

'Not that can be seen above the tree line,' Colonel Bismarck answered.

'If we'd spotted them, we would have gone straight there, because they'll draw Dr Burrows like a cavern mouse to cheese,' Rebecca One said.

'That's where we'll find the people we want,' Rebecca Two told the colonel with complete certainty. 'And that's where we should start the search.'

A ripple of agitation passed through the New Germanian soldiers.

Colonel Bismarck looked at the map. 'As I was about to say, we don't tend to venture into that quadrant. It's a high-radiation area, and it contains nothing of any strategic value.' The colonel drew a breath. 'And there's something else.'

'What?' the Rebecca twins asked in unison.

As he stroked his moustache, he seemed reluctant to answer their question. 'We've lost troops in there. Although we've never made any direct sightings of them, it's generally believed that the indigenous people still linger there – concealed, somehow.'

'Ah, a mystery. I like a mystery,' Cox cackled, fluttering his two misshapen hands under his shawl.

Colonel Bismarck furrowed his brow. 'It's no laughing matter. In light of the number of men who have gone missing over the years, and that they were all combat trained and operationally equipped, these natives should be considered highly dangerous. Every so often we send a spotter plane over to sweep the quadrant. They never find anything.' He fixed Rebecca Two with his grey eyes. 'So, in all probability, your quarry will have already perished.'

'But who exactly are these natives, as you call them?' Rebecca One said. 'Guerrilla fighters?'

'No, on the contrary – if they have weapons, then they must be very rudimentary. Our archaeologists believe they're the descendants of an ancient race which, many centuries ago, lived in huge cities on all the major continents in this world. Indeed, the archaeologists believe their society to be the origin of the Atlantis myth.'

Rebecca One made a '*pah*' noise. 'If he's cottoned onto that, boring old Dr Buckwheat's gonna be in seventh heaven.'

'Seventh?' Colonel Bismarck asked, not understanding the idiom.

'Don't worry about it.' Rebecca Two's face was resolute as she went closer to the map to examine where the pyramids were marked. 'Whatever you say about the risk, we need to initiate the search right there,' she said. 'That's where the people who stole our virus will be.'

'And if Will Burrows isn't already dead, he soon will be,' Rebecca One added, placing a hand on her stomach as she remembered the pain from her gunshot wound. 'When I hack his guts out.'

Eliza filled a spoon with the gruel and, with her other hand, yanked down on Mrs Burrows' jaw so that her mouth gaped open. As she regarded the contents of the spoon, Eliza seemed to hesitate for a moment. Then she nodded to herself, and deposited the gruel at the back of the unconscious woman's tongue.

'You may be as dumb as a Coprolite, but that doesn't stop you gobbling our food, does it?' Eliza said.

But something seemed to be wrong with Mrs Burrows' swallowing reflex, and her throat tensed and the gruel spewed out of her mouth.

'For goodness' sake, you messy cow!' Eliza fumed. 'It's gone all over me!' Jumping up, she quickly wiped the drops that had landed on her face and blouse.

'Second time lucky,' Eliza said, as she returned to her chair and tried to force-feed Mrs Burrows another spoonful. But she rejected this as well. Eliza persevered again and again, but the outcome was the same – Mrs Burrows coughed them up with a spasm that seemed to emanate deep within her chest. Defeated, Eliza dropped the spoon into the bowl and placed it on the side table.

'Well, if you don't get your nourishment, you really are going to be in trouble,' she proclaimed to Mrs Burrows' slack face. She gave the woman's chin a quick wipe, then picked up the bowl and began for the door.

'She knows,' the old woman said, appearing from the hallway. She was agitated, wringing her arthritic hands together.

'Don't be daft – look at her – how can she?' Eliza replied to her mother.

'She's always taken her food down before – why not now? She knows, she does,' the old woman maintained, with absolute conviction.

'What codswallop! She's got a cough – a touch of fever – that's all,' Eliza said. 'But if she's stopped eating, she won't last long, and we'll get the result we're after anyway.' She glanced at the bowl in her hands. 'Better get rid of this – we don't want anyone else helping themselves to it. I'll wash it down the drain.' Eliza headed for the kitchen to dispose of the gruel, which had been lightly dusted with slug poison, while the old woman hung back in the doorway.

'There's more to you than you're lettin' on,' she accused Mrs Burrows' slumped form in the bath chair. She may have been in her dotage, but the old woman's intuition hadn't been dulled by age. Her wrinkled face was fearful – she'd almost been complicit in a crime that went against everything she believed. 'You know what we were up to . . . you know we were tryin' to give you poison, don't you?' With a whimper, the old lady scurried away.

Of course I know, Mrs Burrows thought as she withdrew to the dark haven in her brain. *And if you try it again, I'll be ready for you then too.*

Against all odds, she'd survived this long, and she wasn't about to let this pair of women get in the way of her escaping Topsoil.

In the quiet of the basement beneath the warehouse, Drake was working at a computer he'd set up on one of the benches. As his fingers moved in a blur over the keyboard, he spoke without looking up from the screen. 'How's he doing?' he asked.

Eddie walked into the light. 'He's a bit frayed around the edges, as you'd expect,' he said, as he approached the bench. 'I had to give him something to help him sleep.'

'I'm not surprised. Poor kid hasn't had many breaks lately,' Drake replied, his eyes still not moving from the computer screen. 'It might've gone a little easier with him if you'd held off telling him about Martha's meals for two in the garden shed.'

Eddie gave a small shrug.

'Ironic really, as it's your old gang – the so-called Hobb's Squad– who have the reputation of being corpse-munchers.' Drake's expression was neutral as he continued to work on the keyboard. 'And how was he around you? I thought he might have had a problem after what the Styx put him through.'

'He warmed to me after I'd said I'd buy him a PlayStation, and get him a cheeseburger and chips when he woke up.'

'At least he's not completely off his food, then,' Drake mumbled, preoccupied with what he was doing.

'Mind if I take a look?' Eddie asked, already stepping around the bench so he could see.

'Sure,' Drake replied. 'I'm just compiling the last line, and . . . voilà, it's done!' he exclaimed as he hit the Return key with great flourish. A box of rapidly scrolling characters opened up on the screen, then cleared to leave a cursor and a line of text proclaiming that the program was '*Locating . . .*'

'It's been a while since I've written code like this, but . . . we shall see what we shall see,' Drake said under his breath as he waited for the program. 'Ah, here we are.' A map opened up in a new window. 'That's north London – somewhere in Highgate,' he noted. Then another map opened over the first. 'Central London – the West End. Let's have a closer look at this one, shall we?' he said, maximising the window and zooming into where a red dot pulsed. 'Got you!' he announced as the name of the street came up – the dot was clearly located within a specific building. 'Well, what do you know – it's Wigmore Street.'

'May I ask what you're doing?' Eddie ventured.

'Remember what I told you about the tubes I stripped out of the Dark Light? How they each emit a particular wavelength, and how the cumulative output from all four gives a unique signature? Well, this morning I connected wirelessly to several masts I've rigged up on buildings round here, so I can triangulate any emissions at this precise frequency.' Drake patted the side of the computer screen. 'With this hardware, I'm able to pinpoint it anywhere in the London area.'

'So you're telling me that a Dark Light is being used right there, right now,' Eddie surmised, indicating the flashing dot.

'Yes, and I wonder who the victim is?' Drake said, looking thoughtful.

The car had drawn up on a double-yellow line in full sight of a parking warden, but the driver didn't care – the passenger in the back was far too important and influential for him to be concerned about something as trivial as a fine.

'Action stations,' the brawny protection officer next to the driver muttered as he got out. Having checked both ways along the pavement, he gave the driver the thumbs up, then went to the rear door of the car and opened it.

'Er . . . we're here, sir,' he said tentatively.

The Prime Minister looked up from his papers. 'So soon? Yes, right,' he acknowledged. 'I was miles away.' Closing the file on his lap, he slid across the seat and from the car. As he stood up, he straightened his jacket, tugging at one of the sleeves. He was a big bear of a man and always appeared a little awkward in his suits, as if he'd forgotten to remove the coat hanger. 'I just don't have time for this,' he grumbled, passing his hand across his forehead to brush his fringe to the side.

The protection officer escorted the Prime Minister across the pavement and up the steps into the building.

'Sorry I'm late – got held up at the Commons,' he announced to the receptionist, without sounding the slightest bit sorry.

'Good morning, sir,' she said, putting on her breeziest smile. It was no surprise to her that the Prime Minister was behind schedule – he always was, so she'd taken the precaution of blocking out the following appointment to make sure other patients weren't inconvenienced.

'In here?' the Prime Minister began, turning towards the waiting room.

'No, no need for that, sir. Dr Christopher will see you straight away.' She pressed a quick-dial button on her phone and Dr Christopher's assistant was descending the Georgian staircase almost before she'd hung up.

'If you'd follow me, sir,' the assistant said, swivelling on his heels to the staircase again.

The protection officer hadn't accompanied his charge upstairs, instead positioning himself in the entrance lobby where he was able to monitor anyone who came into the building. He took out his radio to check in with the driver in the car outside. 'Big Chief has just gone up for his examination. ETD is likely to be—'

He stopped as he heard a door open behind him. Wheeling round, he saw a woman emerge from a room at the end of the lobby. She was razor thin, and wore a sleek black suit over a white shirt with a large collar.

'Come in, Twenty-three,' the radio crackled, but the protection officer wasn't listening. Spellbound by the woman, he was hardly breathing. The geometry of her face – the unnatural slope of her high cheekbones – made it almost inhuman, almost cat–like but, at the same time, feminine and bewitching. As her black and stunningly beautiful eyes locked on to his, he felt their sheer force, and a coldness spread through his body. He shivered. Hers was the look of authority – and such absolute authority that the protection officer was overcome by it.

And although there was no way he could have known it, he was one of very few Topsoilers to have laid eyes on a fully-grown Styx woman.

'Twenty–three, say again?' the radio burbled.

As the Styx woman turned away and began to glide up the staircase, the protection officer finally took a breath.

'Twenty-three,' his radio demanded. 'Is there a problem?'

'No, everything's fine . . . I just saw this, er, lady,' the protection officer answered without thinking.

'A lady, huh? Having fun in there, are we?' the driver said roguishly.

Once on the first floor, the assistant knocked lightly on the door of the consulting room and opened it for the Prime Minister, then stepped aside.

'Gordy, how are you?' Dr Christopher asked, getting up from his desk.

'Oh, not too bad. Same old shenanigans, you know,' the Prime Minister replied as they shook hands. 'Very good to see you again, Edward. Hope the family are well.'

'They are, thank you. I know you're on a tight schedule, so would you mind if we went straight to my examination room?'

'Fine by me,' the Prime Minister grunted – he'd been about to sit himself in the chair by the desk, but now reversed direction and straightened up again.

'Any problems with your vision?' Dr Christopher asked.

'It's not so good later on in the evenings, but I suppose that's just fatigue. Too many cabinet papers read by candlelight,' the Prime Minister laughed, as he followed the doctor down the corridor and into another large room filled with equipment.

'Let's take a look. If you'd sit yourself down here,' Dr Christopher said, indicating a chair behind the retinal imaging system, 'and please remove your contact lens – there's a receptacle on your left for it. Then if you'd rest your chin on the pad, we can see how your eye's doing.'

'Yes, no need to bother with the other one, is there?' the Prime Minister said. He was referring to his left eye, in which he was completely blind. Dr Christopher braced himself for the usual joke, and the Prime Minister was not to disappoint him. 'You should be charging me half your normal fee – especially with all the flak we had over our expenses,' he added.

'Quite so, quite so,' Dr Christopher chuckled dutifully. 'Now if you'll look straight ahead, please.' He was sitting directly opposite the Prime Minister, peering at his eye through what looked like part of a microscope.

'All very high tech these days,' the Prime Minister commented, as Dr Christopher fiddled with the machine.

'Yes, only the best for my patients,' he replied. 'I'm going to turn on a light – you might find it a little bright to start with.' He flicked a switch, and the Prime Minister's eye was suffused by a dark purple beam. His body went rigid.

Watching the Prime Minister carefully, Dr Christopher rose to his feet. 'Lights out, huh, fatty?' he said unpleasantly. He stepped round to the man and pinched his cheek to make absolutely sure he wasn't conscious. 'At least I won't have to listen to your inane chatter for a while.'

The Styx woman slipped into the room.

'He's Darklit – amazing how quickly it affects him these days,' Dr Christopher commented. 'There's no resistance at all.'

'That's the beauty of frequent top-ups,' she replied, as they both contemplated the Prime Minister.

Dr Christopher clapped his hands together, then began towards the door. 'Anyway, over to you now. I'll be in my room down the corridor when it's time to bring him out.'

'I know where you'll be,' the woman said with a beguiling smile, then closed and locked the door behind the doctor.

———❦———

'So, if you're right about this and my people are Darklighting someone, what do we do? Rush over to Wigmore Street and catch them in the act?' Eddie asked. 'Then what?'

Drake considered the situation. 'By the time we arrived it will probably be all over. No, let's just hope the poor sap they're brainwashing doesn't croak in the process. I heard it's not unusual, particularly if the subject has a weak heart or a serious medical condition the Styx don't know about.'

'Or pregnant like your friend at university,' Eddie suggested.

Drake shook his head, his expression sad as he remembered. 'Yes, Fiona,' he said quietly. For a moment he stared at the red dot as it continued to pulse on the map, then he abruptly jabbed the Escape key to close the program. 'No, there's no time for this right now – we've enough on our plate as it is. In any case, it's probably just some lowly official having his will bent.'

———❦———

The Rebecca twins were seated opposite each other on the bare aluminium benches extending along either side of the helicopter. Accompanying the girls were the Limiter General, and a further eight Styx soldiers, with Tom Cox crammed in at the far end. With all the personnel and their equipment onboard, there wasn't much space left.

'Door gunner,' the Limiter General observed as a New

Germanian soldier took his position in the seat behind a large-bore weapon mounted by the main door. 'Looks like they're ready for trouble.'

'They're a cautious lot,' Rebecca One agreed. 'I thought that briefing was never going to end.'

'Buckle up,' the pilot shouted from his cockpit, as he worked his way through a bank of switches, thumbing them down one by one. Everyone had tightened their safety harnesses as he hit the last switch and the rotors began to trundle slowly around. They built up speed until the whole aircraft was vibrating like an old washing machine.

'Here we go,' Rebecca Two said, but after a minute they still weren't in the air. And as she peered through the port behind her, she could see that none of the other twelve helicopters had lifted off from the runway either. 'Is there a problem?' she asked finally, shouting so the Limiter General could hear her over the din.

'The motor takes time to warm up,' he replied.

'What an old bus!' she laughed.

Then as the Bramo engine reached the right temperature, the helicopter juddered and they were finally airborne. The twins were watching the other helicopters as they also began to climb.

'We're off,' the Limiter General said, and the nose of their helicopter dipped. Then they were moving forwards, sweeping over the sprawling metropolis.

Rebecca Two was just gesticulating at her sister to tell her that they were passing right over the Chancellery when an aircraft rocketed past from the opposite direction. It looked like a sleek, black bat.

'Look at that thing go!' Rebecca One shouted.

They hadn't seen anything like it on the airfield. It consisted of one large flying wing with no fuselage or tail plane, and from the flames leaping out of the afterburners it was clearly powered by a pair of jet engines. The closest thing the twins could compare it with were the spy planes of the US military – some of the most technologically advanced aircraft used Topsoil. This flying wing was moving at such speed that in less than a second it was no more than a small dot above the ocean.

'What the hell was that?' Rebecca Two asked.

Both the twins looked to the Limiter General for an answer. He was nodding to himself. 'I suspect it's a Horten 229 – built by the Horten brothers for the Nazis in the 1930s, at least three decades before the Americans began to develop their stealth bombers,' he said. Although he didn't smile, the lines around his eyes crinkled as if he was amused. 'I reckon I must have dented the Chancellor's pride about his air capability, and he's trying to impress with his hardware.'

As the engine powering their helicopter continued to hammer away, they left the airspace above the metropolis and rose over the mountain range that extended behind it.

Rebecca Two was keeping an eye on the other helicopters following behind them in neat formation, while her sister was more interested in what lay ahead. She was looking past the pilot as he pulled on the joystick, and the helicopter banked and then straightened out on a new course. Through the large area of Plexiglass at the front of the cockpit, the incredible vista unfolded before her as the full extent of the jungle came into sight – a sea of green that seemed to go on for ever. 'A virgin world,' she said to herself. 'What we could do with this.'

Rebecca Two began to take an interest in what the navigator

was doing on the other side of the cockpit. Tucked behind the pilot, he was obviously in constant touch with him over his headset as he studied a circular screen set into an equipment panel. Unbuckling her safety harness, she used a handrail to steady herself as she went over to him.

Tapping him on the arm to get his attention, she pointed at the screen. 'What are those dark patches there?' she shouted.

He looked surprised to see her there, but nevertheless slid his headset off so he could hear her.

'What are those dark areas?' she shouted again.

'*Ein Sturm ist im Kommen*,' he yelled in response.

She shrugged – good as her German was, the noise of the engine was making it difficult for her to understand him.

'Storm front,' he said, finding the right words in English. 'We have to steer around them in these copters as the wind currents and electrical discharges . . . they are so strong. This is a tracking—'

'It's a radar system for weather patterns,' Rebecca Two anticipated, nodding. 'But then what's that?' she said pointing at a small and indistinct area of light which slowly faded up, then just as slowly faded away again on the monochrome screen.

Rebecca One had now joined her sister, and was listening to the exchange.

'*Wir wissen nicht* . . . we don't know. Some weeks ago we sent a spotter plane over for a reconnaissance, but he finds nothing. Could be a magnetic field . . . how do you say . . . *eine Abweichung von der—*'

'Some sort of anomaly,' Rebecca One translated, meeting her sister's eyes.

Rebecca Two frowned. 'Maybe – just maybe – it's one of Drake's gizmos?' she suggested, and turned to the navigator again. 'Is it close to anything – any features or landmarks?'

The navigator swivelled in his chair so he could consult a map on a metal shelf by the side of his screen, laying a protractor over it. 'The closest feature is the third pyramid . . . the furthest from our current position.'

'It's near a pyramid! Why weren't we told about this?' Rebecca One demanded.

The navigator shrugged. 'Anyway, you'll see the area as it's the last drop point scheduled for this operation,' he replied.

The twins didn't need to make eye contact – they were both thinking precisely the same thing.

'No, it's not,' Rebecca Two said unequivocally.

'We're going there first,' Rebecca One ordered. 'Tell your pilot to re-route us . . . right now.'

Chapter Fifteen

'I'll be out here in the car if you need me. Just speak into this,' Drake said, as he made sure the microphone was attached to the inside of Chester's sleeve. Chester was with Drake in the back seat while Eddie was behind the steering wheel. 'And Eddie will take up position at the rear,' Drake went on.

'What . . . in my garden?' Chester said disbelievingly. Through the side window of the Range Rover, his eyes were glued on the house further down the street. He tore himself away from it to look at the microphone in his sleeve and then the handgun in Drake's lap. 'Do we really need all this?' he asked.

Eddie twisted round to Chester. 'Yes, we do. Be ready for anything,' he said ominously. He checked the street behind in his wing mirror. 'And we can't hang around here for long. It's not safe.'

'Look, Chester, I completely understand why you want to do this,' Drake began, then sighed. 'You want to put your parents' minds at rest that you're okay. But, as I keep trying to tell you, it's really not a good idea.'

Chester set his jaw resolutely but didn't reply.

Drake's unease was evident as he clenched his fingers into a fist and then opened them again. 'You've got ten minutes tops with them – there's no way you can stay any longer than that. The Styx will come and they won't grab only you – they'll grab your mother and father too. Everyone – and I mean *everyone* – you come into contact with is put at risk.'

'I understand that,' Chester mumbled. 'I'll make sure they do too.'

Shaking his head, Drake made a last effort at dissuading the boy. 'You must realise how this is going to play out. Your parents aren't going to let you breeze in and then just go off again. They'll want to know where you've been all this time, and with whom – they'll demand an explanation. But you can't tell them. Then, when you do try to leave, they'll kick up one hell of a fuss and probably contact the authorities, and that's tantamount to making a direct call to the Styx.'

Chester began to say something, but Drake spoke over him.

'And afterwards, when the alarm's been raised and you've vanished into the sunset again, the Styx will round up your parents and interrogate them to see what they know.'

'No, I'll make my mum and dad listen to me,' Chester replied hoarsely. 'They'll do what I ask, because they trust me.'

'It's going to take a lot more than trust,' Drake said. 'These are your parents we're talking about. They'll fight tooth and claw to stop you from leaving.'

Chester let out a tremulous breath. 'No, I have to let them see I'm all right. I owe them that much, don't I?' He looked beseechingly at Drake, who merely shook his head again.

'Some things are better left as they are,' the man replied, but Chester had gone back to watching his house.

'Right now, I bet my dad will be having his cup of coffee in front of the evening news on the TV. My mum will be in the kitchen, with the radio on as she makes the supper. But whatever they're doing, they're probably thinking about me. You see, I'm all they've got. My sister Annie died in an accident when she was little, and there's only me. I can't let them go on suffering, believing that something terrible happened to me too. Nothing can be worse than . . . than the *not* knowing.'

Drake worked the slide of his handgun. 'Well, don't say I didn't try to talk you out of it.'

Eddie started the car and edged it down the street. When he was several houses away from Chester's home, he pulled up.

'Let's go,' he said, and they all climbed out at the same time. As Drake took Eddie's place behind the steering wheel, the Styx escorted Chester along the pavement.

'This is it,' Chester said, as they reached his home.

'Good luck,' Eddie whispered, then peeled off to go around the side of the house.

Taking a few steps up the crazy-paving path, Chester stopped to gaze at his front door. Then he noticed the blind pulled down inside the kitchen window, and that there was movement behind it. 'Mum,' he said, and beamed.

He walked slowly along the remainder of the short path. Everything looked exactly the same – the small areas of grass either side of the path had been recently cut. During the summer months his father always got the mower out on Sundays, in the evenings when it was cooler.

Chester looked for the squat concrete frog that was poised

in the border, its tongue protruding as if it was lying in wait for a concrete fly to buzz past it. The grey colour of the frog, specked in places with dried lichen, was rather dull in contrast to the envelope of eye-catching flowers surrounding it. These were his mother's work – she made regular trips to the local garden centre and completely replanted the border every couple of months whether it needed it or not, choosing the brightest and most dazzling blooms. 'Well, it makes me happy,' she would declare to Chester's father when he inevitably queried the cost. To which he would say nothing, because if it made her happy then he was happy too.

Nothing has stopped. Everything's gone on as usual without me, Chester realised quite suddenly. The rituals that were unique to the Rawls' family life, all the routines and activities that had filled the in-between times as he'd grown up were still continuing, even though he wasn't present. These touchstones to his life had persisted even though he hadn't been around to enjoy them. Part of him felt that somehow they should have come to an end, or have at least been put on hold until he returned home again, because they were *his* rituals too.

These thoughts made him all the more desperate to see his parents. He wanted them to know he was still part of the family, even if he hadn't been around.

He entered the porch, and took a second to run his hand over his hair so it wouldn't look too messy before he pressed the button.

The sound of the bell ringing inside made his heart beat faster. He knew its loose tinkling so well.

He heard voices.

'I'm home!' he said out loud, his face split by a broad

smile. 'I'm really home,' he said even more loudly.

He saw someone behind the mottled glass of the front door – a shifting human outline.

He felt as though he was going to explode.

The door opened and his mother stood there, drying her hands on a tea towel.

Chester stared at her, so overcome with emotion he was unable to speak.

'Yes, what can I do for you?' Mrs Rawls asked, glancing him over casually.

'Mu . . .' he managed to squeeze through his quivering lips as the tears began to fill his eyes. She looked exactly the same – her dark brown hair cut very short, and the reading glasses she was always mislaying balanced on top of her head. 'Mu . . .' Chester tried to say again, drinking in her face, which was exactly how he'd pictured it during all those weeks and months he'd been underground. Perhaps it was a little older than the last time he had seen it, with recently acquired worry lines around the eyes, but Chester didn't notice these because it was the face of someone he loved like no one else. He raised his arms, wanting to throw them around her and hug her.

But she didn't show any reaction, except for her brows, which lowered in a frown. 'Yes?' Mrs Rawls repeated, giving him one of those askance looks he'd seen her give people in the street who asked for money. Then, even more unbelievably, she took a step back from the doorway. 'Oh, I know – you've come for the clothes, haven't you?' she announced crisply. 'It's all ready for you to take.' She gestured at a white plastic bag behind the milk bottles in the corner of the porch. It was full and there was a printed name on it, but Chester couldn't read it clearly because his eyes were flooding with tears.

'Who is it?' Mr Rawls called from inside.

'Dad,' Chester swallowed.

Mrs Rawls had been too distracted to hear him. 'Just someone from the charity to collect our old clothes,' she shouted back down the hallway.

'I hope you haven't tried to chuck out my favourite cardigan again,' came the rejoinder from inside, followed by a loud chuckle. The chuckle was all but drowned out by a sudden burst of music. Chester had been right; his father, a creature of habit, was watching television in the sitting room. And, ironically, the music sounded like a marching band playing a bombastic homecoming tune.

By now, Mrs Rawls had noticed that Chester was crying. He took half a step towards her, but she sidled defensively behind the front door, which she began to close.

'You *are* from the charity, aren't you?' Mrs Rawls asked, becoming suspicious.

Chester found his voice. 'Mum!' It came out in rather an ugly croak. 'It's me!'

But she still didn't show any sign that she recognised him. If anything, the concern on her face became more pronounced.

'You haven't come to collect the clothes at all, have you?' Mrs Rawls decided, now set on closing the door.

Not knowing what else to do, Chester stuck his foot inside the threshold to block it open. 'What's wrong, Mum? Don't you recognise me?' he demanded.

'Jeff,' Mrs Rawls said weakly, her voice choked with panic as she called her husband.

'But it's *me* – Chester!' Chester exhorted her.

For a moment anger supplanted fear, and Mrs Rawls' face flushed red. 'Go away!' she snapped. She put her weight against the door, but Chester pushed back, resisting her efforts to shut it.

'Mum, I can't have changed that much,' he whined. 'Can't you see who I am? It's me – your son.'

As Mrs Rawls swore at him, the sheer insanity of the situation was too much for Chester, and something snapped in his head. 'Let me in,' he growled, shouldering the door all the way open. His mother was thrown back as far as the kitchen entrance, where she caught hold of the jamb to regain her balance.

Chester strode into the hallway and thrust his finger at a large photograph on the wall. He hadn't seen it before – it was from the very last family outing they'd gone on, in the weeks before Chester had disappeared.

In the photograph they were standing together in a pod on the London Eye, Big Ben visible behind them. He remembered how a Japanese tourist had taken the photograph of the three of them using his father's camera. The outing had been a special treat for him, his parents picking him up straight after school. And there he was in the picture, still wearing his uniform.

'Look – that's me! With you and Dad!' Chester shouted. 'What's wrong with you?'

'Get . . . out . . . of . . . my . . . house!' Mrs Rawls said, emphasising each word, and then giving a strangled, strange laugh. 'You're not my son!' She called for Mr Rawls again, but this time she screamed his name at the top of her voice. Chester had never seen her like this before. He couldn't believe what was happening.

There was a crash as Mr Rawls came flying out of the sitting room, a dark stain down his white shirt where he'd spilt his coffee. This time he'd heard his wife's call for help over the television.

'What's going on?' Mr Rawls barked.

'This boy's disturbed or something! He's saying he's Chester,' Mrs Rawls shouted as Mr Rawls advanced toward him.

'He's what?' Mr Rawls exclaimed, throwing a glance at his wife. Still gripping the tea towel, she was twisting it anxiously between her hands.

'He saying he's our son,' she confirmed.

Mr Rawls turned on Chester. He was normally a very shy man, barely even making eye contact with people he didn't know well, but he was angry now, and was staring directly at Chester. 'How dare you? You . . . you sick person!' he fumed. 'How dare you come here and say things like that? Our son is missing, and you're nothing like him.'

'But Dad . . .' Chester pleaded. He was cowed by his father's fury, but thrust a finger at the photograph again. 'I'm me . . . that's me! Can't you see who I am?'

'Get off my property right now, or I'll call the police. In fact, Emily, go and call them anyway. Tell them a madman's loose in the neighbourhood.' As Chester's mother rushed into the kitchen, Mr Rawls seized an umbrella from where it was propped against the wall and brandished it at him. 'You lowlife!' he snarled. 'After some money for drugs or something, are you?'

'Dad, Dad,' Chester was begging, holding out his hands.

'Get out – or, so help me – I *will* use this on you!' Mr Rawls shouted.

But Chester didn't move.

'Right, you asked for it!' Just as Mr Rawls began to swing the umbrella at Chester, Drake pushed the boy aside. Catching Mr Rawls' wrist, Drake twisted his arm and forced him down onto his knees.

'I'll take that,' he said, as he wrenched the umbrella from Mr Rawls' grip, then spun round to Chester. The boy was staring dumbly at his father, who was still threatening blue murder, but unable to get up because Drake had him in an arm lock. 'Snap out of it, Chester,' Drake said. When Chester didn't react, he raised his voice. 'Back to the car – now!' he ordered.

Eddie was suddenly there, bundling Chester away.

Drake heaved Mr Rawls over on to his back, then slung the umbrella down the length of the hallway. 'Sorry to bother you. Wrong house,' he said as he left, slamming the front door behind him.

As they drove away at some speed, Chester was slumped against the car door. He was shaking as he mumbled, 'I don't understand,' over and over again.

Drake put a hand on his shoulder and the boy flinched.

'They've got no idea what they're doing, Chester. Your parents have been Darklit – that's why they didn't recognise you. Isn't that right, Eddie?'

'Yes, that's correct,' the Limiter replied, without a moment's hesitation.

'Their behavioural patterns have been modified – rewired, if you like – and I bet they've been conditioned to contact a Styx agent the moment you showed your face,' Drake said.

'They'll believe they're calling the police, but it'll be a different number. They'll have no conscious control over what they're doing. So I'm afraid to say the Styx have already got to them, Chester.'

'Which means we need to make ourselves scarce,' Eddie said, accelerating straight through a set of red lights.

Chapter Sixteen

Will saw the flash of lightning through his closed eyes. As the whole tree shook with an almost simultaneous crash of thunder, he and Dr Burrows were wrenched from their sleep.

'That was an almighty one,' Dr Burrows declared, getting up and stretching his arms.

'Yeah, another megastorm,' Will agreed. Beyond the reach of the tree branches where he expected the sky to be over-shadowed by thick cloud cover, he saw with some surprise how bright it was. 'But it seems to have completely blown over – we must have slept through the worst of it.'

Despite the incredible amount of foliage in the gargantuan tree above the base, the odd raindrop was making its way through and landing around Will. He became transfixed as these drops ended their marathon journeys, splattering on the floor and leaving dark patches as the moisture seeped into the rough timber.

'Time to get on,' Dr Burrows announced. 'But first, I think some brekky's in order.'

Although Will felt like going back to sleep, his hunger got

the better of him. He followed his father's lead and stumbled towards the Bergen, which Elliott had suspended by a single cord from an overhead branch in an effort to keep the food away from ants. Will and Dr Burrows each helped themselves to a mango fruit from the crop that Elliott had gathered the day before. There was no sign of her or Bartleby, and Will assumed she'd gone off to do some hunting.

Sitting cross-legged by the table, Dr Burrows was scribbling in his journal as he bit into a hunk of mango. Will knew he was unlikely to get an answer if he asked what his father was working on, so instead he sat on the very edge of the platform. He looked over at the pyramid through the overhanging branches. In the intense sunshine, both the pyramid and the margin of grassland surrounding it glistened from the recent monsoon. The heat was already having an effect on the moisture, turning it into clouds of water vapour, which were whisked away by the occasional breeze.

'It's funny how nothing ever changes here, isn't it?' Will said, still not yet fully awake and already perspiring from the heat. 'I mean it's always sunny . . . always the same weather, except for these thunderstorms, and there are no winters or seasons or anything. It's like the clock stopped in some baking hot summer.'

His mouth full, Dr Burrows mumbled something unintelligible in response.

Will began to kick his feet out, swinging them alternately. It reminded him so much of the outings to a rather basic adventure park in Highfield, when he'd been much younger. Covered in a film of sun block, he'd always made a beeline for the swings in the hope that they hadn't been vandalised. But even if they were in working order, Mrs Burrows very rarely offered to push him, preferring instead to browse her glossy film and TV magazines on a nearby bench. So he'd had no alternative but to learn how to swing himself, or just sit there, while other children were pushed by their mothers or fathers.

'I wonder how Mum is,' Will began as he thought about the last time he'd seen her in the motorway cafe. 'I wonder how she and Drake are getting on. I hope she's—'

'Oh, do shut up,' Dr Burrows snapped. His face had turned puce, and Will noticed that he'd crushed the section of mango he'd been eating in his clenched fist. The juice dripped from his hand as he lurched to his feet. 'Can't you live in the present? Can't you make the most of the incredible opportunity you've been given here? You're always harking back to the past, and that's not healthy, especially for someone your age!' He stomped towards the large tree trunk they used to enter and leave the base, then paused. 'In this world, none of us have shadows,' he said, then began to climb down to the ground.

'What does that mean?' Will mouthed at the space where Dr Burrows had been, but he knew very well that he'd touched a raw nerve when he mentioned Mrs Burrows. It was clearly painful for his father to think about the wife who had rejected him when he and Will had returned Topsoil. But there was no way Will was going to turn his back on his mother – he'd seen a new side to her, and she was constantly in his thoughts. The brief time he'd had with her had made him realise, deep down, just how much he loved her.

Although these days he didn't go there as often as he would have liked, Will had found himself a secluded spot near a small spring where he'd set up crosses to honour the members of his family he'd lost. And while he was there, lying in the grass and remembering Uncle Tam, Sarah Jerome and Cal, he would also think about his mother, and pray that she was safe from the Styx. He had a permanent reminder of them nearby because, sealed inside an old medicine bottle to protect them from the damp, he'd buried the phials of Dominion virus and vaccine on the other side of the spring.

So this spring was a place of contradictions for him – on the one side all that had been good in his life, and on the other the lethal virus that the murderous Styx had been preparing to use to commit genocide, and decimate the Topsoil population.

Unlike his father, Will didn't want to forget the past. He felt he owed the people who had lost their lives, possibly as a result of the chain of events that he'd put into motion when he'd first crashed through the door into the Colony with Chester at his side. Will mulled over whether to visit the spring now, but then decided he should probably go and help his father. If he'd upset him, then he needed to patch things up between them, and offering his assistance was a sure-fire way of doing this. So Will washed his face with water from one of the canteens, swung his Sten gun over his shoulder, and began for the tree trunk in order to descend from the base.

He'd crossed the grassland and was climbing the side of the pyramid when he first heard a sound that made the hairs on the back of his neck stand up. Certain he'd picked up the throb of a distant engine, he paused for a moment. He listened hard, then shook his head. If there had been anything, it seemed to have stopped now, but nevertheless he began to take even bigger leaps up the tiers, frantically trying to locate his father. As he reached halfway up the pyramid, he ran along the tier, scanning the clearing below just in case Dr Burrows was working on their recent finds down there. Turning the corner at the end of the tier, Will finally spotted his father. He'd been on the far side of the pyramid, where he was examining the moving stones.

Dr Burrows appeared to have already got over his irritation with his son as he looked across at him. 'Ah, there you are,' he shouted, his hand on one of the stones as he pulled it out as far as it would go. 'I'm seeing if—'

'Dad! Did you hear that?' Will yelled at him, pointing urgently at the sky.

'Just a minute,' Dr Burrows said, mistaking his son's gestures as a greeting and giving him a small wave in return. As Will reached him, Dr Burrows had taken hold of the next stone along in the row and was adjusting its position. 'I'm trying out a new appr—'

Just then, carried on a gust of wind, the sound came again for a few seconds. This time there was no doubt in Will's mind that he'd heard it, although Dr Burrows seemed oblivious to everything but the moving stones.

'For God's sake, just leave those alone! Didn't you hear that?' Will pressed him.

'Hear what?' Dr Burrows answered, retracting his hand from the stones and cocking his head to one side.

He didn't have to try too hard to hear it this time.

A helicopter thundered into sight, flying so low it was scattering the rainwater from the tops of the trees. It climbed, coming to a halt directly above the pyramid. With all the force of a minor tornado, the intense downdraught from the rotors blew in Will and Dr Burrows' faces, and churned up rain-soaked grit and dust from the pyramid. Father and son crouched low as they tried to prevent themselves from being swept off the side.

'Who is it?' Dr Burrows shouted, as he tried to creep further out on the ledge for a better look.

'No, you idiot!' Will cried, yanking his bemused father back against the side of the pyramid in an attempt to hide them both.

'But who's in it?' Dr Burrows was asking.

'Just shut up!' Will ordered him. Now they were tucked in and less obvious to anyone above, Will didn't have a line of sight on the helicopter, and in any case he didn't much care who was in it – there was no question in his mind that it was a military aircraft. And coming on top of Dr Burrows' previous sighting of a Stuka, its arrival on the scene was hardly likely to be good news.

Nevertheless, Will ventured a small distance out from the wall. Blinking against the dust and the wind from the rotors, he caught a brief glimpse of the pilot wearing a helmet and dark goggles. Then, as the helicopter rotated slowly around, Will saw that the side door of the helicopter was open. A soldier manning a substantial-looking gun was poised in it.

As he kept watching, coils of rope were flung from both sides of the helicopter and unravelled to their full length.

Then Will saw something else that made his heart skip a beat. Behind the door gunner, he spied the gaunt faces of Limiters dressed in their characteristic camouflage. Then he saw one of them aiming his rifle – it was directed straight in Will's direction.

'Styx! There are Styx in it!' Will babbled, throwing himself back against the wall and wrenching the Sten gun from his shoulder. He cocked it ready to fire.

We've got to get out of here!

Will hurriedly scanned the jungle across from them. As he was trying to calculate whether they had any hope of crossing the clearing to reach it, he thought he glimpsed Elliott. She seemed to show herself from behind one of the massive tree trunks.

He didn't have time to look further.

At that instant, a whole host of other helicopters appeared over the trees, stopping in a circular holding pattern around the first. They maintained a low altitude just above the tree-tops, their blades stirring up the branches and causing a whirl storm of scattered leaves.

Above the clamour of the massed helicopters, Will heard the unmistakable crack of rifle fire. Shards of stone splintered over him and his father. They were being pinned down by precise firing. He knew then that the Styx wanted them alive – Limiters didn't miss.

Will threw a glance back at the jungle. There was no way they could reach it, even if he and his father took advantage of the low gravity and pitched themselves off the side of the pyramid. The distance was just too great – the Styx sharp-shooters would have plenty of time to pick off anyone fleeing across the clearing. It wasn't an option.

Dr Burrows seemed completely lost, cowering against the wall and hugging his journal in both arms, as if preserving it was all that mattered to him. Will peeked out again at the helicopter directly overhead. He wished he hadn't, catching a glimpse of the dark forms of Limiters silhouetted against the white sky as they abseiled down the ropes. There were six of them, all sliding towards the top of the pyramid at speed.

Acting on impulse, Will pointed his Sten at the Styx soldiers, but a hailstorm of bullets rained down. Shots were being fired by Limiters in the other helicopters, striking the ledge mere metres from him. He lowered his weapon and slumped back against the wall. What was the point against all this fire-power and such numbers?

'We've had it,' Will muttered to his father.

There was no escaping from this, and he felt listless, as though all his energy had been sapped.

He heard a shout from the top of the pyramid. It was a Styx directing the other soldiers to the ledge where he and his father were trapped.

The Limiters had landed.

They were so close now.

'It's all over, Dad.'

Will put his arm across his face and shut his eyes, waiting for the inevitable.

Waiting for capture.

Then the inexplicable happened.

The wall they were pressed against and the stone floor below them gave way.

'Whoa!' Dr Burrows shrieked.

They both plunged into blackness.

'Hey!' Rebecca Two exclaimed, as they continued to hover above the pyramid. 'Where'd they go?'

'What?' Rebecca One snapped from further inside the heli-copter, where she'd been unable to see as much as her sister. She squeezed in between the door gunner and her sister in order to get a better view. 'Don't tell me we've lost them! How can that be?'

The first wave of Limiters to alight on the plateau–like area at the top of the pyramid were already searching the tier where Will and Dr Burrows had been. Other helicopters were setting down in the clearing, men leaping from them the moment the ground was close enough. And the barks of stalkers echoed around the trees as their handlers began to pick up on the many scent trails.

'They won't get far,' Rebecca Two said.

In unbroken darkness, Will was rolling over and over as he tumbled down an incline. He tried not to yell out as his elbows and knees knocked against multiple corners – he realised they were the edges of a flight of stairs, and thankfully each step was relatively shallow or the pain would have been that much worse.

As he landed face down on a stone floor, the wind was completely knocked from him. Managing to get his lungs working again, he immediately cast around for his Sten, which he'd dropped on the way down. With the image of the Limiters descending on their ropes still fresh on his retinas, Will knew how vital it was he located his weapon.

But what had happened?

The Styx soldiers had almost been on them, but by some incredible stroke of luck, he'd managed to escape.

But where was he now? And where was his father?

Having got his breath back, he rolled over onto his side and began to shout, 'Dad, Dad, are you there?'

There was a moan and something clouted Will on the top of his head. He reached out and grabbed it. He discovered it was Dr Burrows' foot. 'Watch it, Dad,' he warned, feeling the leg above it, then pulling himself alongside his father, who was lying on his back and clearly stunned. 'Are you okay?' Will asked, shaking him by the arm.

'Ow!' Dr Burrows complained after a moment, then spoke in a disgruntled voice. 'Please, just let go of me, Will – that arm's bloody sore.'

Satisfied his father didn't seem to be too badly injured, Will released him, then tried to get his thoughts in order. 'That was close – I thought we'd had it.'

Their escape had been nothing short of a miracle, and he still couldn't work out how it had happened.

'You got us inside the pyramid, Dad! How did you work out the code on the stones?'

'I didn't do anything,' Dr Burrows admitted, as he sat up, feeling his leg gingerly. 'And I'm getting too old for this. My poor knees.'

'If it wasn't you, then . . . then how did we end up in here?' Will asked, trying to see what lay in the darkness around them.

'Search me,' Dr Burrows responded, groaning as he stood up and began to rummage through his pockets.

The instincts Will had honed during the months he'd spent deep in the Earth were returning, and he clapped his hands together, gauging the extent of the resultant echo. 'Quite big in here,' he observed.

Dr Burrows was still going through his pockets. 'Yes, but we need to have a proper look at where we are, and for that we need some light. Got anything on you?'

'Um . . . don't think so,' Will said, also standing up to check his trousers, although he knew it was unlikely that he did – the permanent daylight had made it completely unnecessary to carry a luminescent orb around with him.

'Aha!' Dr Burrows said, as he came across a small tube of matches he'd helped himself to from the stores in the fallout shelter. 'Windproof matches. Good old army issue. Here we go,' he declared as he took one out and struck it on the base of the tube.

Will saw they were in a chamber, its roof some ten metres above them. Only two of the walls were visible in the flickering light cast by the match, and set into the one directly behind him he could see the stone steps they'd fallen down.

'The floor,' Dr Burrows whispered. 'Look at it.'

They were both standing on what appeared to be shapes carved into the floor, but unlike the plain reliefs on the exterior of the pyramid these ones were coloured.

Dr Burrows began to investigate, taking several steps as he held the match down low. 'I think it's a map. There are features like rivers and mountains, and what must be cities on this. Look – it certainly is a map! It's of the outer world! Here's Asia. And here's Europe.' As he tried to see more of the map, he was sidestepping so quickly he nearly lost his balance. 'All these continents are shown so accurately – how is that possible?' He scuttled even further along. 'And here's North America!' He whistled expansively. 'No! So then these people – the Ancients – were there millennia before Columbus!'

'Before Columbus?' Will repeated, too preoccupied to fully grasp what his father was saying.

'Yes – and they could reach all these continents because they didn't have to navigate the oceans – they came from *inside* the globe. They had the whole world at their feet!'

'Dad, I could do with some light over here,' Will said, his patience wearing thin as his father continued to babble excitedly. At that very moment, Will's priority was to locate his

Sten gun, but there was no sign of it anywhere.

'Damn it!' Dr Burrows said, as the match burnt his fingers and went out. As darkness swamped them again, Will could hear him scrabbling with the packet.

With another match lit, Dr Burrows moved over the map in the direction of the far wall. What was on it immediately caught his attention. There were more painted carvings, but this time it wasn't a map.

A long procession was depicted on it. The figures were at least twice life size, and from their finery and the elaborate crowns on their heads they had to be sovereigns. Behind the king – if it truly was a king – was the queen, and she was being borne along in a sedan chair. Then came soldiers or possibly the royal guard, some in chariots that were each being pulled by four white stallions.

And with this discovery, even Will forgot that he'd been trying to find the Sten for a second as he took in the spectacle. Then he noticed something in the scene. 'Dad,' he whispered. 'It's the symbol from my pendant again.'

'Yes, it's in the ruler's cartouche,' Dr Burrows said, pointing at the panel below the kingly figure, where the three-pronged emblem was picked out in gold alongside some other pictograms.

'Not just there – it's all over the place,' Will corrected him, spotting it on the crowns of the king and queen, and on a sceptre the king was holding.

In fact, the trident symbol was also emblazoned on the shields and breastplates of many of the royal guard, the gilding on them reflecting the last light of Dr Burrows' dying match. 'Exquisite,' he whispered, but as he moved further along the wall, the flame spluttered and went out.

'Blast! I've got to see more!' he said, fumbling for another.

As they were plunged back into darkness again, Will woke up to their current situation. 'Dad, this is crazy. We just don't have time for this. There are Limiters out there, and they'll be trying to work out where we've gone. They won't just *stop*. They'll try everything to get at us inside here. And Elliott's all by herself too. We've got to reach her somehow.' Will's voice became muffled as he turned to peer into the gloom behind him. 'I have to find my Sten gun. It's our only weapon.'

'Spare me the lecture, Will,' Dr Burrows replied. 'I've got a whole box of matches, and it won't hurt to have another quick peek at these scenes. Then we'll try to find a way out. Okay?'

Will didn't say anything as his father attempted to strike yet another match. Dr Burrows couldn't get it lit on the first or second attempts. 'Oh, come on,' he said.

But as he finally managed it, the chamber was suddenly filled with more light than could have come from a single match.

Will and Dr Burrows were encircled by burning torches. And behind those torches were what, at first glance, could have been trees, covered in rough bark.

That was until Will noticed that they had limbs – arms and legs – which approximated to the human form. And although completely covered by the woody, flaking bark, faces were discernable beneath it. Will could make out their mouths, and their small eyes with brown pupils, which glinted in the torchlight.

With a rustling, the figures closed in on Will and Dr Burrows.

'E-E-E-Elliott's trees,' Will stuttered, terrified out of his wits.

Several patrols of Limiters had taken up position along the four sides of the plateau at the very top of the pyramid, while the Rebecca twins strolled behind them, surveying the activity down at ground level. As the Limiter General climbed up onto the plateau, he conferred briefly with one of his men, who passed something to him, and then he came straight over to the girls.

As he reached them, he held out a small black box. 'First off, this is the radio emitter that was registering on the weather radar system. It was hidden over there, lodged in a crevice,' he said, glancing behind the twins.

Rebecca Two took it from him, and examined the length of wire dangling from it.

'We haven't opened it to assess the technology, because we didn't want to disrupt the signal,' the Limiter General told them.

'Yes, leave it running,' Rebecca One agreed. 'Odds-on Drake's behind this device – he'll have sourced it from one of his techie mates.'

'And what else?' Rebecca Two urged the Limiter General.

'We've carried out an evaluation of the tracks left in the vicinity. There are four sets in total: three human, one of which is adult and the other two younger, and they're some-times accompanied by an animal, which is likely to be the Hunter,' he replied.

'That figures . . . so it is just Dr Buckwheat, Will and Elliott we're dealing with here,' Rebecca Two concluded.

The Limiter General nodded, then resumed. 'Stalkers are finding multiple scent trails on all points of the compass,' he said with a wave of his hand at the surrounding jungle. 'We located the targets' camp in a nearby tree at the edge of the clearing.' He made a quarter turn to show the Rebecca twins where he meant. 'It's down on the south side.'

'Anything there?' Rebecca Two enquired.

'Food, water, spare clothes and a limited amount of ammunition, but we haven't finished searching it yet. There was an improvised device with a tripwire rigged across the main approach, which we made safe. The explosive utilised in the device was C4 – the powerful Topsoil explosive.'

'Follows. Also provided by Drake, no doubt,' Rebecca One surmised.

'And it tells us that Elliott is still up to her old tricks,' her sister added. 'How predictable.'

The Limiter General continued his report. 'There are numerous items – bones, coins, pieces of pottery and glass – that don't appear to have been out of the ground for long.'

'Dr Buckwheat,' Rebecca One snorted. 'Some things never change.'

'And we've also found some human skulls, three of which look fairly recent. They appear to have been impaled on stakes, and one shows damage to the temple consistent with a gunshot wound, possibly inflicted at close range.' The Limiter General glanced at Colonel Bismarck, who was out of hearing distance. 'Perhaps they belong to the New Germanians who went missing.'

'Let our friends discover that for themselves. It's not our problem,' Rebecca One said, flicking her head impatiently. 'Tell us about Dr Buckwheat and Will? Where are they now?' she asked.

'If you'll come with me,' the Limiter General requested,

leading them from the top of the pyramid and to the next tier down. 'The last sighting of the targets was here, on this ledge. The dust raised by the helicopter restricted visibility, but after some rapid movements, the two of them simply dropped out of view,' he reported. 'And the dogs have been unable to pick up any fresh tracks leading from the area.'

The twins were digesting this information as they began to pick their way along the ledge.

'So we had them on a plate – they were caught out in the open – and yet, somehow, we still lost them,' Rebecca One said, a vindictive tone to her voice.

Her sister blew through her lips, shaking her head reproachfully. 'Take us to where they were,' she ordered. 'The *exact* spot.'

As the Limiter General showed them the place, the four-man patrol of soldiers assigned to protect the Styx girls hurriedly moved out of their way.

Rebecca Two examined the wall, while her sister knelt down, running her fingertips along a narrow gap between two blocks of stone on the ledge itself. She clicked her fingers at the nearest Limiter, indicating she wanted the combat knife on his belt. He unsheathed it and handed it to her. 'Do you think your men might have been distracted – maybe they failed to notice as our two friends hotfooted it down the side of the pyramid?' Rebecca One enquired, as she used the tip of the knife to probe several places along the gap, but was unable to penetrate very far into it. 'The lower gravity would have helped them make a quick getaway.'

'And there aren't any obvious signs of a concealed opening in this old heap,' Rebecca Two remarked as she watched her sister.

The Limiter General hovered uneasily behind the Styx twins. He didn't like it that the reliability of his report was being called into question.

'So, what do you say?' Rebecca One asked the Limiter General, showing her dissatisfaction by looking away as she addressed him.

He set his shoulders, confident of his information. 'From three different viewpoints in three different helicopters, my men were zeroed in on the two targets. As you know, my men were laying down fire in a containment pattern, to ensure the targets remained in place. There were no sightings of them escaping into the jungle,' he stated clearly. 'And there's no question in my mind that this was their last known position.'

Appearing from nowhere, Cox glided over and stopped by the wall. Lifting the shawl from his face, he inclined his mis-shapen head, and began to waft air towards his nose with his hand. Sniffing noisily, he shuffled a few steps along the ledge and again sampled the air, repeating this until he was directly below Dr Burrows' moving stones. But Cox wasn't interested in the stones. He sniffed deeply for one last time, as if making absolutely sure. 'Right 'ere, my girls,' he proclaimed, raking his feet over the ground in the same way a chicken does before it begins to peck some unfortunate worm into pieces.

Cox was precisely where Will and Dr Burrows had been tucked into the wall as they'd tried to hide from the heli-copter. 'Right 'ere, I smell fear . . . this is where the quarry went to ground.'

'I give you Tom Cox . . .' Rebecca One announced melo-dramatically, with a sweep of her arm, '. . . better even than any stalker.'

Her sister turned to the Limiter General, who nodded at

the girl's unspoken command. 'We'll bring up the munitions,' he said. 'We'll flush them out, even if we have to tear this whole pyramid apart.'

The strange figures had Will and Dr Burrows completely surrounded.

'Dad, the trees . . . they've got weapons . . . and they don't look too friendly,' Will warned in an incredulous whisper as he saw they had swords drawn, and a couple of them were armed with spears. The iron of their weapons glinted dully in the bizarre hands of the figures, which Will was studying as they came closer. It was as if the skin had grown so profusely that it was raised from their digits in whorls, making their fingers appear swollen and cumbersome.

'Don't panic . . . don't do anything to alarm these . . . um . . .' Dr Burrows whispered back, hesitating as he came up with a name for the strange beings, 'these bushmen.'

'Alarm *them*?' Will replied, then noticed something that made him do a double take. 'Dad, that one's got my Sten, and he looks like he knows how to use it!' Will was right – the bushman was holding the Sten correctly with his unwieldy hands, and was pointing it straight at Will and Dr Burrows.

'Hmm,' Dr Burrows said, trying to give his son the impression that he was calm. 'Yes, they seem to be humanoid – perhaps their appearance is down to some sort of skin mutation? And I agree with you that they definitely seem to be intelligent. I'm going to have a shot at communicating with them.'

Dr Burrows opened his journal slowly, so as not to startle them, and then, after a few seconds, began to speak in a language the likes of which Will had never heard before. The words sounded harsh and epiglottal.

The bushmen rustled a little, but otherwise there was no reaction.

'Might be my pronunciation is wrong, if indeed they are capable of language,' Dr Burrows remarked.

'Whatever you're going to do, just get on with it!' Will urged.

Dr Burrows tried again. This time there was no rustling, but somewhere from the circle of bushmen came a reply, in the same ugly language Dr Burrows had used.

'Yes, yes, yes!' Dr Burrows was beside himself with excitement, getting his pencil stub out and scribbling in his journal. 'Did you see which one spoke?' he whispered to Will, as he translated the response. 'He or she said that . . . we have . . . trespassed and if we don't leave the temple . . . the guards – or more accurately – guardians . . . are going to . . .' Dr Burrows glanced nervously up at Will. '*Kill us*. Christ, Will, they're going to kill us.'

The bushmen began to shuffle slowly forwards, closing in on the two Burrows.

'Is it all right to panic now?' Will asked, frantically scanning around the circle of bushmen to see if there was anywhere he could break through it.

Dr Burrows didn't offer an answer, but gulped loudly.

Will had a brainwave. 'The symbols on the wall . . . I'm going to try something,' he whispered urgently. He stuck his hand inside his shirt and tore the pendant Uncle Tam had given him from around his neck. Then he brandished it at the bushmen, showing it to as many of them as he could, as if he was fending off a gang of blood-crazed vampires with a crucifix. 'Quick – tell them something, Dad . . . tell them I'm their ruler, their king or something, and that they have to obey us and let us stay here.'

Dr Burrows was no help. 'Er,' he'd just mumbled, when one of the bushmen lashed out, sending the pendant spinning from Will's hand. Another of them said something which sounded curt, even in their ungainly tongue.

'Oh,' was all Will could manage, noticing that the bushmen's eyes now looked even more hostile, and how they were raising their weapons.

'That didn't do us any good,' Dr Burrows said. 'He just swore at you – he called you a thief. There's no way they're going to let us stay here now.'

'Thanks a bunch, Uncle Tam,' Will muttered.

As one of the trees stepped forward and raised his sword, there was a massive thump, which made Will's teeth rattle. The whole chamber seemed to shake, rafts of dust showering down over the Burrows and the circle of bushmen.

'What the hell was that?' Dr Burrows asked.

A few pieces of masonry crashed onto the floor. Then a larger block of stone detached from the ceiling and struck a slightly shorter bushman on the head. He simply toppled backwards to the ground. His fellow bushmen turned to look at him, but none of them went to his aid.

'Timber?' Will quipped. The hopelessness of their current predicament was beginning to get to him – he still couldn't quite believe that he and his father had eluded the Limiters and almost certain death, only to be plunged into another equally dangerous situation. Talk about out of the frying pan and into the fire. And even though the bushmen now seemed to be backing off a little as they talked amongst themselves in rapid exchanges, he couldn't see how he and his father were going to escape and rejoin Elliott.

'What *was* that?' Dr Burrows repeated, blinking at the ceiling above. 'An explosion?'

'Yes, Dad,' Will replied resignedly. 'It's the Limiters . . . they're trying to blow a hole through to get at us.' He sighed. 'So if these freaky trees don't do us in first, the Styx will. Great. Bloody great.'

* * *

Under the reduced gravity, the explosion sent sections of the pyramid hurtling so far into the sky that it seemed as though they would never come down again. And even before the smoke and dust had cleared, the Rebecca twins were leaping up the tiers of the pyramid with the Limiter General close behind. As they reached the upper tier, they inspected the damage their charges had inflicted. The facing stones with their carvings had been completely blasted away, but the underlying structure was still intact.

The Limiter General was unperturbed. 'There's the outline of an opening,' he pointed out. 'Tom Cox was right. Now we know where it is, we'll drill a few holes into the surrounding structure and plant some more charges.' He waved his men up. 'One more go, and we'll have Dr Burrows and the boy.'

* * *

From the tree line, Elliott had been watching the helicopter as it hovered over the pyramid. She'd been in the jungle when she first caught the sounds of its engine, and had immediately raced back. Keeping under the cover of the trees, she'd eventually located Will and Dr Burrows crouching on the upper tier.

'Oh, no,' she said. They couldn't have been in a worse position, caught in a hopelessly exposed place. And she was too far away to help them. If she ventured out into the open, she knew that she'd be in plain view of whoever was in the helicopter.

She saw Will glance her way, and edged forward a little, waving wildly to attract his attention. But he was too preoccupied with the thundering machine above, and didn't seem to notice her. She withdrew back into the jungle, checking Bartleby was where she'd told him to wait – she couldn't have him bolting out into the clearing. He gave her a meow to let her know that he wanted to join her, but she shook her head.

'Let's knock this thing out of the sky,' she said, swinging her rifle from her shoulder and wrapping the strap around her arm to steady it for a shot. She lined up her telescopic sight on the helicopter. Although she'd never seen anything like this flying contraption in her life before, her first view was of the pilot. She didn't know if he was actually flying it, but at least she had a human target. And he was as good as dead, caught squarely in her crosshairs.

Taking a breath and holding it in, she was on the point of squeezing the trigger when the helicopter rotated. Through her sight, she had a glimpse of a Limiter inside it. Her blood ran cold. She grimaced, thinking she'd take out the Styx soldier instead. Then she glimpsed something else that made her blood run even colder. A diminutive figure was beside the Limiter. Elliott could see her so clearly that there was no question in her mind.

'Rebecca,' she spat, unable to believe one of the Styx girls had survived the ambush. 'It can't be!' She was still trying to come to terms with this when the other helicopters rumbled over. Within seconds a barrage of rifle fire was landing around Will and Dr Burrows, preventing them from going anywhere. And then ropes were flung from the first helicopter and Limiters began to abseil towards to the top of the pyramid.

'I can't take them all out! What do I do now?' she asked herself, lowering her rifle.

She knew the chances of extracting Will and Dr Burrows from the situation were nigh on impossible, and that she had to get herself to a safe location from where she could plan her next move. Issuing an order to Bartleby to follow her, she began to move through the jungle, travelling around the edge of the clearing in the direction of the base camp.

Sprinting between the huge tree trunks, she kept moving until she arrived at the camp. She heard shouting from the pyramid, but didn't stop to see what was happening, instead snatching a few items to take with her, and quickly rigging a booby trap before she was off again. Elliott kept telling herself she'd made the right decision to withdraw from the area, and any lingering doubts in her mind were completely assuaged as she heard the howls of the stalkers behind her. She retraced her footsteps several times to leave a few false trails, then made straight for the stream, wading into the middle of it where the stalkers couldn't possibly track her.

Once in the hideaway she hurriedly grabbed a couple of the Browning Hi-Power pistols and the spare ammunition she'd stashed there. And she also packed what she had left of Drake's explosives in her Bergen, along with enough food and water to last her for a day – if she was going to be out in the field she needed to keep her strength up.

As she descended the vines from the hideaway to the

stream below, Bartleby was where she'd left him, looking decidedly unhappy. She led him to the undergrowth further along the bank.

'Sorry,' she told him, 'You're staying right here.' She repeated, 'Stay here,' several times, indicating the ground with her finger. The Hunter reluctantly sank back onto his haunches, his tail flicking impatiently from side to side behind him. He knew that they were in trouble, but he didn't understand why he was being excluded from the running. His eyes were on Elliott as she rubbed his head affectionately. 'Can't have you picking a fight with a stalker. And I still don't know if I can trust you with Styx around. You've been Darklit – remember what happened last time?'

As Elliott waded back into the stream, she heard a mournful meow from the Hunter. She held quite still. She felt completely alone. Only yesterday her life had seemed perfect, and now she was going to have to face almost insurmountable odds to save her friend. It all felt so hopeless – a lost cause.

She looked around at the towering trees on either side of the stream. Nothing had changed – the jungle was just the same as it had been a day ago, the profuse vegetation thrumming with life – but to her, it was different now. It was a theatre of war, a place of life and death.

She allowed herself to imagine what her friend might be going through at that precise moment . . . capture . . . torture . . . death.

'Will,' she croaked, trying not to cry as she thought of him in the clutches of the Limiters. 'No,' she said, 'I can't fall apart now . . . there *has* to be a way through this.' She drew herself up, squaring her shoulders. 'I have to think like you, Drake.'

Chapter Seventeen

'They want us to go with them,' Dr Burrows said, as he observed how the bushmen were behaving. 'They know what the situation is outside, and they're taking us somewhere safe!'

Will could hear the optimism in his father's voice as the circle of strange beings rustled with activity. He glanced over his shoulder as they advanced stiffly towards him and Dr Burrows like an animated hedgerow, their feet scuffing over the stone floor. At the same time, the bushmen in front of them were also on the move. And in the middle of the circle, the two Burrows were clearly meant to follow them.

'Yes,' Will whispered. 'But where are they taking us?'

The phalanx was all around them as they reached the far corner of the chamber, and a passageway was revealed by the light from the burning torches. This led to some steps, which they began to descend.

After a while Dr Burrows spoke up. 'These stairs go on for ever. Feels to me as if we'll end up somewhere *below* the pyramid,' he suggested, his voice full of wonder. Will had no sense if this was the case or not, and within a few minutes he and his father found they had come to the last of the steps and were back on a level surface again.

From the light of the flickering torches, Will could make out that they were at some kind of intersection. But they didn't stop there for long as the bushmen conducted them into yet another passageway, its walls adorned with more brightly coloured reliefs. Will and his father glimpsed one of a coastal city, its centrepiece a majestic palace. This palace was vaguely reminiscent of the Taj Mahal, with a large domed roof and slender minarets at the four corners. And in the bay itself, there was a colossal statue of a robed man facing out to sea, with what appeared to be a telescope in his hands.

'Look at the scale of that place – it's remarkable enough to be the eighth wonder of the world. I'll tell you one thing for certain, Will,' Dr Burrows announced, turning to his son.

'What?'

'Once this is all over and we're out of danger,' Dr Burrows said, 'oh boy, we've got to come back here.'

'Sure, Dad,' Will answered, but without a trace of enthusiasm. He wasn't thinking more than a few seconds ahead, let alone that far into the future. He had a very bad feeling about the situation. His fears intensified as, without any warning, the torches around them were extinguished and they were swallowed up by darkness again. 'Why have we stopped here?' Will asked his father in a whisper. 'They're not moving.'

There was no longer any rustling around them. The bushmen were standing completely still.

'We'll be fine. You see,' Dr Burrows told his son. 'These are the descendents of a once-great civilisation. They recognise us for what we are – fellow seekers of knowledge. They'll treat us with respect. We're no threat to them, and we've done them no harm.' He genuinely didn't seem to be concerned by their predicament. After a moment of silence, he spoke again. 'You know . . . waiting here in the dark like this has reminded me there's something I keep meaning to ask you.'

'What's that, Dad?' Will replied distantly, not taking much notice of him.

'Cast your mind back to when you were in the Deeps . . . on the Great Plain . . . did you by any chance come across a Coprolite barge on the canal system? It had three Coprolites on it?'

'*What?* I don't think this is the time or the pl—' Will began to object.

'No, listen – at the beginning, there were three of you, right? You, Chester and whatsisname . . . Col . . . Colin?'

'Cal,' Will said, an edge to his voice because he found it inexcusable that his father couldn't even get his dead brother's name right. 'Yes, we were all together when we saw a Coprolite barge,' he said with a sigh.

'I knew it! I just knew it!' Dr Burrows exclaimed, his voice rising a tone in his excitement. 'I was on that barge, in a Coprolite dust suit. As I think back to that moment, I'm certain I saw the three of you! I saw *you*!'

'No?' Will replied, with genuine amazement as he recalled the incident. Cal had remarked that one of the Coprolites was acting completely out of character. 'I don't believe it! We came that close, and had no idea. That's so weird! If only we'd known.'

Dr Burrows laughed. 'Yes, but we're together now, and that's what really matters. Will, I can honestly say that working with you in this incredible world has made it, without question, one of the happiest times of my life. If not *the* happiest. I'm so very proud of you.'

'Dad,' Will managed, overwhelmed by emotion as he absorbed his father's words. He didn't quite know how to respond to this overt show of affection from him. 'Yes, it's been . . . such . . .' Will began, but trailed off as, all of a sudden, there was frenetic rustling all around them. Will completely forgot what he and his father had been discussing as he became anxious again. 'Why are they doing that?' he asked in an urgent whisper. 'You should light a match so we can see.'

'Better not – I might set fire to one of them. Just keep your nerve, Will,' Dr Burrows replied. 'I'll stake my reputation on there being an underground network connecting these pyramids, and that's where they'll take us, in just a minute. Somewhere away from the Styx.'

Will became even more unnerved as the rustling reached fever pitch around them. 'No, I'm not going to just stand here and do nothing. Give me the matches, Dad, right now,' he insisted.

He never received a response from his father. There was a grinding sound from close by, and they were enveloped in dazzling light. Simultaneously, they were propelled forwards with such force that both of them lost their balance, tumbling over. But far from landing on a hard surface as Will had expected, he encountered soft ground and felt grass under his hands.

'Too bright,' he groaned, as he attempted to open his eyes in the glare of the sunlight. He caught a glimpse of the edge of the jungle some distance away.

'The pyramid!' his father cried in alarm. 'We're outside the pyramid again!'

Will flicked his head around. His father was right. They were at the foot of the pyramid. He was able to distinguish vague shapes on it – shapes of men, and they were coming towards him. Then he heard a voice he knew only too well, and his heart almost stopped.

It was a voice that he thought he'd never hear again.

'Where did you two spring from?' it shouted down at them.

'Rebecca!' Will gasped.

Then there was another voice, identical to the first but from a different part of the pyramid. 'Oh, looky here, I do believe it's the dynamic duo!'

'NO!' Will shrieked, as it clicked that not just one, but both of them were still alive.

As he tried to crawl away, he came across his Sten gun in the grass. The bushmen had thrown it out at the same time as he and his father were ejected. Snatching it up, Will wheeled around and pulled the trigger. He managed to loose off some shots, blindly spraying the pyramid in the hope he'd hit one or other of the Rebeccas. The rounds were ricocheting off the stonework in all directions.

He was halfway through the magazine when he was struck on the back of the head, pistol-whipped by a Limiter.

Then there was no more blinding light.

<hr />

'Got to take it easy,' Elliott said, forcing herself to move more slowly as the howls of the stalkers came from all over. She didn't want to blunder into one of the attack dogs or be ambushed by a Limiter patrol. Too much was depending on her. She hadn't gone straight to the pyramid as there were a couple of things she'd needed to do first, to prepare herself. But now, as she headed towards it, she heard a short burst of automatic gunfire.

She halted on the spot. 'Sten . . . Will's Sten?' she asked herself out loud, wondering if it had actually originated from his weapon, or whether the Limiters were using similar light machine guns, which would have been most unusual. But it made no sense for it to have been Will – if he and Dr Burrows had already been captured, why was there an exchange going on now? She had to get closer so she could find out precisely what the situation was. But how was she going to do that, with so many Styx soldiers in the area? It was at that point that she happened to glance at the branches up above her.

'The trees! Use the trees!' she said to herself. She chose a trunk and began to haul herself up.

After a while she stopped climbing and instead began to move parallel to the ground by hopping from branch to branch, always in the direction of the pyramid. Her idea was working; she knew it was highly unlikely a stalker, even with its ultra-sensitive sense of smell, would detect her up here.

As she landed on the gnarled branch of one of the mightier trees, she began to climb again, further and further up, until the odd finger of sunlight percolated through the foliage above her. And as she rose higher, she was amazed to find butterflies as large as paperbacks flapping their brightly coloured wings, and caterpillars the size of pencil cases gorging themselves on the bountiful fruit.

At one point, as she was heaving herself up onto a branch, she found herself face to face with something covered in shaggy brown fur. Three eyes blinked simultaneously at her as the animal, just as surprised as she was by the encounter, gaped its mouth slowly open. Dr Burrows would have identified it as a type of sloth from the hook-like claws it was now using to manoeuvre itself ponderously away from her.

Although Elliott didn't have time to marvel at the incredible wildlife she was finding, she realised that at ground level she'd only been seeing a small part of the ecosystem. A whole other world existed above it.

After another twenty minutes of climbing, she was at such a great height that she could see over the remaining jungle. Bracing herself against a bough, she sighted her rifle on the top of the pyramid.

She didn't like what she saw.

Will came to. He raised his head to find he was being supported on his feet by a pair of Limiters.

'Hello, l-o-o-o-o-ser,' Rebecca One mocked him, swinging her hips as she stepped in front of him.

'Dad?' he said groggily.

'Daddy's over there,' the Styx girl indicated with a flick of her head. Will tried to focus on his father – the Limiters had brought them to the very top of the pyramid, and he could just about see a group of figures on the far side of the plateau. His head hurt from where he'd been struck, and he also realised that he could feel the heat of the sun keenly on his arms and shoulders. He looked down at himself.

'Yes, I thought you might want to soak up a few rays,' Rebecca One smirked. 'I had your shirt taken off. Pale and interesting is so last year's look.'

Will could feel his skin beginning to burn – the Styx girl knew very well he had no natural protection against the ultraviolet.

'You little bitch,' he growled.

'Definitely,' she agreed. 'But I reckon I'll have graduated to Big Bitch by the time you and I are finished. When you put that bullet in me, I can't tell you how much it hurt.' The way Rebecca One was talking about it made Will's blood chill. He of all people knew how vindictive she was. She had something horrible lined up for him. Nevertheless, he wasn't going to let her see how incredibly frightened he was.

'Boring, boring, boring,' he replied, through an exaggerated yawn.

She ignored his taunt. 'Will, as you may have gathered by now, the way we Styx go about things is very *Old Testament*.' She bent her knees in a near perfect *demi-plié*, then straightened up again – it reminded Will of the hours of ballet practice she'd do at their house in Highfield, using the garden because there wasn't the space inside. 'We believe in an eye-for-an-eye, a tooth-for-a-tooth, and all that jazz,' she said, then drew in a breath as if she was wildly excited about something and didn't want it to be over too soon.

'What are you yapping on about?' Will said, struggling against the Limiters' grip and trying to get an arm free so he could deal with the girl before him.

'I'm telling you this so you won't be surprised that I'm going to collect from you now, with interest,' she went on.

'As I said – boring,' Will muttered.

'Knock yourself out, Coxy,' she announced abruptly, then simply smiled at Will.

He noticed someone had appeared beside her. He'd seen the unnerving face before in the Deeps, with its pupil-less eyes and multiple growths. 'Tom Cox?' he gasped.

'One and the same,' the distorted voice concurred. Then Cox slid towards Will, slashing a scythe down the side of the boy's bare stomach.

It may have been a superficial wound, precisely inflicted so as not to cause too much damage to him, but the pain was still excruciating. Will screamed until his breath ran out.

'A little taste of what's in store for you, dear brother,' Rebecca One laughed, leaning in towards him. 'Does it hurt? I hope so. Imagine that, but a million times worse, and you'll know what I went through when you shot me.'

The sweat was streaming down Will's face as the Limiters continued to hold him tightly. 'You . . . you . . .' he began, but unable to find a word strong enough to express his hatred for her, he instead spat in his former sister's face.

'Lively one, ain't 'e?' Cox said, licking Will's blood from the highly polished blade of the scythe. Some of it ran on his blackened and cracked lips, the crimson beads sparkling in the intense sunlight. 'Do you want me to cut 'is tongue out for that?' he offered.

As she wiped Will's saliva from her face with a sleeve, Rebecca One considered this. 'No, maybe later. We need him to talk to us first,' she said, then beckoned to her sister to bring Dr Burrows over.

'Will, you're bleeding! What have they done to you?' he burst out as he was allowed to approach his son. Unlike Will, he wasn't being restrained by Limiters, but was being held at gunpoint by the second Styx girl, who was armed with a New Germanian pistol.

Will saw his father was still hugging his journal as if his life depended on it. 'I'm all right, Dad,' he replied grimly.

'Hey, bro,' Rebecca Two greeted him as she stepped around Dr Burrows. 'Want to make life easier for us all and tell me what you've done with our Dominion phials? Dr Buckwheat here swears he knows nothing about them – he's such a bad liar, I actually believe he's telling the truth. So does Elliott have them?'

'Elliott who?' Will snarled back at her

'Why don't you give us our phials back, and we'll leave you alone with your silly old stones and the tree men, who obviously don't want you either?'

Dr Burrows opened his mouth as if he was about to speak, but Will interrupted him.

'Yeah. So you'll let us go? Do you *really* think I'm going to swallow that? Yet another lie?' he said, rolling his eyes at the sky.

'Okay. So we'll do it the hard way. Suits me,' Rebecca One said coldly. 'I'm going to enjoy every minute of this.'

Weighing the scythe in his shrivelled hand, Cox edged closer to Will.

'Not quite yet, Coxy,' Rebecca One told him. 'By the way, I've got some news for you. Your mate Drake tried to pull a stunt on Highfield Common. So we wiped out his whole team.'

'He's dead?' Will asked in a low voice. 'No, you're just lying again.'

'Does *Leatherman* mean anything to you?' Rebecca One shot back, winking at Will as she let the name sink in. 'And we're told there's a new addition to the Colony – a slimmed-down cabbage.'

'Celia the Cabbage,' Rebecca Two chimed in.

'Mum?' Will said.

'My wife?' Dr Burrows mumbled, slow to pick up on what he was hearing. 'What's happened to her?'

'As if you care,' Rebecca Two replied coldly. 'We're told she attempted to resist during her interrogations. The Dark Light messed her up badly.'

'Really badly,' Rebecca One tittered. 'In fact, *sliced* cabbage would be a better description – remember, Will, like the stuff in those gross kebabs we used to pick up from the local take-away and feed you for supper, back in the good old Highfield days.'

'Sauerkraut, even,' Rebecca Two suggested as she thought of it.

'Better keep it down,' her sister advised her. 'These New Geraniums might think you're talking about them.'

'New Geraniums?' Dr Burrows asked, looking down at the parked helicopters and the soldiers milling around them. 'Who are they? They aren't Styx, are they?'

Both girls fell silent as they saw the Limiter General was on his way over to them. He was accompanied by Colonel Bismarck and one of his men, who was carrying a piece of bulky equipment.

'Think we're needed for a second,' Rebecca One said. 'Keep the two prisoners warm for us, Coxy.'

'Nice 'n' toasty,' he confirmed, squinting up at the sun as he bobbed from foot to foot in eager anticipation.

As Colonel Bismarck and the New Germanian soldier held back, the Limiter General brought the twins up to speed.

'You need to see this,' he said, speaking quietly so he wouldn't be overheard by Will or Dr Burrows. He produced a pouch and emptied its contents into his gloved hand. There were pieces of both a phial and another bottle of brown glass, along with some desiccated blades of grass.

'White stopper,' Rebecca Two noted, exchanging glances

with her sister. 'But what's this?' She carefully picked out a label still stuck to a fragment of the brown glass and held it up.

'It's in Russian, so it must be from the medicine bay of the submarine you found,' the Limiter General replied. 'I'd hazard a guess that both the phials were being kept in the bottle, with a wad of grass around them for protection.'

Rebecca One considered this. 'So if that's all that's left of the phial with the white top, we're down one vaccine. And there's no sign at all of our virus?'

The Limiter General continued with his report, 'No. Our stalkers made short work of ferreting out where this had been buried in the ground. Someone's been there very recently – in the last hour or two, we estimate. The earth's been freshly dug, and the turf was laid back over it in an effort to hide it from us.'

'So we can assume that Elliott tried to retrieve both phials and, in the process, the idiot broke one. Either accidentally or on purpose. And she probably has the Dominion with her right now,' Rebecca One concluded. She contemplated the white stopper in the Limiter General's palm. 'Pity about that, but it doesn't really matter – we can always manufacture more vaccine after we've got the virus back.' Then she glanced over to where the New Germanian soldier was attaching a large khaki-coloured speaker to the top of a tripod, and one of his comrades was connecting up a box with dials on it to a large battery. 'Is the PA system ready?' she asked, directing the question at Colonel Bismarck.

'Almost,' he confirmed. 'We're just bringing up the rest of the speakers now.'

Elliott was watching from her treetop vantage point when the amplified voice carried towards her.

'Elliott – whether or not you've got a visual on us, we know you'll be hearing this.'

It was so loud it startled a flock of birds, which took to the air from a nearby tree. Elliott zeroed in on the Rebecca twin holding the microphone. An array of large horn speakers had been set up on the top of the pyramid, not far from where Will and Dr Burrows were being held.

Elliott had been watching as Cox lashed out at Will with the scythe, and her trigger finger had tightened. But she didn't fire, knowing she should let things play out for a little longer, just in case an opportunity presented itself. If Will and Dr Burrows were moved, she might be able to jump in and rescue them. She knew the Styx weren't about to helicopter them out, not until they'd got their hands on the Dominion virus. In the meantime, she thought it unlikely any real harm would come to them. Not while the Rebecca twins were attempting to negotiate and needed their two hostages as leverage. And Elliott's instincts told her she wouldn't have to wait long to hear what the deal was. There was always some sort of deal with these two conniving Styx girls.

Elliott nodded to herself as one of the twins continued. 'Bring us the Dominion virus, and all three of you will be spared. You've got five minutes to give us a sign that you agree to this . . . all you have to do is fire your weapon twice. Then we want the Dominion virus here at the pyramid within the next hour. It's that simple.'

'Yeah, sure,' Elliott muttered.

'To show you we're serious, your boyfriend here, with such a fetching tan, is going to do a karaoke act . . . especially for you,' the Rebecca twin said.

Elliott watched as the twin put her hand over the microphone to confer with Cox, then they both moved to where Will was. As the Rebecca twin stood before him, she spoke over the PA again. 'Elliott, we want you to listen to this. It's called *The Nine Finger Rap*.' The twin giggled, then held the microphone in front of Will.

'Stay away, Ell—' he managed to get out before one of the Limiters tightened an arm around his neck.

'What are they up to?' Elliott asked herself. She could see that Dr Burrows was gesticulating madly as he pleaded with the Rebecca twins, but they were both ignoring him. One of the Limiters guarding Will seized his arm and held it out. Will was straining and trying to wrest it away from the soldier, but it was hopeless – the Limiter was just too strong.

'If you haven't caught on yet, we're gonna chop his finger off,' the Rebecca twin announced. 'And for every ten minutes it takes you to show up here, he's going to lose another.'

'Oh, God,' Elliott exhaled. She couldn't just stand by and watch Will suffer like that. She knew that the Rebecca twins probably hadn't the slightest intention of letting any of them go free – that wasn't how the Styx ran things. She remembered the moment on the Great Plain, back in the Deeps, when she and Will had thought they were putting Drake out of his misery by shooting him. She hadn't been able to do it then, but she was ready now. She sighted up on Will's head, her finger poised on the trigger.

Cox took Will's hand and held the scythe above the base of his index finger.

'No! I can't!' Elliott cried, as she saw Will's face contort with fear.

As he opened his mouth to yell, she switched targets and pulled the trigger.

Chapter Eighteen

Everyone on the pyramid heard the distant report of a weapon going off. There was a fraction of a second's delay before the bullet found its mark.

Cox's face exploded with the sound of an overripe melon bursting open. The grimy shawl over his head billowed as if the wind had suddenly caught it. He wavered on his feet for an instant, then keeled backwards, the scythe dropping from his hand.

All those with military training had either flung themselves to the ground or were crouching low, leaving only the Rebecca twins and a bemused Dr Burrows still standing upright.

'Nice to hear from you, Elliott,' Rebecca Two said into the microphone as she regarded the body several metres away from her. The twin was completely composed as she went over to it and bent to pick up the scythe. 'Poor old Coxy. That was uncalled for. And I'm also rather disappointed with you, Elliott, because I was sure we'd be able to come to some sort of agreement. We both want th—'

Rebecca Two was interrupted by a second shot from the jungle. The military contingent reacted to it again, and there were shouts from the Limiters around the base of the pyramid.

'Anyone down? Has anyone been hit?' the Limiter General called out several times, but everyone was accounted for.

The Styx girls' eyes met, and Rebecca One laughed. 'I guess that was the second shot we were looking for. I guess Elliott's just given us the signal that we *do* have a deal.'

Rebecca Two joined in with her sister's laughter. 'Suppose so. It's quite amusing really, but bad manners can't go unpunished.' She took her hand from the microphone and spoke into it.

'All right, we have a deal, but that was very rude of you. You killed one of our friends without our permission . . . and so you've changed the terms of the deal. And, be warned, if you're thinking of sniping anyone else up here, we'll execute both Will and Dr Buckwheat.' She took a breath. 'Right, the new deal is that we'll do the exchange for *one* of the hostages – I repeat – *one* of the hostages, and I'm betting you'd want that to be Mole Boy here, unless you've developed a thing for older men? We give you our word that we'll stick to the new deal. Just come in with the virus, okay?'

Dr Burrows seemed to recover from the shock of Cox's shooting. 'This is all so unnecessary,' he exhorted the Rebecca twins. 'Can't we talk it over before anyone else loses their life?' He glanced at his son, who was being held on his knees – Will's eyes were wide with fear.

'You want to talk?' Rebecca One said, in a voice that sounded like something from a cartoon as she opened and closed her raised hand to mimic a flapping mouth. Then she lowered her hand and reverted to her normal voice. Her eyes were cold and unamused. 'Maybe I don't want to talk to you,' she said. 'Because you're so old and boring.'

'No, I mean it – I'm sure we can agree something. Give me the microphone and I'll persuade Elliott to bring the phial to you,' Dr Burrows volunteered.

Will found his voice. 'Don't do this, Dad. Please. You don't know who you're dealing with.'

Dr Burrows was resolute as he went over to Will and placed his journal on the ground in front of him. 'Look after that for me.' Then he took the microphone from Rebecca Two and spoke. 'Is this turned on?' he asked, his voice booming across the jungle.

'It's turned on,' Rebecca Two answered wearily.

Dr Burrows continued. 'Right, Elliott, this is me. I want you to do exactly what I tell you.' He floundered, unsure what he was going to say next.

'Tell her again that we're going to execute one of you,' Rebecca One said casually, as she examined her nails.

'I will do no such thing!' Dr Burrows snapped, straight into the microphone. 'That's just silly. What could you possibly hope to achieve by that?'

'Revenge. We're going to exact our revenge because of what *she's* done. In case you hadn't noticed, Elliott whacked poor Coxy. She hurt one of our pals, and we really don't like that,' Rebecca One continued, her voice hard. 'Go on . . . tell Elliott what I've just told you.'

Dr Burrows blew through his lips with disbelief. 'Oh, fine. If you're going to murder someone, then let it be me,' he offered, not taking the threat seriously.

Will shouted at his father as he saw Rebecca Two's hand with the pistol begin to move. 'Dad, for Christ's sake, give them the microphone back and stop—'

'No, son, I've had enough of this posturing. They don't mean it. And Elliott will bring the virus here and we can all get on with our lives. The work we've been doing together is far too important for all this tomfoolery to get in the way.' He raised the microphone to his mouth. 'Elliott, I've just told them they can kill me if one of us has to die. I know they're bluffing, so—'

'No, we're not,' Rebecca Two said.

She lifted the pistol and, without flinching, emptied it into Dr Burrows' back.

The multiple shots were broadcast by the PA, reverberating through the jungle as if some colossus was thumping on a kettledrum.

For a moment, Dr Burrows just stood there, swaying.

'Will?' he gasped.

Then his legs buckled and he flopped forwards.

'Oh, no! Dad! DAD!' Will cried out, breaking from the Limiters' grip and falling on top of his father's journal. He reached out his hand to where Dr Burrows lay dead. 'NO!'

Chapter Nineteen

Will was in no state to notice what was going on around him. He was sitting slumped over by his father's body, left where it had fallen. Still without a shirt, he didn't seem to care about the sun on his shoulders. In fact, Will had only moved once from Dr Burrows' side, to retrieve his father's glasses from where they'd spun off after the shooting. He was now holding these in one hand, Dr Burrows' beloved journal in the other.

From time to time he shook his head. He just couldn't accept what had happened. Less than an hour ago they'd been inside the pyramid, and his father had been bubbling with enthusiasm about how they would return there for a proper look at the murals they'd discovered.

It may have been an uncertain one, but nonetheless there had been a future in which his father would have played no small part. All that had gone with Dr Burrows' death. All that commitment, passion and energy his father had shown in his single-minded pursuit of knowledge, often with scant regard for his own safety, had been cut short in the millisecond the Styx girl had pulled the trigger.

Looking sideways at the sky, Will was struck by the realisation that everything was continuing without his father there; time was still trundling along on its relentless path without him around to witness it.

Nothing had changed.

Everything had changed.

He'd wept at the beginning, but now there were no tears, and no interest in what was going to happen next. A single Limiter had been left to watch him, while the Rebecca twins had moved to a lower tier of the pyramid.

He heard steady footsteps as someone approached behind him, but he didn't turn to see who it was. If the twins had come back to torture him or kill him, then there was nothing he could do about it. He had little doubt they would, when it suited them.

'You should wear this,' a man's voice said, and a green towel was put over Will's shoulders. 'Otherwise you'll get sunstroke.' A second towel landed beside him, along with an aluminium canteen, which made a noise as if it was full of water as it fell on top of the towel. 'Your wound is still bleeding – you might want to clean it and bandage it with this, or *die Fliegen* . . . the flies . . . will get to it.'

The voice was efficient and speaking English with an accent that sounded somehow too proper and old fashioned, similar to the BBC archive recordings Dr Burrows used to listen to back in Highfield. It just didn't sound right to Will. Only now did he turn to see who was there. Shielding his eyes, he stared up into Colonel Bismarck's face, taking in his military moustache and his kindly grey eyes.

'I watched my father die too,' Colonel Bismarck said, squaring his shoulders with a deep breath. 'I was about your age. We were in a stockade town across the ocean when it was overrun by the pirates. Most of the settlers were slaughtered, and I only escaped by hiding up in the rafters of the roof in our house.' He checked himself, as if he was saying too much, then clicked the heels of his brown patent leather riding boots together with a small bow. 'You have my condolences.'

Will watched the man stride away across the top of the pyramid, then turned back to his father.

At the insistence of the Limiter General, the Rebecca twins had taken cover on the next tier down. He'd been concerned for their safety if they remained on the very top where they'd be in Elliott's sights.

One by one, Styx search parties were reporting back to the Limiter General. The four-man patrols, most of them using stalkers, had been following precise search patterns in the jungle, but were returning without any news of Elliott's whereabouts.

The Rebecca twins were half listening to these progress reports as Colonel Bismarck came over to them.

'My troops are at a state of readiness if you wish to deploy them – just give me the word,' he said to Rebecca One, indicating the soldiers in the grass clearing below with a nod of his head. So far the Limiters had been doing all the running, while his New Germanian soldiers stood idly by. Rebecca One glanced down to where he'd indicated. A handful of his troops had been tasked with guarding the helicopters, but the rest were sheltering from the sun in the lee of the trees at the edge of the jungle, where they sat around, playing cards and smoking.

'Thank you. We'll see how this pans out,' the Styx girl

answered, but remained facing the Colonel as she sensed he wanted to say more.

He frowned. 'Do you mind if I speak to you about something?'

'Go ahead,' she replied.

'In my view you acted precipitately when you shot the father. You had pledged your word on the exchange, but then you reneged on it.'

Rebecca One smoothed her sleek black hair with her hand. She respected this man, and was prepared to take the time to explain herself to him. 'No, to be accurate, Elliott moved the goalposts when she took the life of one of our side. What she did to Coxy couldn't be allowed to pass, not without reprisal.'

The Colonel's tone was earnest and fervent as he spoke; he clearly believed that this was a matter of principle. 'We would not have conducted ourselves as you have. We belong to the Bayard Order, and are proud of our Prussian roots. We adhere to a strict moral code, on or off the field of war. *Ehre vor Allem* – honour above all. When that girl out in the jungle shot your comrade, it was because you were about to harm her companion. You gave her just cause for what she did.' A fly buzzed close to his face and he waved it away as he continued. 'So why now do you think she's going to believe anything you say?'

Rebecca One nodded. 'The girl Elliott shouldn't be underestimated. She's been living in one of the most dangerous environments imaginable – she's young, but she's a survivor, and a resourceful and skilful fighter. In order to get her where we wanted her, we had to raise the stakes . . . we had to threaten someone who really matters to her. We need to corner her, like a hungry rodent, because then she'll begin to act predictably. When she thinks she has no choice, she'll either go into hiding in the jungle, or she'll come up with some sort of plan. If it's the former, we'll hunt her down, and if it's the latter then she has to make contact – and then we'll be in play with her. Either way, we'll win the contest,' Rebecca One said. The Colonel was about to speak again when she swung round to the Limiter General. 'Aren't we close to the witching hour, anyway?' she asked. 'The time limit must nearly be up.'

'Five minutes to go,' he said, consulting his watch.

'Then no more Will Burrows,' Rebecca One said, rubbing her hands together. She twisted back to the Colonel. 'When it comes to those that oppose us, we believe in zero tolerance. We don't give concessions bec—'

There was an explosion like a thunderclap from the jungle on the other side of the pyramid. Foliage and broken branches were ripped from the trees and thrown into the sky.

'What's going on?' Rebecca Two shouted. 'Damn it! We can't see a thing from here.'

'Get over to the north side,' the Limiter General yelled at a couple of patrols of Limiters, who emerged from the tree line.

'Come along. We'll get a better view from up here,' Rebecca One said. Both twins swung around as if they were about to clamber back onto the top of the pyramid.

'No, not a good idea,' the Limiter General advised them. 'This might be a ruse to coax you out into the open again. Better you stay down on this level.'

The twins did as he said, but began to run along the tier of the pyramid. They'd gone around the corner and were halfway along the next stretch when there was a second explosion. More foliage burst into the air, followed by a creaking as a tree crashed down into the clearing. This time it was much closer, and to the south of the pyramid – on the side the Rebecca twins had just left.

'This is like musical chairs,' Rebecca One scowled as they slid to a halt and did an about turn.

As Limiters ran in different directions below, the Rebecca twins retraced their steps. The Limiter General was still standing in the same spot as they arrived.

'No question it's Elliott,' he told them. 'Doing party tricks with her C4.'

'Little show-off. What's she hoping to achieve with these theatricals?' Rebecca One said.

'Why don't you ask her?' Rebecca Two replied, thrusting a finger at the small figure walking purposefully towards the pyramid from the south. 'Here comes the original Drain Baby herself.'

Elliott appeared to be unarmed. She had a Bergen on her back, and was holding one hand out in front of her, with something gripped in it.

'How nice of you to join us!' Rebecca One shouted gleefully, then her voice changed as she adopted a cold tone. 'Now stop right there!'

'Don't tell me what to do!' Elliott retorted, as the Limiters in the clearing regrouped and began to assemble around her, their rifles trained on her. 'And tell your goons that if one of them comes too close, I'll release this. And . . .' She raised her clenched fist to head height. 'And . . . bang!' she said, a wry smile spreading across her lips. 'The charge in my rucksack will go off and you can kiss goodbye to your virus. I've packed a good twenty pounds of explosive around the phial.'

'What do you advise?' Rebecca Two asked, speaking to

the Limiter General from the corner of her mouth. 'Take her out with a head shot?'

'If we do that and she's using a dead man's trigger, her grip will relax and the C4 will detonate. As she says, our virus will be incinerated,' he replied.

'Dead man's trigger?' Rebecca One repeated.

'It's a *fail-deadly* mechanism,' the Limiter General explained to her. 'If she loses motor control even for a second, her hand comes off the switch and contact is made. It's a suicide bomber's favourite.'

'So we find out what she wants,' Rebecca Two decided. 'Come up here!' she shouted to the girl.

Elliott walked at a leisurely pace to the east side of the pyramid, then used the steps to ascend it – she didn't want to risk leaping up the tiers in case she slipped and let go of the dead man's trigger.

The Rebecca twins, the Limiter General and Colonel Bismarck were waiting for her on the top of the pyramid as she arrived there. She hardly gave them a glance, going straight over to Will.

'I'm so sorry,' she said in a subdued voice as she stood beside him.

He jerked his head round to look up at her, blinking as if he'd woken from a deep sleep. 'Elliott! What are you doing here? You should've made a run for it,' he said hoarsely. 'You know we can't win.'

As Elliott offered no response, he gave a small shrug, then turned away from her.

For a moment she remained beside him, looking at Dr Burrows where he lay face-down in an ever-increasing pool of blood. Then she swung about, her expression determined. She slid her eyes over the girls, then the Limiter General, finally allowing them to rest on Colonel Bismarck. 'Who the hell are you?' she demanded.

'I'm a colonel in the New Germanian army,' he answered.

'So they're your flying machines. How did you get mixed up with these butchers . . . these murderers?' Elliott asked. She didn't give him time to respond as she spoke again. 'I want you to get one of your men to bring up a dressing and tend to his injury,' she said, inclining her head towards Will.

'I'll summon a medic,' Colonel Bismarck confirmed, already moving towards to the edge of the pyramid.

'No way!' Rebecca One intervened. 'You stay put, Colonel.'

'Oh, really,' Elliott retorted. 'You're in no position t—'

'Nothing – I repeat – *nothing* happens until we agree a way forward,' Rebecca One interrupted her.

Elliott surveyed the two dozen Limiters spread out along the side of the plateau, every one of them waiting for the order to attack her. They were like coiled springs, ready to burst into action. Their numbers were steadily increasing as additional Styx soldiers scaled the sides of the pyramid. Despite the fact that these gaunt faces, so full of violence, were quite terrifying, Elliott shook her head with a dismissive chuckle.

'Ha! Just look at you! You're all longing to kill me, aren't you? But the boot's on the other foot – I've got your lives right here – right in the palm of my hand,' she declared, raising her fist. 'If I let go of this, every one of us will be blown to kingdom come.' Maintaining a safe distance from the Styx soldiers, she began to parade in front of them, waving her fist in their faces.

'You're enjoying this a little too much,' Rebecca Two said.

'How very Styx of you. By the way, you told us your father was a Limiter, but we're not sure we believe you. Who was he, exactly?'

'Why, it was the Crawfly,' Elliott replied, a mischievous glint in her eye.

'No, it couldn't . . .' Rebecca Two began.

'My father's dead, and don't try to distract me,' Elliott said, making straight for the twin.

'You haven't got what it takes to blow yourself up,' Rebecca One levelled at her.

'No?' Elliott replied. Without a moment's hesitation, she unfurled her little finger. 'Well this little piggy has. He's bored and wants to come out to play.'

There was complete silence as the sun beat down on the top of the pyramid. Everyone there was transfixed by Elliott as she straightened out a second finger. 'Oh, look at that – another little piggy's joined him,' she said matter-of-factly. 'Can you see the device now?' She was peering at the black object just visible in her hand now two fingers were clear of it. 'And I think you're forgetting what happened at the submarine the last time we bumped into each other? Remember how I set off a shed load of Drake's explosives? I didn't hesitate then, and I'm sure as h—'

Will chose that moment to speak up. 'Just do it, Elliott!' he shouted, without even bothering to turn around. 'Fry those little bitches.'

Elliott and Rebecca One locked eyes, their expressions uncompromising. 'As I was saying, you're in no position to dictate terms to me,' Elliott sneered.

Rebecca One didn't respond.

'That's a first. I don't hear any of your snide little comebacks?' Elliott taunted her. 'Stalker got your tongue?'

From behind her sister, Rebecca Two was regarding the cable coiled around Elliott's arm that led from her clenched fist and into the Bergen. She nodded. 'Let's all just calm down. You can have your medic for Will,' she said to Elliott.

Chapter Twenty

As Drake left the bedroom area to return to the main room of the warehouse apartment, Eddie was at his desk and working on one of his model soldiers. He was peering through a large magnifying glass mounted on a retractable arm as he carefully dabbed paint on the soldier, but stopped the moment he heard Drake enter.

'How's Chester doing?' he asked.

'Not so good,' Drake replied. 'I did warn him about any approach to his parents. It was never going to have a happy ending.'

Eddie nodded as he pushed the magnifying glass to one side. 'Is it a good time to talk about how we're going to move things forward? Chester's appearance on the scene has side-lined our plans, and my people will doubtless be doing all they can to find us, so there's an additional pressure.' Eddie rested his brush on the plate he'd been using as a palette and wiped some paint from his hand. 'I want to fulfil my side of the bargain and help you in whatever you're intending to do, then we need to go after Elliott.'

'Funny you should say that – I'm putting something

together, and I've got a meeting on it, right now,' Drake replied, as he consulted his wristwatch. 'I need to see a man about a snail.'

Eddie looked at him askance. 'What?' he asked.

'My pesticides supremo is cooking up something special for me,' Drake answered, as he took his car keys from his pocket and rattled them in his hand. 'I'll be a couple of hours at the most.' He turned to leave, then stopped. 'And later this evening it would be useful if you would show me the way down to the Eternal City you mentioned. Near the cathedral.'

'St Paul's or Westminster?'

'Personally,' Drake said, 'I rather like the sound of the Westminster entrance.'

***

'So what's her next move?' Rebecca One asked the Limiter General in a low voice.

At the other end of the pyramid Elliott was kneeling beside Will, who'd hardly seemed to notice as the young medic had cleaned his wound and applied a dressing to it. And Will had only cooperated and put on a New Germanian shirt and peaked cap because Elliott had badgered him into it. But although Elliott was now talking to him, he was completely uncommunicative, as if he wasn't hearing a word she was saying to him.

'Her options are limited, and she knows it,' the Limiter General replied to the Styx twin. 'The moment she hands the phial over, she's lost her ace, unless she's planning on taking a hostage so she has safe passage out of here.'

'What – like one of us?' Rebecca Two said, exchanging glances with her sister. She smiled. 'If she chooses either of us to accompany her, then you know exactly what to do. Kill both her and Will, regardless of who else gets hurt. We're all expendable when it comes to recovering the virus.'

'I know that,' the Limiter General confirmed.

'Oh, here we are – some activity,' Rebecca One observed.

Elliott was trying to get Will onto his feet, but it was only on the second or third attempt that he staggered up. Still gripping the detonator, she used her other hand to lead him across with her.

As she stopped before the Rebecca twins and the Limiter General, Will had a faraway look on his face. Clutching his father's journal to his chest, he kept turning back to where Dr Burrows lay. All the fight seemed to have gone out of him, as if he couldn't even summon up any animosity towards the Styx girls.

'We're getting really tired of hanging around on this heap of old stone,' Rebecca One said. 'Tell us the deal.'

'Tell you the deal?' Elliott repeated, and laughed dryly. 'I don't trust any of you Styx as far as I can throw you,' she said. 'Hey, you! Over here!' she suddenly shouted at Colonel Bismarck.

He immediately did as she asked.

'I don't know anything about you, or where you come from, but I want you to witness this,' she said.

The Colonel nodded.

'I'm prepared to strike a deal, but with conditions attached,' Elliott continued. 'I'll give you your Dominion—'

'Tell us something first – what happened to the vaccine – the phial with the white stopper?' Rebecca One butted in.

'I couldn't get the lid off the medicine bottle. I was in a hurry so I had to smash it open with a rock. I was a little heavy-handed, but luckily for all of us, only the vaccine phial was damaged,' Elliott explained. 'As I was saying before you interrupted me, I'm prepared to give you the Dominion virus if—'

'No!' Will exploded. 'No, you sodding won't!' He seemed to be focusing on what was happening around him for the first time since his father's killing. 'They'll just take it Topsoil and use it!'

'Leave this to me, Will,' Elliott said.

'You can't be serious! You're not actually going to give it to them, are you?' Will was incandescent now, as if Elliott and not the Rebecca twins was the enemy. Dropping his father's journal, he lurched towards her.

Elliott took a step back from him, shocked by the ferocity of his outburst. 'Will—'

But he was still advancing on her. 'Release the trigger now, Elliott! Destroy the Dominion! Remember what Drake said we had to do. They,' he stuck his thumb in the direction of the Styx girls, 'are not getting their stinking hands on it. All those people – Drake and my mum – have died trying to stop them,' he ranted. 'And we will too!'

As she took another step away from him, he dived at Elliott, knocking her to the ground. Now on top of her, he seized hold of her arm. 'Help me!' the girl cried, as Will concentrated all his efforts on her hand, trying to lever her fingers open and activate the trigger.

'You're not going to let them have it!' he seethed. 'You bloody traitor!'

Elliott struck Will in the face with her elbow, but it was going to take more than that to stop him. Colonel Bismarck was the closest to the two of them as they struggled with each other, and reacted before anyone else. He grabbed Will by the neck and arm, trying to pull him off Elliott. Realising that they had the perfect opportunity to disarm her, Rebecca One and the Limiter General also entered the fray. If either one of them could take hold of her hand and keep it closed, they would have regained control of the situation again.

But as Colonel Bismarck heaved Will away, Elliott managed to keep the Styx at bay. She was fending them off with kicks and blows with her free arm and, just in time, backpedalled across the ground to escape from them.

'Not so fast,' she shouted breathlessly as she scrambled to her feet.

They backed away.

'Nice try, White Necks!' she jeered at them.

Will was beside himself with fury. 'Come on, Elliott, do it! Destroy the bloody virus!' But the Colonel was making very sure that he kept a firm grip on the thrashing boy.

'That was close.' Elliott composed herself for what she was going to say next. 'Right, my conditions are . . . you are to put Will and me on one of those flying machines—'

'They're called helicopters,' Rebecca One informed her.

'On one of those helicopters, and when we're up in the air, I'll give you your Dominion back. We'll be accompanied in the helicopter by the Colonel and his men – but no Styx.'

'And when *precisely* will you . . .?' Rebecca Two began, but then rolled her eyes in Will's direction.

Already burnt by the sun, his face now turned an even deeper red as he began to rage at the top of his lungs.

'Colonel, can you please stop that idiot from yelling. I can't hear myself think here,' Rebecca Two said. A pair of Limiters came to Colonel Bismarck's aid.

'No – not them! Get a couple of your men up here!' Elliott snapped at the Colonel. 'I won't have Limiters touching him. And he's to stay right beside me – he's not to leave my sight. And you too, Colonel. I want you beside me, too.'

'So, as I was saying . . . when do we actually get the virus?' Rebecca Two asked.

'I told you – I'll hand it over when we're in the air, then Will and I will be flown away from here and put down at another location in the jungle. It's as simple as that,' Elliott finished.

'Fine,' Rebecca Two agreed. 'Let's get the show on the road.'

Will was taken down the side of the pyramid, struggling every inch of the way with the two New Germanian troops tasked with moving him. As Elliott and the Colonel followed behind, she was careful not to lose her footing in case she slipped and let go of the dead man's trigger. The two of them caught up with Will and his New Germanian bearers as they reached the first helicopter in the rank. Still swearing his head off, Will was passed up to a pair of soldiers inside.

'Keep hold of him,' Elliott told them. 'Tie him up if you have to.'

Colonel Bismarck held Dr Burrows' journal up to Elliott. 'The boy might regret leaving this behind. It was his father's.'

'Thank you,' Elliott said. 'I'm sure he'll appreciate having it once he's calmed down . . . if he ever calms down.'

The Colonel boarded the helicopter, Elliott right behind him.

'So where's our phial?' Rebecca Two demanded, her sister and the Limiter General either side of her.

'Start this thing up,' Elliott said to the Colonel, then turned to the three Styx, waiting like a delegation next to the helicopter. She pointed at the grass clearing beside the pyramid. 'I want all your Limiters out of there. The stalkers, too.'

'Evacuate the west side?' the Limiter General asked.

'Why are you asking for this now?' Rebecca Two said, with a bemused expression. 'It wasn't part of the deal.'

Elliott raised her hand with the trigger. 'Just do it, if you want your phial in one piece.'

The Limiter General issued orders to his men who quickly withdrew. As the pilot threw the switches and the Brama engine coughed and sputtered into life, the two Rebeccas and the Limiter General began to pull back to a safe distance. They hadn't gone far when Elliott put the fingers of her free hand into her mouth and blew a piercing wolf whistle.

Rebecca Two wheeled around. 'What are you up to?' she shouted. 'Just give us the phial.'

Rebecca One was visibly agitated. 'If you're trying to trick . . .'

At that moment, Bartleby tore into the clearing vacated by the Limiters. Coming to a sliding halt, he looked for Elliott. He was distracted as one of the stalkers on the far side of the pyramid spied him and began to bark fiercely.

The rotors were gathering speed as Elliott whistled again. Bartleby's ears pricked up as he located her, then he galloped at full pelt towards her.

'What's the Hunter doing here?' Rebecca Two said. 'What do you need him for? There's something fishy about all this.'

'Too bloody right,' her sister agreed. She began to shout at the top of her lungs. 'Bartleby, here!'

Hearing her, the cat hesitated, then changed direction away from the helicopter.

'Come on, boy! Come to me!' Elliott yelled.

Rebecca One had a worried look on her face. Something didn't add up. Why would Elliott be bothering about the Hunter when so much depended on making good her escape with Will? Somehow, and the Rebecca twin couldn't figure out quite how, the animal was vital to Elliott's plan. She now began to shout in the Styx tongue, issuing a series of unintelligible words. She was attempting to control the cat by using the Dark Light programming he'd been subjected to during his time in the Colony. And she expected unconditional obedience. She was to be disappointed.

Elliott, also able to speak the Styx language, repeated Rebecca One's words, adding, 'Bartleby, I'm telling you to come to me.'

The cat stopped.

It had come down to a battle over his will.

Rebecca One made another attempt to summon the Hunter using the Styx trigger words.

But Elliott called him again, and the tug of war came to an abrupt end as Bartleby made his choice. He bounded towards her. He hesitated by the door to the helicopter, shying away from the wind from the rotors.

'Get in, Bartleby!' Elliott ordered him. As the cat came on board in a single bound, she grabbed him in her arms. 'And get us into the air!' she screamed at Colonel Bismarck.

Too late to do anything about it, the Rebeccas noticed the length of rope looped around Bartleby's neck. Elliott tore a small bundle from it.

'All this time . . . and she didn't have it on her!' Rebecca Two realised.

'The Hunter was carrying the phial,' her sister said.

The helicopter was ten metres off the ground and rising.

'Throw it to us,' Rebecca Two shouted, stepping forward. 'Or the deal's off!'

Limiters had emerged from beneath the trees and others were poised on the pyramid, every last man of them with his rifle aimed on Elliott in the helicopter.

Elliott dangled the small bundle enticingly in front of her. 'Okay, it's all yours . . . you'd better not drop it,' she said, tossing it down to the twins.

As Rebecca Two caught it, the helicopter was gaining more height. 'One of Will's stinking socks,' the twin said in a disgusted voice, but nevertheless wasted no time in ripping the threadbare sock open. Inside was a single black-topped phial, which she held up to the light to examine. A massive grin spread across her face as she gave her sister and the Limiter General the thumbs up. 'We've got it!' she howled triumphantly.

The helicopter was some fifty metres from the ground as Rebecca One spun around to the waiting Limiters, about to give them the order to open fire on it.

'I wouldn't recommend that,' the Limiter General said, laying a hand on her arm. 'Look over there.'

The New Germanian troops had come out to watch the proceedings. Sensing their commanding officer might be in trouble, many of them had their weapons drawn, and those around the remaining helicopters were pointing them loosely at the twins.

'Don't worry,' the Limiter General said. 'These old whirly-birds guzzle fuel, so even if the Colonel doesn't take Elliott and the Burrows child back to the city, he can't get very far with them.'

Rebecca One nodded, then waved the Limiters to stand down.

'It's over,' Elliott whispered as she lingered by the doorway to watch the pyramid retreating into the distance, the Limiters on it fast becoming harmless little dots. She exhaled with relief, and then sat back on the floor of the helicopter.

'Was that the genuine article? Was that the Dominion phial they wanted?' the Colonel asked. 'They seemed satisfied it was, but I need to know – or I'm honour bound to take you back.'

'It was the real thing,' Elliott confirmed. 'I kept my side of the bargain.'

The Colonel nodded to the navigator, who let the pilot know he should continue on course. As the helicopter soared above the treetops, Elliott opened her clenched fist and put something on the floor, before using the same hand to wipe the perspiration from her brow.

'What!' Colonel Bismarck exclaimed, as he leant forward to peer at the black metal object. 'I thought that was a detonation device?'

'I'm afraid not,' she replied, picking up Dr Burrows' compass and flicking it open so the Colonel could see. 'I didn't have a dead man's trigger, so I had to bluff my way through with this.'

Colonel Bismarck laughed.

Elliott smiled wearily back at him. 'And I didn't have any explosive in my rucksack either. I used everything I had with me for my big entry at the pyramid.' She unwound the cable from her arm and shrugged the rucksack off her back. 'Other than a couple of handguns, this is full of dirty clothes.'

The Colonel laughed even louder, but Will was far from amused. He tried to jump up, but the two New Germanians either side of him on the metal bench held him back. The soldiers were both stronger than he was, on top of which his wrists were bound, so he didn't put up a fight.

'For God's sake,' he fumed, as he stared daggers at Elliott. 'You gave the Dominion to them. Why, after all we've done to stop them getting it? Either you've completely lost the plot, or you're a bloody traitor! Or both!'

PART THREE

Restitution

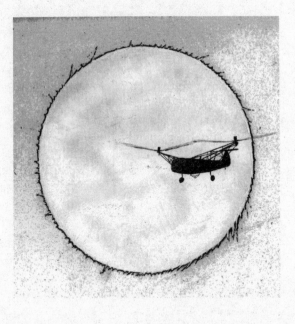

Chapter Twenty-one

'Eddie, I'm going to take Chester for a spin in the car,' Drake said. 'All he does is mope around in his bedroom, zapping things on that PlayStation you bought him.'

Eddie put his paintbrush down and pushed the magnifying glass aside. 'A change of scene might do him good,' he agreed. 'Do you want me to come too?'

'No, that's fine,' Drake replied.

As Drake crossed the Thames over London Bridge, Chester was in the passenger seat next to him, enjoying the breeze on his face through the open window as he peered at the river. But as they approached the banks of cameras at the perimeter of the City, London's financial district, Drake closed all the windows. Chester watched as the tinted glass slid up, sealing them in the car.

'Keep your head down through here,' Drake advised Chester. 'Damned CCTVs everywhere, and they have facial recognition programs now. You'd think the whole country was run by the Styx.'

'I'm beginning to get the feeling it is,' Chester mumbled pathetically.

Drake gave him a sharp look. 'You can drop the Eeyore act right now. Unless Eddie's bugged the car – which he hasn't – there's no need to keep the charade going.'

'Okay,' Chester said, his voice brightening. 'But why all the pretence, anyway? What's going on with him?'

'All will be clear, in time,' Drake said, glaring at a black cab, which had swerved in front of the Range Rover.

They were heading northwest out of London and into the never-ending suburbs. As he regarded the throngs of people on the streets, Chester still hadn't adjusted to the sight of so many of them after his months underground. His head soon began to hurt as he tried to scrutinise each of them in turn, wondering how many were either Styx in disguise, or had been conditioned with the Dark Light and were their agents. Maybe he'd become paranoid, but – he told himself – that was probably a good thing.

As they passed the end of a parade of shabby-looking shops, Drake turned into a run-down industrial estate, one side of which was formed by a line of old railway arches. Built from Victorian brick, stained soot black from decades of pollution, the arches were either boarded up, or cheap glass and aluminium frontages had been fitted across them, with signs that proclaimed, 'Pine Furniture – U Won't Find Cheaper!' or 'Office Equipment – Best Deals in London'. Drake drove on until he came to a unit that appeared to be some sort of car body shop, and pulled up outside.

'This way,' he said, and Chester followed him through a door in the metal pull-down. The interior was littered with discarded car panels, and in the middle of the floor there was a van up on a stand with a man working under it, energetically whacking its exhaust pipe with a hammer.

'Morning,' Drake said loudly, and the man stopped what he was doing and emerged from beneath the vehicle. Dressed in faded blue overalls, he was heavily built and completely bald.

'Mr Smith,' he greeted Drake, tucking the hammer away in his tool belt.

'Everything ready?' Drake asked.

The man didn't answer, giving Chester a lingering glance.

'It's all right – he's with me,' Drake assured him, then took two glittering objects from his wallet. As he dropped them into the man's palm, smeared with engine oil and dirt, Chester saw they were a pair of large diamonds. 'As I told you before, be careful how you dispose of them.'

'Sell 'em? Not a chance, mate, I'm keepin' these,' the man grinned, revealing one of his front teeth was gold. 'Pension fund for me and the missus, these are.' He began to move to the back of the workshop, and Chester trailed after Drake as they penetrated deeper into the arched cavern.

'If all goes according to plan, I might need another vehicle soon,' Drake said, as they passed through into a combined office and storeroom, with boxes of car components stacked high around a table with a telephone on it.

'Somethin' sporty this time?' the man enquired. 'Somethin' with a bit of oomph?'

'Nope, a plain vanilla estate would do me fine. A high-mileage family car – like a BM or Merc. And untraceable, of course, just like the Range Rover,' Drake replied.

'No problem. Leave it to me, mate,' the man confirmed, as they entered a dingily-lit room with lockers in it.

On a crate, in a crumpled pile, Chester spotted something familiar. 'My school uniform!' he exclaimed. 'What's that doing here?'

The man unlocked another door at the end of the locker room and thrust it open. From the echoes it sounded as though there was a much larger space beyond. As he passed the key to Drake, he said, 'I'll leave you to get on with your bus'ness, Mr Jones.'

'It's Smith,' Drake corrected him. 'The name's Smith.'

'Sorry, yes, Mr *Smith*,' the man chuckled, flashing his gold incisor again. 'And I'll keep my eyes peeled. If any strangers come by, I'll sound the buzzer. Right-oh?'

'Cool. Thanks,' Drake confirmed. After the man had left, Drake turned to Chester, who was hovering by his school uniform. 'I want you to put that lot on. Then come and join me.'

'But why?' Chester said. As he lifted his blazer to look at the grey trousers beneath it, several large photographs slipped to the floor. The uppermost one was a copy of the family picture taken in the pod on the London Eye, which he'd seen for the first time when he had tried to go home. And another was of the Highfield High School football team, featuring a much younger Chester in his goalie uniform. 'And Drake, why are these here?' he asked.

'Oh, yes, bring them with you too,' Drake replied.

Chester was becoming very uncomfortable with the situation. 'Can't you tell me what's going on? My school clothes . . . these pictures – this is all a bit freaky.'

'Just keep calm, and do precisely what I tell you,' Drake answered. 'It'll be okay, I promise you.'

'I suppose,' Chester agreed uneasily. As he picked up his blue-and-green striped school tie, it was as though he was holding something from a different lifetime.

Drake went through the door and closed it behind him.

'Completely hat stand,' Chester muttered, as he began to get changed. Now he was alone, he felt a hollowness in the pit of his stomach. He had no idea what Drake had in store for him – from his brief glimpse of the next room, it was ominously dark in there. And as he got ready as quickly as he could, it didn't help that he caught odd noises coming from the room – some shouting, then the sound of something being dragged across the floor. He'd grown since he'd last worn the uniform – the trousers were ridiculously short and difficult to do up at the waist, and the blazer hardly fitted across the shoulders. Walking a little like a Frankenstein monster in the tight clothes, he went to the door and knocked on it, before gingerly pushing it open. Then he entered.

'Come in,' Drake bade him from the shadows.

The space was large – it was surprising how far back the cavern reached – but Chester couldn't gauge its full length, because there was only a single light with a coolie shade illuminating a small area approximately twenty metres from where he was standing. And directly under the cone of light there was a person bound to a chair. His head was down, but it was moving from side to side in small jerks.

Drake appeared from the darkness to loosen a gag from around the man's mouth.

Then Chester realised who it was.

'Dad,' he croaked, blundering into a second chair he hadn't noticed in the gloom.

Chester moved into the penumbra cast by the light. His father took a moment to register someone was there, then lifted his head to look straight at his son.

Chester took a step forward.

'H—' he trailed off. Mr Rawls gave him such a glare of

pure hatred that Chester closed his mouth. It was all the more shocking to him because his father was normally one of the gentlest and most reserved people you could ever hope to meet.

But the look Mr Rawls was giving Chester made him feel as though his father was a complete stranger. Despair spread through him, as if his father's love for him had withered away to nothing.

'What have you done with Emily, you animals?' Mr Rawls cried. He strained against the ties holding his arms behind the chair, and tried to kick his legs out, but it was useless.

'Don't struggle, Jeff, or we'll work your wife over,' Drake threatened.

'My mum! Where's my mum!' Chester asked Drake.

Drake went over to Chester and leant close to him, but made no attempt to lower his voice, as if he wanted Mr Rawls to hear every word he said. 'She's in a cubicle at the back and she's fine, as long as Jeff here cooperates. Now pull up that chair and plant yourself on it.'

Chester hesitated.

'Do what I say,' Drake growled.

The boy dazedly took his place opposite his father, who continued to stare daggers at him. 'What are you after, you little thug? Are you trying to get money out of me?' Mr Rawls asked. His voice became high-pitched and slightly hysterical. 'Look, don't you realise I'm an actuary . . . I work for a minor insurance company . . . I don't earn much. You're barking up the wrong tree!'

Drake intervened at this point. 'If you're an actuary, Jeff, I'd expect you to have a highly logical and analytical mind. I need you to use that mind right now, for your and Emily's sakes.'

Chester wanted to cover his ears at the ugly torrent of invective that came out of his father's mouth. Mr Rawls tried to turn his head to get a proper look at Drake, who grabbed him and forced him to face the front again. 'Hold the first picture up, so Jeff can see it,' Drake ordered Chester, moving beside Mr Rawls now he was staring at the photograph from the London Eye. 'Tell me, who's that with you and your wife?'

Mr Rawls spat contemptuously, then answered. 'My son. That's my son, and—'

'And who is this?' Drake switched on a torch and shone it at Chester's face. The beam was powerful, making the boy squint.

'I HAVE NO IDEA!' Mr Rawls screamed. 'HOW SHOULD I BLOODY KNOW?'

Chester still couldn't believe it. He was even wearing the school uniform he'd had on in the photograph, and yet his father was still unable to recognise him.

'Look at him really carefully, Jeff, because you *do* know who he is, and if you don't tell me I'm going to kill Emily. She's in a room just behind us, and I'll walk right in there and slit her throat. In fact, I'm going to make you watch me do—'

'No, Drake!' Chester exploded, aghast. 'You wouldn't do that!'

Switching off the torch, Drake went over to Chester. 'Shut up,' he growled at the boy. Chester did as he was told – he wasn't about to argue with him.

'Who are you people?' Mr Rawls asked. 'Are you canvassing for new BNP voters or something?' He laughed viciously.

'I don't think you understand how serious the situation is,' Drake said to him, unsheathing his knife. It was a terrifying weapon, with a serrated edge. Drake angled the blade so the light caught it, reflecting it straight into Mr Rawls' eyes. 'If you don't cooperate, and fast, neither you nor your wife is going to leave this place with your internal organs.'

Mr Rawls blinked as if he was having a bad dream and wanted to wake up. He began to shout for help at the top of his lungs.

Drake marched straight over to him and slapped him hard across the face, then stuck the tip of the knife into his throat. Chester jumped up from his chair, but said nothing.

'You can shout until you're blue in the face, but nobody's going to hear you. Nobody's going to come to your rescue. So go on, let it all out, Jeff,' Drake dared him. As Mr Rawls fell silent, Drake re-sheathed his knife.

Drake ordered Chester to return to his seat and to hold up the other photographs. He made Mr Rawls describe the boy in each of these, then to describe Chester before him. He forced him to do this over and over again, making him look at the photographs and then Chester himself. If Mr Rawls refused, Drake would threaten him with the knife or cuff him across the face, until it became red and bruised.

As they went through this routine, Chester began to understand what Drake was up to. He was attempting to deprogramme his father, to purge him of the cognitive patterns the Styx had implanted with the Dark Light. And because Chester understood that Drake needed to be so brutal, he began to feel a little better about the physical abuse the man was dishing out to his father.

Then, as Drake slapped Mr Rawls once again, all that changed.

'Go to hell!' Mr Rawls shouted, clearly reaching the end of his tether. 'You can do what you want to me, but I'm not going to listen to this rubbish any longer.' Then he looked down at his lap, steadfastly refusing to answer any more questions.

'We're not getting anywhere with this,' Drake snapped. He swept over to Chester and wrapped his arm around his neck, squeezing it so hard that the boy couldn't breathe, let alone object.

'I'm now going to strangle your son, Jeff. This is Chester, right here in front of you.'

The heels of Chester's school shoes scraped against the concrete floor and the photographs slid from his lap. The chair went over as Chester desperately tried to break free from Drake's choke hold.

'I'm going to throttle him,' Drake promised, his voice so cold and unemotional that Chester really believed that he was going to go through with it.

Mr Rawls was still staring at his lap, shaking his head. Then he glanced up and his eyes widened.

'Chester!' he said, barely audibly at first.

Chester was turning blue.

'Sorry, can't hear you, Jeff,' Drake taunted him in a singsong voice.

Chester's eyes were bulging, and he no longer had the strength to kick out.

'You got a few seconds left before he dies, Jeff,' Drake said. 'You can save him. Just tell me who he is. Tell me, who can you see?'

'CHESTER!' Mr Rawls shrieked.

Drake released his grip on Chester, straightened the chair, and helped the gasping boy back on to it.

'Chester! It's you!' Mr Rawls was crying now, tears running down his cheeks. Still not fully recovered, Chester was both laughing and coughing as he staggered over to his father and flung his arms around him.

'Dad, it's over . . . we're together again . . . I dreamt of this,' Chester croaked as Drake sliced through Mr Rawls' bonds with his knife. 'My dad's back. How can I thank you for getting him back?' Chester poured out to Drake.

'Don't thank me quite so fast,' Drake said, as he retrieved the photographs from the floor. 'We've still got your mother to go yet, and I might really have to kill you this time.'

Elliott noticed the helicopter had changed course and that the flight seemed to be becoming choppier. She immediately looked at Colonel Bismarck, who was talking to the navigator in the cockpit. Shaking his head, the Colonel came over to her.

'There's a problem,' he said. 'We were en route for the jungle east of the pyramid you wanted, but a storm front is showing up on the navigator's screen. It's blowing our way fast, and it's a major one. We've already taken evasive action to skirt around it, but we can't even stay on this new bearing for long. We can't risk being caught in it.'

'What are the alternatives?' Elliott asked.

'There's a clear corridor straight through to the city. Why don't we take you there, where you'll be safe?'

'Can't do that, Colonel,' Elliott replied. 'We need to be east of the pyramid.'

Even as Colonel Bismarck left to consult with the navigator and the pilot, the helicopter entered the storm fringes, and rain began to lash in through the open door. The Colonel had to hang onto the sides as he came back to Elliott again, such was the buffeting they were already experiencing from the powerful wind currents.

'The pilot's going to look for an area somewhere close to here, where there's been a recent jungle fire – we can put you down there,' Colonel Bismarck told her. 'I'm afraid you'll have to make the rest of the journey on foot.'

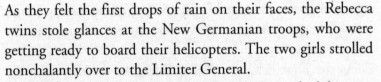

As they felt the first drops of rain on their faces, the Rebecca twins stole glances at the New Germanian troops, who were getting ready to board their helicopters. The two girls strolled nonchalantly over to the Limiter General.

'You put the word round?' Rebecca One asked him, as both of them intentionally kept their backs to the New Germanians. They didn't want the troops to suspect what might be coming next.

'I did. My men have been instructed to spare the helicopter crews, but the rest of the troops are to be eliminated if they resist,' the Limiter General replied in a low voice.

'And that young officer who helped us,' Rebecca Two put in, 'I want him unharmed.'

The Limiter General peered up at the rapidly darkening sky. 'Understood, and if this is a storm coming over us, our job will be made that much more easier. These old birds can't take off in inclement weather, and you never know – maybe we'll be able to assume control of the New Germanian troops without spilling any blood.'

Rebecca Two rubbed her hands together with relish. 'That would be good. More fresh recruits for the first stage in our new offensive.'

Her sister grinned broadly. 'Yes, with a few small but

crucial changes, I think we're going to be happy in our new home. Very happy indeed.'

Colonel Bismarck struggled to get his words out against the slipstream as the helicopter sped along. 'There! Do you see it?'

Elliott was right beside him, hanging onto the safety bar by the open door, as the jungle zipped below her. 'Yes – I see it,' she confirmed, catching the first glimpse of the tract of jungle recently ravished by fire, like a carbon scar amongst all the lush greenery.

As the pilot headed at full throttle for the clearing, they seemed to get ahead of the storm for a moment, and the air currents became less turbulent.

'Colonel,' Elliott began, now they had both pulled back from the doorway. 'You've been very straight with me, and I'd like to do the same for you.'

The Colonel frowned.

'I'll say just one thing: watch out for the Styx – don't underestimate what they're capable of. They won't be best pleased that you've let us go. And from what I've heard of your city, they might decide they like it there,' Elliott said.

'Thank you, but with their numbers I don't think they pose much of a threat to us,' Colonel Bismarck replied, although something in his eyes told Elliott he'd taken her warning to heart.

As the helicopter began its final descent, Elliott threw a glance at Will, who had his head down. She switched her attention to the view through the door. The recent fire had reduced the dense jungle to nothing more than a blanket of ash, which the wind from the rotors now lifted into the air. It was as if they were in the eye of a grey-black tornado, a dense smokescreen that all but blotted out the sun.

With a thump, they finally touched down, but the pilot didn't cut the engine – the Colonel clearly wasn't intending to stop for long. As Elliott leapt from the helicopter with Bartleby following behind her, Will was untied and led over.

'What if I don't want to go with her?' he said to the Colonel, as he rubbed his wrists to restore the circulation. 'I'd rather see this city of yours. You're all Germans from World War Two, aren't you?'

'Yes, from before the war ended,' Colonel Bismarck replied. 'How do you know that?'

Will inclined his head towards the Colonel's sidearm. 'That's a Luger.' Then he turned towards the other soldiers. 'And they've got Schmeissers, haven't they? I want to come and see what else is in your city. My Dad would've wanted that too.'

Will had been refusing to look at Elliott, but now eyed her coldly. 'And I don't want to be anywhere near *her*.'

Elliott knew that he was still reeling from the loss of his father, but she'd had enough of his comments.

'Will Burrows, you can be such a pain,' she fumed. 'Sure I gave them the Dominion phial – I had to, but only because you went and got yourself captured. You forced my hand. And you seem to be forgetting that I've just saved you from your vile sisters. Once again.'

'Yeah, sure, but at what cost?' he shouted back at her.

'It's not over yet,' she replied quietly, her voice barely audible over the engine.

'What do you mean?' he asked, jumping from the helicopter and advancing belligerently towards her. 'Oh, I suppose you've got some great plan for us to waltz in and snatch the virus back from them? Like that's going to work! They'll never let it out of their sight now, and we've also got a gazillion Limiters to get through, too.' He punched his fist into his open palm with a growl. 'I don't understand it. You of all people, just dropping it into their hands like that. Drake would be bloody ashamed of you!'

Elliott's face went blank for a moment, as if she was on the verge of crying, then she lashed out at Will, slapping him in the face.

He gasped with shock as Bartleby, upset that they were quarrelling with each other, gave a faltering meow.

'How dare you say that,' she said in a low, tremorous voice. 'It sounds as if Drake's dead, and you haven't got the faintest idea what he would've done in the same situation. And why aren't you listening to me? – I told you we're not finished. It's not over yet.'

'Oh, sod off!' Will shouted. 'I don't want to know.'

'You're looking for someone to blame for what happened to your dad. Well, don't blame me! I did all I could to save him!' Elliott shouted. 'I might just as well blame you for Drake's death. If you hadn't shown up on the Great Plain when you did, none of this would have happened. He might still be alive.'

Will spat into the ash. 'You can believe that if you want to. You never liked me anyway. Right from the start it was you and Chester, you and Chester . . . going out on patrol together all the time, like bosom buddies,' he yelled at her, so livid he didn't know what he was saying any more.

'Maybe that's because he needed to learn more than you did,' she shouted back.

'Or maybe you just liked him more than me,' Will levelled at her.

'Far be it from me to intrude on your – what do you call it – your *tiff* with you girlfriend, b—' the Colonel began to say to Will, but was cut off by another eruption from him.

'Hah! You've got to be joking!' Will spluttered, touching his smarting cheek where Elliott had struck him. 'She's not my girlfriend and never will be!'

This elicited chuckles from the soldiers inside the helicopter, who fell silent as their colonel gave them a stern glance.

'And you'll never be my boyfriend, because Chester's right – you're a freak!' Elliott countered.

'I'm sorry to hurry you, but we have to take off,' Colonel Bismarck continued. 'The storm is coming this way, and we don't have much fuel in the reserve tanks.'

Breathing stentoriously like an angry bull, Will stomped across the dry ash. But he didn't go far, stopping to look at the horizon with his hands on his hips. The Colonel sorted out some rations for Elliott, then tried to give her some weapons.

'I've got a couple of pistols in my rucksack,' she said, declining his offer.

But he wouldn't hear of it, and provided her with a pair of Lugers and one of the Schmeissers Will had admired, along with spare ammunition. 'In case you come across any unfriendly animals,' he told her, with a wink.

'Thank you. I won't forget this,' Elliott said, then shouted across to Will. 'Make your mind up! Are you staying? Or are you going with them?'

Although he kept his back to her, he shook his head. 'No,' he grunted in response.

The Colonel wished Elliott good luck, and gave her a salute as the helicopter returned to the air. She watched it go, shielding her eyes from the thick clouds of ash that the blades had swept up from the ground. Only when the helicopter had passed out of sight, and all was silent except for the sound of the howling wind, did Will finally turn to Elliott. He appeared to have calmed down a little as he picked his way slowly towards her. 'So tell me . . . why did you say it's not over yet? What's this genius plan of yours?'

Ignoring Will, Elliott began to make a fuss of Bartleby, wiping the layer of fine ash from his bald head. 'Back there at the pyramid, you were a very good cat. You did what you were told, didn't you?' she said, kneading his temple.

As Will heard the deep purring of the Hunter, he was becoming increasingly frustrated that Elliott was shutting him out. 'Why won't you answer me? It's the least you can do!' he ranted, his temper flaring all over again. 'I have a bloody right to know what you're planning. If it's true what they said, I've lost both my parents now. My mum's probably dead, and that foul scum just murdered my dad.'

'I know. I saw it,' she said, glancing at Will. 'And you must know how sorry I am, but now's not the time to think about it. You can do that later.'

'You've got something up your sleeve, haven't you?' Will asked. 'Tell me what it is.'

Elliott nodded once. 'Okay. I'm going Topsoil – through that tunnel I found by the waterfall.'

'Topsoil? What the hell for?' Will said, his brow furrowed as he tried to work out what she was intending to do. 'That doesn't make any sense. The Dominion's here . . . in this world.'

'I'm going Topsoil because whether or not Drake's still alive, I've got to get the vaccine to someone there.'

'But . . . but . . . I don't get it.' With an expression of pure bemusement, Will took a few steps towards her, hesitating for a moment, before taking a few more. 'But you smashed the vaccine phial – the one with the white top?'

'Yes, I did,' Elliott confirmed, as she used Dr Burrows' compass to check the bearing. Then she strode away from Will, who broke into a run to catch up with her, raising a trail of dust behind him. 'But not before I'd swallowed the contents,' she added, almost as an afterthought.

Will came to a sudden halt as the penny dropped. 'Then . . . then we *have* got the vaccine!' he exclaimed. 'It's *in* you!'

Chapter Twenty-two

Chester was completely exhausted and not paying much attention to his surroundings. But as Drake drove them through the London streets on the way back to the warehouse, the boy was so exhilarated that he felt as if he was floating along. His parents had been returned to him. 'Mum and Dad,' he murmured to himself, then began to hum to the tune on the radio.

The process to deprogramme his mother had been a lot less fraught, greatly helped because Mr Rawls also took part. Chester couldn't stop grinning to himself as he thought about the moment his mother's eyes had lit up and she'd finally recognised him.

After that, he'd sat with his parents for as long as Drake had allowed him, telling them how he and Will had stumbled across the Colony and the events that had followed. To start with they'd looked at him in horrified disbelief, but their own experiences helped to persuade them that what Chester was saying was true. Although it was rather hazy in their minds, they both had vague memories of being overpowered, and then of ghoulish men shining intense purple lights in their faces. And their recollections of events following this incident were also a little unclear to them, as if they were unable to tell what was real or what they'd dreamt.

But they were both so overjoyed that their son was still alive, they were just about ready to believe anything – that and the fact that they were still absolutely terrified by Drake, and wouldn't have dared to question anything he said.

Now that the spell of the Dark Light had been broken, Drake wasn't taking any chances. He wanted Mr and Mrs Rawls kept under lock and key for at least the next forty-eight hours, and the bald mechanic had eventually agreed to sleep at the premises to keep a close eye on them. In fact, after Drake offered him another diamond, he said he was going to move his 'missus' into the arches to wait hand and foot on Chester's parents.

'It's weird,' Chester said to Drake. 'I thought about being back with my parents all the time I was underground but, you know, I'd almost given up hope.' Then he thanked Drake yet again.

Drake nodded. 'Don't mention it. I couldn't just leave them under the Styx's control.'

'But will they really be all right? Has the Dark Light stuff all gone now?' Chester asked.

'Reversion therapy isn't a science – you never know what else in the psyche has been tampered with. But the Styx might not have gone too deep, and we've certainly taken care of what we know about.'

'You did the same for Will, didn't you?' Chester said.

'Yes, with him it was a death wish triggered by heights, so it was sort of handy I cottoned onto it when we were up on the roofs in Martineau Square. I forced him to visualise the outcome if he jumped – made him face his hidden demon – and it did the trick, eventually,' Drake replied. 'He broke the impulse. Strong kid, that.'

'He is,' Chester said. 'And the most stubborn person I've ever met.' Despite his fatigue, Chester was beginning to think clearly. 'But what will happen to my mum and dad?' he asked. Although his parents were safe for the moment, they couldn't stay in the lock up indefinitely.

'I'll move them somewhere else tomorrow. They're in the same boat as the rest of us now – there's no way they can ever go home,' Drake said, then glanced at Chester. 'Do you think they can lead the sort of life we do?'

'They haven't got a choice, have they?' Chester replied. 'Until we beat the Styx.'

Drake nodded. 'Talking about the Styx, you can't breathe a word to Eddie about any of this. How's your neck feel? I did my best not to leave any bruises. Let me have a look.'

Chester opened his shirt collar to show Drake.

'No, you're fine,' Drake said. 'I don't want Eddie to pick up on what we've been doing.'

'So you don't trust him completely?' Chester asked.

'I don't trust *anyone* completely,' Drake replied. 'And we've got to get the story straight in case he asks anything. We drove around for a while – that'll explain the mileage on the car if he checks – then we zipped over to Regents Park for a walk, where you had some lunch followed by an ice cream.' Drake leant over to release the glove compartment in front of the boy. 'Take the wrapper in there and drip some of the melted ice cream down your front – make sure it shows.'

As Drake continued to drive, Chester followed his instructions – rubbing the wrapper on the clothes he'd put back on after he'd changed out of his school uniform.

'You said we had lunch?' Chester enquired wistfully. He realised that with everything that had happened during the day, he hadn't had anything to eat for hours.

Drake gestured at the glove compartment. 'You'll find some sandwiches in there too. Tuck in, but just remember, when we get to the warehouse, you have to go back into your act and make like the world has ended. Got that?'

'Maximum Eeyore,' Chester confirmed, reaching for the sandwiches.

Will and Elliott began to get an idea of just how widespread the jungle fire had been as they continued through the barren fields. In places the wind had gathered the ash and charred wood into drifts, and the going here was difficult as they sank up to their knees in it.

And every so often they came across what remained of the trunks of the mighty trees. Shorn of their branches and a fraction of their original height, these had the appearance of giant sticks of charcoal that had been rammed into the ground.

What had begun as a light breeze was rapidly turning into a powerful wind. Large raindrops began to fall, hitting the ash around them and sending it up in little puffs, as though Lilliputian bombs were going off.

Then they were plunged into an eerie half light as the sun became choked by clouds. No wonder Colonel Bismarck had been concerned; the storm of all storms was upon them. A searing arc of lightning jagged into one of the charcoal tree trunks several hundred metres away, and with a groan it began to pitch over, as if in slow motion. Almost instantaneously there was a crash of thunder, so loud it was like a physical force, knocking them off course as they went.

'Run!' Elliott screamed.

'I am!' Will screamed back.

Apart from the fact the thunderclaps made him anxious, Bartleby seemed to be enjoying himself, scampering around in the rain and getting himself covered in ash as if it was all some game.

Then they came to a steep slope and followed it down. The rain was now torrential, and the combination of water and loose ash was treacherous. They kept losing their footing and slipping down the grey incline.

As they reached the bottom, they found themselves in some kind of hollow, where many more of the charcoal trunks were standing. They were racing between these as they heard a screech.

'Bartleby!' Will yelled, and they both ground to a halt. 'Where is he?'

The rain was pelting them with such force that they had to protect their faces as they scanned the surroundings for the Hunter.

There was another screech.

'He's in trouble,' Will shouted, gesturing to where he thought the sound had come from.

As they retraced their steps between the carbon tree trunks, they spied movement.

They crouched low.

Black creatures slightly larger than rugby balls were crawling slowly over the carcass of a dead buffalo. Its stomach was split wide open, and its intestines had been spread over the ground. The creatures were feeding on these intestines, nudging at the coils of gut and other body organs as they stuck spike-like proboscises into them and sucked.

'Fleas? Mega Fleas?' Will mumbled to Elliott.

They did resemble huge versions of these insects, with crooked rear legs and segmented carapaces that shone dully under the reduced light. But these creatures appeared to be scavengers and not parasites, as they fed on the felled buffalo. Will estimated that there were around thirty of them in the pack, and a low humming noise was emanating from them, as if they were communicating with each other. The sound seemed to be coming from their forelegs as they rubbed them together.

Another yelp.

Ten metres from the dead buffalo, Bartleby was rolling on his back, one of the fleas gripped between his paws as it extended and retracted the dark spike from its mouth parts. It was trying to bite or sting him. And other fleas were slowly leaving the buffalo carcass to head towards the thrashing cat. They clearly weren't just scavengers – they were predatory too.

Elliott realised Will was unarmed – after they'd argued, she'd kept the weapons to herself. Worse still, the Browning Hi-Powers were buried at the bottom of her Bergen, and she only had the New Germanian weapons to hand.

'Here!' she hissed, whipping out one of the pistols she'd tucked into her belt.

Will turned just in time to catch the Luger she'd lobbed at him.

He pointed the weapon at the flea in Bartleby's paws, steadied his aim, and squeezed the trigger.

Nothing happened.

'Safety's on!' he growled through clenched teeth, and had begun to fumble for the lever on the unfamiliar weapon when Elliott fired her pistol.

The flea in Bartleby's paws was slammed away by the shot, as if it had been swiped with an invisible bat.

As their antennae twitched, the other fleas turned slowly, their jointed legs twitching and humming, until they were facing Elliott. Then they began to advance towards her.

Running between the blackened tree trunks, Will skirted around the back of the dead buffalo in order to reach Bartleby. The Hunter was dazed and unsteady on his feet, but otherwise unharmed. Getting hold of his scruff, Will was dragging him up onto his paws as one of the fleas at the edge of the pack noticed him.

'Come on, Bart!' Will urged the cat.

Bartleby was standing now, but he hadn't recovered sufficiently to move at any speed.

The flea hopped, landing just in front of Will. It happened so quickly, he reacted completely on instinct. He shot it at point-blank range. Its hard exoskeleton cleaved open, exposing its white flesh as a milky fluid splashed the ground around it. It reminded Will of a coconut he'd won in the shy in the travelling fair in Highfield, which he'd cracked open with a hammer.

He was trying to drag Bartleby away with him as he heard Elliott shout his name and then gunfire. Swapping her pistol for the Schmeisser, she was firing short bursts at the advancing horde of fleas. Every so often one of them hopped at her, but she was able to shoot it out of the air before it reached her.

'Go!' she yelled, as she spotted Will and Bartleby, who was now moving under his own steam, although rather drunkenly.

She wheeled around and they fled together. Within minutes, they'd clambered up the other side of the hollow and were in the ash fields again. The edge of the jungle loomed before them – they were tantalisingly close to it.

'They're coming!' Will puffed, as he threw a glance behind them.

The fleas hadn't given up on the prospect of catching some fresh prey. Now that they weren't restricted by the charred tree trunks, they really began to show what they were capable of. They began to make tremendous leaps.

Even above the sound of the rain and the wind, Will could hear the thump of their powerful hind legs against the ground as they launched themselves in high arcs. They were dropping out of the sky and landing all around.

Will and Elliott would run ten metres, then stop to deal with the fleas pursuing them, repeating the manoeuvre over and over, but making agonisingly slow progress towards the tree line. They hoped that when they reached the jungle, they'd be able to shake the insects off their trail.

Elliott was despatching most of the fleas with her Schmeisser, and Will picked off any that got past her with his Luger. He was just thinking that they had the situation under control when one of the fleas struck his back. It immediately gripped onto his shirt with its pincer-like claws. As he tried to shake it loose, he lost his balance and flopped face first into the ash.

Bartleby's yowl alerted Elliott that something was wrong. Will was rolling over and over, and also trying to strike the insect with the butt of his pistol, but it clung resolutely onto him. Worse still, the flea was gradually edging towards the exposed nape of his neck.

Then it drew back its proboscis, making ready to bite him.

Elliott didn't have time to switch over to her handgun, which would have allowed her to make a more accurate shot.

'Stay face down!' she screamed at the struggling boy. 'And stay still!'

She crouched, aimed, then unleashed a volley with the Schmeisser.

With a loud crack, Will was showered with white gunk. He hauled himself to his feet, shook his head, and began to sprint again. Elliott took care of several more fleas, but then they appeared to give up on the pursuit. Glancing over his shoulder, Will saw the surviving fleas were springing back towards the hollow, probably to return to the buffalo carcass.

And within twenty minutes, Will and Elliott were under the jungle canopy, where they paused to recover their breath.

'Thanks,' Will panted, tearing off some leaves to wipe the remains of the insect from his hair and neck.

'No problem,' Elliott replied, slapping the side of her Schmeisser. 'It was a bit hit or miss – these things aren't that accurate.'

'You used *that*?' Will said, still trying to catch his breath.

'It did the trick,' she said.

'It did,' he panted, raising his eyebrows. 'But . . . one thing.'

'Yes?' she asked.

Will glanced suspiciously at the jungle around them. 'If any of these trees look at you with mean little eyes . . . just let them have it too, will you?'

'What?' she asked.

Will kicked at the roots of a nearby tree. 'Those Bushmen only cared about their bloody pyramid . . . they didn't help us

. . . and I'll never forgive them for what they did to Dad and me.'

'I haven't got the faintest idea *what* you're talking about!' Elliott said, as she checked their bearing with the compass. 'But I'm sure you're going to tell me,' she added, 'when we have time.'

After another hour's trek, they'd arrived at the hideaway in the cliff face.

'Thank God you made sure the Styx didn't get their mitts on any of this,' Will said gratefully. He was very tired, but his spirits were buoyed as he took inventory of the equipment Elliott had carried to the cave for safekeeping. 'I reckon we've got enough hardware to deal with *anything* along the way,' he said, as he began to pack his Bergen. Then he came to the pistol-shaped tracking device Drake had given him. 'And this is more important than anything else – this is our ticket home,' he announced, holding it up.

'I hope so,' she said, shoving a fresh magazine into a Sten and cocking it. 'I truly hope so.'

Colonel Bismarck was shown into the room by the Chancellor's private secretary, tottering on her incredibly high heels.

'Ah, Bismarck, all done and dusted with those dreadful people, I trust? A successful outcome, so we can wash our hands of them?' the Chancellor asked. He was lounging in an armchair as a barber put the finishing touches to his hair, and a woman in a grey smock gave him a manicure.

'Yes, the Styx recovered their virus. There was a limited exchange of fire, and although we suffered no losses, the Styx had a single casualty. One of the three targets they were searching for was, however, unnecessarily put to death during the operation – he was a civilian from the outer world.'

'As long as he wasn't one of ours,' the Chancellor exhaled.

'No. And although there weren't any direct sightings of them, it seems as though the indigenous people were somehow involved with the targets. They took two of them inside the pyramid, then expelled them again.'

Not the slightest bit curious about this, the Chancellor sniffed dismissively. 'Well, they haven't been a major threat to us, not like the pirates or the Inquisitors were. And, anyway, that area has nothing of value in it. But the academies might want to know what happened. It'll give them something to cluck about,' the Chancellor suggested with a perfunctory smile. 'Is that all?'

'I'm compiling a full report for you, sir,' Colonel Bismarck replied. 'But you should know—'

'A moment,' the Chancellor said, holding up his hand as the barber carefully snipped at his moustache. Once the barber had finished trimming it, the Chancellor spoke again. 'Continue.'

Colonel Bismarck cleared his throat. 'The Styx agreed to an exchange for their virus, as part of which a young boy and girl were to be allowed to go free. I'm afraid to say that the Styx do not appear to be people of their word, so I had no option but to remove the boy and girl in one of the Fa 233s, and drop them in a remote location. The rest of our troop detachment and the remaining helicopters were left at the pyramid, with orders to return to the airfield after I'd gone.'

The barber held up a mirror in front of the Chancellor so

he could admire his moustache and his heavily oiled hair. 'Very acceptable. Thank you,' he said, and then the barber took the towel from his shoulders with a flourish. 'That all sounds – OW!'

The manicurist recoiled at the Chancellor's shout.

'Careful, woman – that was very careless of you,' he complained, rubbing his finger where the woman had inadvertently cut into the flesh. He turned impatiently to the Colonel. 'And that must be all from you?'

'Yes, except that I've just learnt that we've lost radio contact with the helicopters,' Colonel Bismarck said. 'I suspect the Styx might have something to do with it. I was—'

'No, I think that improbable – they've got what they came for,' the Chancellor interrupted. 'No, it's either that massive storm I'm told is heading our way, or it's equipment failure again.' He closed his eyes for a moment, as if exhausted. 'I suppose you're going to nag me for that increase in your military budget, so you can have the new communications system? Just put it all in your report, Colonel.'

'But we should be wary of the Styx,' the Colonel said. The manicurist had risen from her stool and was dragging it noisily across the marble floor so she could work on the Chancellor's other hand.

'Yes, yes, as I said – awful people. And now I must get on. Thank you, Bismarck. Sterling work,' the Chancellor said, as he shook his newspaper open.

Chapter Twenty-three

Tower Bridge flashed by as a pair of leather-clad riders raced their powerful motorcycles through the empty London streets. As they passed the other bridges across the river, they were vying with each other for pole position.

Once in Parliament Square, they were forced to skid to a halt at a set of traffic lights. Drake flipped up his helmet visor and gestured at the floodlit Houses of Parliament. 'It's said in the Colony that passages lead directly there from the Styx Citadel. People say you have direct access into its basement vaults.'

Eddie lifted his visor. 'Not after Guido Fawkes took the fall for our aborted black op.'

'What? You mean the *Gunpowder Plot*?' Drake said quickly. 'You're kidding me!'

'The tunnels were filled in after that,' Eddie replied, then dropped his visor again. The lights changed and he was first off the mark, leaving Drake behind to wonder at his answer. As Big Ben began to ring in five o'clock, he shook his head once in disbelief, gunned his motorcycle, then let out the clutch to speed after the Limiter.

After parking in St Anne's Street, they went on foot, taking a right and a left to end up on Victoria Street. As the western facade of Westminster Abbey loomed in front of them, Drake had no idea where Eddie was taking him. In the event, the Styx led him almost to the abbey, then reversed direction. Now walking more slowly, he was heading towards a row of sandstone buildings, which looked every bit as old as the abbey itself. Between the buildings was a short alleyway and, as Drake shot a glance down it, he glimpsed a square beyond. Although it was around an hour before sunrise, the street lamps in the square allowed him to make out trees and a number of cars parked there. Then he spotted a sign at the entrance to the alleyway. '*Dean's Yard*,' he read out loud. 'I don't think I've been here before.'

'Keep behind me, and stay quiet,' Eddie told him in a low voice as, halfway down the alleyway, someone in uniform stepped out in front of them. Drake tensed, thinking it was a policeman, but then saw from his uniform that he was some kind of porter. The man was standing beside a small red-and-white barricade designed to restrict vehicles from entering the square.

'Evening, gentlemen,' the porter said. As he looked the two of them over, Drake knew from the way he'd squared his shoulders and had his walkie-talkie ready in his hand that he was expecting trouble. There was no way he was going to allow two bikers clad in leathers into the square at that time of the morning, not without explaining themselves properly.

Eddie showed no hesitation in going straight up to the surly man and, when he was close enough to him, he spoke a few words into his ear. The porter said nothing back to Eddie, but seemed to immediately lower his guard. He pocketed his walkie-talkie, then rubbed his hands together, opening them a little to blow on them as if he was feeling the cold. Then, to Drake's surprise, he turned to regard Victoria Street down the alleyway, staring straight through both him and Eddie as if they didn't exist. As the man sang '*I did it my way,*' in a woefully tuneless way, he simply wandered back to his cabin, whistling more of the song before closing the door behind him.

Drake came abreast with Eddie as they entered the square. 'He's been Darklit, hasn't he? You gave him some trigger words to let us through. What were they – *Frank Sinatra*?'

'No, they were words you wouldn't be able to pronounce. You may not have noticed it, but I was concerned that the sequence had been changed. Thankfully, it hasn't,' Eddie replied, striding straight across the grassed area in the middle of the square.

'I think I've heard of this place before,' Drake pondered, as he scanned the many doorways in the Georgian buildings around them. 'There's a famous school close to here, and wasn't the father of the real *Alice in Wonderland* its headmaster at one time?'

Eddie didn't answer as he went straight to one of the doors and pushed it open. Inside was a gloomy corridor with a floor of pitted flagstones. They continued down this to another door at the very end, where Eddie took out a luminescent orb so he could use a key. Once unlocked, the door creaked open and Drake smelt the mustiness of the damp cellar below. They descended a flight of stone steps to find the place was crammed with packing crates filled with mildewed school textbooks.

Eddie squeezed between these to reach the wall at the end

of the cellar, where he located a rusty hook at head height and tugged on it. Drake was inspecting an ancient ale bottle from the top of one of the crates as, by Eddie's feet, a panel around a metre square swung open in the lower half of the wall.

As he saw the size of the opening, Drake laughed to himself. 'And it doesn't even say DRINK ME on the label,' he muttered, and tossed the bottle back into the crate.

Eddie threw him a quizzical glance. 'Sorry?'

'No, nothing,' Drake answered. 'I was just thinking how unsophisticated this portal is. All expenses spared – no bells or whistles.'

Eddie nodded in agreement. 'At the time this was dug in the early nineteen hundreds, we were a bit thin on the ground – the events in Russia were our main priority.'

They crawled into the opening and, once on the other side, Drake was able to stand again. He found they were in a white-washed passage several metres across, which led to another flight of steps constructed of crumbling red brick.

Drake was going down these steps when he realised Eddie wasn't with him. The Styx was waiting at the top, showing no sign that he was prepared to go any further.

In the light cast by Eddie's luminescent orb, beads of moisture sparkled like diamonds on an elaborate spider's web spun between the wall and a crumbling wooden joist. Noticing the web just above his head, Drake blew gently on it. A rather obscene spider with a bloated abdomen emerged from a crack in the wall, creeping between the exoskeletons of long-dead flies stuck in the web.

'I take it we're not going any further?' he enquired, as he watched the spider, disappointed there was no new victim for it to suck dry, return to its hiding place.

'There isn't much point – now we know we can access this route. And this is how it goes for the rest of the way,' Eddie answered. 'Just more steps and passages.'

'Fine, as long it gets us down to the Eternal City with a couple of fully loaded Bergens,' Drake replied.

Eddie nodded again. 'Then we're done here,' he said.

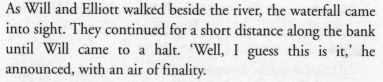

As Will and Elliott walked beside the river, the waterfall came into sight. They continued for a short distance along the bank until Will came to a halt. 'Well, I guess this is it,' he announced, with an air of finality.

He gazed at the crystal-clear water, and the exotic dragon-flies darting over its surface. 'It's very special here, isn't it?' he said, raising his eyes to the lower branches of the huge trees, where a flock of emerald-green birds chattered away. 'And this is probably the last time we'll ever see it,' he added.

Will swivelled around and glanced at the waterfall. Although it was hidden in the shadows, the passage was waiting there for them. The passage that would, they hoped, take them to the outer crust.

Stooping to pluck a blade of grass, Will twirled it between his fingers. 'You know, I never told Dad that there was a tunnel here,' he said disconsolately.

Elliott nudged a stone with her boot until it fell into the river, but remained silent.

'Do you think if I *had* told him, things might be different now? If he'd jumped at the opportunity to go back to the surface . . . he would still be alive,' Will posed, his forehead creasing with guilt and regret.

'No, not the Doc. Not him,' Elliott answered, without

hesitation. 'He wasn't about to go anywhere, not until he'd finished his work. You know that.'

Will smiled wanly at her. 'Yes, that's true.' He took a deep breath. 'Okay, Little Miss Vaccine, we need to get you to a Topsoil hospital so the doctors can bottle your blood.' He slipped off his Bergen and took out his night-vision device, easing the band around his forehead and making sure the lens was positioned correctly, ready to flip down over his eye. 'And as you're so super-duper important now, I'm on point. So if anything tries to eat me, at least you'll be safe.'

Elliott raised her eyebrows, her face mock serious. 'Sounds like a plan to me,' she said, not able to stop herself from laughing.

'Wait – I forgot about Bartleby!' Will exclaimed. They both regarded the Hunter. He'd remained further down the stream where he was trying to catch one of the small silvery fish with a paw as it swam past. 'On second thoughts, we should let bozo go first,' Will chuckled.

'It's weird being here,' Chester said, licking the ice cream Drake had bought him from a vendor near the Royal Festival Hall. He and Drake were walking at a leisurely pace beside the Thames, in the midst of the crowds out that day. 'Feels so normal, as if I never left,' Chester added, as he looked out over the water, the odd ripple glittering as it reflected the brightness of the midday sun.

As they followed the walkway further along, they moved into the shade provided by Waterloo Bridge, where the second-hand booksellers had set up their stalls.

'All these people, from so many different places . . .'

Chester commented, as he caught smatterings of conversation from passers-by. 'And not one of them has the slightest idea what's below them,' he continued, glancing down at the pavement.

'Maybe it's better that way,' Drake replied. 'Most people find this world complicated enough as it is.'

A group of kids on skateboards hurtled past, weaving their way between the somnambulant tourists as if they were a mobile slalom. Chester gazed after them, watching as a tall youth in a baseball cap with a large 'D' on it came to an abrupt halt. He skilfully kicked down the tail of his board, so it flipped up into the air and did several revolutions before he caught it.

'That was cool. You know, I asked Father Christmas for a skateboard just before Will and I discovered the Colony,' Chester said pensively. 'I've never learnt how to use one.'

'Can't say I have, either,' Drake admitted. He went across to the raised wall by the water's edge and leant against it, taking off his dark glasses to enjoy the warmth of the sun on his face. 'But just think what else you've learnt instead.'

Chester joined him by the wall. 'So are my mum and dad really all right?' he asked, changing the subject.

'In the lap of luxury. I put them up in a hotel with room service. As long as they stay put, you've got nothing to worry about – they're safe,' Drake assured him. 'I know you want to see them again, but you have to be patient. We need to get a couple of things done, then I'll move them to a new location where you can be with them.'

'With Eddie too?' Chester said. 'After you've finished the operation with him in the Eternal City, is he still going to be part of the team?'

'That's rather up to him,' Drake replied, angling his head so the other side of his face caught the rays.

Chester frowned as he had a thought.

'I take it your silence means you want to ask something else?' Drake divined.

'Er . . . yes,' Chester answered. He realised some ice cream had dripped down his chin and wiped it off with his hand before he spoke. 'I've never understood why you stayed underground for so long – you could have gone Topsoil any time you wanted, couldn't you?'

'The original plan was that I infiltrate the Colony and collect as much intelligence as I could on our dear friends,' Drake explained.

'Yes, I know that,' Chester said.

'I found out that the network up here had gone south when one of the Scientists told me the Styx had caught and killed a member of my cell. That meant the whole thing had unravelled, and there was really no reason for me to return Topsoil again. As the Styx had got just about all they wanted out of me anyway for the development of their rifle scopes, my usefulness had come to an end, and I knew that my days were numbered. It was too dangerous for me to stick around in the Colony any longer.' Drake cleaned the lenses of his sunglasses and put them on again. 'So, after a weapons trial in the Deeps, I made my move and ran for it. I decided to stay there for a while and continue to gather as much intel as I could. And, to be honest, when Elliott came along, it gave me a real reason to remain there. I couldn't leave her by herself.'

A tall thin man with a scrawny beard suddenly stopped on the walkway several metres away, eyeing Drake, then Chester.

Chester was immediately suspicious. 'I don't like the look

of him,' he whispered. 'Styx?'

Drake laughed. 'No, he's not Styx – he's being too obvious. Besides, can't you see the copies of the *Big Issue* under his arm – he's trying to work out if we're potential customers.'

Nevertheless Chester continued to watch the bearded man until he'd moved on. Now down to the cone of his ice cream, he crunched loudly. 'And there is something else I can't figure out.'

'What's that?' Drake asked.

'You can get your hands on explosives when you need them,' Chester said.

Drake nodded.

'So I was thinking . . . with Eddie's maps of the layout down there, why don't we just sneak in and do a mother of a demolition job on the Citadel?' Chester proposed. 'You could take all the Styx out in one fell swoop.'

Drake nodded again. 'Good question, but it's not that simple. Ever gone into a room with a bad infestation of cockroaches – I mean a really bad one – and switched the light on?'

'No, I haven't,' Chester said.

'Well, I have, many times. Even if they're all over the floor, you can only stamp on a few of them, because they disappear, just like that,' Drake said, with a click his fingers. 'They shoot back to their hiding places, where you have absolutely no hope of finding them.'

'Right,' Chester replied slowly as he pictured the scene.

'Well, it would be just the same with the Styx. You might manage to kill a handful of them, but the rest would just vamoose. As you know, there are quite a few operating on the surface at any given time, anyway.'

'It wouldn't work, then,' Chester put in.

'Isn't it better to know where they are, down there in the Colony, rather than scattered all over the country, where they might become even more active – if that's possible? And besides, how could you live with yourself if any Colonists got caught up in the attack? It's inevitable that at least one civilian would lose his or her life in the size of explosion you're talking about.'

Chester popped the last piece of cone into mouth. 'Yes, but wouldn't it still be worth it?'

'So you could live with what politicians call "collateral damage"? The death of innocent people?' Drake put to the boy.

Chester chewed thoughtfully. He could see exactly what Drake was saying, although he wasn't sure if he agreed with it. 'But if we prevent maybe millions of Topsoil deaths because we've stopped them spreading something like Dominion, then I wouldn't feel too guilty about it. Of course, it would be awful if any Colonists were killed, but overall it would be a good thing to do. The right thing.'

'The right thing,' Drake repeated, then looked at Chester. 'There was a time I might have agreed with you. But not anymore.'

'Oh,' Chester mumbled, unsettled by the intensity in the man's voice.

'This is for you.' Drake reached into his pocket and handed Chester a mobile phone. 'Tuck it away and, whatever you do, don't let Eddie see it,' he said. 'We're going back to the warehouse now, and on the way I'll tell you what I want you to do.'

Chapter Twenty-four

The front door shook on its hinges, the pounding on it so excessive that nobody could fail to hear it – not even in the rooms at the back of the house.

'Ooo's that?' complained the Second Officer's mother from the kitchen.

Mrs Burrows, propped up in her bath chair, already knew that it wasn't a neighbour calling around so early that Sunday morning.

The pounding on the door came again, more impatiently this time.

'I've got me 'ands full in 'ere! Get it, someone – might be Mrs Evans with the needlework she wants doin',' the Second Officer's mother shouted. She always rose before her son or daughter each morning, but she was even earlier on Sundays – a special day throughout the Colony when they might splash out on a choice cut of meat for their midday meal, rather than their weekday fare, the slimy pennybun mushrooms.

Indeed Mrs Burrows could smell the fresh rat as it began to cook. Eliza would have bought it at the market the day before, and likely as not it wouldn't be the sightless variety, but bog-standard sewer rat, because they were less costly. And Mrs Burrows would reap the benefit because rather than the usual fungal slop, she would be treated to a thin broth made from boiling the stripped carcasses.

'Coming . . . coming,' Eliza called as she stomped down the stairs, annoyed that she'd been interrupted while doing her hair. She was still trying to rearrange a few wayward strands as she opened the door.

'Oh!' she said, soft as a sigh.

The old Styx was standing there, his chin raised as he looked to the right and scrutinised the other houses in the terrace along the side of the street. His young assistant was hovering directly behind him, and on the pavement there were even more Styx – ten of them, all so similar in appearance that Eliza couldn't tell them apart. The way they were observing their surroundings with small, jerky movements of their heads made them resemble a recently alighted flock of birds. But these were terrifying birds of prey. Eliza also couldn't help but notice curtains moving in the houses opposite as neighbours tried to see what was going on.

The old Styx slowly turned to look at Eliza, who bowed her head and stepped back. It wasn't done to meet a Styx's gaze, particularly one as supremely important as this man. In the Colony this was the closest thing to a royal visit. Indeed, it was rumoured that the old Styx was now the most important person in their hierarchy, but nobody knew for sure.

His black, full-length leather coat creaked as he stepped lightly across the threshold and into the hallway.

His young assistant followed on his heels. 'Your brother's home,' he said abruptly.

Eliza didn't know how to respond to this – she wasn't sure

if it was a question or an assertion. In a state of terrible indecision about what she should say, she began to mumble, but was saved by her mother, who had emerged from the kitchen and was doddering down the hallway.

'If that's Mrs Evans with 'er mendin', tell 'er she's a day early,' she shouted. 'We agreed it would be tom—'

As her rheumy eyes fell on the old Styx, she gave a croak not unlike an asthmatic frog. She too averted her eyes, clasping her hands at her waist.

'We've come to see the Burrows woman. She's in here,' the young assistant said, already making for the sitting room. Again, it was impossible to tell if he was enquiring where Mrs Burrows was, or if he already knew, but both women believed it was probably the latter. The Styx seemed to know everything that was going on, down to the very last detail, even if they kept their distance from the Colonists.

As the young assistant pushed the door open and then drew to the side to let the old Styx enter, Eliza stole the briefest glance at this most important of people. She noticed his pale white skin was as creased as a crumpled page, and his obsidian-black hair had traces of silver at the temples. But as the subdued light from the room fell on his face, what was so shocking was that the hollowness of his cheeks and his sunken eye sockets made him resemble an animated corpse.

Although he was first in the room, he held back as his young assistant went over to Mrs Burrows and lifted her limp wrist. For a moment the young assistant held it aloft in his gloved hand, then simply let it drop again. He glanced at the old Styx, who gave him a single nod in response.

Just then the Second Officer arrived at the bottom of the stairs. Dressed in his shirtsleeves, the big man spotted the Styx outside on the pavement and also the way his mother and sister were standing mutely, with their heads bowed. Without a moment's hesitation, he strode across the hallway and into the sitting room.

He saw the old Styx and his assistant but didn't announce himself, waiting just inside the doorway. In his job as a policeman in the Quarter, the Second Officer had daily dealings with the Styx, so he didn't show quite the same degree of awe as rank and file Colonists did when confronted by one.

The young assistant acknowledged the presence of the Second Officer with a half look. 'It was never expected that this woman would live past the first day, let alone for the weeks she has. She's going to remain in this vegetative state – there's no prospect of any improvement.'

The Second Officer cleared his throat. 'Yes, the doctor told us that, but I think she's getting a lit—'

The young assistant continued as if he hadn't heard a word the Second Officer was saying. 'Of course, it's remarkable she was able to resist the battery of Dark Lights – many more than we've used on a subject in a long time – but it's even more remarkable that she's somehow still alive,' the young assistant said. 'You're to turn her over to the Scientists,' he added abruptly.

'The Scientists?' the Second Officer repeated, taking another step into the room.

'They're going to examine her brain. They're interested in her neural physiology and how it conferred resistance to our interrogation techniques. She will be taken away for dissection when they're ready to receive her,' the young assistant said. 'You've done a good job.'

The Second Officer couldn't help himself. He uttered the

word 'But', nearly following up with a 'No', an act of insubordination against the Styx that would probably have landed him in his own gaol at best – or, at worst, with Banishment to the Deeps.

Perhaps sensing the strength of the Second Officer's feelings, the old Styx fixed him with a stare and spoke for the first time. 'When you offered to care for this woman in your home, you took rather too much on yourself and your family. Look upon this as a blessing.'

The old Styx and his assistant were moving towards the door to leave as the Second Officer managed to say, 'Thank . . . you,' but only because it was expected of him. Inside, he was yelling, 'Keep your bloody hands off her, you filthy White Necks! Haven't you done enough already? Let her live out her days here, in peace!'

He took a few seconds to compose himself before he went out into the hallway. The old Styx and his young assistant had already left and were moving down the street with the rest of their entourage, curtains twitching in the windows of the houses as they passed them.

Eliza closed the front door, then banged her head against it as if the world had ended.

'What 'ave you *done*? You brought them to our 'ouse! To our 'ouse!' the Second Officer's mother accused him. 'Ohhh,' she groaned, sinking down onto the bottom step of the staircase as she fanned herself with her hand. 'I feel all funny. I'm 'avin' an 'ot flush. I think me dodgy ticker's givin' out.'

'I hope you're satisfied – you've made our mother ill!' Eliza said, as she wheeled around from the door. She groaned as if she too was suffering from some painful affliction. 'The shame of it all – the Styx in *our* house, as if we were common criminals or troublemakers. What will people say?' She shook her head. 'Everyone will know – I can just imagine all the tongues wagging in the market tomorrow.'

The old lady puffed, then looked enquiringly at the Second Officer. 'What did they say to you, anyway?' she asked.

The despair evident on his face, the Second Officer didn't answer right away. 'They're taking Celia for a medical examination,' he eventually replied.

'What sort of *exhamation*?' his mother demanded.

The Second Officer couldn't contain his despair any longer. 'They're going to put her on a slab and cut her up!' he blurted.

There was a moment as Eliza met eyes with her mother and they absorbed this piece of information. Then their faces cracked into huge grins and the old lady, apparently forgetting her 'dodgy ticker', leapt to her feet. She and Eliza began to dance around one another, chanting, 'She's going, she's going'. They were like two children who had been told that they were let off school tomorrow because it would be closed for the day.

As the Second Officer returned to sit with Mrs Burrows, the sounds of jubilation were still coming from the hallway. 'I'm so sorry, Celia,' he said. 'It's out of my hands now.'

'There's another of them,' Will noted, slowing as he pointed at the three-pronged symbol carved into the side of the stone passage. He automatically put his hand to his neck, although Uncle Tam's pendant no longer hung there.

He turned to Elliott. 'The effort that must have gone into hollowing out this passage is simply mind boggling. I suppose the Ancients wanted a link between their "*Garden of the*

Second Sun" and the outer crust. Maybe for a trading route between both worlds?'

'When you come out with stuff like that, you have no idea how much you sound like your father,' Elliott remarked.

'Do I?' Will replied, quietly pleased that she should think that. He hiked his Bergen up on his back. 'At least I've got Dad's journal in here – thanks to you. You saved it. After he was shot I wasn't thinking straight . . . in fact . . .'

Will was constantly aware that he was now the guardian of Dr Burrows' journal, the sole record of all his investigations. If he could get it to the appropriate people on the surface, it should secure his father's place in history as one of the greatest explorers of all time and, in some way, guarantee him immortality. And this notion helped Will to cope with the immense sense of loss he was feeling for the man who'd been the single most important person in his life.

'. . . in fact, I wasn't thinking at all,' he mumbled, his expression vacant.

'Nobody'd blame you for that,' Elliott assured him.

Will came out of his short reverie and frowned. 'And do you know, we haven't gone that far yet, and I'm already beginning to feel lighter. The gravity's definitely less.'

'Definitely,' she agreed. 'Now can we get a move on? We've got so far to go, I don't want to think about it.'

Chapter Twenty-five

The Limiter General timed it perfectly. As the storm receded, the fleet of helicopters swept in low and put down in the middle of the stadium. The massive complex had been built outside the city limits several decades ago for a celebratory rally. But now the previously well-kept area was overrun with weeds – and a perfect spot for the Fa 233s to land without being seen by anyone in the city itself.

The Limiter General was supervising his men as they escorted the New Germanian prisoners from the helicopters, corralling them down one end of the field where three long, vertical banners stirred in the dying wind. Each of these banners had once proudly displayed the New Germanian national symbol – an eagle against a stark red and black background. However, in the intervening years they had become so sun-bleached and tattered, the eagle and the stark colours had faded almost to nothing.

The prisoners were standing with their hands on their heads, their eyes downcast as they waited for instructions.

'Load of wimps,' Rebecca Two commented.

There hadn't been a single casualty at the pyramid as the

Limiters had taken the whole complement of New Germanian soldiers by surprise and assumed control of their fleet of helicopters. The Rebecca twins had been far from impressed by the soldiers' willingness to lay down their arms and surrender.

'It's a failure of leadership,' Rebecca One agreed, curling her lip disdainfully. 'That's something we can fix.'

'Leadership? You mean the fat bloke who lives in the arch, with his shiny hair and a taste for the good life?' Rebecca Two asked, raising an eyebrow.

Rebecca One tittered snidely. 'Yes, him – the fat Chancellor. Though Coxy seemed to have a soft spot for him.'

'Poor old Coxy. Did we bring his body back with us in the end?' Rebecca Two said.

'We did. Why?'

Rebecca Two was thoughtful for a moment. 'Because I think the first official engagement the fat Chancellor presides over – as our puppet, that is – should be a full state funeral for Cox. You know, a band playing, military honours, and an aircraft fly-by and—'

'Yes, and a statue. A very lifelike and a damned great statue, in that square where the Chancellery is,' Rebecca One proposed, then chuckled. 'And it should be just outside the fat Chancellor's window, where the doofus has to see it every day. Coxy would be amused by that.'

The merriment suddenly left her face and she gave a small hum, as if irritated.

'What is it?' her sister asked.

'It's Will and Elliott. I can't believe we let them slip through our fingers again. It was fun despatching Dr Buckwheat, but we were just getting into our stride when Elliott caved like that, and gave us back our virus. Pity . . . we had

Will right here.' Looking at her hand, she clenched it into a tight little fist. 'We had him right here, and we let him go.'

Rebecca Two smiled sanguinely. 'Don't be disheartened. We achieved the main objective, and there will be time enough, time to mop up the little annoyances later. One needs something to look forward to – that's what makes life worth living.' She stopped speaking as she watched the young blond-haired officer being conducted away from where the other New Germanian troops were being held. He was between two Limiters, a third following close behind with a small case in his arms.

'So the processing begins,' Rebecca One observed.

Her sister nodded in the officer's direction. 'That's the soldier who met us when we first entered the city. He's a good man – he saw sense when I threatened him. He saved your life with his quick thinking.'

'Right,' Rebecca One said in a drawn-out way, a slight smile playing on her lips as she threw a sideways glance at her sister.

'I hope that they're not too rough, and they don't break him,' Rebecca Two said earnestly, still watching as the group headed towards one of the archways set into the banked ramps of seats at the side of the stadium. 'You know, if you don't mind, I think I'd like to sit in on his session . . . make sure they do it properly.'

With a knowing cackle, Rebecca One prodded her sister. 'Don't you come over all serious with me and pretend that this is purely business – you really like him, don't you? You've got a thing for Captain Goldilocks over there.'

'Captain Franz,' her sister said, then regretted it.

'Ha! You even know his name!' Rebecca One cawed, then

dissolved into peals of laughter.

'Don't be silly,' Rebecca Two mumbled, making an embarrassed tutting sound as she began to walk quickly towards where the Limiters were leading the officer.

Due to their increasing weightlessness, Will and Elliott were moving through the Ancients' passage at a rate of knots.

They merely had to kick themselves off and they were literally flying through it. For the greater part the passage was straight, with only gentle curves to negotiate, which they did by fending themselves off the sides. And when they did encounter sharp bends, Will would spot these first with his headset and shout a warning to Elliott to slow down.

It was if they were falling, only sideways, or maybe upside down. Will wasn't quite sure how one classified *up* or *down*, any more.

And it certainly helped that they had both mastered a similar form of spacewalk locomotion during the months they'd spent in Martha's level back at the Pore.

The only hazard along the way was if they ran into a dust cloud or some of the loose debris floating freely in the air. It wasn't a regular occurrence but, nevertheless, it could be a painful one as they hit it at the speeds they were going.

And to keep himself occupied, Will tried to calculate how fast they were actually travelling. He reckoned it might even be as much as fifty kilometres per hour.

'The radius of the Earth . . . six thousand, three hundred kilometres . . . but this tunnel will be shorter . . . because of space the inner world takes up . . . therefore . . . we might have a total distance of . . . oh, I don't know . . . four thousand kilometres to go,' he said out loud, as he thought it through. 'At this speed,' he yelled at Elliott, 'we're going to get there in no time at all!'

'Don't count your lizards 'til they've spawned,' Elliott advised him.

Some time later, Will saw that Bartleby had come to a stop up ahead.

'BRAKES ON!' he yelled at the top of his voice to alert Elliott. He reached out to grab the side of the passage as he tried to slow himself.

But it didn't go according to plan, and he began to spin through the air until he was close enough to the side again to reach it and bring himself to a halt.

He heard Elliott's screech from behind, and shot a hand out to seize hold of her as she rocketed past. He managed to catch her, but her momentum swept him off the side again.

'Didn't you hear me?' he asked as they both finally came to a rest.

'No, I didn't. Shout louder next time, will you?' she snapped back at him.

They were so tired that tempers would occasionally flare, and they'd end up arguing over the smallest thing, but this time they were both distracted by what lay ahead.

Just beyond where Bartleby was performing slow revolutions in the air, there seemed to be something across the passage, blocking it.

Will approached, finding that it wasn't rock, but thick and slightly shiny filaments projecting from the side walls. They weren't that dense, but as far as he could make out they continued for some way along the passage up ahead.

He used the barrel of his Sten gun to probe them. The

filaments were flexible, wavering as he pushed against them.

'I have no idea what this is,' he admitted, yanking on a single filament to snap it off from where it was anchored. It was grey in colour and about seven centimetres in diameter. 'Maybe some type of plant? Dead plant? Or maybe a mineral of some kind, which has formed here due to the low gravity environment?' He whistled through his teeth for a moment as he examined it. 'But whatever it is, it could slow us down,' he said.

'It didn't slow the two Rebeccas down much, did it, when they came this way?' Elliott disagreed. She pushed herself towards the filaments and yanked another strand from the rock, then moved back and took her Bergen off. She proceeded to try to set fire to the filament, calling over to Will as she was successful.

'Yes! It burns really well! Hot food!' she announced.

'Brilliant. I could do with some,' Will replied, taking the tracker out and switching it on. As he pointed it in different directions and it emitted a variety of slow clicking sounds, he was studying the dial on top of the device. 'The signal's weak, but we're still on course,' he said, nodding to himself.

There had been a number of passages branching off from the main route, but these were generally smaller, so there was little confusion about which way they were meant to go. And although he was curious to find out where the side passages led, Will knew that their priority was to finish the journey before their supplies of food and water ran out. There was the other consideration that the Styx might not be far behind in the tunnel as they raced back to the surface to use the Dominion virus there. Will didn't much like the idea of bumping into them, and it made it all the more imperative he get

Elliott Topsoil as soon as he could.

As Bartleby floated past him on his way over to Elliott, a trail of sparkling beads of saliva spilling from his open mouth, Will caught the smell of meat cooking.

'God, I am starved. Don't let that cat get mine,' he said, putting the tracker away again.

A day later, Will began to notice tiny flickers of light. At first he thought his headset was malfunctioning, but as he flipped the lens up and slowed, he saw that small blue sparks were creeping along the top of his Sten.

Elliott had pulled up beside him. As her rifle came close to his Sten, a thin blue spark leapt between the barrels.

'What's that?' she exclaimed.

'Turn your lantern off,' he told her.

She took her Styx lantern from where it was clipped to the shoulder strap of her Bergen and extinguished the light.

Any object on them made of metal, including the Styx lantern itself, had eerie blue waves of light creeping over it.

'I think it's some kind of electrical charge. Might be static?' Will said. 'And can you hear that?'

In the darkness, they listened. There was definitely a low rumble, a vibration filling the passage.

'Yes, I hear it,' Elliott said, as she switched her lantern back to its lowest setting.

'I wonder . . .'

'What?' she asked as Will stared into middle distance, frowning.

'No, I was just thinking – I wonder if, right now, we're level with the crystal belt. This build up of electricity might have something to do with the triboluminescence – those huge flashing crystals we went past before on our way to the inner world,' he suggested. 'So where we are now, we could be right next to the void.' He glanced at the rock of the passage wall. 'Maybe it's through there somewhere.'

'So you're saying we could be halfway across?' she asked.

'Could be,' he replied.

PART FOUR

On the Offensive

Chapter Twenty-six

There were two sets of equipment spread out on the floor, and Drake was carefully checking off each item from a list as Eddie watched him.

'We'll both be carrying fifteen of these,' Drake said, pointing with his pen at some silver canisters, each the size of a small thermos flask. 'They contain pesticide at incredibly high pressure, and at incredibly high concentration,' he explained. 'We'll plant them at regular intervals in the margins around the Eternal City, with radio-detonated charges strapped to them. As they go off, the pesticide will be released in aerosol form, and the convection currents will ensure that full dispersal takes place. By my calculations, the whole area should receive blanket coverage in sufficient strength to do the job.'

'Pesticide bombs,' Eddie reflected.

'Precisely,' Drake said. 'No more snails . . . so no more nasty little viruses for the Scientists to cherry-pick.'

Chester slouched into the room, his shirt hanging out on one side of his jeans as if he'd got dressed in a hurry. Drake glanced up at him, but went on without a pause, nudging a bulky coil of rope with his foot. 'Eddie, you said we should bring this – there's probably more here than we'll need, but I've erred on the side of caution.' Then Drake indicated a pair of small black boxes, leaning forward to lift up the wires trailing from the closest one with his pen. 'Throat mikes. We'll keep in constant touch throughout the op with these – they're current issue Specfors kit.'

'Specfors?' Eddie enquired.

'Special Forces,' Chester chimed in.

Both Drake and Eddie looked at him, somewhat surprised that he knew this. He inclined his head towards his bedroom. 'From the PlayStation game I was on this morning,' he grunted.

'Right,' Drake said, as he resumed. 'Anyway, these units are far less cumbersome and more reliable than conventional headsets.'

'And those?' Eddie asked, indicating the two piles of folded green uniforms. On top of each Drake had laid a gas mask. 'I already have my Limiter respirator and fatigues.'

'These are better – they're the latest issue NBC kit,' Drake answered.

'Ah, that's one I don't know,' Chester piped up.

'It stands for *Nuclear, Biological and Chemical*, but the military refer to them as Noddy suits,' Drake said, with a brief smile. 'And they're essential down there in the Eternal City – you know what happened to Will when he passed through the city the first time without a respirator?'

'He and Cal only just managed to avoid being chewed to death by a stalker?' Chester said sourly. 'Or do you mean he was nearly grabbed by those killers from the Division?'

Drake fixed him with a stare to let him know he was overstepping the mark.

'Yeah . . . I know – he was pretty ill,' Chester finally said.

'There are some thoroughly unpleasant pathogens knocking around down there, which is the point of this whole exercise,' Drake said, now shifting his gaze back to the gas masks. 'And, to be frank, if you're wearing one of these Noddy suits and we're spotted, then you're less likely to be recognised by your old oppos. On that topic . . .' Drake indicated the pairs of pistols and rifles. 'These fire tranquiliser darts in case we bump into anyone from the Division once we're inside. The dose in the darts is enough to put a man out for a good fifteen hours.' Drake glanced up at Eddie. 'So no lethalities, just as we agreed. The worst that will happen is your former buddies wake up with a blinder of a headache.'

'Thank you,' Eddie said.

'I don't get it, Drake,' Chester snapped, his head lowered as he glowered at Eddie. 'Just because you're working with a Styx, you're prepared to let the rest of them off the hook?'

'Now just a second,' Drake objected.

'No, let him say his piece,' Eddie put in calmly, his normal implacable self. 'I can see he needs to get something off his chest.'

Chester was red in the face as he went on. '*They* wouldn't think twice about killing any of us – or my parents for that matter – if it came to it, but you're happy to let them off the hook because you've thrown your lot in with your new best mate.' He flicked a glance at one of the dart guns on the floor. 'You should be using real bullets, not these kids' toys.'

Eddie nodded. 'I don't know what I can say that will change the way you feel, not after what you've been through,' he said.

'Yes, what can you say?' Chester scowled.

Eddie walked to the wall of windows and looked down at the view of the Thames, and then across to the buildings on the opposite bank. 'But what I will say to you is that this world you've built yourselves is doomed. It's not sustainable. You strive for growth at any cost – more technology, more people, more freedom, and all the time you're strangling the planet, the basis for all life.'

'But we're doing things to save the—' Chester began to object.

'Save the environment?' Eddie rebuffed him, then laughed loudly. Both Chester and Drake were taken aback at this – neither had heard him as much as chuckle before. 'Your politicians are weak, and have neither the will nor the power to make the changes in time, because the people themselves are weak and won't forgo their luxuries. But my people, the Styx, would take immediate and complete control of industry to slash pollution levels, and also implement a feudal system so that every member of this nation knows precisely where he or she stands.'

Chester frowned. 'A feudal system?'

'Yes, just as there was in the past. Everyone would work for the common good, and there would be no unemployment, because those who refuse work would be consigned to ghettoes, and be excluded. We will change everything. We will save everything. We will save you from yourselves.'

Chester was completely thrown by all this, glancing at Drake, who said nothing. 'But that's rubbish. If you really want to *save* people, why do you go round *killing* them all the time?'

'Because it's the only way we can achieve our aims. I grant you that using the Dominion virus is not the right approach, which is why I'm here, but remember . . .' Eddie turned to Chester and locked eyes with him, 'we have to share this world with you, so you're defiling our home too. Why should we just stand by and let you do that? If we're forced to take a few lives along the way in order to rescue this planet from a foul, lingering death, wouldn't you say we were just acting in self-defence?'

Chester shook his head emphatically. 'No, what you're saying is crazy. It's twisted. Everything will be okay without all this stuff you're suggesting. Nobody has to *die*.'

Eddie swept his hand at the vista through the windows. 'You won't be telling me that in twenty years' time when the sea levels have risen, and all this is under thirty metres of water. When the food riots start, and you have to kill for your next meal.'

'Drake, tell him he's wrong,' Chester implored.

'You started it,' Drake replied.

Eddie left the window and went over to his battle scene, taking something from the corner of the table. 'Chester, I bought you these films to watch.' He glanced at the upper-most DVD. 'This looks like an interesting one – it's all about these giant robots that come to Earth from outer space and have to battle its population in order to save it . . . to avert an ecological disaster.'

Chester had no idea how to react to this, simply going over to Eddie to take the films from him. 'Er . . . great . . . thanks,' he mumbled. He turned to Drake, looking more than a little sheepish. 'This operation . . . are you sure you don't want me along with you? I could act as lookout? Or I could just help carry some of the kit?'

'No need, Chester – we've got it covered,' Drake replied.

'Two of us will be enough – we're just going to slip in and get the job done – shouldn't take more than a couple of hours once we're on the ground.'

'S'pose I'll go and watch my films then,' Chester said, as he shuffled out of the room.

⚬━━◦☠◦━━⚬

'Hallelujah!' Eliza shouted as she heard the clack of horses' hooves on the cobbled road outside. She ran to the window to peer out. 'Yes, they're here!' she confirmed with another exultant shout as the cart drew up outside.

'The day we've been hopin' and prayin' for 'as finally arrived,' her mother proclaimed as she tore out of the kitchen, drying her hands on her pinafore.

A thickset Colonist in a grey smock coat jumped down from beside the driver, the cart rocking as it was relieved of his not insignificant bulk. In a workaday manner, he began to trundle towards the house. After a few paces he stopped abruptly, swearing as if he'd forgotten something, then swung around to the cart again.

Eliza was still watching through the window. 'No . . . what is it now? Don't go back! Can't we just get this over with?' she urged, as he went to the rear of the cart. Leaning over the side, he retrieved a clipboard, then resumed his lumbering walk towards the house. He had raised his meaty, club-like hand, and was about to rap on the door when Eliza whisked it open.

'Oh,' he said. Eliza couldn't help but stare at the man's eyebrows – they were so full and white and bushy they reminded her of the blight of giant penny-white caterpillars the rural areas of the North Cavern had suffered a few years ago. Surprised at how promptly the door had been opened, the man's

348

eyebrows now seemed to be moving independently of each other, and it was all Eliza could do to fight the temptation to swat them.

'G'd morning,' he mumbled, his hand still poised in the air. He slowly lowered it, and the twin caterpillars ended their act of levitation as they settled on the ridge of his brow. Then he squinted at the printed papers on the clipboard. 'Is this the residence of the Second Officer?' he enquired.

'It is,' Eliza answered eagerly. 'But he's not here. He's at work.'

'No matter. I can serve this notice anyway,' the man said and, clearing his throat, began to read. 'Under Order 366, Edict 23, for the furtherance of the Scientists' knowledge, you are hereby required to provide—'

The Second Officer's mother poked her head out from behind her daughter. 'You've come for the Topsoiler,' she cut him short.

'Er . . . I have,' the man confirmed.

'Then don't bother with all that offissal 'ogwash. She's in 'ere,' the old lady said. Although her aged body was small and shrunken, she pulled hard on the man's arm, tugging him into the sitting room where Mrs Burrows was in her bath chair. 'Just get rid of 'er.'

'This is the person?' he enquired.

'She's not a person, she's a Topsoiler. Now, please, just get her out of here,' Eliza said impatiently. 'But leave the bath chair because it's not ours and we have to give it back.'

Placing his papers on the sideboard, the man rolled up the sleeves of his smock. He made clicking noises with his tongue as he looked Mrs Burrows over, trying to work out how much she weighed, as if she was a piece of unwieldy furniture.

However, the oversized dress that swamped her slim frame made it rather difficult for him to make an assessment. With a last click of his tongue, he stepped closer to her, tentatively lifting her arm in the billowing sleeve of her dress.

'And we want to keep the clothes, undergarments and all,' Eliza informed him.

Aghast at the suggestion, the man turned to her, one of his caterpillars almost doing a handstand on his sloped forehead. 'What do you expect me to do – take them off her? I can't do that – wouldn't be decent.'

'No, not *now*,' Eliza laughed. 'My brother can pick them up later.'

Relieved, the man continued his assessment of Mrs Burrows. 'She doesn't walk?'

'No,' Eliza laughed bitterly. 'She's deader than a slug in a pint of New London – where she is now, there's no coming back. So just take her out and throw her on your cart!'

With a nod the man wrapped his arms around Mrs Burrows' waist and hoisted her limp body from the chair.

There was a threatening growl from the corner of the room and Colly reared up at the man, baring her sharp teeth.

As the man swung Mrs Burrows' body round to shield himself from the cat, the Second Officer's mother was flabbergasted. 'Colly – what *is* wrong with you?'

'Is she on heat or something?' the man said, looking decidedly worried.

'To your basket! Now!' the old lady scolded the cat.

Under her loose skin, Colly's muscles were bunched like knotted ropes as she made ready to pounce at the man.

'Colly!' Eliza shouted, raising her hand to cuff the animal. Still she showed no intention whatsoever of backing off, so

Eliza seized hold of her by the scruff of the neck and began to drag her into the hall. The cat's extended claws snagged a threadbare Persian carpet on the floor so that it came out of the room with her. But Eliza eventually managed to get the hissing animal into the kitchen where she shut her in.

'I don't know what come over that 'unter,' the Second Officer's mother apologised. 'She's normally good as gold, and never that way, not with no one.'

'No matter,' the man said, hurriedly slinging Mrs Burrows over his shoulder as if she was a sack of potatoes, and heading for the door. He stopped with a muttered curse. 'Nearly forgot again – pass me my papers, will you?'

The old woman tucked the clipboard under his arm and he continued on his way.

Eliza and her mother went to the door to watch as the man deposited Mrs Burrows in the back of the cart. And, all the time, there was frantic scratching, interspersed with low, baleful wails from the kitchen.

'What *'as* got into that animal?' the old lady said. 'I don't understand it.'

'Maybe she feels the same way about the Topsoiler as my dear misguided brother?' Eliza replied maliciously. 'He's going to be heartbroken that he didn't have a chance to say a final farewell to his darling basket case. And in no time at all the Scientists will be opening her head like a cess oyster.'

'Cess oyster?' the old lady repeated, not catching on.

'Yes – you know – CRACK!' Eliza said, moving her hands as if she was using a hammer and chisel, which was the only way to prise one of those hardy crustaceans open.

She and her mother could hardly stand as they descended into howls of hysterical laughter. The noise they were making prompted the neighbours across the street to come to their windows to see what all the merriment was about.

'CRACK! CRACK! CRACK!' Eliza shrieked, tears in her eyes.

Chapter Twenty-seven

As the clicks came fast and strong from the tracker, Will and Elliott stopped by a side passage. She looked at him questioningly, and in response he gave her a broad smile.

'Through here – somewhere – is the submarine,' he said. 'I planted a beacon on the conning tower.' His face lit up as something occurred to him. 'Want to take a look at it? At the submarine? We could find out how the Rebecca twins managed to get into this pass—'

'I absolutely DO NOT,' she snapped, her voice rising into a shout.

'Oh, all right,' he said meekly.

Elliott's eyes were hard and uncompromising as she stared at him. 'Come on, Will – what if one of us slips and we get stranded in the middle of nowhere again, floating around like last time?'

Will was about to say that if this happened they could use his father's method of firing a weapon to propel them back to the side again, but thought better of it. 'Let's just keep going, then,' he murmured.

As the gravity began to return, their jumps along the

passage became shorter and shorter, until they were covering the distance far more slowly than before.

Then they came to a place where the rock had fractured and shifted, and had no choice but to worm through a tiny crawlspace before they could continue on their way again. And shortly after this, they found a seam had opened up and split the rock all around the passage. There was nothing but a yawning, dark chasm. Although it was approximately thirty metres from side to side, they still managed to jump across the gap and resume their journey.

'There are more signs of tectonic movement in this area,' Will had said to Elliott. He didn't say any more, wondering if it had occurred to her that they might hit a dead end. If he was right and they'd passed beyond the Russian submarine, then the Rebecca twins hadn't been down this stretch of tunnel. And in all likelihood, somewhere up ahead, the flexing of the Earth's crust over the centuries could have been so extreme that the passage was blocked altogether.

Many hours later, the gravity had become even more pronounced and they were forced to walk along in bounding steps. Sometimes they even had to heave themselves up sections of the passage, which was turning through a series of alternating bends.

'Oh, no,' Will exhaled as they went around one of these bends.

They'd come to what he'd been dreading.

The way ahead was completely blocked by a cave-in.

He took out the tracker and checked the signal emanating from the next beacon. 'It's so close,' he said.

'And I'm so tired,' Elliott whispered. She slumped down

into a sitting position, her head bowed, as Bartleby settled beside her, panting hard.

'But the signal,' Will began.

'Don't tell me. I don't want to know,' she murmured, then closed her eyes.

'Elliott,' Will said, but there was no reaction. She was fast asleep.

Weighing up the options, Will stumbled over to inspect the plug of debris in the passage. They could try to find a way around it by taking one of the smaller offshoots, but as far as he could remember they'd passed the last of these some kilometres back. And even if it did prove to be an alternative route, the prospect of retracing their footsteps now they were so close was just the last straw.

Or they could try to dig their way through, although it was impossible to tell how much rock was in the way.

'Re-excavate,' Will muttered to himself, making up his mind to see how far he could get. He glanced again at Elliott as she slept. He didn't want to wake her. Slipping his Bergen off and rolling up his sleeves, he began to move the rocks, lifting them aside one by one. At least the reduced gravity meant that he could shift even the largest slabs, something which would be unthinkable on the surface.

After several hours, Will was soaked in sweat and still hadn't made it through. He was so weary, his legs were like jelly. Flopping down, he closed his eyes and experienced the sensation that he was falling through the ground, a sensation he knew came of chronic fatigue. 'Stop for a few minutes,' he said to himself, 'then get going again.'

'This is one of those life or death moments. Stay there, and you might never get up again,' a rumbling voice announced.

'You and Elliott haven't been sleeping or eating enough. Neither of you are in great shape. You might not have the strength when you finally come to again.'

'Shut up, Tam,' Will whispered, catching the outline of someone sitting beside him as he fought to keep his eyes open. 'Not real . . . I know . . . you're . . . not . . . real.'

'I'm as real as you want me to be,' Uncle Tam replied with a measure of indignation, then blew out a mouthful of pipe smoke. It drifted into Will's face, and he coughed.

'That really stinks,' Will mumbled. 'And it's bad for you.'

Uncle Tam's response was to blow another cloud at the boy. 'I'm dead, Will. It's hardly going to do me any harm now,' he chuckled. 'And if you lie down on the job now, you'll be joining me soon. Don't just jack it in, Will. Too many Topsoilers are depending on you.'

Something occurred to Will, which suddenly made him extremely annoyed. 'Hey, yes! That pendant you gave me was a bloody joke. It didn't help at all – the Bushmen . . .'

As Will sat bolt upright, he thought he could hear the faint echo of laughter, but there was no sign of the big man. However, he was wide awake now, and Tam's words stuck with him.

Too many Topsoilers are depending on you.

'Oh, come on then,' Will urged himself as he got to his knees, and then clambered to his feet. He renewed his attack on the cave-in, whistling to himself and sometimes counting each rock he extracted until he reached a hundred, then starting over again.

An hour later, he was really beginning to flag as he prised a large slab loose and it set off a small avalanche. He jumped back, not wanting to be caught as the stones rolled towards him. Then, as he crept back to where he'd been working, he found that there hadn't been an avalanche at all. Instead he saw an opening there. 'I'm dreaming, aren't I?' he said to it. 'You're not real – just like Tam.'

But as he stretched his hand into the opening and spread his raw and dirty fingers, there wasn't anything there. And his headset allowed him to see that there was a bigger space on the other side.

'YES! Result!' he exclaimed, punching the air.

He crawled through the opening, careful not to disturb the rocks around him, then clambered out onto a level passage. It was coated in fungus. As he knelt down to touch it, it took him back to the weeks they'd spent with Martha – there was little doubt in his mind it was the same type of fungus that grew on her level, but could he be that close to the surface again?

He took the tracker from his pocket and found that the signal was strong. Very strong.

He knew he should really go back and tell Elliott what he was intending to do, but he didn't, instead following the source of the signal. It wasn't sensible – he didn't have his Sten or Bergen with him – but at that moment he was determined to keep going and find out where they were.

A gust blew, chilling the sweat on his brow.

Then, before him was a place he recognised.

And a tall boulder he knew only too well. He went up to it, locating the face with the three-pronged symbol carved into it.

Moving beyond the boulder, he stepped to the edge of the ledge, where he peered into the gargantuan pore he'd named Smoking Jean. Water fell in showers and the wind was strong.

He was standing on the precise spot from which his father

had made his leap. And both Will and Elliott had done the same, as they'd followed him.

'Dad,' Will said, remembering.

Dr Burrows had been right to jump – as he'd told Will at the time, one had to have faith in one's convictions. And as a result, he'd made the discovery to beat all discoveries, another world at the centre of the Earth.

But what had been his reward?

To be murdered in cold blood by a pair of insane girls, who had once masqueraded as his daughter.

Will's anger boiled up, finding no outlet but tears.

Blinking them away, he peered up towards the top of the pore.

As he caught a flash of something white moving in the far distance, his anger evaporated and he immediately pulled back from the opening. He'd totally forgotten about the Brights. This was their lair.

'Oh, Jesus!' he said, realising he didn't have a weapon with him, or any of the cans of the aerosol that Drake had provided.

He began to retrace his footsteps, at first managing to remain calm as he went, then breaking into a trot. He didn't want to have come all this way just to be picked off by a Bright.

As he wormed back through the opening and re-entered the passage where he'd left Elliott, she was still fast asleep, with Bartleby curled up by her feet.

Will was completely and utterly exhausted. He slumped to the ground beside Elliott and gave her a nudge.

'Wha . . .?' she said eventually.

'Found Smoking Jean,' he yawned, barely able to string a

sentence together. 'And the boulder . . . the place we jumped . . .'

'What?' she replied groggily, then jerked her head up. 'How?'

'Tam was here . . . I . . . cleared a way through . . .' Will said.

'Tam?' Elliott asked, her eyes now wide open. 'But if you've got through to Smoking Jean . . . then you've done it! You bloody hero! You've done it! Let's get moving!'

'Yes . . . but . . . Brights,' he mumbled. 'Spray . . . us . . . with . . . the . . . ca—'

He never finished as he rested his head on the hard rock, and was instantly asleep.

As he waited for Eddie to get ready, Drake happened to glance at the battle scene on the table. He walked over to it, trying to work out what was different. 'The layout's changed. This must be later on, when Napoleon's forces were being routed?'

'Yes, it's the final day of the engagement,' Eddie replied.

Drake frowned. 'But Wellington's skipped off again. Where's he gone?'

'He's back on my desk. I'm still not satisfied with him,' Eddie said, hiking his Bergen onto one shoulder.

'He looked pretty damn good to me,' Drake shrugged. 'Right, time to hit the road.' He went to the doorway that led through to the bedrooms and called softly. 'Chester, we're off. We'll be back later in the morning.' He waited for a response, but none came. 'Typical teenager – he'll be sleeping the sleep of the dead. I won't disturb him,' Drake said to Eddie, as he turned away from the doorway, and then they made their way out of the flat.

The last thing they needed was to be flagged down by an over-zealous policeman, so they took the journey at a much more sedate pace than the last time. In any case, their heavily-laden Bergens didn't make riding their motorbikes the easiest of tasks.

They parked in the same place in St Anne's Street. 'Onwards and downwards,' Drake said, as he collected a rifle case from the back of his bike. Then they walked the short distance to the alleyway that would take them through to Dean's Yard. They were identically dressed in Noddy suits, with thick hooded jackets and trousers of a matching colour. This, combined with the climbing rope and the other equipment they were carrying, gave them more than a passing resemblance to a pair of mountaineers setting out on a new challenge. Not exactly what you'd expect to see on the approach to Westminster Abbey at any time of day, let alone at that hour in the morning.

Not surprisingly, the porter burst into action the moment he laid eyes on them. 'Stop right there!' he ordered, hurrying straight for them with his palms raised. He was just about to grab hold of Eddie when the Styx repeated his trick. As he uttered the trigger words, the porter's face went blank, all concern erased from it. Then the hefty man simply swung round on his heels and, tucking his hands into his pockets, wandered nonchalantly back into the empty square.

'Good thing old Frankie was on duty again tonight,' Drake whispered, putting his pistol away as he watched the transformed porter.

Making their way through to the small trap door, Drake and Eddie readied themselves for the long trek down to the forgotten city far below London. As they negotiated the numerous flights of brick steps and jogged along kilometre after kilometre of the straight passageways, neither of them spoke, their boots drumming a regular tattoo on the damp flagstones.

When they came to the start of a circular stairway, its treads running with water and treacherously slippery, they broke off to carry out the usual routines any soldier would before going into the field. They checked each other for 'flashing' – anything reflective that might give them away if it caught the light – and then they jumped up and down several times on the spot as they did the similar 'rattle test', to ensure their Bergens and belt kits were packed properly.

Drake extracted the two rifles from the case he'd been carrying, handing one to Eddie. As with their pistols, these weapons only fired tranquiliser darts, and Drake had fitted night scopes to both of them. Last of all, they donned their gas masks and turned on their throat mikes.

'Once more unto the breach, dear friend, once more,' Drake said, speaking in a whisper as he tested the radio link.

Eddie turned to him, his dark pupils barely visible through the eyepieces of his mask. 'Yes, receiving you loud and clear,' he acknowledged.

Contrary to what Drake had said, Chester hadn't slept a wink. And the instant Drake and Eddie left the flat, he emerged into the main room and went over to the bank of CCTV monitors. He watched as the two of them wheeled their motorbikes out onto the street, then mounted them and took off into the night.

'Right . . . things to do,' he said to himself, as he sat on the sofa with the mobile phone Drake had given him. His hands were shaking with excitement as he called the number in the memory. His father answered on the first ring.

'Chester – thank God!' Mr Rawls blurted.

Chester sat bolt upright – it was obvious something was wrong. 'Dad, what is it? Drake told you to expect my call, didn't—'

'Yes, yes,' his father babbled. 'But your mother – she's gone.'

'What do you mean *gone*?' Chester said. 'Gone from the room?'

'Worse than that – gone from the hotel.'

'Are you sure?' Chester pressed him.

'Yes, I've been down to the lobby to check. I know Drake told us not to step outside the room for anything, but I had to . . . I spoke to the concierge, and he said he saw Emily leave the hotel, via the main entrance. She just walked straight out.'

'But why would Mum do that?' Chester asked. 'She knew how important it was that she stay hidden.'

'Yes, of course, we both did. But she was acting strangely yesterday – she wasn't herself at all. Then after Drake dropped by in the afternoon, she seemed to accept that he had to speak to me in private . . . and that I couldn't tell her what it was about . . . it was on a . . . you know . . . how does Drake put it?'

'It was on a *need to know* basis,' Chester helped him. 'Don't worry – Drake does the same with me – it's in case the Styx get hold of you and make—'

'Last night she went very quiet again,' Mr Rawls inter-rupted. 'It was as if something was on her mind, something was troubling her. And when I got up an hour ago, I only turned my back on her for a second and she'd gone.'

'Oh, no,' Chester whispered.

There was a moment of silence as neither of them spoke.

'Dad, you can't stay there,' Chester said decisively. 'You've got the keys for the car Drake gave you – go to it right now and meet me where he said. Don't stop for anything.'

'But . . . I can't leave . . . not without knowing where Emily is,' Mr Rawls disagreed, his voice trembling. 'What can we do?'

'Nothing, Dad. There's nothing we can do. Either she's just miffed about something and she'll come back when feels like it, or . . .' Chester couldn't finish what he'd been about to say, the words dying on his tongue. 'Just get out of there and do what Drake told you – meet me at the RV.'

Mr Rawls followed his instructions and, half an hour later, pulled up several blocks away from the warehouse in the old estate car Drake had recently bought. Mr Rawls' face was grim but he still managed a weak smile as he spotted his son waiting for him.

'So what's the plan?' he asked as soon as Chester slid into the passenger seat.

'Same as it was. It hasn't changed. We have to do exactly what Drake told us,' Chester replied.

Mr Rawls opened his mouth to object, then closed it, shaking his head as if all this was more than he could handle.

'But, actually, there is one thing,' Chester realised. 'You can't go anywhere near the hotel after you've dropped me off.'

'No, I . . . I . . . what if Emily comes back?' Mr Rawls replied. He really was flustered now.

'Listen, Dad, if everything's fine, then she'll wait for you. But if something's wrong and the Styx have got control of her again, that's the last place you want to be.' Chester was trying to sound as composed as he could, when just below the surface he was in as much turmoil as his father.

But Chester also knew, when it came down to it, Drake was the only person who could help, and there was absolutely no way he was going to fail him now. 'We should go. Take a right here so I can show you the warehouse. Later on, when we're finished, you have to come back to the flat and stay there, where you'll be safe. You'll need these,' Chester said, passing the keys to his father.

'We could sell tickets for this one, we could,' one of the Scientists commented to the other, as they stood either side of the inspection table on which Mrs Burrows had been laid. Both men wore the regulation scarlet lab coats edged with black piping, and on their breast pockets were numbers, the means by which they referred to each another.

One-Six-Four, the Scientist who'd been speaking, was a stooped man with a long, pink face and a lugubrious manner. 'This Topsoiler's a minor miracle. She was roasted good and proper under a whole bank of Dark Lights, and yet here she is, heart still beating . . . still drawing breath . . . quite remarkable.'

He adjusted his glasses and regarded his colleague over Mrs Burrows' body. Two-Three-Eight, his junior by some twenty years, was a shorter man with a much livelier disposition. Whenever he spoke, it was in rapid bursts, as if he was articulating his thoughts the moment they occurred to him. And he was, by all accounts, a rising star in the Laboratories.

'Surprising,' Two-Three-Eight agreed, as he scrutinised Mrs Burrows with his small eyes, eyes which missed little.

Mrs Burrows' clothes had been removed and a grey sheet draped over her. Two-Three-Eight leant forward to examine her arm, then moved down to her calf, humming frenetically as he poked and kneaded her with his stubby fingers, so roughly he left red marks on her skin.

'For someone who has been cataleptic as long as is claimed, the subject exhibits minimal wasting of the muscular tissue. I would have expected a far greater degree of muscular atrophy consistent with her current state would you not agree?' Two-Three-Eight burst forth in one, unbroken stream. As he drew breath, he glanced up at One-Six-Four, wrinkling his piggy nose distastefully, as if he didn't like what he was seeing. 'The Colonists who took her in have they been subjecting her to any form of manipulation or treatment because I would have said that some kind of physiotherapy must have been administered in order for her to be in this condition?'

One-Six-Four took a step back, wondering if the verbal volley from the other man had come to an end, or if more was on the way. Two-Three-Eight was now humming to himself again, and the older man took that as a sign that he'd said all he had to say, for the time being. 'I very much doubt that,' One-Six-Four responded ponderously. 'After all . . . they're just Colonists . . . a policeman from the Quarter and his family . . . what would they know of such things?'

'Too true, too true,' Two-Three-Eight conceded so quickly it sounded as if he was sneezing. 'The explanation could be perhaps that she was on peak physical form when the Styx brought her in and so the degradation is less marked than it would be for a normal subject.'

One-Six-Four rubbed his forehead as if he was developing a headache. 'Desist! All this conjecture is a waste of my time,' he rebuffed Two-Three-Eight, growing weary of the other man, who was forgetting his position. It wasn't Two-Three-Eight's place to speculate on such matters – he had years before his apprenticeship would be served. 'As you know we're cutting open her cranium in the morning . . . to undertake a multiple-section investigation of her cerebral tissues. It will be intriguing to see which areas of her brain were destroyed or disrupted by that intensity of Dark Light exposure.'

'I'll put my money on the rear lobes being porridge,' Two-Three-Eight chirped up. 'Once we make the first incision there'll be slop dribbling out all over the examination table so some sort of capture tray may be necessary as we don't want to be treading the neural matter all over the floor or losing it down the drain before it can be fully analysed.'

That was it. Two-Three-Eight really had overstepped the mark this time – neural physiology and the application of interrogation technology was One-Six-Four's specialist area, and he didn't like some fast-talking young whippersnapper attempting to usurp his authority. Particularly if he might be right.

'Enough . . . prepare her for dissection,' One-Six-Four ordered coldly. 'Shave her scalp and hook her up to a drip. I don't want her popping her clogs before tomorrow – I like to dissect my subjects while they're still fresh and the heart's still pumping.'

Chastened, Two-Three-Eight nodded in a suitably sub-servient manner, then beetled over to the instrument cabinets that lined the wall. He didn't much care for the way One-Six-

Four lorded it over him, but he was prepared to bide his time. One day it would be different. He would have his own specialist area, his own apprentices to bully, and his own bodies to hack up.

Mrs Burrows was perfectly aware where she was. She'd emerged just sufficiently from the dark refuge inside her brain so she could listen to the exchange between the two Scientists. Although she had no way of knowing what they looked like, for some reason she'd pictured a pair of Dr Burrowses standing there and discussing her, as if she was nothing more than a piece of meat they were about to carve up. These academic-types were so engrossed in their subject, they reminded her a little too much of her husband, with his all-consuming, selfish passion for his blessed archaeology.

She felt Two-Three-Eight's rough handling of her head as he sliced randomly at her hair with a pair of scissors. Then he threw a bowl of water over her scalp, slapped on some soap, and began to scrape a cut-throat razor across it. Another ignominy – losing all her hair – but she wasn't going to do anything yet. Not quite yet.

Drake tore down the spiral steps on Eddie's heels. He was sweating so heavily beneath the thick Noddy suit that his eye-pieces kept fogging up. And the fact that his breathing was restricted by the gas mask didn't help matters much, either. So when the Styx stopped without any warning, Drake nearly collided with him.

'What is it?' he asked over the radio link, straining to see what lay ahead.

'Have a look for yourself,' Eddie replied, parting some dark skeins of vegetation. It could have been ivy, except for the fact that the numerous lobate leaves on each stem were glowing with an eerie greenness. 'I give you the former kingdom of the Bruteans,' the Styx announced. 'The most feared race in the whole of Eurasia in the twelfth century BC.'

Drake came alongside him, pushing more of the vegetation aside as he regulated his breathing so his eyepieces would clear.

'Holy God!' he exclaimed, as he appreciated just where he and Eddie were poised.

They were peering out of an opening in a sheer-sided cavern wall, around a hundred metres above ground level. At first glance, it was difficult to come to terms with the immense scale of the cavern. For Drake, it was similar to looking across London from one of its tallest buildings at dusk or dawn on a hazy summer's day. As he leant out a little more, he could see the unimaginably large and twisted buttresses of rock that speared up from the ground and extended to the canopy above, like drunken pillars.

The vegetation, which he had to keep pushing aside as it settled back and blocked his view, was everywhere. Not only did it cover the cavern walls, but it was also encroaching on the mud flats surrounding the city. Everywhere too it was emitting its soft luminous glow, the overall intensity such that he realised he'd have no real need for the torches he'd brought with him.

And in the middle of this colossal halo of light, the dark mass of the Eternal City itself rose up. Drake used other routes to get in and out of the Colony, and had never needed to investigate any new ones that would have taken him through this deserted city. So, until this moment, he'd never seen it for himself. And although Will had told him about it in great detail, from what he was glimpsing even at this distance, it almost defied description.

Eager to see more, he took up his rifle and used the scope to pan around the city, spotting fantastically imposing buildings wherever he looked. 'Mind-blowing,' he whispered. Everywhere he turned he saw gargantuan temples with colonnades, and buildings with towers like something out of a fairy tale – but one that would scare the living daylights out of any child. He saw ranks of statues, and also rivers that wound their way through the city like lazy black serpents. And between the buildings were broad avenues, which was precisely where Eddie was focusing his attention as he too used his rifle.

'I can't see any Division foot patrols, but it doesn't mean they aren't there,' he said. 'They're mostly routine, to check for breaches in the border, but every so often they —'

'They escort parties of Scientists on their specimen-gathering outings,' Drake finished for him, recalling what Eddie had said before. 'There was a rumour flying round the Colony that your lot were planning to relocate everybody here,' he added. 'It seemed to have some credence, but was there any truth to it?'

'The Panoply has never completely dismissed the idea – it's one option if the Discovery were to happen.'

'You mean the fateful day when the Colony gets rumbled by Topsoilers?' Drake asked.

Eddie nodded. 'It's bound to happen sooner or later. But the reality is that the Colony doesn't have the manpower to make this cavern habitable.' He lowered his rifle and peered at the roof, several thousand metres above them. 'The canopy up there is formed from a plug of exceptionally dense granite, which is why your Topsoil geologists have never detected this cavity. It also means that a major seismic movement might one day cause the plug to fracture and collapse, which would be disastrous for both the Eternal City . . . and for Topsoil London above.'

'Doesn't bear thinking about,' Drake agreed, as he glanced down and noticed a thick hoop of rust-scarred metal set into the stone by his foot. Although it was almost completely covered in the glowing foliage, he could see that there was a heavy chain attached to the hoop, which extended over the lip of the opening and down the cavern wall below them. He knelt to tug on the chain, but wasn't able to move it the slightest degree, his gloved hand slipping from the substantial links.

'The chain isn't serviceable, which is why we brought this,' Eddie said. He took the coiled rope from his shoulder and then tied one end to the iron hoop. He threw the rest out of the opening. 'I'll go first,' he said, as he prepared to abseil down.

Drake waited until he couldn't feel any tension on the rope and then followed after Eddie. As soon as he touched the bottom, Drake became aware of the drizzle falling from above. It was by no means constant, occasional gusts of wind sweeping the light showers this way and that. As he took a moment to get his bearings, he made out rectangular structures on the ground all around him, swathed in the glowing vegetation and another darker, non-luminous weed. He went over to one of the structures that wasn't completely engulfed by the foliage. It was raised from the ground by four stone legs, and the object itself was approximately the size of a phone box, but one that had been tipped over. As he ran a hand over the matt surface of its longest side, he thought he could make out a dim light coming from or through it.

Eddie's voice crackled in his earpiece. 'Mica panel,' it said.

Drake heard a squelch beside him, and Eddie appeared from nowhere as he stepped into his field of view. Drake was so startled that he instinctively whipped his rifle up.

'Easy,' Eddie said.

'Sorry,' Drake replied. 'But if you will sneak up on me . . .'

'I didn't,' Eddie countered.

Drake realised then that Eddie probably hadn't meant to take him unawares; the Styx was in his element here – he'd been trained to operate in environments such as this, and stealth was second nature to him. 'You said something about mica,' Drake asked him.

'Yes, it's a translucent mineral,' Eddie answered. 'These are graves – the Bruteans laid their dead warriors to rest behind the closest thing they had to glass, possibly so their grieving relatives could come and watch the bodies decay.'

'Novel idea . . . like *Death TV*,' Drake said, looking around at the graves which, as he thought about them, resembled a bunch of widescreen televisions all facing in different directions. He chuckled. 'Certainly a welcome departure from *Big Brother*, but I can't see it catching on. Unless there's more audience participation.' He glanced over at the city. 'More to the point – any sign of Division activity?'

'Nothing – seems clear,' Eddie replied, as he stooped to grab a handful of the dark weed from a sludge-filled depression in the ground. 'Rub some of this over yourself to cloak your scent. It'll help keep the stalkers off our trails.'

'Okay,' Drake replied, following his example. When he was

finished, he took a pair of what appeared to be wristwatches from his pocket. 'Here are the locators so we can find each other,' Drake said, activating the devices before handing one to Eddie, who buckled it on.

Drake examined the small screen on his. 'I've got your marker.'

'Check – I've got yours too,' Eddie confirmed.

'Fine . . . so we'll use these to make sure we RV on the other side of the city,' Drake said. 'As we discussed, just do your best to plant the canisters at regular intervals as you go – although it won't matter too much if we get the intervals wrong and clump them.' Wiping his eyepieces, he peered up at the swirling showers above them. 'The air currents in here are stronger than I thought they'd be – they'll do an excellent job of dispersing the pesticide.' He looked at Eddie, standing there in his Noddy suit. 'And if it doesn't work and some lucky Plague Snails make it through, we can always try something else.'

'It'll work,' Eddie said confidently. 'Good luck, Drake, and I'll see you on the other side.'

'Yep, barring any of your old mates gatecrashing our party,' Drake laughed.

Then, with a final wave, they set off around the margins of the city, heading in opposite directions.

Chapter Twenty-eight

Chester and his father were carrying a trunk between them as they entered the alleyway leading into Dean's Yard.

'Morning,' the porter announced as he stepped straight into their path.

'And good morning to you,' Mr Rawls replied with forced cheerfulness. 'I'm just delivering my son to the school. I'm afraid our charter flight from Switzerland was plagued by engine problems, so we had to make a detour to Paris-Orly for emergency repairs. As a result we didn't touch down until an hour ago, and my son's awfully late for school. Aren't you, Rupert?'

'Yes, father,' Chester responded, trying to sound as if his mouth was crammed full of marbles.

'Awfully late,' the porter repeated. He slid his eyes over Mr Rawls, then Chester, taking in the striped rugby shirt and jeans the boy was wearing. He didn't appear to be convinced.

Mr Rawls coughed, raising his head towards the square in a gesture of impatience.

'Can I ask your surname, sir?' the porter said.

'Prentiss,' Mr Rawls answered.

Having noticed the initials *RP* painted on the trunk, this piece of information was enough to settle the porter's suspicions. 'Of course, gentlemen, you must be worn out. Please come through,' he said. 'Can I give a hand with that, sir? Looks heavy.'

'No,' Mr Rawls answered a little too quickly, then slowed down. 'Thank you . . . jolly kind of you . . . but we can manage.'

'Very good, sir,' the porter said, stepping to the side and allowing them to pass. As Chester and his father went into the square and out of earshot, the porter muttered 'Private jets . . . Paris Oily . . . how very *la-di-da*,' under his breath. 'Bloody toffs. It's all right for some, while I'm stuck here all night freezing my brass monkeys off.'

As he carried the front of the trunk, Chester glanced over his shoulder at his father. 'Nicely handled, Dad, but Rupert? *Rupert?* What made you pick that name?' he whispered.

'It had to begin with an R and, anyway, that's what I wanted to call you when you were born. Always thought Rupert Rawls sounded rather good,' Mr Rawls replied, then shook his head. 'But your mother wouldn't hear of it.'

'I'm bloody glad she stopped you. Good old Mum,' Chester said, filled with concern as he thought about her. 'I just hope she's okay.'

Chester had no problem in recognising the doorway Drake had described to him, and they carried the trunk inside. They made their way directly to the second door, which led down to the cellar.

'Don't we need a key for this?' Mr Rawls asked as he saw the lock.

'No, Drake said he'd take care of it,' Chester replied,

placing a hand on the old wooden door and pushing. As it swung inwards, he glanced at where the bolt from the mortice lock should have engaged in the door frame. 'Sometimes the simplest solutions are the best ones,' Chester whispered, recalling Drake's words as he'd taken him through the plan. Chester prised out the small metal wedge Drake had inserted in the gap in the faceplate, and pocketed it.

Mr Rawls nodded. 'He must have been here earlier and jammed it open?'

Chester winked at his father. 'Just make sure it doesn't shut behind us, or you'll never get out of this place,' he warned him.

They took the trunk down the steps and to the end of the cellar, where they placed it out of sight behind the packing crates. Chester turned to his father. 'That's it, Dad. Drake doesn't want you to see any more, just in case . . .'

'Yes, I know, I know – in case I'm abducted again,' Mr Rawls guessed. He gave his son a desolate look. 'Chester, I'm not cut out for this. Most of my life has been spent behind a desk, working on actuarial reports. And I'm so worried about your mother, I can hardly think about anything else.' He sighed forlornly. 'I know I'll never be any good at this cloak and dagger stuff. And I don't know how you can do it.'

'Okay, Dad, can we talk about this later?' Chester said, feeling terrible that he was cutting his father short. 'I've got a schedule to meet.'

'Yes, of course,' Mr Rawls replied resignedly. 'And are you absolutely sure I can't do anything more for you? Feel like a fifth wheel.'

'You've done more than enough already, Dad. You'll help me if you just go back to the warehouse and wait for us there,'

Chester said. 'Soon as I see Drake I'll tell him about Mum.'

'All right, son,' Mr Rawls mumbled.

Chester watched as his father turned to go out of the cellar, ambling between the crates with his head hung miserably. He looked so fragile and vulnerable, and Chester realised how protective he felt towards him. It was as if the parent-child relationship had been completely reversed, and now Chester was the one who had to look after him, and tell him what to do.

And much as Chester wished there was something he could do to take the sadness away from his father, there wasn't, and he couldn't let what had happened with his mother make him lose focus. Not now.

Opening the trunk, he took the rifle and belt kit from the top. Next he lifted out the two heavy Bergens by the shoulder straps, and put them to one side. 'They weigh a ton – wonder what Drake's got in them?' he asked himself, then shook his head, grumbling, 'Need to know basis,' several times. 'I never really liked Noddy,' he announced to the empty cellar, as he reached in to get the NBC suit that lay in the very bottom of the trunk.

It took Drake and Eddie a good two hours to make their way around the weed-covered margins. They both planted the last of their canisters and then rendezvoused as they'd arranged.

'That's our way in,' Eddie said over the radio, as he and Drake approached the thick wall that encircled the city. Drake saw where he meant; massive blocks of masonry had collapsed, leaving an opening through which a large windowless building the size of an aircraft hangar was visible. Drake would have had reservations about cutting straight through the city without Eddie to guide him, but the Styx knew its layout, and it was the most direct route back to where they'd entered the cavern.

Once through the opening, they dropped into a water-filled culvert. As they began to move along it, Drake glanced at the wall of the building beside them. A good three storeys high, its entire surface had been carved with a huge relief of a procession of fierce-looking bearded men. Their long hair flowing out behind them like unruly snakes, they were dressed in loincloths and carrying spears. 'Glad we don't have to tangle with that mob,' Drake commented to Eddie, as they emerged from the last of the dark water. Drake held back while Eddie crept to the corner of the building, where he crouched down to survey the way ahead with his rifle.

'Clear,' Eddie said, and they walked out into one of the wide avenues Drake had only glimpsed from a distance. But now he was actually inside the city, he caught his breath as he took in what lay around them.

'Jesus Christ! It's *Land of the Giants*!' he exclaimed. He couldn't believe the incredible scale of the place. The door-ways of the buildings were several times the height of any normal man. All the temples and palaces appeared to have been constructed by a race of phenomenally tall beings. And in sheltered areas along the edges of the avenue where the wind didn't penetrate, patches of shifting mist trailed over the ground, moving like the long lost ghosts of the former inhabitants of the city.

Drake and Eddie travelled down several avenues, keeping to the sides where they were forced to climb over chunks of fallen masonry from the buildings. Every so often, Eddie called a halt as he checked ahead. On one of these occasions, Drake spied something in a clearing several hundred metres away.

'Is that the Prisoners' Platform Will told me about?' he asked, indicating a structure raised high in the air on multiple stone piles. On top of it there were vague human forms, all in various contorted attitudes as if they had been fashioned from a light-coloured rock. 'He said those are real people, who've become somehow fossilised,' Drake added, as he used his telescopic sight to examine the petrified bodies, and the remains of manacles and lengths of rusted chain still attached to them.

Eddie didn't answer as he waved Drake on. They entered an echoing building with a marble floor, climbing flight after flight of stairs until they could go no further because the way was blocked. Instead Eddie took them down a corridor and out onto a balcony. 'This is a favourite observation post for the Division. They often station a couple of men up here. Take a look,' he offered.

'I can see why,' Drake said. From this vantage point he was able to look down on the layout of the city, and was struck again by just how extensive it was. He gazed across at the large domed building, which Will had also mentioned to him – it really did resemble a second St Paul's, although this one had been built many centuries before the Topsoil version Drake knew.

'May I?' Eddie asked, and Drake drew back to let the Styx scrutinise the avenues below. When he was satisfied he couldn't see anyone, they retraced their steps down the stairs and into the open again, where Eddie led Drake into some sort of flooded underpass. 'Watch it in here,' he warned, taking out his Styx lantern.

Drake didn't ask why, but turned his torch on and held it beside his rifle. He wished he could have worn one of his light-gathering lenses, but it would have been impractical under his gas mask. They'd gone several hundred metres when something rolled at them through the water, throwing up spray behind it. Eddie reacted with lightning speed, and leapt back. As it kept coming for them, he trod straight on top of it.

It ruptured into a pulpy mass of flesh, as if a slug the size of a pumpkin had been squashed. Through a rend in its thick black skin, its exposed body organs were visible – they were leaking a dark purple liquid, which mingled with the stagnant water.

'Whoa! What the hell is that?' Drake exclaimed.

Eddie rolled it over with his boot, so they could see its ferocious teeth. 'The Scientists believe it's some sort of unique fungus which has evolved in this city. It's carnivorous, and it's capable of locomotion.'

'You don't say,' Drake gasped. 'Anything else I should know about? Flying mushrooms, for example?'

'No, they can't fly,' Eddie replied in a flat voice, as if he thought Drake was being serious.

They resumed their journey, eventually coming to the city wall where Drake called a halt. 'I reckon this is as good a spot as any. Time to see if my wireless detonator does what it's supposed to.' Unbuckling a pouch on his belt, he slid out a small box, then extended the aerial from it. He lifted up a cover on the front of the box to reveal its fascia, and pressed one of the buttons. A green LED came on. 'Armed. Why don't you do the honours?' he said, handing it to Eddie. 'Predictably, it's the big red button.'

Eddie held it before him, then hit the button.

With muffled explosions there were bursts of light all around the perimeter of the cavern. Plumes of vapour rose from each of the thirty ruptured canisters, lit momentarily by the fiery glow of the charges, and then just as quickly fading away again.

Drake shrugged as he turned to Eddie. 'That wasn't very impressive – don't get much bang for your buck, do you?'

'As long as it does the trick,' Eddie remarked. 'Now we need to evac. If there's anyone here from the Division, they'll want to know who was responsible for that.'

'You bet they will,' Drake replied, and they began to move quickly through an archway in the city wall and out into the flats, on a course that would take them to where the rope hung.

As they came to the graveyard of boxlike tombs, a shot rang out.

'Contact!' Drake yelled.

Passing straight between them, the bullet slammed into the side of one of the tombs, the mica panel crazing with fissures. Almost instantly, it shattered into a thousand tiny pieces, revealing something dark and rotted inside.

Drake and Eddie threw themselves in opposite directions, rolling behind the tombs for cover. 'Where was it from?' Drake asked urgently over the radio. He heard Eddie's voice – it was completely emotionless.

'As you face the city, a four-man patrol at two o'clock. I—'

Eddie's voice suddenly cut out, and Drake couldn't see him anywhere as he used the light-gathering sight on his rifle. He took a moment to wipe the eyepieces of his mask. He wasn't up against amateurs here, and he needed to draw on all his senses. The trouble was that the hood of his Noddy suit was restricting his hearing – he took the risk of yanking it down. The gas mask would still be protecting him from any airborne pathogens.

He listened and watched. Seconds turned to hours as he strained to make out the tiniest thing, but there was only the wind and the steady dripping of water around him.

Then he caught a noise.

It was barely audible, the sound of a breath being taken. Drake spun around just in time to see a huge stalker bearing down on him, its slitted eyes reflecting the eerie green light.

Almost losing his footing on the slimy weed as he stepped back, Drake fired from the hip. The tranquiliser dart caught the dog in the flanks, where it lodged. The massive animal came to a sliding sideways halt as its paws ploughed through the weed. But it didn't seem to be the tranquiliser that had stopped it, but more the surprise at being tagged by the dart. Drake realised he wasn't out of trouble as he watched the stalker snort and shake its huge head like a bull in the ring. Twisting its heavy body around, it pounded towards him again as it resumed the attack.

Then, with a growl, the several hundred pounds of hellhound were airborne as it sprang at Drake. But he was ready – he fired, catching it in the eye. The tranquiliser seemed have more effect this time, the stalker's body instantly going limp. But the dog's momentum was such that it slammed against Drake. Like a bowled tenpin, he whacked hard against the waterlogged ground, the air knocked from his lungs.

Although he wasn't hurt, he stayed on the ground, seeking refuge under the nearest weed-covered tomb. 'One stalker down,' he puffed into the radio once he'd got his breath back.

Despite the suppressor fitted to its muzzle, the rifle still made a sound similar to a punctured football when it was discharged, and Drake was concerned that it might have been enough for the Styx soldiers to get a fix on him. He needed to move to a new position, and fast. He peered out from the other side of the tomb. As the coast seemed clear, he crept into the open. He realised how lucky he and Eddie had been – at least the Division patrol hadn't had time to mount a full ambush – at least the situation was still fluid.

As Drake scanned the immediate area through his night sight, he caught a fleeting movement no more fifteen metres away – as if a shadow had flitted past. He gave the locator on his wrist a quick check. He didn't want to nail Eddie by accident. Seeing that he wasn't anywhere close, Drake whispered into his throat mike.

'Think I've got a target – seven o'clock to the city,' he said. 'He's behind our position – they're trying to cut us off from the exit.'

Drake watched where he'd seen the movement.

Seconds ticked by.

The Styx soldier broke cover from behind a tomb and Drake reacted instantly. The dart clipped the man on the upper arm. Yanking it out, the soldier staggered a few paces, then collapsed. As Drake reached the soldier, he kicked the man's rifle out of his reach.

The soldier was wearing a long coat, and Drake immediately recognised the characteristic grey-green camouflage of the Division. He had large circular goggles over his eyes, and a Styx breathing mask covered the lower half of his face.

'You're going sleepy-byes for a good long while,' Drake whispered, and fired another dart into the man's leg at point-blank range. He didn't want to run the risk that the soldier hadn't received a full dose of tranquiliser. 'One Division soldier down,' Drake reported to Eddie over the throat mike, wondering why he hadn't heard back from him yet.

Drake moved again, in a crouched run towards the wall where he and Eddie had entered the cavern, and where he hoped the rope would still be hanging. The plan depended on it being there. 'Checking area between six and nine o'clock,' he informed Eddie over the radio link. As he glanced at the locator, he was surprised to find that Eddie's marker was almost on top of his.

'I've dealt with the others,' Eddie said, as he appeared beside Drake, depositing three of the long Styx rifles on the ground at his feet. 'But th—'

A shot rang out, and they both ducked down.

'That came from above,' Eddie said, scanning the upper reaches of the cavern wall.

But Eddie didn't spend any time on this as they both spied a figure no more than twenty metres away. He'd been lying in wait for them, close to where the rope was suspended. Clutching his shoulder, he went down on his knees, then fell face first.

'He's a Limiter. Watch my back,' Eddie said, as they both stole towards the prone body.

Drake saw that Eddie had been right as he flipped the man over. His coat was quite unlike those worn by the Division – this one had a camouflage pattern which consisted of blocks of different browns. There was blood over his chest from a wound to his shoulder. 'He's been shot with a live round – a tranquiliser dart hasn't done this. And I know this man – he's a Limiter officer.' Eddie threw a glance at Drake. 'They don't usually accompany the Division patrols in here.'

'You did,' Drake replied.

But Eddie wasn't listening as he felt the man's neck to take his pulse. 'He's still alive,' he said, and immediately pointed his rifle at the opening where the rope was tethered. 'But who's up there?'

Before Eddie knew it, Drake was behind him with an arm around his neck.

Eddie struggled, trying to swing an elbow into Drake's face.

'No you don't!' Drake growled, applying more pressure to Eddie's windpipe so he could barely breathe and, at the same time, twisting his neck almost to breaking point.

'You can't get out of this. Drop your rifle or I'll kill you,' Drake told him in no uncertain terms. 'Then hold your hands up, where I can see them.'

Eddie knew he had no option, and complied.

'Why? What is it?' he gasped.

Drake whispered into his ear. 'You slipped up twice. Your first mistake was that no one – and I mean *no one* – knew Fiona was pregnant. It was too early for her to tell anyone. So how come you knew all about it? I might have given you the benefit of the doubt and assumed you'd picked up on that from your Topsoil surveillance, but then you let something else slip. You referred to my friend at university as 'Lukey'.'

Drake tightened his grip as Eddie tried to speak.

'No, shut up and listen!' Drake fumed. 'Only Fiona called him Lukey – it was her pet name for him. And I was only aware of it because I happened to overhear them a couple of times in their room.' Suffused with anger, Drake's voice was low and cold. 'But you knew because she said it when she was under duress, didn't she? It was when she was being interrogated. That places you right there when she was being Darklit – when she died from internal bleeding. And that nickname is the sort of tiny, trivial thing that I doubt even you Styx would bother to share with each other.'

Drake let out a breath and fell silent for a moment, as if he was trying to regain control of himself.

'Funny, really – although you were once my enemy, I thought I'd found someone I could trust.'

Eddie groaned as Drake increased the pressure on his windpipe.

'I thought I'd found someone I could work with. A friend.'

As Eddie slipped into unconsciousness, Drake laid him on the ground.

Straightening up, Drake reached for the radio unit on his belt and switched the frequency over. 'Chester, can you hear me?'

'Yes,' Chester confirmed from the opening in the cavern wall above, where he'd been watching Drake through his rifle scope. The boy was obviously shaken after firing on the Limiter, and spoke so quickly Drake could hardly understand him. 'Was that okay? That Limiter was about to take a shot at you – I couldn't just let it happen. And what was that with Eddie? I saw what you did to him.'

'Just cool it – you did well – everything's under control.' Drake checked the time. 'We need to get through the Labyrynth and into the South Cavern before daybreak. I want to catch the Colony asleep.' He used his rifle scope to locate where Chester's head was peeping out from the vegetation over the opening. 'Send me down the weapons first,' he said. 'Then lower the Bergens. And, whatever you do, be gentle with them.'

'Yup . . . okay,' Chester acknowledged, then glanced at the pair of loaded Bergens on the ground beside him. He'd been forced to make two trips all the way down from the Topsoil cellar, because there was no way he could have carried both of the rucksacks at once. They were too heavy for that.

Drake regarded Eddie, sprawled at his feet. 'I must be going soft . . . letting you live,' he muttered, as he aimed his rifle and shot a dart into the Styx's arm. 'But, in any case, there's no way you'd let me do what I intend to do next,' he told the unconscious man.

As they quickly made their way around the Eternal City, Chester told Drake how his mother had walked out of the hotel. Drake assured him that he'd been right to tell his father to wait at the warehouse. But he could offer little in the way of comfort about Mrs Rawls' plight, except that he would look into it the moment they were Topsoil again. And Drake was reluctant to talk about what had happened with Eddie, except that he stood in the way of the second phase of the operation, and had to be 'removed from the equation', as Drake put it.

Now, as they lingered on a muddy bank in the far reaches of the cavern, Chester shivered. 'I'm so glad we didn't have to go through there. Spooky-looking place,' he said. They were in a slightly elevated position and Chester could see over the city wall and into the Eternal City itself. He shivered again and made a ghostly *Whoooo* noise as he gazed at it. Even though he knew the inhabitants were long gone, the buildings had such a strong aura of power and menace that they made him feel distinctly uneasy. It suddenly dawned on Chester that he'd been so preoccupied with his mother's disappearance, he hadn't given his own situation much thought. Drake refused to tell him what he was planning to do in the Colony, but it was bound to be dangerous. Chester didn't even know if he himself was going to make it through the day and see his father again.

'Come on, kid! Snap out of it! What are you daydreaming about?' Drake's voice crackled in his ear. 'I was speaking to you.'

'Sorry,' Chester said, as he turned to see Drake waiting for him at the mouth of a cave.

Drake swept his hand into the opening as if he was a showman. 'Step this way, sir. You're about to experience one of the most complex mazes in the unknown world.'

'I am?' Chester swallowed, hurrying over to join him. 'But how do you know the way through?'

'Your mate, Will – he gave me the schematic his Uncle Tam drew for him. That, combined with several extremely helpful Limiter maps in Eddie's basement, has all gone onto this piece of . . .' Drake whisked something dramatically into Chester's limited field of vision, 'bang-up-to-date technology.' Chester caught the dim light coming from the iPod screen.

'What? We're going to watch some music videos now?' he chuckled, his mood lifting.

'No, not until this is all done and dusted. You see, a compass is useless in the Labyrynth due to the iron deposits and, of course, GPS is out of the question, so I had to get creative. I put all the maps together on this, then linked it to a pedometer. I even get spoken directions over my earpiece. So it should be a cinch to get to the other side, but we're going to have to move like greased lightning. I hope you've got your running shoes on.'

'Oh, great,' Chester groaned comically, adjusting the heavy Bergen on his back. 'Somehow I just knew this wasn't going to be easy.'

And run they did, flying through the passages of cherry-red stone, turning through so many left and rights it wasn't only the exertion that was making Chester feel light-headed. And it didn't help matters that they were constantly moving up a slight incline, their feet crunching in the fine sand for hour after hour.

Drake noticed the boy was beginning to flag. 'Hold up!' he ordered over the radio. 'Right, you can take that respirator off – we should be far enough now for it to be safe.'

Remembering how ill Will had become, Chester wasn't so sure about this, but Drake didn't show any hesitation as he wrenched the gas mask from his head. Then Chester followed suit, realising his hair was soaked through with sweat.

'Drink something or you'll start getting cramps,' Drake advised him.

Chester took the canteen from his belt and gulped down several mouthfuls, then sighed. 'Talk about rugby training,' he said.

After another hour of running, made easier because they could breathe more easily, Drake stopped again.

'Is that a door? Are we there?' Chester managed to get out as he slumped onto the ground, puffing hard and absolutely exhausted.

Drake, on the other hand, was hardly out of breath. 'Nearly, but this door is welded solid,' he said, then shrugged off his Bergen. From one of the side pockets he extracted what appeared to be a string of sausages, certainly to Chester's rather bleary vision.

'What's that? Food?' Chester asked.

'Not quite.' Drake held it across his chest. 'Necklace explosive. It's directional, so the force is maximised, while the sound of the blast should be kept to a minimum.' He proceeded to stick it around the bottom of the door in a rough square, then stood up. 'Time to get back,' he warned Chester. 'I'm going to detonate the sausages.'

'I can see where Elliott gets her habit of blowing things up,' Chester commented drily.

They took cover behind a bend in the passage, where Drake used a wireless detonator. There was a more of a *whomf* than a full-blown explosion, followed by the clang of iron on stone.

'We're in,' Drake said. 'Weapons at the ready in case someone heard that.'

They ducked through the still-smoking opening in the door and came out in a passage, which led through to a small circular grotto.

'Yeuch – what's that smell?' Chester said, pulling a face as he trod across the ground, which was covered in a layer of straw-like material.

Drake pointed at some low sheds. 'Colony pigsty.'

Chester could hear the grunting coming from the iron sheds as they walked through the area. They were halfway across it when a scrawny little piglet poked its nose out of a clump of straw and spotted Chester. It must have got the fright of its life as it squealed plaintively, and bolted into one of the sheds.

Chester had been equally frightened by the piglet's squeal, and jumped into the air with shock. 'Shuddup!' he snapped

angrily at it, then proceeded to step straight into a large heap
of pig manure, which squelched unpleasantly under his boot.
'Rank,' he muttered, as Drake straddled a fence. Chester followed him over, then they passed along a short passage, which
opened into a much wider one.

'This is the main haul – you must have come this way
when they brought you down from the Quarter. See the ruts
in the rock over there,' Drake said. 'It's from all the centuries
of carriages that have shuttled back and forth along this route.
Strange thought that, isn't it?'

Chester stared at the twin grooves worn deep into the
bedrock. 'I'm actually in the Colony again,' he realised, inhal-
ing the air.

'Yes, the Skull Gate is up that way,' Drake informed him,
pointing to the right.

Chester wasn't listening. All of a sudden, the reek of the
over-recycled air hit him. It was the essence of all the thousands of people who lived there in the Colony.

'I never thought I'd smell that smell again. I prefer the pig
pooh, any day,' he mumbled. An uncontrollable shudder ran
through his body. He was only too familiar with this smell
from the Quarter, where he'd spent months locked up in the
Hold. It evoked vivid recollections of one of the bleakest and
most desolate periods of his life. Things had looked so bad
he'd begun to prepare himself for the very real possibility that
he might die.

But he'd never given up on Will. He'd prayed and prayed
for rescue, and when by some miracle his friend had shown
up, springing him from the prison, fate had been cruel to
him. His bid for freedom had been thwarted and he was
recaptured by the Styx, only to be frogmarched straight back

to the Hold again. All his hopes had been raised and then dashed – it was almost worse than if he hadn't been presented with the opportunity to escape in the first place. Although this hadn't taken place very long ago, he'd somehow managed to put it out of his mind, until now.

'Are you all right?' Drake asked, noticing how quiet the boy had become.

'S'pose so,' Chester answered. 'Can we just get this over with and go home as quickly as possible?'

'That's the plan,' Drake said. 'Next stop, the Fan Stations.'

Chapter Twenty-nine

With Mrs Burrows out of the house, Eliza and her mother were moving the furniture and putting the sitting room back to how it had been before their unwelcome guest had arrived. With much heaving, struggling and grunting, Eliza had managed to drag the bed up the first of the stairs to the next floor, but there she'd given up, defeated by its weight. She just wasn't strong enough. And her mother couldn't be expected to help, especially not with her 'dodgy ticker' as she kept reminding Eliza. Eliza was becoming more and more incensed that her brother wasn't there to give her a hand.

'You know where he's gone, don't you?' she growled as she squeezed past the bed, now stuck at the bottom of the stairs.

Her mother frowned at her. ''E said 'e was poppin' out for a swift 'alf at the tavern.'

'Hah! That's hardly likely – he never takes Colly with him when he goes to Tabards,' Eliza said.

The old lady trailed after her into the sitting room. 'Tell me then – where 'as 'e gone?' she demanded.

'Bit obvious, isn't it? He's gone to say a fond farewell to his basket case. Didn't you notice he was still in uniform when he rushed out? When does he *ever* go to the tavern in uniform?'

'Well I'll be . . .!' the old lady said, as she considered it. 'It's never-endin', this folly of 'is.'

'It's going to end soon enough,' Eliza chortled unpleasantly, as she carried an occasional table to the corner of the room. Then, wiping the sweat from her forehead, she contemplated the sideboard. 'I reckon we can manage that together, can't we? We only have to shift it a few feet along the wall, then I can put the rug back where it used to be.'

They took up position at either end of the sideboard. 'Move it out from the wall first – we don't want to scrape the wallpaper,' Eliza said. 'One, two, three . . .'

The legs grated on the bare floorboards as they slid the sideboard out.

There was a loud crash. Eliza assumed one of the legs had broken off the rickety sideboard, as the old lady let out a piercing shriek. 'Jesus, me foot! Somethin' fell on me foot!'

Eliza rushed over to where her mother was hopping around. There was absolutely no damage to the sideboard, but then she spotted Will's gleaming spade where it lay on the floor. She stooped to pick it up, glancing at the maker's label on the shaft. 'Looks Topsoil to me.' She shook her head, her expression one of bafflement. 'What the blazes was it doing there? Must have been wedged between the wall and the sideboard.'

'Ow! Me foot! Me foot!' the old lady continued to yelp, still hopping around with the pain.

Eliza was more intent on the spade. 'But how did it get there? Unless my halfwit brother wanted to hide it from us for some reason?'

'I don't care 'ow it got there! Don't bother about that bloody shovel, what about my bleedin' foot!' the old lady shouted indignantly.

'There's no need for that profanity,' Eliza reprimanded her. 'Anyway, it's not a shovel. It has a pointed end . . . see,' she said, holding the blade up to show her mother. 'This has a pointed end. It's a spade, for digging.'

'I don't bleedin' care what it's bleedin' well called, you silly cow,' her mother grumbled, heading to the kitchen with a combination of hops and hobbles, swearing blindly as she went.

'That's where we're going. Up there,' Drake whispered, as he and Chester tucked themselves into the side of the passage. 'Main control room for the Fan Stations.'

Chester craned his neck, locating the zigzag flights of cast-iron steps bolted to the wall that resembled an old fire escape. Then he peered some fifty metres further up, to the very top of the cavern, which was filled with dense clouds. As he saw the constantly-moving waves of dusky grey smoke, it gave him the impression he was looking at some sort of inverted sea. He also noticed where the waves were lapping over into funnel-type structures set into the roof of the cavern. Inside each of these something was spinning around. 'So those are the fans?' he guessed.

Drake nodded. 'You hear that low humming? Those things up there are like giant extractor fans. This is one of several locations where the stale air is drawn out of the South Cavern and vented to the surface via disguised flues.'

'So we get all this filthy smoke Topsoil, instead? That's not right,' Chester decided, frowning. 'I thought Eddie was dead against pollution? Remember all that stuff he said to me?'

'Forget it – he was playing mind games with you. Never trust anything a White Neck tells you,' Drake replied. With a '*shh*', he held his hand up. 'Like clockwork – the changeover is precisely on the hour,' he whispered. 'Stay down. Make sure he doesn't eyeball you.'

As Chester remained pressed against the wall behind Drake, he caught a glimpse of a squat man trundling up the track. The man couldn't see them where they were hiding as he made for the flights of steps, then began to ascend to the control room.

'Do we go now?' Chester asked.

'Not quite yet,' Drake said.

Then Chester saw that a different man was coming down the steps. He lingered at the bottom to light a long-stemmed pipe before setting off.

'Right – the next shift has just taken over, so we're good to go,' Drake announced. With Chester close behind, he hurried over to the steps and then mounted them two at a time, his tranquiliser pistol ready in his hand. He stopped as they reached the door at the top. 'The control room is always manned. That Colonist's in here, and there may be more, so keep your eyes peeled.'

The old iron door was unlocked, and Drake gently pushed it open so they could slip inside. Chester found that they were in a long gallery, with a row of windows in wooden frames down one side. It was similar in appearance to a train carriage from a bygone era, although it was wider and longer than any Topsoil carriage. And to the other side, the wall was formed by an incredible latticework of archaic pipes, all of highly-buffed brass and secured to panels of dark oak. Not only were there numerous levers and valves on these pipes, but also dials and gauges that clicked and twitched in unison.

The noise Chester had heard below was far louder up here – a regular and very low thump, which made his skull reverberate. The impression that he was actually inside some gargantuan beast recalled to him his favourite story from the Bible, *Jonah and the Whale*. However this was different – it was as if he'd found his way not into the belly of the beast, but its lungs.

Drake took it slowly as he crept further into the gallery.

Then, tucked away in an alcove amongst all the pipework, they came across the Colonist.

With a shout, the stocky man leapt up from a table, a pack of playing cards flying from his hands and into the air. Dressed in dark grey overalls, he had bristly white hair and a red scarf tied around his neck. He shouted again, grabbing a ludicrously oversized spanner from the side of the table.

'Sorry,' Drake said, then fired his pistol, dropping the man where he stood with a tranquiliser dart. Out cold, the Colonist fell forward onto the table, which splintered under his not inconsiderable weight. Drake rolled him over to make sure that he hadn't been injured in the fall. The dart was still stuck in his massive chest.

'Colonists,' Chester murmured, his lip curling in disgust. 'I really hoped I'd never see one of those head cases again in my life.'

'This man isn't your enemy,' Drake said, noticing how the boy's hands had tightened around his rifle. 'He's just doing his job.'

'Yeah – just like that creep in the Hold,' Chester scowled.

'He was called the Second Officer – and he was just doing his job too.'

Taking a folded piece of paper from inside his jacket, Drake shook it open and passed it to Chester, who was still staring at the unconscious man. 'This is important. I need you to concentrate,' Drake ordered the boy. 'Look at this drawing.'

'What about it?' Chester asked, as he relaxed his grip on his rifle and turned his attention to the line drawing. It showed a panel with five large gauges on it, and a whole series of pipes below it.

'This measures the pressure of the air being pumped into the cavern.' Drake swung to the wall of pipes. 'We'll start from either end, and work our way into the middle until we find it,' he said.

It took a few minutes before Chester eventually located it. He called Drake over.

'Good, that's it. Right – slip your Bergen off and put it down here,' he said, pointing to the floor next to the panel. Then he opened up the Bergen, and ever so carefully lifted out a pair of objects encased in sleeves of a blanket-like material.

'Are those gas cylinders?' Chester asked.

Drake nodded as he screwed transparent plastic pipes into the valves on the top of each of the cylinders, which were both around thirty centimetres in length. He placed the cylinders under the panel, then stopped as he thought of something. 'You should have these . . . just in case,' he said, extracting a couple of small khaki-green tubes from his belt kit and handing them over.

Chester examined the writing on the sides of the tubes, but had no idea what it meant. 'Atro . . . atrop . . .'

'They're atropine injections. If something goes wrong, and you're exposed to what's inside the cylinders, yank the end off one of those field hypodermics and whack it into your thigh. It'll give you a shot of the atropine compound, which will counter the effects of the nerve gas.'

'Nerve gas?' Chester said, glancing nervously at the cylinders. 'I was carrying nerve gas on my back?'

'Yeah, under monstrously high pressure, too,' Drake replied, as he saw Chester's horrified expression. 'But what's in the other Bergen you lugged down to the Eternal City is far worse – enough plastic explosive to vaporise every molecule of your body. If that'd detonated, there'd be nothing left of you to bury,' he added, with a wry smile.

As Chester shook his head, Drake took a box from the Bergen and opened the lid. Chester saw that it contained clamps. Getting down onto the ground, Drake slid below the panel and began to attach the clamps to the brass pipes, screwing each of them into place. 'I'm cutting into the air lines now. Just keep an eye on that door in case anyone decides to show up,' Drake said, his voice muffled as he continued to work under the panel.

It took him a few minutes to make sure the clamps were firmly attached, then he slotted the transparent pipes from the two cylinders into them.

'Time for the gas masks again, Chester,' he said, as he emerged from under the panel. 'And we don't take them off, not for anything.' Once they had both donned their respirators, he loosened the valves on the cylinders of nerve gas. Each time there was a small hiss, but nothing more as the thrumming noise of the machinery in the gallery continued unabated.

'Is that it?' Chester said, expecting more.

'Yeah, that's it,' Drake confirmed. 'I've tapped the nerve gas straight into the air supply for the South Cavern – it'll circulate everywhere but the Styx Citadel and the Garrison, which have their own supplies. You see, just a few parts per million of this stuff in the atmosphere down here will be enough. And it's odourless, so nobody will be able to tell it's there.'

'But what will it do to the Colonists?' Chester asked. 'Will it harm them?'

'No, nothing serious, except maybe for some nausea and vomiting in a handful of cases. No, in less than half an hour, the Colonists will be waking up with flu-like symptoms – chronically watering eyes and runny noses – which will last for the rest of the day. The main point is that they won't be able to see anything much, and certainly won't be in any state to stop a couple of Topsoilers trespassing on their manor.'

Drake checked his pistol. 'And if we happen to bump into anybody, we only use the tranquiliser rifles and handguns,' he told Chester. 'We're not here to injure any Colonists.' He lifted his Bergen onto his back. 'Right, Chester old man, let's go and have some fun.'

⌐○⌐

'What in earth are you doing round here so late?' the guard in the sentry box asked, standing up. He frowned at the Second Officer, and then noticed Colly by his side. 'Ah, I've got it. You took the Hunter out for a walk, and you wandered a bit too far from home? You're lost!'

The guard's broad shoulders shook, but he didn't make much sound as he laughed. The notion of anyone who'd spent their whole life in these underground caverns losing their way amused him, although there was also concern in his eyes as he regarded the Second Officer.

'I have been walking around for a while – that's true,' the Second Officer admitted, as he scratched the white stubble on his chin. He averted his eyes from the guard, as if he was ashamed of what he was about to do. 'I have a favour to ask of you, old friend,' he began softly.

'And what might that be?'

The Second Officer raised his head to glance beyond the iron gateway to where the Laboratories lay, an almost identical pair of rectangular buildings connected by a walkway. They were both two storeys high and constructed from dirty-looking grey granite. The main difference between them was that behind the right-hand building, known as the South Block, a large chimney duct of red brick ran up the cavern wall. Resembling a swollen vein the way it stood proud of the smooth rock, it was said to convey fumes away from an incinerator in the basement and up to the surface. An incinerator where the Scientists burnt their experiments that had gone wrong.

And also people.

And according to the rumours in the Colony, sometimes even a combination of the two.

However, the rumours weren't that fanciful because the South Block was where the Scientists practised eugenics and genetic manipulation – specifically the controlled breeding of Styx and the modification of their genome for the betterment of their race.

'I need you to let me through,' the Second Officer ventured, finally meeting the eyes of the guard. 'I need to go into the North Block.'

The guard blew through his lips. 'Let you through? Let you through? Now why would I put my job – and my life – on the line, and allow you to do that?' he asked.

'Because I have this.' The Second Officer unbuttoned a pocket in his tunic and produced his warrant card. 'As far as you're concerned I'm here on official business, and if there's any comeback, I'll take the blame.'

'Well, in that case . . . I suppose I could . . .' the guard considered, then gave a shake of his head. 'Look, don't think I'm making a judgement of you, but I know why you want to go in there. I saw the Topsoil woman being carried in.' He stepped outside his sentry box and towards the Second Officer. 'But just let me say this.' He laid his hand on the arm of his friend. 'Maeve and I were talking about you at the weekend. I know in your job you've seen and heard a lot of what goes on – just as I have at this butchers' palace – but you mustn't let it get to you. You've still time to find yourself a wife, a nice wife from *below grass,* and settle down . . . and have some children. You need that . . . some good to balance out all the bad. You shouldn't be spending your life like this – taking pity on lost causes and half-dead Topsoilers.'

The Second Officer patted his friend's hand before pulling his arm away. 'Thank you.' Then he put his warrant card back into his pocket. 'If anyone happens to ask, just say I'm here to collect some clothes for my sister.' He glanced at Colly. 'And maybe I should leave old puss-in-boots here with you.'

The guard gave a small smile. 'You'd better. It's late and there's no one in the North Block at the moment, but if they were and they came across an unattended Hunter, they'd probably throw her on the slab and cut her open just for laughs. That's what those damned people do in there.'

The Second Officer seemed to look unwell at this.

'Are you all right?' the guard asked him.

'In time I will be . . . maybe,' the Second Officer replied as he started towards the grim building.

Once inside, he took the stairs to the second floor. He'd been in the North Block many times before when he'd been assigned the task of escorting Topsoilers there, most of them abducted from the surface by the Styx. As a matter of course, they were kept in the Hold for a few weeks while they were softened up and Darklit, to make them more 'amenable' (in Styx parlance) to lending their skills for the benefit of the Colony. Often he found he was transporting Topsoil scientists, because these were the people with the expertise that the Styx wanted to exploit, but the journey was nearly always one way – they were rarely, if ever, returned to the surface afterwards.

He walked down the wide corridor, glancing through the observation ports in the doors on either side as he went. There didn't seem to be anyone in the rooms to his right where the abducted Topsoilers were usually locked up as they toiled on Styx projects. For the last six months, since the incident when Mrs Burrows' son and his younger brother had broken out, the Styx had locked the Colony down and there wasn't nearly as much to-ing and fro-ing from the surface. Not that he'd been aware of, anyway.

Then he came to the rooms where he thought that they might have brought Mrs Burrows – the operating suites at the far end of the floor. Sure enough, as he lifted the handle on the door and entered the first of these, he saw her lying on the table in the middle of the room. His boots clacked on the white-tiled floor as he went over to her.

She had a variety of tubes inserted into her arms. He gasped as he saw she'd been shorn of all her hair, and that black dotted lines had been inked on her scalp, showing where they were going to make the incisions into her cranium.

'I'm so sorry,' he whispered, as he touched her face. There was absolutely nothing he could do for this woman he'd known for such a short time, and yet had made such an impression on him.

Chapter Thirty

A ided by the slope, Chester and Drake sprinted down to where the ground levelled out and the buildings began. They made no effort to conceal themselves as they went through the deserted streets, all of them packed with houses. It had never really occurred to Chester that the Colony operated on a different time from that of London above. From his reckoning it must have been around seven or eight o'clock up on the surface, but it was apparently still the early hours of the morning in the South Cavern.

Chester was looking at the lines of bizarre street lights – iron poles each with a football-sized luminescent orb on top of them, held in place by metal claws. 'You know . . . I saw those lights up in the Quarter and some of the buildings there . . . but I've never actually seen the Colony before,' Chester tried to tell Drake as he ran. 'They put a hood over me . . . when they took me . . . to the Miners' Station,' he puffed.

'They didn't bother to use a blindfold on me,' Drake replied. 'Probably because I was a dead man the moment they'd got all they wanted.'

Chester was now taking in all the terraces of stone-built

houses as he and Drake continued to race along. The houses were all rather basic, but well built. They gave Chester the same feeling as he got from the older areas of London, the feeling that every surface, down to each brick and each piece of masonry, had been carefully crafted to withstand the ravages of time. And more than that, these houses had been tended to, repaired and scrubbed clean for century upon century, as generations of people had lived out their lives in them. People who had never as much as experienced the warmth of the sun.

'It's all like some weird dream,' he said to Drake.

Just then a man pushing a two-wheeled cart turned the corner and trundled it into the road directly in front of them. He was wearing a flat cap and one of the waxy-looking jackets the Colonists dressed in. He didn't notice Chester and Drake straight away as he had his head down and was sneezing loudly.

'The nerve gas. It's already irritating his nasal membranes,' Drake observed.

The man looked up, wiping his eyes. He'd evidently managed to clear his vision sufficiently to see Chester and Drake, both in their gas masks and bristling with weapons, as they pounded towards him. His jaw gaped, and he seemed to be about to shout when Drake dropped him with a tranquiliser dart. Drake didn't even stop to check him as they kept going.

'This is so cool,' Chester said. Helped by the fact that his Bergen, now emptied of the gas cylinders, weighed significantly less, and that he was getting second wind, he was finding it easier to keep up with Drake. 'I swear it's like a shoot-'em-up videogame. Will you let me deal with the next one? Please?' he begged.

'Sure – knock yourself out,' Drake agreed.

Chester didn't have long to wait.

Two men in bowler hats and dark blue aprons emerged from a passage in front of them. They were both rubbing their eyes and stumbling around blindly.

And they didn't have any idea what had hit them as Chester tagged both men with darts in quick succession.

'Nice work,' Drake complimented him.

Chester was chuckling away to himself as he watched the Colonists fall against each other and collapse in an untidy pile on the pavement.

'At this rate the high score's going to be *mine*,' he announced, spinning his pistol in his hand like some gunslinger in a Western. 'All mine.'

'Sometimes I worry about the younger generation,' Drake muttered under his breath.

They stole into the bedroom and, treading lightly over the thick carpet, stood around the bed. It was dark, the windows shuttered to keep out the permanent day on the other side. A couple lay sleeping in the kingsize bed, the man snoring gently.

A bright light flicked on.

The woman woke up immediately. A Limiter seized hold of her, cupping a hand over her mouth to stop her from making any noise.

'He must have a clear conscience . . . look at him, sleeping like a baby,' Rebecca One whispered, as she peered down at the Chancellor.

'A very spoilt baby,' her sister said, surveying the extravagantly furnished room. 'It's like something in a palace.'

Rebecca One felt the silk sheets where they lay over the Chancellor's portly body. 'Certainly is. But what's that on his face? Some kind of eye mask?' She sniffed at it. 'Smells of fruit . . . mango.'

'No! Not a mango eye mask! The fat Chancellor is preserving his youthful good looks!' Rebecca Two said, trying unsuccessfully to stop herself from sniggering.

'Time for a rude awakening,' Rebecca One decided. She took hold of the mask and pulled it away from his head as far as the elastic would permit, then released it. It slapped back against his eyes with a small splat.

He let out a cry and sat bolt upright. '*Gott im Himmel!*' he shouted, tearing the mask off and squinting because of the bright light directed at him.

Then he made out the Styx girls by the side of his bed, both of whom were looking with some amusement at his lemon-coloured satin pyjamas and the embroidered K on the breast pocket.

'*Was machen* . . . What are you doing here?!' He jerked his head around to his wife, who was still being restrained by the Limiter. He whipped his head back to the Rebecca twins, breathing heavily, both from anger and fear. 'Have you taken leave of your senses? What are you doing in my house?' he demanded. 'How dare you!'

Rebecca One perched on the bed beside him. 'We've decided that we want to help you, and that you and your lost nation are going to help us. Cooperation is the name of the game.'

The Chancellor wiped some mango juice from his eye, and

snorted. 'Get out of my bedroom! And tell your soldier to take his *Hände* – hands – from my wife! I'm not going to help you! Never!'

'Oh, but you are,' Rebecca Two said calmly, beckoning with her hand.

A Limiter advanced from the corner of the room and placed a large case on the foot of the bed. He undid the catches and lifted off the top of the case.

'What is that?' the Chancellor asked, eyeing the gunmetal-coloured box with dials on it. 'What are you doing?' he said, panic creeping into his voice, and still watching as the Limiter straightened out the flexible stem, which was attached to the rear of the box. At the end of the stem was a shade that housed a dark purple bulb.

'This is called a Dark Light. It's our latest model, portable and much more powerful than its predecessor,' Rebecca One replied in an upbeat manner, as if she was advertising a new product on a shopping channel. Then her tone changed, becoming frosty. 'If you relax, it'll go easier for you . . . and it'll also do wonders for your baby-face complexion.'

'But if you try to resist it, you're history,' Rebecca Two chimed in. 'We don't really need you. We're only keeping you around because you're funny.'

'Whatever that is, you are not going to use it on me!' the Chancellor shouted, sliding back over the shiny sheets so he was up against his button-upholstered bedhead of purple satin. 'And how did you get into my house anyway? How did you know where to find—?'

'Ah, that would be because of our bestest friends, Captain Franz and his men,' Rebecca Two said. She clicked her fingers and he and three other New Germanian soldiers entered the room. 'In fact, we've already got one of your regiments with us, and it won't be long until all the rest of your army is brought into line.'

'*Was machen Sie da?*' the Chancellor bellowed at Captain Franz.

The young soldier remained silent, deferring to Rebecca Two.

'He's not answerable to you any longer,' Rebecca Two said. 'He's already seen the light.'

In no time at all, Drake and Chester had the Laboratories in sight. Drake made them stop across the road from the two buildings while he investigated the area. Chester still didn't know what they were doing there – Drake had refused to tell him in case they were captured by the Styx – but the Bergen full of explosives was a pretty big clue.

'The night guard's still on,' Drake whispered pointing at the Colonist hovering outside his cabin. The nerve gas had begun to take effect and the man was coughing and spluttering, but he was nevertheless puffing determinedly on a cheroot, as if the smoke was somehow going to allay the symptoms.

'That's irregular – although he's on duty, he's got a Hunter with him,' Drake said, observing the guard as he went over to Colly and patted her on the head.

'Looks a lot like Bartleby,' Chester whispered back.

Then the guard took out a handkerchief and dabbed his eyes, before turning to give the North Block a glance.

'Let's do our worst,' Drake declared, as he walked straight out into the open, with Chester following close behind. 'Tag him, will you?'

The guard only saw them at the last moment. Spitting his cheroot from his mouth and holding up his hand in alarm, he seemed at a loss what to do as the two bizarrely-dressed figures appeared before him, armed with pistols and rifles.

Chester might have been showing off or it might have just been his less-than-perfect aim, but he shot the dart bang smack in the centre of the man's raised palm. He toppled like a felled tree.

'Don't get too flash,' Drake cautioned. 'Aim for the trunk of the body – there's less chance you'll mess up.'

'Okay. Sorry,' Chester agreed, as they slowed in front of Colly, who hadn't moved from where she was sitting. She cocked her head to one side as she watched them curiously. 'Nice kitty,' Chester said.

'Keep your distance – these animals can be volatile, and you might have just blatted its master,' Drake warned.

Colly also seemed to be affected by the gas, attempting to rub her saucer–sized eyes with her paws, as bubbles of snot foamed at her nostrils.

As he gave her a wide berth, Chester observed, 'This one's smaller than Bartleby. And better looking.'

'That's because she's female,' Drake said.

'Female? How can you tell?' Chester queried, throwing a backwards look at Colly as they neared the steps of the North Block.

'Chester,' Drake replied, as if exasperated, 'Hunters don't have any hair – you can see *everything* – did you really not notice that she was missing a few things Bartleby has?'

'Um . . . no . . . didn't actually,' Chester mumbled in embarrassment, as they entered the building and took a left turn. They hurried down a short corridor and through a pair of swing doors. Chester found they were in a huge room – the walls were covered in white tiles, and the lino underfoot was so highly waxed it resembled a sheet of dark water. The room was brightly lit, not by the usual luminescent orbs, but by long, strip-light versions of them arranged in several rows across the ceiling. And along one wall stood glass-fronted cubicles, each large enough to accommodate a bench, a couple of chairs, and racks of Petri dishes and test tubes.

'Isolation cabinets,' Drake informed him, as he noticed where Chester was looking. 'You can see the air-extraction units on top of them – it's where they handle infectious agents and prepare cultures. And these are the cold stores where they keep all their specimens,' he added, as he turned to the far wall. There were three very substantial steel doors from around which a light mist was issuing.

'So what goes on in this place?' Chester asked.

'It's the main path lab – there's a smaller one on the floor right above us, but this is where they modify viruses and bacteria, developing them into weapon-grade pathogens, like Dominion.'

Drake had slipped off his Bergen and placed it on a bench. From inside he produced a series of packages the size of telephone directories. They were completely wound in black tape, each with a small keypad, into which he began to type a series of digits. 'Setting the timers on the charges,' he informed Chester. When he'd finished the last of them, Drake took three with him to the nearest cold store. Opening its door, he was engulfed in a cloud of freezing mist as he slid a charge across the frost-covered floor. Then he slammed the door shut and was just about to move onto the next when he stopped. 'Chester, make yourself useful, will you, and put one of these

411

in each corner of the room?'

After all the explosives were in position, Drake and Chester returned to the main entrance.

'Right, we've got around twenty minutes until this place is reduced to hardcore. Keep a look out for anyone while I distribute a few charges along here.' Drake glanced at another pair of doors, which led to the opposite side of the building. 'After that, we'll do a quick recce upstairs, then it's a wrap,' he said. 'And we're outta here!'

'Cool,' Chester replied.

The Second Officer had pulled up a stool and was sitting beside Mrs Burrows. Not knowing what else to do – and knowing there was nothing he could do – he'd put his hands together and begun to pray. The Book of Catastrophes, dealing mostly with vengeance and retribution, didn't exactly offer him much inspiration when it came to mercy or compassion. However, like most Colonists, he knew the majority of the book off by heart, and was able to scrape together a few passages which he now mumbled in the hope they would make a difference. But try as he might, he couldn't stop himself from shedding tears as he reflected on the great injustice of Mrs Burrows' situation.

After a while, he began to cough and his eyes became red and inflamed. He knew this wasn't due to his anguish, and assumed that one of the chemicals used by the Scientists must be causing it. Nevertheless, he resolved to stay a little longer. And still he continued to pray.

As they arrived at the top of the stairs, Drake motioned to the left. 'I'll look down here. You take the other side.' He started to move off, then hesitated. 'And, hey, Chester, if you happen to bump into any nerdy-looking types in red lab coats, feel free to use live ammo on them. They'll be Scientists.'

'Really . . . but aren't they Colonists too?' Chester asked, giving him a quizzical glance. 'And how is it that you know the layout of this building so well?'

Despite the fact that his face was obscured by his gas mask, Chester saw Drake's eyes narrow in anger.

'You were here,' the boy realised, recalling what Drake had told him and Will in the Deeps. 'The Scientists made you work for them in this place.'

Drake was silent for a moment and then nodded. 'And if you find any poor sods in the rooms along the right-hand side, let me know. That's where the Styx torture Topsoilers until they agree to work on their weapons of selective destruction. One of those dingy little rooms was all I knew for a year.'

'So we'll free anyone in them before the whole place blows,' Chester suggested.

'You got it,' Drake said, and headed off.

Chester pushed through the swing doors. He found that all the rooms Drake had referred to were unlocked. Nevertheless, he gave each of them a quick inspection to make absolutely sure they were unoccupied. Finding they were all empty except for lab equipment, he moved further down the corridor.

That was when he heard a voice.

For a second he deliberated whether to fetch Drake, but then decided he'd investigate it for himself.

His dart gun at the ready, he stole towards the source of the voice. It seemed to be coming from a room near the end of the corridor. He pulled the heavy steel door open a fraction and peered in.

He was greeted by a most peculiar sight.

It was evidently some sort of operating theatre. In the middle of the room there was a woman on an examination table. Chester's first thought was that she must be dead, but he revised this when he spotted the array of fluid-filled bags on a stand behind her. The bags were feeding tubes inserted into her arms.

The scene brought back unwelcome memories of a visit he'd made to his sister in intensive care, following the car accident. It was the last time he'd ever seen her. So he didn't dwell on the woman, but switched his attention to the heavy-set man on an aluminium stool at her side. The man's elbows were propped on the table, and his head was cradled in his hands. He was dressed in a dark blue uniform and, for some reason, he struck Chester as being vaguely familiar.

The man, clearly a Colonist and not a Styx, was wiping his eyes repeatedly. And, as Chester continued to spy on him, he saw the man's shoulders were shaking. Chester couldn't tell whether this was due to the nerve gas, or whether the man was actually upset and crying. He certainly seemed to be making small sobbing sounds, punctuated by the odd sniff or unintelligible grunt.

Chester heard as the man spoke again – he couldn't make out precisely what he was saying, but it sounded as though he was reciting something from the Bible. He seemed to be praying.

Chester's hand tightened on his dart gun. From Drake's description, this wasn't a Scientist, so neither he nor the person on the table deserved to perish in the explosion.

Keeping his gun trained on the man, Chester opened the door wider, then eased himself into the room. The man must have heard him, half turning to look. His face was red, and it certainly did appear as though he'd been crying.

And, at that moment, Chester recognised exactly who he was.

'You?' Chester gasped.

The Second Officer was on his feet in an instant, the stool crashing to the floor behind him.

'You!' he bellowed back at Chester. 'I know that bloody voice!'

He launched himself at the boy who managed to squeeze off a shot but, in the heat of the moment, missed completely. The dart shattered the glass in a steel cabinet behind the Second Officer, who was moving with all the belligerence of a stampeding bull.

Chester didn't get the opportunity for a second shot as he was bowled over, and the gun sent flying from his hand. The Second Officer fell on top of Chester with such force that the boy thought his ribcage was going to be crushed.

As the two of them writhed around on the floor, the Second Officer was trying to get a grip on Chester's throat, and in the process dislodged his gas mask. For the first time Chester found out what it was like to inhale the nerve gas.

'I'm going to kill you, you bast-*choo*!' Chester spluttered as he sneezed. He meant it too. With the Second Officer's bulk on him, Chester couldn't get at his rifles or his sidearm, but his knife was a different matter. He managed to slip it from the sheath on his belt. He had no compunction about hurting this man who had – he believed – been complicit in his horrible ordeal for all those months in the Hold.

Chester was manoeuvring the knife into position to jab the Second Officer in the ribs, and they were shouting and swearing and struggling with each other, when a woman's voice cut through the air.

'Stop it! Both of you!' Mrs Burrows commanded, as she sat up on the table.

Drake had heard the commotion and was sprinting as fast as his legs would transport him. Passing the stairs in the central well, he had just entered Chester's side of the building when he saw someone rotate a bar into place on a large stainless steel door to lock it shut.

Then the last person he expected to see stepped into the middle of the corridor.

'Eddie?' Drake said, squealing to an startled halt on the highly polished floor.

Quite calmly, the Styx stood before Drake. Still dressed in his Noddy suit, Eddie had a Styx rifle slung over his shoulder, but otherwise he was unarmed – his hands were empty. And Drake noticed he wasn't wearing a mask, yet seemed to be completely unaffected by the nerve gas.

Maybe it was because Drake couldn't believe his eyes, but he tore off his respirator as he brought his pistol to bear on the man. And it wasn't his dart gun, but a Beretta, which was loaded with live ammunition.

'I wouldn't do that if I were you, Drake,' Eddie said, as he saw Drake had removed his respirator.

'The gas?' Drake asked. 'Why aren't you—?'

'You're not the only one with access to atropine,' Eddie interrupted him.

'But . . . but what are you doing here?' Drake demanded.

416

'Thought I'd come and see how you were getting on,' Eddie said nonchalantly. 'I know you feel you're justified in ending our alliance because of what happened to Fiona, but you've crossed me. And I'm not the type to turn the other cheek.'

Drake's eyes had begun to smart from the nerve gas. 'You sound very confident,' he said. 'For someone who has a weapon drawn on him.' Without lowering his pistol, Drake fumbled a syringe of atropine from his pocket. He flicked the cap off with his thumb before ramming it against his thigh. 'And you obviously took something to counter my tranquiliser, in anticipation that I might use a dart on you.'

Eddie nodded.

Drake blinked his tears away, already feeling the atropine counteract the early symptoms of the nerve gas. 'But you're not going to get up afterwards if I shoot you with live rounds,' he said.

Eddie shook his head. 'You won't do that.'

Drake tightened his finger on the trigger. 'Really? You're in my way, and we've only got a short time until the ground floor of this building blows out from under us. I'm not intending to hang around until it does.'

Chester and the Second Officer instantly stopped struggling with each other.

'Mrs B . . .?' Chester asked, staring wide-eyed at the bald woman who pulled the tubes from her arms, then swung her legs around so she was sitting on the edge of the examination table. 'Is that really you, Mrs Burrows?'

'Celia?' the Second Officer gasped, his hands still around Chester's neck. 'You can speak . . . and move . . . you're well again! How did this happen? It's a miracle – it's the Book of Catastrophes doing its good work, it is!'

Mrs Burrows looked completely composed and otherworldly as she held the grey sheet around herself.

'It may be a miracle, but it's not because of your Book of Catastrophes,' she said. 'In truth, I recovered some time ago, thanks to the way you looked after me . . . you kept me alive.'

'You did . . . I did?' blathered the Second Officer, in utter confusion.

'Yes. And I knew my time was running out when I was brought here. I was just about to try to escape when you showed up.' She stopped abruptly, putting her head back as she sampled the air with a long sniff. 'A Styx,' she announced.

'What do you mean?' Chester snapped, whipping his head round to the doorway. 'Where?'

'He's very close, but I can't be too precise. Whatever's in the air is hindering my sense.' She turned towards the boy, but her eyes weren't on him as she slowly swept her hand in front of her face, as if she was seeing something Chester and the Second Officer couldn't. 'Do you know what this is? It wasn't here a few hours ago.'

Chester glanced at the Second Officer, unsure whether he should say anything in front of him, then decided it wouldn't make much difference now. 'Nerve gas – we're piping it into the Colony air system.'

'If I allowed it, this gas of yours would be playing havoc with my eyes and nasal membranes,' Mrs Burrows said.

'You're doing what?' the Second Officer boomed, as he caught the implication of what Chester had just said.

'And this whole building is rigged to go up,' Chester told the Second Officer, with relish. 'So we'd better get out as quickly as we can. Or we'll all go up in smoke.'

The Second Officer was still on top of Chester as he began to puff with rage. Chester suddenly realised just how heavy the Colonist was. 'And get off me, you fat lump!' he spat.

Without a word, the Second Officer rolled off – as he did so he spotted the knife in Chester's hand. 'You weren't going to use that on me, were you, you jackanapes?' he said.

'You better bel—' Chester began, bristling again.

'The Styx is here,' Mrs Burrows announced.

That was the moment at which the door slammed shut, and Eddie locked it from the outside.

'I don't want to have to hurt you, Eddie,' Drake said. 'But if you try to stop me, I'll take you down and leave you here to die.'

Eddie uncrossed his arms as he saw Drake's trigger finger tighten.

He said something under his breath.

'What was that?' Drake asked, taking a step towards him.

Quite clearly this time, Eddie uttered a few words in the Styx tongue.

Drake went completely rigid, as if seized by a spasm. As he did so, the handgun went off, but Eddie had been ready for this, stepping deftly to the side to avoid the shot.

Swaying where he stood and stiff as a board, Drake began to topple forwards. Eddie moved quickly in to catch him.

'You can still hear me, can't you? And you know why you're paralysed, Drake, don't you?' Eddie asked. 'I put you through some Dark Light sessions of my very own devising while you were still our guest down here. I implanted a few behavioural patterns in you that I thought might come in useful one day.'

Eddie levered Drake's fingers from around the pistol, removing it from his hand and chucking it down the corridor. Then he lowered Drake into a sitting position on the floor. Drake's head was slumped forward and resting on his chest, although his eyes were still open.

'You see, I play the long game. Now that it doesn't matter, I can tell you that I was responsible for the untimely demise of Tam Macaulay and Sarah Jerome's father. I recognised in brother and sister the propensity for causing trouble – I wanted them and all the other hares I'd set running to become rebels, and to stir the population of the Colony from its torpor.' He nodded to himself. 'You see, we Styx had become too settled, too complacent, in our underground fiefdom. We needed a wake-up call to make us look outwards again, to the surface, and to do what the Book decrees is our duty.'

There was a hammering on the door and Eddie glanced casually at Chester and the Second Officer, who were jostling with each other to see him through the observation port. Then he simply looked away from them.

Eddie shrugged at Drake's recumbent form. 'But if all my handiwork did make a difference, I'll be the first to admit I misjudged how events would play out. It might have served to galvanise the leading Styx family into action, but on an extremist path, which was not the right path for us to pursue.' He sighed. 'I got it wrong.'

Taking a few steps as if he was about to leave, Eddie checked himself and stopped. Without looking at Drake, he laid a hand on top of his head. 'And once that misguided family – those Rebecca twins as you call them, and their grandfather, the old Styx – have been shown for the fools they are . . . once they have been bested by the likes of you and

Will Burrows – a mere boy – then they will lose their grip on power, and I will return to the Colony to take the helm. I'm patient – I'm prepared to wait for that day.' He tucked his hands in his pockets and strode towards the stairs. 'So long, Drake,' he said.

Chester rushed to the door the moment Eddie closed it, but couldn't get it open. 'We're locked in! Where's Drake?' He tried to use his throat mike to speak to him, but the radio had been damaged in the struggle and was completely dead. 'This whole bloody place is going up in a matter of min—' Chester trailed off as he caught sight of something through the observation port. 'What!' he exclaimed, then wiped his streaming eyes for another look. He saw Eddie out in the corridor, and Drake edging towards him with a pistol. 'Oh no, it's him again!' Chester shouted. 'Mrs Burrows, you were right. It is a Styx!'

Having taken off his tunic and put it around Mrs Burrows' shoulders, the Second Officer now joined Chester. He spotted Eddie on the other side of the door and started to thump on it to attract his attention. 'Ha! Now your puffballs are pickled,' he declared to Chester. 'The Styx will do for you and your friend. They'll get me out of here.'

'Nope,' Chester replied, elbowing the Second Officer aside for another look at Eddie. 'That was *our* Styx – he's not on your side anymore.'

'So he's on your side,' the Second Officer said, with surprise. Chester shook his head.

'Well, whose bloody side is he on then?' the Second Officer demanded, his broad face a picture of confusion.

'I honestly don't know,' Chester admitted.

They couldn't hear the exchange between Drake and Eddie, but Chester gulped as he saw Drake freeze statue-still, and his pistol go off randomly. He gulped again as Eddie went over to him and pried the weapon from his hand, then lower him to the floor and out of sight. 'Dark Light . . . Drake's been Darklit,' he whispered, as he realised what he'd just witnessed. 'We're in big trouble. We can't have longer than a few minutes before the charges go off!'

'But . . .?' the Second Officer said, jabbing his thumb in Eddie's direction.

'No, why don't you listen to me! He won't be in the mood to help us. Not after what we did to him,' Chester ranted. 'We're well and truly snookered!'

'Then we'll just have to think of something ourselves,' Mrs Burrows declared. As she stood up, the policeman's tunic was almost like a coat on her.

Chester and the Second Officer worked together, doing their best to force the door open, but it was far too solidly constructed. By now, Chester was coughing as much as the Second Officer, and his eyes had become so irritated he could hardly see.

'We could smash that,' Chester suggested, as he slapped the circular inspection port in the door. He knew it was a long shot. The port was less than ten centimetres in diameter and positioned too high up for them to reach the handle through it, but it was still worth a try.

'Budge out of the way,' the Second Officer said.

Chester stood back as he seized the aluminium stool and swung it at the glass in the observation port. But the stool broke into pieces after several attempts, and the glass wasn't even marked.

'See what else is in here,' Chester instructed the Second Officer, as he began to rummage through his Bergen, searching for something they could use to break their way out. 'I haven't got any explosives, but . . . yes . . . this might do it,' he said, snatching up one of his rifles from the floor. 'Keep your heads down – I'm going to use real bullets!' he warned. He cocked the weapon and tried to aim at the window, but his vision was so impeded he stopped himself. 'This is no good,' he muttered. Then he remembered the atropine syringes Drake had given him and quickly fished them out of his pocket, lobbing one to the Second Officer. 'This will help you see again. Use it like this!' he told the Colonist, as he put his rifle down and, removing the cap from the syringe, thumped it into his thigh.

He bent to retrieve his rifle, then stood up again. 'Whay! Feel really dizzy now,' he said. But with a few deep breaths his head cleared, and he aimed at the observation port and fired. The sound was deafening in the room. Although the first shot did minimal damage to the window, a small crack appearing at the edge of the glass. 'Must be toughened or something! Damn it!' Chester cursed, then fired twice in quick succession. On the third attempt the glass shattered.

The Second Officer was immediately there, knocking out the remaining shards with one of the legs from the stool. 'That Styx has gone,' he observed, then he stuck his hand through the now unglazed port. 'The handle . . . can't get to it . . . too far down,' he grunted.

'Let me have a go. I'm thinner,' Chester said, pulling him out of the way.

But it was still no good – even with his whole arm through the door, Chester's hand was a good twenty centimetres off, and besides that it was going to take a firm grip on the bar to swing it open. While the Second Officer ransacked the cabinets around the walls to see if there was something to help them reach the handle, Chester tried to rouse Drake, shouting and screaming at him, although he could only see his feet through the port. He was still shouting when Mrs Burrows appeared at his side.

'I don't know what Eddie's done to him . . . he might even have killed him,' Chester said, his voice hoarse with desperation.

Mrs Burrows breathed in deeply. 'No, I can't smell blood,' she said.

Chester realised what was wrong with her. 'Oh, no! You're blind! Those creeps blinded you!' he burst out.

'Just tell me what you can see out there,' she pressed him.

He was doing this as the Second Officer returned with a length of rubber surgical tubing and proffered it to Chester. Chester took it from him and stretched it, then shook his head. 'That's no good, is it?' he shouted.

'Calm down, Chester,' Mrs Burrows told the boy. 'First things first. We need to get Drake back into action. How do we do that?'

The Second Officer bumbled over with what appeared to be a pair of extended metal forceps. 'Not *nearly* long enough – won't reach,' Chester said to him, turning back to Mrs Burrows again. 'Well,' he began, thinking hard, 'My dad was Darklit, and Drake sort of shocked him out of it . . . Drake was hitting him and—'

'Yes, that's it . . . use pain to bring him round,' Mrs Burrows cut the boy short. 'That could work.'

'But how? Should I shoot him? Or tag him with a tranquiliser dart?' Chester said in a single breath. 'But what good would that do?'

Mrs Burrows swivelled to the Second Officer, who was still going through the cabinets, turfing their contents out onto the floor. 'Colly!' she said. The Second Officer stopped. 'Your Hunter's close, isn't she?' she asked.

'Left her outside with my friend,' he answered. 'How did you kn—?'

He was interrupted by Mrs Burrows as she put two fingers in her mouth, and gave a piercing whistle through the observation port.

'That won't do anything. Colly's a disobedient little cuss,' the Second Officer grumbled.

But within seconds, there was a meow from outside the door.

'Colly – good girl!' Mrs Burrows said. 'Now, listen to me – see that man outside – I want you to bite him.'

With Mrs Burrows at the observation port, Chester had no idea what was happening out in the corridor. But there was another meow, and the intonation was such that it sounded as though it should have had a question mark after it.

'Yes, I'm telling you to bite him. Just do it,' Mrs Burrows urged the Hunter.

In the corridor, Colly circled around Drake several times. It wasn't in her nature to harm a human, and she was decidedly uncomfortable about what she was being asked to do. But she also knew from Mrs Burrows' tone that it was vitally important. The Hunter approached Drake, then gave him a quick nip on his thigh just above the knee.

Mrs Burrows sniffed. 'No, it's got to be harder – bite harder!' she shouted.

'Jesus – I don't think we've got long now,' Chester said, as it hit him how much time had elapsed. 'We're not going to do this.' He and the Second Officer met each other's eyes, and it dawned on Chester just how ironic it was that he was working alongside someone who only minutes ago he'd wanted to kill. But now they were both going to perish, if Mrs Burrows' idea didn't work out.

'Go on – BITE HIM!' she yelled.

Colly ventured back to Drake, her tail flicking uneasily behind her as she lowered her muzzle. Then she closed her jaws on his lower leg and bit hard.

'HARDER!' Mrs Burrows screamed.

Still clamped onto Drake's leg, Colly shook her head, just as she would if she was despatching a large rat.

There was a roar as Drake's head came up. Colly was so startled by his reaction, her paws were slipping and sliding on the waxed floor as she tried to bolt away.

Drake staggered to his feet. 'Chester,' he shouted. He saw the locked door and rushed over.

As he swung the bar up and wrenched the door open, he took in Mrs Burrows, and the Second Officer and Chester's delighted faces.

Only then did he glance at his watch. 'No time for pleasantries,' he said. 'We've got about a minute to get clear.'

Without a moment's hesitation, the Second Officer grabbed Mrs Burrows and threw her over his shoulder.

Drake gave him a nod. He hadn't known what to expect when he first saw the Colonist, but at least the man wasn't going to be a problem. Drake spotted Chester's Bergen and rifles on the floor. 'Take your kit . . . and don't forget your gas mask!' he barked at the boy.

Then they dashed along the corridor, down the stairs and out into the open. As they came to the guard's cabin and the

Second Officer saw his friend sprawled on the ground, Drake spoke to him. 'I'll take Celia from here,' he said. 'You deal with him. He's too heavy for me to move.'

The Second Officer did as he was told, and they'd crossed the road and were just moving down the nearest street when the first of the charges detonated. They didn't go off simultaneously, but in a ripple like a series of fireworks on Bonfire Night. The sound of the explosions echoed all around them as the sudden onrush of air made them totter forward. As the last boom reverberated throughout the cavern, they stopped to watch the building sink into a cloud of dust.

The Second Officer had put his friend down, and now stepped in front of Drake, squaring up to him. 'If I was doing my duty, I should rightfully arrest you.'

Chester had been prepared for this moment, the dart gun ready behind his back.

'But if letting you two Topsoilers go means Celia's safe, then so be it,' the Second Officer continued.

'Why don't you come with us?' Mrs Burrows asked him. 'There's nothing down here for you.'

'There's my mother and sister,' he shrugged. 'I couldn't leave them.' He glanced up at the smoke rising from the remains of the Laboratories building. 'I'll just have to think up something convincing to tell the Styx, and cover myself.'

Drake scanned the streets around them, a worried expression on his face. 'We've got to scram,' he said. 'We should've been long gone before the charges went off. The Styx will be out looking for us now.'

'Oh, Christ,' Chester mumbled.

But Mrs Burrows didn't seem to be overly concerned. 'Thank you for saving me,' she said to the Second Officer, and leant forward to kiss him. 'You're a good man, a truly good man.'

He held one of his hands to his cheek where she'd planted the kiss, and Chester could have sworn that he was blushing.

As Drake and Mrs Burrows began to move away, Chester held back for an instant. 'Yeah, maybe you're not so bad . . . for a total meathead,' he told the Colonist.

'Be off with you, Topsoiler,' the Second Officer said, pretending to cuff the boy and smiling. 'Now where's that damned Hunter got to? I just hope she wasn't hurt in the explosion,' he added, his smile vanishing as he began to look for her.

Refusing any help, Mrs Burrows was having no trouble in keeping up as the three of them dashed through the streets in the direction of the Fan Stations.

Despite Drake's fears about the Styx, there weren't many yet in evidence, and those that were already patrolling the streets could easily be avoided as Mrs Burrows used her sense to full effect.

'Not that way,' she said. 'With all this gas around the place, I'm not as accurate as I should be, but I think there's some Styx down there.'

Drake peeked around the corner and quickly withdrew. He nodded at Chester. 'How are you doing this?' he asked Mrs Burrows, as the three of them immediately reversed back down the street.

'The Dark Lights did something to me – I think they rewired my brain,' she told him, then laughed. 'I might be blind and never able to watch TV again, but I wasn't intending to anyway.'

There was no time for more conversation as they entered a

road full of rather sleepy people milling around like confused cattle. Chester almost found it funny – with the men in their ludicrous night caps and shirts, and the women in flowery dressing gowns, it was like some slumber party that had gone wrong. They'd obviously been woken by the multiple explosions – it would have been impossible not to hear them within the limits of the giant cavern.

Drake and Chester didn't once have to use their tranquiliser guns. The Colonists were so badly affected by the gas that they were no threat. And Drake took the opportunity to snatch a pair of slippers from a rather rotund woman, who screamed loudly. It was only when, a little further on, he gave them to Mrs Burrows, that Chester realised she'd been barefoot up until that point.

They were forced to make one further diversion when Mrs Burrows again warned about the presence of Styx. Then, before Chester knew it, they were on the thoroughfare with the cart tracks worn into it and within sight of the side passage where the pigsty lay.

'Never thought I'd ever be so grateful to smell pig pooh again,' Chester said.

As they entered the Labyrynth, Drake took out his iPod to guide them. Mrs Burrows held onto Chester's Bergen to help her keep to the route. But, after an hour of walking, Drake noticed she was dragging on the boy. He assumed her ordeal in the Colony must be catching up with her.

'We should take a breather,' he said. As they sat in the red sand, they had some water from the canteens.

'Tell me about Will – tell me about my son,' Mrs Burrows asked suddenly.

Drake looked at Chester, prompting him to answer.

'Um . . . he was okay . . . just fine . . . when he . . . er . . . left. You see, he went after Dr Burrows, deeper into the Earth,' Chester explained, not feeling this was the moment to let her know that both of them had jumped headfirst into Smoking Jean, a colossal void, and that he had no idea if they'd survived the fall or not. Chester had never before been in the situation that he'd had to inform someone their husband and child might be dead.

Mrs Burrows appeared to be unsatisfied with the answer. She turned her sightless eyes on Chester, and almost imperceptibly, her nostrils flared. 'You're not telling me the full story, are you?' she said gently.

'Maybe we should do this later,' Drake intervened. 'We're a bit pressed for time right now.'

Chester noticed that Drake seemed preoccupied and gave him a small shrug.

'There might be a complication,' Drake said finally, grimacing as he toyed with his respirator.

After all the excitement, Chester was feeling completely drained and just wanted to return to the surface. 'What do you mean?' he asked, then noticed what was in Drake's hand. 'The gas masks! We haven't got enough of them for the journey through the Eternal City!'

'No, it's not that. There's a spare in my Bergen,' Drake answered in a subdued voice. 'It's Eddie. He was ready to let us all die back there and if, as I suspect, he's returned Tops—'

'The warehouse!' Chester burst out, leaping to his feet. 'My dad! He's there. If Eddie gets to him first . . .!'

'Yes, so we need to get our skates on,' Drake said.

'If this is about me,' Mrs Burrows spoke up. 'I won't hold

you back. I've been waiting for someone to catch up with us.'

Chester and Drake simply looked at her.

'She has now, but you frightened her, Drake, and she's keeping her distance.' Mrs Burrows turned to the passage they'd just come down. 'It's all right – you can come out now,' she called.

'Why am I not surprised?' Drake sighed, but he was smiling. Chester had no idea who Mrs Burrows or Drake were talking about.

'Well, how could I leave her behind, in that house with those two dreadful women?' Mrs Burrows said, then she shouted again. 'Come and join us, Colly!'

The cat slunk out from the shadows, looking like a black panther as she regarded Drake with her cautious, amber eyes.

'That's all we need . . . when we resurface back in Westminster!' Drake said, chuckling.

Chapter Thirty-one

William and Elliott leapt together across yet another of the wide ravines. As they both landed on the other side, their feet skied through the silt until they came to a stop. Elliott tottered a few steps, then glanced at Will.

'Are there many more of these?' she asked, as Bartleby, deciding it was time that he jumped, launched himself from the other side of the ravine. Unfortunately, he'd misjudged where he would touch down, and thudded into Will's legs, knocking him forward.

'Oi! Be careful, moggy!' Will reprimanded the cat, who lolloped off to investigate the new stretch of seam.

'Well, are there many more?' Elliott asked again, barely moving her mouth as if it was numb.

Will looked at her, recognising that she'd hit another low. The effects of sheer fatigue came in waves; for the most part there was an overwhelming detachment from everything around you. But occasionally you went on roller-coaster rides into the most crashing bleakness and despair, when even the smallest task seemed like a Herculean undertaking, and when you had no sense of there being any light at the end of the tunnel. Will suspected this was where Elliott was right now.

'No, I think that's the last of the big jumps. And thank God for the low gravity,' he said, attempting to sound as positive as he could. 'I don't know how we'd have got across otherwise.'

Elliott gave a yawn. 'I am *so* tired,' she slurred. 'And so hungry I could eat a cave cow . . . two cave cows.'

'Yeah, me too, but I wouldn't go that far. You wait until you get to the fallout shelter – there aren't just nice, clean beds there, but loads of food too,' Will told her, his stomach rumbling at the prospect of bully beef spread on dry biscuits, which, at this very moment, seemed to him like a feast sent from heaven.

In less than a kilometre they'd reached the end of the seam and begun along the constricted passage that led from it. As they squeezed between the rough stone walls, Will turned the tracker off and stowed it in his pocket; it was impossible for them to lose their way now. But it was odd not to have the sudden bursts of clicking to punctuate the slow and weary rhythms of their boots clumping and scuffing on the ground.

An hour went by before Will and Elliott spoke again. 'Not far now,' he announced.

'Oh, right,' she sighed.

Recognising that Elliott still sounded rather down in the mouth, Will made another effort to lift her spirits. 'Yep. Really not far to go. Have you spotted the signs above us?' he said. Coming to a halt, he held his luminescent orb high so its light fell on the upper reaches of the wall. 'See . . . almost home and dry.'

Elliott leant back against the passage wall, and angled her lantern upwards. 'A red triangle,' she observed, as the circle of light revealed the peeling red paint of one of the symbols.

'They run at about five-hundred-yard intervals,' Will said, as he set off again. But the moment he'd uttered these words, they resonated in his head, as though a tuning fork had been struck.

With Elliott following behind him, Will continued to walk mechanically along. Without being aware of it, he was whistling distractedly through his teeth, just as his father had done when they'd been in this very same passage only months before. Dr Burrows had been the first to notice the direction markers, pointing them out to Will.

Will ceased his whistling. 'They run at about five-hundred-yard intervals,' he repeated barely audibly, but in his own head he was hearing his father's voice, as distinctly as if Dr Burrows was standing right beside him.

Will began to slow his pace as he recalled how his father had been forced to persuade him along this leg of the route. At the time, Will had been filled with self-recrimination that he hadn't made more of an effort to find Chester and Elliott, so they could regroup after the explosion by the submarine. And he'd become argumentative and lashed out at Dr Burrows, venting all his frustration and resentment on him, when in fact he'd been furious with himself. Furious and extremely confused about what he should be doing.

Will now came to an abrupt halt, making Elliott pull up sharply behind him.

'What is it?' she asked.

'I . . .'

Before Will knew it, he'd dissolved into floods of tears. He couldn't stop himself from crying, crying so hard that he could barely draw breath. 'Dad, oh, Dad,' he moaned and twisted quickly away from Elliott to hide himself against the wall. He was thoroughly embarrassed and ashamed that she should see him lose control of his emotions like this.

Padding back to find out why his travelling companions weren't keeping up, Bartleby regarded Will through his large coppery eyes, not understanding what was wrong. The cat tried to push his muzzle between Will and the wall to get his attention. When Will wouldn't move and let him in, Bartleby sat on his haunches beside him, his head cocked to one side as he began to make low mewing noises in sympathy with the sobbing boy.

'Being such an idiot,' Will murmured, as Elliott stepped over to him.

'No, you're not,' she said softly. She put an arm around him, then laid her head on his shoulder.

'Don't know what . . . why now . . .' he got out between quick, shallow breaths, still unable to regain any measure of control over himself.

They remained like that for some time, Elliott holding him.

'What a muppet,' he managed to say, his chest heaving.

'It's all right. You're just sad,' she said, and gave him a comforting squeeze. 'You shouldn't try to fight it. Do you remember what I told Cal on the island, about how horrible experiences make you tougher, and more able to survive?'

Will mumbled a 'yes'.

'It's not really true. Only time makes things better,' she admitted.

As Will became calmer, Elliott lifted her head. She was about to kiss him on the cheek when he edged back from the wall, disengaging himself from her.

Unaware what she'd been about to do, Will stared at his feet. His voice was strained and hoarse as he tried to express himself. 'I used to get so cross with Dad. I was so bloody sure of myself, so absolutely certain that I was right. *Silly old man*, I used to think to myself. *You silly, stupid old fuddy-duddy* – getting everything wrong – making such a bloody mess of things,' Will said, wiping his wet face with his sleeve. 'Sometimes I was horrible to him, and now I can't tell him that I was the one who was wrong, and how sorry I am.' Will tried to chuckle as he used a thumb to rub the tears from his eyes, but it didn't sound very mirthful. 'Well, tell him I was wrong *some* of the time,' he added. He began to sigh heavily, but it morphed into a hiccup, so loud it made Bartleby's ears prick up.

'Do you want some water?' Elliott offered. 'We can stay here for a while, if you like?'

'No . . . I'm okay now,' Will said. 'Thank you.' He moved off into the passage, sniffing every so often as he led the way, still thinking about his father.

'We made it!' Will called to Elliott as he burst from the gap in such haste he almost fell onto the concrete platform. With his luminescent orb poised before him, he was just about to turn to the right when Bartleby cannoned through the opening, galloping at full speed.

'Nooooo!' Will warned with a shout, but it was too late. There was a huge splash as Bartleby shot off the concrete platform and hit the water in the harbour.

As Elliott arrived, she and Will watched the Hunter. His ears were flattened against his head and he was holding his broad nose stiffly out of the water as he doggy-paddled back towards the side.

'I had no idea he could swim. And he seems to quite like it – he's not really a cat at all, is he!' Will said. As Bartleby came close, Will knelt down to give the animal a hand to clamber back onto dry land again. After Bartleby had shaken himself down, splattering both Will and Elliott, Elliott directed her lantern beam into the lagoon of clear water and then at the cavern wall to their left.

'So this is it?' she said.

'You haven't seen the half of it yet. We need to get the floodlights on,' Will replied, drying his hands on his front. 'Come on, it's this way.'

They moved down the platform, climbed over a pile of rubble, and then turned left along the quay. In no time at all they had reached the low building with its dusty windows.

Will approached the heavy grey-blue door. 'It's already open!' he exclaimed.

Elliott swung her rifle from her shoulder and cocked it.

'Someone in there?' she asked.

Will took hold of the circular locking mechanism and pulled the door a few centimetres towards him. 'This was definitely shut when we left here,' he said. Frowning, he turned to Elliott. 'And I know it was locked – Dad told me to make sure it was locked.'

As she crouched down, Elliott's finger was on the trigger.

'No, I don't think there's anything to worry about, not in this place. It won't be the Styx,' Will said to her. 'But what this means is . . . I suppose . . . that Chester made it back here, with Martha.' He grinned. 'So he's okay then.' He shook his head. 'You know, with everything else, I haven't given him much thought lately. I just sort of assumed he must have got Topsoil again with that kooky woman, and that he's up there on the surface somewhere.'

But as she observed Bartleby, Elliott wasn't so relaxed about their current situation. 'The Hunter is sensing something. Keep your voice down,' she whispered to Will. 'And pull the door further back so I can see inside.'

Will did as she asked, and once she'd checked the interior with her rifle scope, they both entered. Will wasted no time in going over to the panel of switches. 'This is the main control panel for the lights. Do I turn them on . . . is that a good idea?' he said to Elliott, who nodded back at him.

'I just don't like the way Bartleby's acting,' she declared in a low voice. The cat was creeping forward, apparently wary of something.

Recalling that the first switch hadn't done anything when his father had tried it, Will selected the next along and swung the handle down. As they met the contacts sparked, and for an instant the room was illuminated by a flash of blue illumination, then the bulkhead lights flared into life.

'Gah!' Will exclaimed. 'Forgot it was so bright.' But despite the brilliance, he still managed to flip down the bank of switches that controlled the lights outside in the harbour. 'Dad said this whole place is powered from turbines in the river,' he informed Elliott.

'Careful,' she hissed, nodding towards the corner of the room.

Will glanced at the metre-thick blast door. 'It's been left open too,' he noted, moving towards it.

'Hold it,' Elliott whispered. 'That looks wet.'

Will sought out what she was peering at. On the way over to the door was a small, grimy-looking object, with grey smear marks on the concrete floor all around it.

As Bartleby inched towards it, Will couldn't understand why he was acting so nervously. 'Dad and I certainly didn't leave anything there,' Will informed Elliott in a whisper, 'But it's just a dirty rag, isn't it?'

While the girl kept her rifle trained on the blast door, Will went over and prodded the object with the toecap of his boot. 'Yes, a rag,' he pronounced, then kicked it over. 'No, watch out – because it is dangerous . . . very dangerous!' Will exploded, barely able to speak he was laughing so much. 'Look at it – that's no rag – it's some really dirty underpants! Chester must have dropped them here!'

As Elliott came alongside him, she saw what was unmistakably a pair of filthy and rather threadbare Y-fronts.

Then the three of them, Will, Elliott and Bartleby, tiptoed through the blast door and into the passageway beyond. It was some fifteen metres high, and brightly lit by the strip lights down the middle of the ceiling. Will threw a glance at the radio operator's booth, assuring himself it was still there. He was intending to pay it a visit later.

He indicated the next cabin along. 'You'll love what's in there,' he said, making no effort to keep his voice down. 'It's the armoury. It's—'

'Bartleby's still acting squirrely. And there's a strange smell,' Elliott warned him sharply.

Will sniffed several times. 'Detergent – that's all,' he decided. 'Probably this,' he added, rubbing his foot on a damp trail which ran down the otherwise spotless lino of the passageway. 'Chester or Martha must have dragged something through here.'

But Elliott was right – Bartleby was still behaving strangely as they edged forward, although Will put it down to his being in unfamiliar surroundings, filled with new odours.

By the doorway at the end of the passageway there were some food packets that had been shredded into small pieces.

'*Always leave a place as you'd wish to find it*,' Will said somewhat disapprovingly, as he quoted Dr Burrows' maxim.

'Your father?' Elliott asked, recognising that the boy's words hadn't sounded his own.

'My father,' Will confirmed. 'But I'm surprised Martha and Chester would make all this mess.'

'There's something else in here,' Elliott whispered, wrinkling her nose. 'There's a smell that—'

'Nah, it's fine,' Will insisted. 'You worry too much. I keep telling you – no one else would come down here. It's a very long way from the Colony or the Deeps, miles from anything.'

'But don't you think the White Necks might've been the teensiest bit interested how you and the Doc made it back to Highfield? And what if Chester or Martha have been caught and Darklit – they'll have told them everything, including about this place,' Elliott reasoned. 'And what about your mother? What if the Styx really Darklit her?'

'No, not my mother – Drake made sure Dad and I didn't say too much about it in front of her, especially about where the river came up under the airfield,' Will replied. 'But I suppose you've got a point.'

They entered the main area, which was filled with ranks of bunk beds. It was the size of a football pitch, and around the edges there were further rooms. With all the lights on, they could quickly see no one was in there.

'What did I tell you?' Will said to Elliott. 'Nobody home. Nobody home. Come with me.' He broke into a run, cutting straight through the area of bunk beds. Elliott trailed cautiously after him, her rifle still at her shoulder. As she caught up with him on the other side of the floor, he pointed at a light-blue door with a number stencilled on it. 'The showers are in there,' he informed her. Then, as he reached the next door along, he let out a whoop of joy. 'And this is what we've been waiting for! The kitchen's in here!' he announced.

He yanked the door open and stepped in.

The whole room seemed to be moving.

Then it stopped.

Hundreds of small eyes were on him.

Whiskers twitched.

Then they swarmed.

A black heaving mass of rats.

'Jesus Christ!' Will wailed as, like a gush of oil, the whole pack fled for the door. Stuck in the entrance, Will gripped the doorjambs on either side of him. He closed his eyes, bracing himself against the torrent of vermin that were flooding past. Even between his legs.

He heard Elliott's rifle crack as she shot one rat, then a second, but it was nothing compared to Bartleby, who was having the time of his life. He was like a spiky tornado as he leapt into action, seizing rat after rat in his teeth. He wouldn't bite them to death, but nip their scruffs and, with a deft shake of his head, despatch each of the rodents by breaking its neck.

'JEEESSSUUUUSSSSSSS!' Will was howling, as he staggered backwards from the room. Only then did he open his eyes and take in the trail of carnage that led to the main door. Dead and bleeding rats littered the way, but there was absolutely no sign of Bartleby.

Elliott was doubled up with laughter. 'You should have

seen yourself!' she exclaimed.

Will didn't find it in the least bit funny. 'Disgusting!' he gasped.

'They're just rats . . . and now we've got something to eat,' Elliott managed to say, still in fits of laughter.

Will was extremely subdued as he went back into the kitchen and surveyed the chaos the rats had left. Shredded ration packets, ripped tea bags – everything and anything they could get their teeth into had been torn open. He spied a plastic tank of detergent on the floor that they had somehow managed to knock from the draining board by the sinks. That explained why it had been smeared everywhere.

He turned his attention back to the shelves, where the tins were stacked.

'At least they haven't got at my corned beef,' Will said, as he tried to console himself, but he didn't feel quite so hungry any more.

'Strip off all your gear and sling it in the trunk with your weapons,' Drake told Chester. 'We'll come back for it later.'

Mrs Burrows and Colly were waiting in the cellar as Chester took off his Bergen and then his belt kit, placing them in the open trunk. Then he contemplated his handgun, reluctant to be parted from it. 'Won't we need our weapons when we get to the warehouse?' he asked.

'You do realise it's lunchtime up here – there'll be people everywhere. And police. We don't want to be caught with any-thing incriminating on us – it's not worth the risk,' Drake replied. 'And I've got some hardware in my Range Rover, not far from Eddie's. We'll stop off there first.'

'Fine,' Chester agreed.

Drake cut a length of rope and fashioned it into a makeshift lead for the cat. Colly seemed to be less frightened of him as he looped and tied it around her neck, then handed the end to Mrs Burrows. 'For appearances' sake,' he said. Slamming the trunk shut and clicking down the catches, he placed a couple of crates of old books on the lid to hide it. 'Time to hit the road,' he announced.

He climbed the steps to the door at the end of the cellar and tried it. As he expected, it was locked. 'This might be a little noisy, but we should be okay,' he said.

He moved several steps down, then executed a perfect side kick at the lock. There was a crash as the wood splintered, and he pulled the door open and went through, Mrs Burrows and the Hunter behind him, as Chester brought up the rear.

As they emerged into the square it was indeed full of people. There were thirty or so pupils from the nearby school, some of whom were kicking a football around on the grassy area in the middle, while others sat about in small groups. In addition, as Chester squinted in the unaccustomed daylight, he could see a smattering of tourists toting cameras, and a couple of elderly men in clerical robes. He took a deep breath and closed the space between him and Mrs Burrows.

Silence descended on the square as people began to notice them.

The initial lull gave way to a ripple of astonished murmurs, the football rolling to a halt as the boys lost interest in their game. Everyone was watching the strange little group make its way along the side of the square. Chester realised that if he and Drake in their green and mud-caked Noddy suits weren't enough to attract attention, then a bald-headed woman with black dotted lines across her scalp, dressed in a blue tunic and wearing ruby-red slippers, was guaranteed to get them more than a passing glance. And Colly, equally as bald as Mrs Burrows and the size of a Great Dane, was the icing on the cake for the transfixed onlookers as she sniffed inquisitively at them.

As they neared the exit to the square, the porter was looking them over with hostile curiosity. He was a different man from the nightshift porter Drake had met twice before, but evidently had the same commitment to his job. Knowing the suspicious-looking trio with their pet would have to pass by him on their way out, he waited, tapping his foot on the ground.

'G'd af'noon,' he said in a clipped way to Drake, adjusting his weight on the balls of his feet as if preparing for a confrontation.

'It's a fine afternoon,' Drake agreed wholeheartedly, with his eyes half-closed as he gave the bright blue sky a glance. And before the porter could say another word, Drake proclaimed, 'If you're wondering, we're a performance art group.'

'Ahh. Artists,' the porter said. Reducing his own personal Defcon, he lowered to his heels and nodded knowingly, as if he required no further explanation.

They passed down the alleyway and out onto the street, where Drake went to the pavement's edge to hail a cab. But the people here were even more numerous than in the square, and were stopping to gawp at the strange foursome. A pair of identically dressed young Japanese punks, with huge and exaggerated coxcomb Mohicans of electric blue, strolled over to Mrs Burrows.

'Crucial look, sister,' the boy punk said, as he regarded her with unreserved admiration.

'Coooool lady,' the girl punk squealed.

'Thank you,' Mrs Burrows said. She'd been talking to Colly, trying to keep her calm in this new environment. The combination of the hubbub from all the people and the busy traffic passing by on Victoria Street was unsettling the Hunter, and her head was darting this way and that as she tried to take it all in.

'Groovy cat too,' the boy punk said to the girl punk, pointing at Colly with an amazed expression. The Hunter gave him a curious sniff.

The girl punk clapped her hands together in glee and jumped up and down. 'Yay! It's Doraemon – like in the manga!'

'Yes, real life Doraemon robot cat!' the boy punk said. He took a quick photograph of the Hunter whilst having an animated exchange with his girlfriend in Japanese, then they finally moved on.

Colly might have been in a state of high confusion, but Mrs Burrows herself didn't appear to be coping that well either. When Drake eventually found them a black cab, she looked extremely grateful as she sank into the back seat.

'Everything all right, Mrs Burrows?' Chester asked her.

'Sensory overload,' she merely replied, then asked for the window to be closed.

As they stopped at some lights, the taxi driver looked over his shoulder at Colly curled up on the floor. 'That really a guide dog? Never seen one like that before,' he said.

'Sure is. Now, we're in a hurry, so please put your foot down,' Drake asked him.

As they drew up beside Drake's Range Rover, he gave

Chester money to pay the fare, then ushered Mrs Burrows and Colly straight from the cab and into his car.

'Don't you want me to come too?' Mrs Burrows offered. 'I can help.'

'Celia, you look done in, and I think we can cope without your early warning system on this one. If I know Eddie, he'll have flown the coop,' Drake replied, then went to the rear of the car and opened the tailgate to get at a kit bag. 'Have a Beretta,' he said to Chester, passing him a handgun before tucking a second one into his belt.

Without speaking, Drake and Chester passed down several streets until they came to the warehouse, where they hugged the wall to avoid the surveillance cameras.

'Watch the shadows,' Drake said, unlocking the door, and opening it a fraction so he could check for any booby traps. Then they both slipped inside and took out their handguns. 'If he's here, he'll have seen us on the CCTV,' Drake warned Chester in a whisper. 'He'll know we're coming.'

They gave themselves thirty seconds to adjust to the dim light in the main body of the warehouse, then Drake led the way up the flight of stairs, continually scanning the various lumps of old machinery below in case Eddie was hiding there.

As they reached the top, they found the door to the apartment was wide open. 'Nice and slowly,' Drake whispered, creeping over the threshold.

The first thing they saw was that the carpet had been removed from the entrance lobby, leaving just bare concrete. As they went further in, their Berettas held in front of them, they found the floor of the main room was exactly the same. 'He's done a runner, and taken it all with him,' Drake said in a low voice. The room was a bare shell – the table with the

Waterloo battle scene, the bank of CCTV monitors, every stick of furniture, and even the wallpaper, had been stripped out.

But something remained on the bare floor in the middle of the room, and Drake and Chester's eyes were on it as they stepped closer.

The shape stirred.

'DAD! It's DAD!' Chester shouted. He tore over and removed the gag from his father, who was bound up with rope.

'Chester! Thank God it's you,' Mr Rawls spluttered. 'I don't know what happened! I just woke up like this.'

'Don't worry, Dad,' Chester said, checking his father over for any injuries as he loosened his ties. 'He's okay. Eddie hasn't hurt him,' he called over to Drake, who had gone to the far end of the room to investigate the bedrooms.

Drake was back within seconds. 'Nope. Nothing left.' He raised his eyebrows. 'I have to give it to him – pretty impressive at such short notice.'

'But how did he manage it?' Chester asked, as he undid the last of the rope from around his father's ankles and helped him to his feet.

'Perhaps he had a band of little helpers – some elves – to shift it all out for him? Who knows?' Drake chuckled. 'I'm just relieved Jeff here is unharmed.' As Drake glanced at Mr Rawls, he noticed something. 'Hold on a tick,' he said. He reached across to Mr Rawls' breast pocket and took out the note tucked into it, then unfolded it.

'*A gesture of goodwill for the future. Your friend,*' Drake read aloud.

Chester frowned. 'Sounds like it's for you, Drake. So did

he expect you to make it out of the Colony?'

Drake looked amused. 'Maybe. Maybe he's not as black and white as I thought he was. After all, he was prepared to leave that Colonist policeman to die with the rest of us in the explosion, but he still saw fit to spare Jeff here.'

'Explosion? Policeman? What on earth have you been doing?' Mr Rawls demanded, looking from Drake to his son.

'Why don't you take him out to the car, where you can fill him in?' Drake suggested to Chester. 'I'm going to drop you all off somewhere, then go back to the hotel to find out if your mother's shown up.' He thought for a second. 'But, first, there's something I need to see.'

Drake left the flat to descend the stairs. As he was making his way through the warehouse, he spotted something on the ground. He nudged it with his foot. It was a slug of a grey material, not dissimilar to old porridge. There was no sign of the motorbikes, but he didn't expect there to be as he and Eddie had left them in Westminster.

He saw the scaffolding frame draped with thick sheets of polythene was still standing in the corner of the warehouse. On his way over to it, Drake didn't stop to press the red button on the lathe's power panel and disarm the explosives – he already had a good idea what he was going to find.

As he lifted the sheets aside, he saw that although the concrete surround in the floor remained, the metal door had gone. Three or four steps of the stairway were still visible, but then the entire opening was filled with a grey slurry – it was the same substance that had been spilt on the factory floor. Drake hunted around until he found a length of wood, which he rammed into the dense slop, then pulled out again. He touched some of the material left on the wood, rolling it between his fingers.

'Quick-drying cement,' he said, and glanced down at the blocked opening, nodding to himself. 'So the whole cellar is pumped full of it . . . clever. You certainly made sure no one's going down there again . . . but I bet you took all that Styx equipment with you, didn't you, Eddie?'

Part Five

Reunion

Chapter Thirty-two

Will was showing Elliott around the harbour when they came across Bartleby, who had settled down on the concrete pier with one of his recent kills gripped between his paws. He was chewing noisily on either its head or rear end – Will couldn't tell which from the state of the gored carcass. Just like any cat, the Hunter was totally engrossed in his prey, to the exclusion of all else. He didn't even bother to lift his head to glance at Elliott as she wandered down the side of the pier and inspected the wreckage of the sunken boats in the bottom of the clear water.

Will had been staring absently at the other side of the lagoon where the old barge had drifted free, when he noticed what was attracting Elliott's attention. He slapped himself on the forehead. 'The launch! What an idiot! Why I didn't think of it before?' he burst out, and raced back up the pier. Once on the quayside, he hurried the short distance to the generator building.

'Yes, it's gone! Chester's taken the launch with the outboard that Dad and I left here,' he said, peering down the side of the building.

'So there's no question he went Topsoil. But where does that leave us?' Elliott asked, as she caught up with Will.

'I can probably get another outboard motor to work and there's gallons of fuel in the tanks down here, but the problem is . . .' Will said, as he scratched his chin. 'The problem is the launch.' He threw a glance at the low building where the vessels were kept. 'There aren't any.'

'No boats,' Elliott said.

'Well, there are, but the fibreglass is really ropey – I know because I had a good look at all of them. I double-checked after Dad picked one out. If I'd left it to him, I might not be here today.'

'Well, you are, and it seems as though *we're* here for keeps, doesn't it? We're marooned,' Elliott said glumly, as she set off down the quayside.

Is that such a bad thing? Will thought to himself before he knew it. Her body language wasn't lost on him as she walked despondently away, no longer taking much interest in her surroundings. *Maybe she hates being here with me. Maybe all she really wants is to be with Chester?* Will scrunched his eyes shut. *And maybe I'm just being a total dipstick. You shouldn't care so much – why do you care so much?* he posed to himself, with a small shrug.

'But I do care very much,' he answered himself earnestly, speaking out loud as he flicked his eyes open again.

Elliott seemed to slow her step at that instant, and Will wondered if she'd overheard him. He hoped not – she was far enough down the quay that the sound of the underground river at the very end should have drowned out his voice. At least, he hoped it had.

Blushing, he made an about turn and jogged back to the

fallout shelter, then entered it, going straight to the radio operator's booth.

'The black one, not the red one,' he said, remembering his instructions as he'd told Chester which of the wall-mounted telephones had, by some miracle, still been working. Will thought of his friend and the last time he'd seen him. It had been just before Will had followed after Dr Burrows with a leap into Smoking Jean, a leap into the unknown.

It was only months ago, but it seemed considerably longer. So much had happened since then. Will was now without a father – he'd lost yet another person central to his life. And, quite possibly, he'd also lost his mother. So many had died. At this rate, he thought to himself, he'd be the only one left, completely alone – a friendless, embittered orphan, always on the run from the Styx. That was if he himself survived.

As he slumped into one of the canvas-backed chairs, Will recalled how he'd been sitting in the same spot when Dr Burrows had surprised him with dry biscuits and a mess tin full of horribly over-sweetened tea.

As Will savoured that moment with his father, he realised how happy he'd been then, despite all the uncertainty surrounding his future. And despite the fact that Dr Burrows had been prepared to sacrifice everything, including his relationships with his wife and son, to his tenacious and single-minded pursuit of knowledge, there *had* been a caring and considerate side to him. Maybe it was hidden deep in Dr Burrows for much of the time – like one of his prized relics buried in the earth – but nevertheless Will had been treated to occasional glimpses of it.

'Dad. Dear old Dad,' Will muttered sadly, as he powered up the ancient radio on the bench before him, watching as the valves on the top began to glow. He didn't know if the radio even needed to be switched on for the telephone to work, although he felt superstitious about it, telling himself it couldn't do any harm. After a minute, when the valves were emitting a pink-orange light, he rose from the chair and reached across for the black telephone. He knew Drake's emergency number without even thinking – after Elliott's fever when she'd repeated it over and over again, it was one number that would forever be indelibly etched on his memory.

Although he had no idea whether Drake was still alive, or if anyone else might pick up the messages, Will dialled and left several for him on the server. He tried to keep them succinct, telling Drake that he and Elliott had reached the shelter, and that they had no means of making the journey back Topsoil. Just like the last time he'd used the telephone, he heard a few crackles and bursts of white noise in response, but otherwise there was nothing to confirm the call had got through.

Despite what the Rebecca twins had said on top of the pyramid, Will then tried his mother's mobile phone. Although he couldn't tell whether it was still connected, he left her a short message.

'Calls made,' he announced when he'd finished and replaced the receiver. It may have all been a complete waste of time, but at that very moment he wasn't exactly spoilt for options. Of course, he and Elliott could return down the inclined seam, but they'd merely end up in the land of the Brights again. And then what? Try to make it across to Martha's shack, and spend the rest of their days eating spider meat?

'Maybe I should try to build a boat,' Will mused to himself. As he thought about it, that didn't seem like such a far-fetched idea. There were enough materials to work with around the place, and even a full machine shop in one of the outhouses on the quayside. 'Yep, maybe make a boat,' Will decided. As he exited the radio operator's booth, he noticed he'd left the main blast door open. He went over and pushed it to. After the incident with the rats, he wasn't going to take any chances.

He headed to the main dormitory area and in the midst of the bunk beds, he came to the table where his father had gathered together all the documents and paperwork he'd been able to find in the place. The detailed survey plan of the fallout shelter and the surrounding area that Dr Burrows had left there was still spread open. And on top of this were a stack of equipment manuals, and a dog-eared paperback.

Will picked it up to read the title of the book, '*Ice Station Zebra*,' he said. Then he studied the colour photograph on the cover, which looked as though it was a scene from a film. In it there was a submarine poking up through the ice pack.

'The submarine we found was *real*,' Will mumbled, holding the book closer so he could see the men in parkas, who were posing around the conning tunnel with guns in their hands. The men appeared so heroic and sure of themselves. Will made a *humph* noise and tossed the book back onto the table. He had no idea what a hero was any more, and he certainly didn't need to read about fictional ones.

Although it was out of character – he'd never once offered to help with any form of cleaning in his Highfield days – he then set to work on the kitchen. He swept up all the shredded packets and rubbish left by the rats and, wearing a pair of rubber gloves he'd taken from the quartermaster's stores, threw it in a dustbin, which he dragged to the generator outbuilding.

As he inspected what was left in the kitchen, he found that the rats had gnawed their way inside most of the crates stacked against the wall and devoured their contents. But there were a few at the top that hadn't been breached, and to his delight these contained quite a number of the crackers in green foil packets, and also boxes of rations, each with a chocolate bar inside. Most of these bars were completely inedible, but as he proceeded to work his way through the boxes, he was finding the odd one in which the chocolate wasn't covered in a white powdery coating, and smelt and tasted all right. And Will's favourite from his last visit – pineapple chunks in syrup – had also been spared from the hungry rodents because it was canned.

'So I've got corned beef and bickies for the main course and, for pudding, pineapple chunks and chocolate. Life isn't so bad,' he sighed, trying his best to convince himself.

But as he weighed one of the rectangular cans of corned beef in his hand, then began to check for signs of corrosion along its seals, his mind wasn't on what he was doing. He was half listening for Elliott, wondering when she was going to come back to the shelter.

And wondering if she was really as discontented as she appeared because she was stranded in this place with him.

Beside Mrs Burrows on the back seat of the Range Rover, Chester was so exhausted that he fell into a deep slumber almost immediately Drake turned the key in the ignition. Mrs Burrows' eyes were shut, but she seemed to still be awake – her arm was over the back of the seat and she was stroking Colly. Laid out in the rear of the vehicle, the Hunter's steady purring was audible over the sound of the car engine.

They were making their way out of central London when Mr Rawls, in the passenger seat next to Drake, finally spoke up. 'What do you think my wife's chances are?' he asked. 'Tell me straight.'

'Okay, Jeff, but this isn't going to be easy for you,' Drake said, as he changed gear. 'She has some minor strategic value to the Styx, because of her connection to Chester, and hence to the rest of us. So, like bait in a trap, I expect she's back at your house in Highfield right now.'

'Really?' Mr Rawls said, the optimism evident in his voice.

'But don't get your hopes up. There are two options; the first is that I try to extract her again. But if I muff it and they take me alive, then you'll all be put at risk. So you wouldn't have just lost Emily, but both you and your son would fall into their hands too.'

'Right . . . and the second option?' Mr Rawls asked hollowly.

As they stopped at a junction, a small terrier on the pavement began to yap loudly. Drake glanced in the rear-view mirror.

'Cat!' he exclaimed. Colly's head had popped up like a jack-in-the-box. She'd fixed her gimlet eyes on the dog and was making a low growling noise, her top lip hiked up to display her glistening incisors. 'Get that Hunter out of sight!' Drake ordered.

'Steady, girl,' Mrs Burrows said, and the cat immediately complied, sinking down again.

'You were saying,' Mr Rawls prompted Drake. 'The second option?'

'Yes. I did all I could to deprogramme your wife, but she's

obviously highly susceptible to the Dark Light. She might be useful to the Styx in the future, as one of their 'drones' or 'sleepers', or whatever you want to call them. My best guess is they'll keep her around for the time being.'

Mr Rawls considered this for a moment. 'So, really, we should leave her be. And there's absolutely no one else we can go to for help to get her back . . . and do something about the Styx?'

'I'm afraid not, unless there's another autonomous group out there somewhere that I haven't heard about, and there may well be. But if you think about it, if they're any good, I won't find out about them anyway.'

'Quite,' Mr Rawls agreed, now staring at Drake. 'So you're not even going to *try* to get Emily back, are you, because of the risk?'

'Look, I'm not saying it's out of the question. I'm going straight to Highfield after I've dropped you off. I'll take a look – from a distance – but I have to tell you, Jeff, that I think we should let things ride, at least for the next fortnight or so,' Drake said.

'Yes, I see the logic in that,' Mr Rawls said. 'Life and death . . . the checks and balances of my new existence,' he added quietly. 'How can you stand to live this way, Drake?' he asked.

'Because, a long time ago, the Styx gave me no alternative,' Drake answered.

In the middle of an anonymous housing estate, Drake drew up in front of a row of garages. As they all disembarked from the Range Rover, he lifted the door to one of the garages just sufficiently for them to duck inside. It was stacked high with cases of equipment, from amongst which Drake produced a pair of fold-out chairs, a single camp bed and some sleeping bags. Telling them all not to go outside for anything, he closed and locked the door behind him, then drove off.

Leaving the car on the outskirts of Highfield, Drake went the rest of the way on foot, always keeping to the backstreets. Putting on a pair of dark glasses, he finally emerged onto the High Street. With a glance at the museum where Dr Burrows had once worked, he continued along, slowing slightly as he saw the Clarkes' former grocery shop on the opposite side of the road, which had become a coffee bar. It wasn't part of one of the major chains, but a cheaply-fitted-out local effort proclaiming itself rather curiously to be '**The Village Coffee Shop**', offering 'Cut Price Internet Access' according to the signs taped inside the window.

As he swung on his heels to go inside the newsagent's, he removed his dark glasses and then pretended to browse the magazines.

The shopkeeper was giving Drake surreptitious glances at the same time as working through a list on the counter in front of him. As he became absorbed in his task and took his eyes off Drake, he started to sing abstractly to himself, 'Dem bones, dem bones, gonna walk around.'

Drake moved to the central display in the shop where there was a selection of stationery and inexpensive toys. As he pretended to examine a padded envelope, he simultaneously felt the underside of a shelf in the display. Retrieving a note that had been stuck there, he palmed it.

'Connected to the thigh bone . . .' The shopkeeper suddenly stopped singing. 'Need any assistance there?' he offered. 'Are you looking for something?'

Drake went over to him with the envelope. 'Found what I

wanted, thanks. I'll take this.'

Once outside the shop, Drake put his sunglasses back on, hesitated for a moment, then crossed the road to the coffee shop where he ordered a cappuccino and half an hour's Internet access. He had no intention of going further into Highfield. There was no need.

'He's back,' Mr Rawls said, as they heard the key in the lock and the garage door raised up. Drake ducked inside, then pulled the door down behind him.

Drake had two carrier bags with him. He passed one to Mrs Burrows. 'Some new clothes for you, Celia, so you don't have to go around in that policeman's jacket. And there's also a hat in there to make you less conspicuous.'

'Did you see her?' Chester asked eagerly.

Drake passed the other bag to Mr Rawls, who was on his feet, looking at him expectantly.

'Coffee and pastries,' Drake said.

'So was my mum there?' Chester asked again.

Drake nodded grimly. 'She's back at home, but I couldn't get close. All the signs are that they're keeping tabs on her. I'm sorry – I'm not going to attempt anything for the moment. It's too dangerous, for all of us.'

He waited for this to sink in, then spoke again. 'But I've also got some good news for you. Will and Elliott are okay. They've come back from . . .' Drake frowned before he continued, '. . . from another world at the centre of the planet.'

'What?' Mr Rawls mumbled.

'That was what Will said in the messages I just listened to. They're stranded in the deep-level shelter, with no way to make the journey upriver.'

Despite the news about his mother, Chester was grinning from ear to ear. 'Will! Elliott! Oh, that's fantastic!' he exclaimed.

'Thank God,' Mrs Burrows exhaled, and sat down suddenly, as if the news was more than she could have ever hoped for. 'And my husband?' she asked quietly.

'There were two messages and the quality wasn't up to much. I might have missed something, but Will didn't mention the Doc, only that Bartleby was with them.'

Mrs Burrows nodded.

Drake clapped his hands. 'Right. You can drink those coffees on the way. We're going to Norfolk.'

As they trooped outside, they were stunned to find a battered white minibus instead of the Range Rover.

'Done a swap with your friend in the garage?' Chester asked, looking the vehicle over. 'It's really not your style, is it?'

'I should reserve your judgement on that,' Drake replied, as he thought about where he was about to take them.

Thirteen miles before the disused airfield in Norfolk, Drake suddenly left the main road, steering the minibus into a bald and muddy field. Around its edges were a collection of motley-looking mobile homes and caravans, with heavily patched canvas tents and even what appeared to be makeshift tepees dotted between them. A large fire burnt in the centre of the field, around which numerous raggedy children and dogs raced.

'A bonfire?' Mr Rawls said. 'What have we stopped here for?'

'That's not a bonfire, it's a car that's been set alight,'

Chester observed uneasily.

'This is where you'll be staying while I go down to the deep level shelter,' Drake said. 'I'm sure it's not what you expected, but the round trip to and from the shelter takes a couple of days at best, and I can hardly put all of you up in some country B&B, can I? Particularly not with the Hunter.'

'Um, no, I'm coming with you,' Chester said, as he regarded the various mobile homes with distaste. 'Besides, you'll need help with the launch, and I know the route. I've done it before. I'm your man for the job,' the boy added.

'I don't need any help, and it's not practical for you to come too. Apart from the fact I'll be carrying spare cans of fuel for the return journey, I don't know how many passengers I'll be bringing back. Even if it's just Will and Elliott on board, there's not going to be a lot of room, is there?'

'I suppose you're right,' Chester conceded.

'And you need to keep an open mind,' Drake said, fixing him with an uncompromising stare. 'Just because they've chosen a different way of life and nobody wants them on their doorstep, it doesn't mean these aren't good people. I've had dealings with them in the past, and they've never let me down. If I can negotiate a price for you all to be put up in one of their homes, they'll look after you well. I guarantee you that.' Drake scanned the scene before them. 'And you should be safe here. They avoid the police like the plague, which is a real plus, but the best thing is that the Styx are unlikely to have infiltrated them. Why would they bother? There's nothing for the White Necks to gain from it.'

Chester nodded.

'Just, please, make sure Colly's kept well away from their dogs,' Drake added as an afterthought. 'They won't take kindly to it if she stiffs one of their prize greyhounds.'

A shout came above the sound of the wind. On the slope leading down to the Pore a cluster of basic huts had been erected, and three Limiter officers now exited hurriedly from one of these. They slowed to look at where their mounts were tethered. The horses were agitated and whinnying as a cave cow, one of the huge insects indigenous to the Deeps, helped itself to oats from the food trough. The cave cow was only a young calf, similar to the one Dr Burrows had befriended, but it still had the dimensions of a small family car. The front pair of its three sets of articulated legs was buried in the grain in the trough as its mouthparts clacked hungrily away; food was hard to come by in these lands of constant night, and it wasn't going to waste the opportunity to gorge itself.

The tallest of the three Limiter officers raised his rifle at the large dome of its carapace, using his scope to seek out its smaller head. Oblivious to the danger it was in, the cave cow continued in its feeding frenzy, its chopstick-like antennae vacillating so quickly they were a blur.

'Leave it – it's no threat to the horses,' one of his comrades told him. 'We'll deal with it later.'

The constant shower of water falling from above grew more intense as the trio approached the edge of the Pore then walked the full length of the wooden platform, which had been built some thirty metres out over the titanic void. At the very end of the platform, two of their subordinates were manning long-range, light-gathering telescopes as they scoured the blackness below.

The three officers now spoke to them.

'You called. Have you got something?'

The Limiter on one of the telescopes looked up. 'Yes. We saw a single flare.'

'You're sure?'

'Positive,' the other observer said, without moving from his telescope. 'We're just waiting to see if there's a second one.' Several seconds passed, then both the observers spotted it.

Although it didn't register on their ghoulish faces, a palpable sense of relief emanated from the three Limiter officers as they went into a huddle.

'Two flares. So someone's made it back. We need to pass this news up the chain of command,' the tall Limiter said. 'Immediately.'

'And we may need more balloons, because we've already lost four in accidents,' his fellow officer remarked.

'Yes, and if we're going to recover our men in relays between the balloons, it's going to take too long,' the third officer suggested. 'The current arrangement is far from ideal. I hate this reliance on such outmoded technology.'

Moving to the wooden rail at the side of the platform, all three officers stared down into the unbroken darkness of the void below. But they had no hope of seeing the hot air balloon thousands of metres below them, or the many others below it, in a chain that stretched all the way down the Pore for hundreds of kilometres.

'We can only pray that down there somewhere, one of our men has recovered the Dominion virus,' the tall Limiter officer said, voicing the concern they all shared.

⚜

'Aren't you ready yet?' Will called out, chuckling as he waited for Elliott to emerge from the quartermaster's stores. Located in one of the rooms around the dormitory area in the fallout shelter, it was an Aladdin's Cave of military uniforms and equipment.

For several hours Will had buried his nose in a book he'd found on fibreglass vessels. Having finished the chapter on repairing hulls, he'd announced to Elliott that he thought he might be able to patch up the least damaged of the launches from those left in the outhouse. On hearing this, Elliott's whole demeanour had brightened, and she'd suggested he take a break so they could try on some of the military gear from the racks in the stores.

And now, as Elliott still failed to make her big appearance, Will adjusted his clothes. He'd had his turn first and was sporting a ridiculously baggy light-fawn tropical outfit, complete with a pith helmet.

'Can't you find anything?' Will shouted, wondering why girls took so long when it came to clothes.

'Ready,' she shouted back, as she sashayed through the doorway. With a mesh scarf tied around her head like a bandana, she was wearing dark green shorts, a white gym vest and the most incredible US Air Force flight jacket of supple black leather. The only comic touch was a pair of combat boots many sizes too large for her, which she was now struggling to walk in.

From all the time she had spent out in the open in the inner world, Elliott's skin was still tanned, and her hair long and glossy – to Will's eye she looked simply stunning in her outfit.

'Wow!' Will gasped.

'What do you mean 'Wow'?' she said, laughing as she took

two clomping steps and then nearly tripped. 'Don't I look funny in this?'

'Well, no actually, I think you look great,' he said.

She stopped trying to walk and smiled at him.

'You left the front door wide open!' a voice announced.

Accompanied by Bartleby, who was wagging his tail excitedly, a figure appeared around one of the bunk beds.

It was drenched and leaving puddles of water behind it.

'Drake!' Elliott shrieked. She ran full pelt at him, managing to trip herself up.

'Ooof!' he exhaled, as she slammed into him.

She held tightly to him as she cried tears of relief. 'The twins said . . . I thought you were dead,' she gasped. 'But I couldn't believe it was true.'

'Well, it isn't true yet, anyway,' Drake chuckled. He extended a hand towards Will. 'I've never seen you both look so good. This place you've been to – this "secret world" – must have really agreed with you.' As Elliott detached herself, Drake gave the boy a hug, then held him at arm's length to take in his outfit. Grinning, he shook his head. 'I'm not convinced by that get-up – it's just not *you*, is it?' He glanced back at Elliott. 'However, I really dig that flight jacket. I hope there's one in my size.' He stopped grinning and turned to Will. 'Tell me about the Doc? Is he—?'

'He didn't make it,' Will said abruptly. 'One of the Rebeccas shot him. In the back.'

'Damn!' Drake said quietly, inclining his head for a moment. 'I gathered something might have happened to him . . . from your message.' He wiped the moisture from his face and looked up again. 'I want you to tell me about it over a cup of tea. I hope you've got some in this place. I need something warm after that hike downriver.'

'We've got loads of fresh rat in the cold store, if you'd like some?' Elliott offered enthusiastically.

Drake hesitated, meeting eyes with Will.

'No, maybe better if I make you something,' Will put in quickly. He removed his pith helmet and lobbed it through the door of the store, then they all headed for the kitchen.

Will and Elliott took Drake through the chain of events at the pyramid.

'I hope I did the right thing?' Elliott asked, referring to the Dominion virus and the exchange she'd been forced to make with the Rebecca twins.

Drake nodded. 'We've got the vaccine, which means the virus is pretty much useless to them,' he replied. 'You did well, both of you.' He took a deep breath. 'Okay, it's my turn now,' he announced, and proceeded to tell Elliott about her father.

She was dumbstruck. 'So, what, he's trying to bring the regime down? A Styx against the Styx?'

'Yes, he's playing his own game,' Drake said. Then he went on to tell them about his foray into the Colony with Chester, and how they'd brought Mrs Burrows out with them.

Will choked on his tea. 'But she's blind?'

'I think she's something else altogether now,' Drake replied. 'I haven't explored what she's capable of, but it's as though she's been given an incredible gift. A new and powerful sense.'

As Will opened his mouth to ask more questions, Drake shook his head. 'Look, rather than sit here jawing about it, why don't I get you home, then you can ask her yourself?'

Will and Elliott rapidly agreed to this.

'But after the operation on Highfield Common cratered,

somehow I never found the time to come down here for a look round,' Drake said. 'So, before we leave, I want you to give me the full tour.'

Once Will and Elliott had shown Drake the dormitory area and adjoining rooms, they took him to the armoury. He was like a child in a sweet shop as he selected a few items to take back with him.

'*Radio Operator*,' Drake read on the door of the next cabin when they were out in the corridor again. 'This has to be where all the comms are based, and the telephone link you called me on?'

'Certainly is,' Will answered, as he pushed the door open.

Wandering in, Drake gave the room the once-over.

He froze.

'What's that?' he said suddenly.

'What's what?' Surprised that Drake had drawn his handgun, Will stepped from behind him to see what he was referring to.

Drake's eyes were fixed on the bench. In front of the main radio was a model soldier, barely more than a centimetre tall.

'Did you know that was there?' Drake demanded urgently.

'No way,' Will replied. 'And I've no idea where it's come from.'

Drake moved closer to it. 'What about you, Elliott?' he asked. 'Know anything about this?'

'Not me,' she said.

Will reached towards the soldier.

'No! Don't touch it!' Drake warned, as he ducked down to look under the bench. Once he was satisfied, he got back up and checked the area immediately around the figure. 'No wires, no traps,' he said under his breath, then very carefully picked the figure up.

As Drake held it to the light, Will could see that it wasn't a modern soldier, but one from an old campaign. Sporting some sort of admiral's hat, and with a cavalry sword hanging from a belt around its waist, it appeared to be writing on a map, or perhaps a battle plan.

But the oddest thing was that the figure's long jacket and trousers had been painted to resemble the camouflage of a Limiter's combats. And it was a perfect copy of this camouflage – the disruptive pattern consisting of rectangular patches of light and dark brown.

Will frowned with incomprehension. It might have only been a model soldier, but it was certainly a menacing one. 'It looks like a Limiter, but it's d—' he started to say.

'It's the Iron Duke. The Battle of Waterloo is his great passion,' Drake cut him short. 'This is the Duke of Wellington, but *Eddie* style.'

There was a sharp intake of breath from Elliott. 'Isn't that what you called my father?'

'I don't understand. Was Wellington a Styx then?' Will asked.

Drake turned to him. 'No, I don't think so – just a brilliant tactician, and Eddie admired him for it, and the way he trounced Napoleon. But tell me – I need to know when you were last in here.'

'More than two days ago . . . when I made the calls to you,' the boy answered, trying to remember. 'But, no . . . hold on . . . I did come in once after that.'

'When, exactly? This is important,' Drake snapped.

'Probably ten or twelve hours ago. And I'm absolutely

positive the soldier wasn't here then,' Will replied.

'So while we slept, my father's been here . . . and he sneaked this in,' Elliott reasoned, then frowned. 'And Bartleby didn't hear him?'

Drake passed her the model soldier. 'He's a Limiter, isn't he?' he merely said in explanation. 'Right, both of you grab yourselves a weapon . . .' he began, then caught himself. 'Elliott, you need to tell me now that you're okay with this? I'm not the best of friends with your old man, and if I come across him here, I will use ultimate force. I will shoot to kill.'

Elliott didn't hesitate in her response. 'Sure, ultimate force. He means nothing to me,' she confirmed.

'Good,' Drake said, with a brief smile, but his eyes were deadly serious. 'Now we're going to comb every damned inch of this place.'

They first went to see if there was another vessel hidden on the quayside or in the harbour, as Eddie would have required one for the journey down the river. But other than the launch that Drake had just arrived in, they found nothing. Then they systematically checked and rechecked the fallout shelter, each of the outbuildings, and every nook and cranny in the harbour. Working as a team and armed to the teeth, it took them several hours to finish the job. And although they'd put Bartleby into play with his acute sense of smell, the Hunter seemed unable to find anything either.

As they made their way back into the shelter, Drake was still looking around nervously.

'Just because we can't find him, doesn't mean he's not here,' he said. 'I suggest we pack up and split from this place.'

'You bet,' Will and Elliott chorused.

Chapter Thirty-three

In one of the upper levels of the Styx Citadel, the corridor outside the old Styx's rooms was filled with a long queue of those he'd summoned to report to him. This was the most important floor of the whole building, from where all the Styx's major operations were orchestrated. Despite this, it was virtually indistinguishable from the rest of the Citadel; with its unadorned white walls and stone floors, dingily lit with only the odd luminescent orb, it had a somewhat monastic feel.

And as the Styx waited in line in the corridor, they could hear furious shouting from behind their master's door. Finally a young officer from the Division emerged. Blood had spilt down the pale skin of his face from a cut on his temple, but he kept his eyes resolutely before him as he marched along the corridor.

The old Styx was still in full flow, even though now alone. 'I will *not* tolerate failure on this scale,' he raged, as he heard a high-pitched sound and then a clunk from the burnished brass pipes on the wall behind him. He leapt from his chair and went to one of the pipes, opening a hatch in it to extract a bullet-shaped cylinder. He unscrewed the top, and took out a roll of yellowing paper, which he quickly unfurled.

It was from the Scientists, and what was written on it only incensed him further. 'NO!' He slung the message carrier across the room, only this time there was no one there to be struck by it. 'NO!' he yelled again, sweeping everything from his desk onto the floor. 'NO! NO! NO!'

His young assistant appeared in the doorway, clearing his throat to announce his presence.

The old Styx had his back to him as he shouted, 'We lost half our lab facilities in a single hit . . . and now my worst fears have been confirmed. That bloody man Drake also fumigated and wiped out the source of any new virus in the Eternal City. Why can't we find and kill him? Why is there never any good news?'

'I think we might be able to help with that,' Rebecca Two said, as she and her sister stepped into the room.

The old Styx wheeled around. He didn't smile and there was nothing approaching relief on his face as he saw that his two granddaughters were still alive, but his eyes glistened with anticipation.

'Do you want our good news first, or our even *better* news?' Rebecca One asked, as she sat in the chair on the other side of the desk. 'Let's start with the good news,' she said matter-of-factly, as she took out the phial of Dominion virus and placed it on the now empty desktop before him.

The old Styx nodded. 'And the even better news?' he enquired.

'We have a brand new army at our disposal. They're called New Germanians, they've had several Dark Light sessions, and they're ready for deployment,' Rebecca Two answered. 'Here's one I prepared earlier.' She clicked her fingers. Captain Franz entered the room and stood smartly to attention. 'There are oodles more like him – thousands, in fact. And we also have control of their air force and naval fleet, and all the hardware you could want to mount a full-scale land war. Some of it's rather time-expired, but it's reliable enough.'

Rebecca One spoke up. 'We just have to work out how to get it all up here. It's in the centre of the planet, where there's another world,' she explained.

The old Styx nodded, as if nothing he was hearing – even the existence of an inner world – came as a revelation to him.

He took a breath. 'First things first,' he said. 'I see the virus on my desk, but I don't see a second phial. Where's the vaccine?'

Rebecca One grimaced as she held up her thumb and index finger, keeping them apart by a whisker. 'There's a tinsy winsy bit of bad news, but we didn't want to fall into that "good news, bad news" routine.'

'No,' Rebecca Two said, as she took a couple of steps across the room, then spun daintily to face the old Styx. 'The vaccine phial was supposedly broken and its contents lost. But when we thought it through afterwards, we realised that Will or Elliott or both of them might have glugged it down – most likely Elliott, as she was unaccounted for when we first arrived at the scene.'

'We're not entirely sure about this, though,' Rebecca One added. 'But if the half-breed or that idiot do have it and they somehow manage to get it into the right hands, say to Drake, th—'

'We know precisely where Drake will try to take it, so we should do some forward planning,' the old Styx interrupted, waving his young assistant over to him.

'Oh, and we offed Dr Burrows, so there's one less fly in the ointment,' Rebecca Two said, as an afterthought.

'Fine,' the old Styx replied distantly, as he wrote on a piece of paper and passed it to his assistant, who scuttled out of the room. 'Now go back to the very beginning. I want chapter and verse on this new army of ours.'

The journey up the subterranean river went without event. For much of the way Will manned the outboard, while Elliott acted as pilot at the bow of the launch, so allowing Drake to get some rest. Each time they pulled into the fuelling stations along the route, they made sure they had some warm food before grabbing an hour or two of sleep.

After a day and a half, they arrived at their final destination, the long quayside, and made their way to the disused airfield above.

At three o'clock in the afternoon they climbed from the shaft and, under a leaden sky, Elliott took her very first steps on the outer crust of the planet. After her time in the unspoilt jungle of the inner world, she appeared unimpressed as she shielded her eyes to look at the derelict buildings. Then she raised her head to squint at the dull circle of the sun. 'So this is your home?' she asked.

'Yeah,' Will answered, 'this is it, all right.'

Drake drove them to the travellers' site, drawing up by one of the mobile homes. They all got out, except for Bartleby, who remained locked in the vehicle, his nose pressed up against the window. As he ogled the many dogs roaming loose in the field, strings of drool began to extend from his mouth and he made vibrato whining noises.

Will and Elliott stood there, not knowing what they were meant to do next. Drake went to the door of the mobile home, then noticed Will wasn't following him.

'Your mother's in here,' he said, and knocked twice on the door.

Will didn't respond as Elliott, looking very unsure of herself, took a step closer to him.

'Is this like the place where you used to live?' she asked Will. She'd seen the towns and villages they'd driven through on the way there, and now frowned as she peered around the site. A fire – a real bonfire this time – had been lit beside the husk of the burnt-out car, and a group of people were sitting around it. From the group, Will could hear strains of a song – a woman was singing what sounded like a ballad as someone strummed a guitar in accompaniment.

'No, nothing like this,' he answered. 'I lived in a city. This is very different. Too much mud,' he added, then tried to laugh.

Nodding once, Elliott took another step towards him.

Will bit his lip. He didn't know if he was reading the situation correctly, but he sensed that she wanted to say more, or perhaps she wanted *him* to say more. And he did want to say something. As this small chapter in their lives – during which they'd only had each other for company – came to a close, it felt to Will as though it needed to be acknowledged in some way.

But Will was at a loss as to what he should say and, even if he had known, how to say it. It was as if he wasn't equipped yet to handle the situation. And the timing was somehow all wrong, particularly with Drake present.

The moment, if it was a moment, was lost as a woman's voice came from inside the mobile home. Drake was about to open the door when Elliott jerked her head as she spotted something. 'Chester!' she exclaimed, the excitement evident in her voice. 'Isn't that him over there? By the fire?'

'Yes, he's with his dad, Jeff,' Drake told her.

Elliott glanced at Will. 'I'll . . . um . . . see you later,' she mumbled, striding off.

'Yes, see you later,' Will replied quietly.

'In here, Will,' Drake said, as he opened the door and ushered the boy in, but didn't enter himself. As the door closed behind Will, he found it difficult to see much in the gloom because all the curtains were drawn.

'Will,' a voice said. 'I knew it was you.'

'Mum!' Will cried, rushing over to where Mrs Burrows was sitting on a padded window seat.

Mrs Burrows hugged her son, tears falling from her sightless eyes. 'You made it,' she said.

'We both made it,' Will choked, then pulled back as he tried to see his mother's face in the near darkness. 'Drake told me what they did to you.'

As she held Will's hands in her own, she squeezed them. 'It was a small price to pay. Roger paid a bigger one.'

'Oh, Mum, it was awful . . . he . . .' Will was saying, then stopped himself. 'But how do you know what happened? How do you know he didn't come with us, and he's not waiting outside?'

'Because I know who's outside,' she answered.

'Really? But how?' Will asked.

She sighed. 'And I could sense the sadness in you as soon as you stepped from the minibus.'

At that moment, Drake returned, dragging Bartleby by the lead. The Hunter's claws were out and his eyes were wild. As soon as Drake took the lead off him, he tore back to the door, head-butting it as he tried to get through it. 'He's going crazy for the dogs. Probably best if I stick him in the bedroom with Colly,' Drake said.

'No, why don't you let her in here instead,' Mrs Burrows suggested. 'Colly's been cooped up for too long, and she's got to meet Bartleby, sooner or later.'

By now, Bartleby had picked up the scent of the other Hunter. Straight away he began to scamper around in circles as he snuffled at the worn carpet inside the mobile home.

As Drake opened the bedroom door, Colly came bucketing out. The two Hunters faced each other, taking inquisitive sniffs, but not coming too close. Then they lurched at each other and touched noses, as Bartleby pawed the carpet. With a rumbling growl, he bared his fangs. Without any warning, Colly gave Bartleby a good, strong nip on the side of the head. He let out an indignant yelp.

But, far from retaliating, Bartleby licked the other cat's ear affectionately.

Mrs Burrows chuckled. 'Just showing him who's boss.'

'Know how he feels,' Will muttered.

'I'll make myself scarce so you two can catch up,' Drake said, leaving Will and his mother together in the mobile home.

Will eventually emerged into the field. He headed for the fire, where a man was now singing. Chester and his father were sitting on a hay bale, listening to the song, but there was no sign of either Drake or Elliott. Will assumed that he'd taken her off to draw samples of her blood. He'd spoken about getting them to a number of London-based hospitals, so at least they'd have the vaccine ready for production if the Styx decided to release the Dominion virus.

Creeping up behind his friend, Will put his hands around his neck. 'Boo!' he said.

'No!' Chester yelled, leaping up from the bale he was lounging on.

He looked terrified until he saw who it was. 'You!' he laughed, pushing Will back, but not aggressively. 'You want to be careful. We're all a bit jumpy round here,' he added in a low voice.

'All right?' one of the larger kids shouted across to Chester, concern on his face.

Will realised then that the singer had fallen silent, and quite a few of the travellers and their children had risen to their feet. They were giving him less than friendly looks.

'Yes, it's okay, really. I know this muppet,' Chester replied. He turned to Will. 'And this is my dad,' he added, indicating his father beside him.

It seemed to be incredibly formal and out of place, but Will and Mr Rawls shook hands and said hello to each other.

Chester leant towards Will. 'This really is the coolest place. Haven't felt so safe in months.'

As the singer resumed, Will scanned the people around the fire. It was a collection of such incredible characters that he suddenly thought of Uncle Tam's gang, whom he'd met outside the tavern in the Colony. Will wasn't sure what had invoked this memory, but decided it was probably because there was a man in the assembled circle who was the spitting image of Imago Freebone.

Shaking his head, Will smiled at his friend. 'Look at us, round a gypsy camp fire. If only our teachers from school could see us now,' he said.

'If only,' Chester replied.

Then they were both laughing, delighted to be reunited again.

When it was time for them to leave the travellers' site, Drake slid open the side door of the minibus. Now that they were more interested in each other than the dogs running around the field, Drake was able to get the Hunters inside without any difficulty. He made sure they went to the very back of the vehicle, where Colly jumped up onto the seat. This didn't leave any room for Bartleby, who was relegated to the floor where Drake had laid an old blanket. But they both seemed to be more than happy, stretching out and making themselves comfortable.

'Celia,' Drake said to Mrs Burrows, 'Why don't you and Jeff take the next row?' He went to guide Mrs Burrows by the arm, but she drew back from him.

'I really don't need any help,' she told him, firmly but gently. 'And why don't you let the others go first?'

'Sure. Elliott, you next, then,' Drake suggested.

Will had been waiting patiently at the back of the line with Chester, but to his surprise his friend suddenly forged ahead and followed Elliott in so he could sit with her. And when Chester was inside, he took off his Bergen and placed it beside him, so that there was no room for anyone else on the seat.

As Mrs Burrows and Mr Rawls boarded and settled themselves in the next row, Drake briefly met eyes with Will.

'Looks like it's you and me in the front, old chap,' he said.

As Drake started up the minibus and they headed towards London, the two Hunters were soon fast asleep, in total contrast to Elliott and Chester who were talking nonstop as they swapped stories. Although Will responded whenever they directed the odd comment at him, he began to feel thoroughly left out.

Mr Rawls and Mrs Burrows didn't speak at all, but as if sensing Will's mood, his mother leant forward and squeezed his arm to comfort him. 'We're safe now, Will,' she said. 'That's the main thing.'

Drake wound his window down a little and turned on the rather basic radio. 'Getting drowsy. Need to wake myself up,' he confided to Will.

Will was happily listening to the songs, but stiffened as a new one came on. '*You are my sunshine, my only sunshine,*' the singer crooned.

'Do you mind if I change the station?' Will asked Drake, grimacing.

At the start of the motorway Drake pulled into the services, and twisted around in his seat to address them.

'Right, that's enough chitchat. I want you all to get some shut eye, and I'm afraid I need you to put these on.' He reached into the foot well in front of Will and pulled out a bag, from which he produced some hoods.

'So we can't see where you're taking us?' Will asked, as he examined the hood that Drake had handed him. 'Why's that necessary?'

'Obviously the Hunters will make it tricky to maintain a low profile anywhere in London,' Drake explained. 'I can't expect them to stay inside all the time. Besides that, there are just too many of us to camp out in one of my safe houses. So I've arranged to go to someone who can put us all up, but it has to be on the basis that I don't expose them to any danger.'

'So if we don't know where we are, we can't lead the Styx back to them if we're Darklit,' Will reasoned.

'Need to know basis,' Chester piped up.

Drake nodded.

'We're going on a magical mystery tour,' Mrs Burrows said mischievously, as she began to pull her hood over her head.

Drake chuckled. 'Er . . . Celia . . . wait a minute – that's not going to work with you, is it?'

'Not . . . really,' she admitted. 'I might pick up a few clues along the way.'

'Thought as much,' Drake said, extracting a small tub of Vicks from his coat pocket. 'So instead, I want you to rub some of this decongestant under your nose. I have no idea how strong this new sense of yours is, but I hope it'll do the trick?'

'You think of everything,' she said.

Chapter Thirty-four

Drake drove for many hours, finally leaving the main thoroughfare for a succession of single-track roads. The junctions he came to lacked signposts, but he was so familiar with the route that he had no need for them. He finally stopped before a pair of metal gates hung between substantial stone columns. Perched on top of these columns were weatherworn griffins, their expressions fierce, as if daring anyone to enter.

'Gog and Magog,' Drake said to them, as though he was greeting long lost friends, then cast an eye over his bus full of hooded passengers, who had slept for most of the way. As the gates swung slowly open, he edged through them and continued on the other side. The rolling pastures of rough grassland to his left and right were dotted here and there with twisted oaks or wind-whipped beeches.

When the gates were out of sight, he spoke loudly. 'Rise and shine, everybody! Hoods off! We're here!'

They began to stir and wake from their slumber, removing their hoods as Mrs Burrows wiped the decongestant from her top lip. 'It'll be a while before I get over that smell,' she grumbled.

Will's vision took a moment to adjust to the light and allow him to see their surroundings clearly. 'We're in the countryside!' he said.

As if to order, the sun crept from behind the clouds, bathing the landscape in its gentle glow and conferring upon the pasture a rich, golden bloom. Accelerating down a steep incline in the track, Drake took the minibus over a cattle grid. Then a small hump-backed bridge came into view, but Drake made no attempt to moderate his speed as he raced across it. The minibus felt as though as it was going to take off – and it did, landing with a bone-jarring thump.

'There goes my stomach!' Chester laughed, as he and his fellow passengers held on to stop themselves from being thrown about.

'Hey! A lake!' Will exclaimed, as his eyes fell on the expanse of water to the left of the track, its banks thick with bulrushes. On a small island in the middle of the lake, nestling between a spinney of sycamores, was a replica pagoda. The combination of this and the faux curved-back bridge that extended a short distance from the island, gave the impression that someone had attempted to recreate the design found on a Wedgwood Willow plate.

Then the minibus began to climb to the top of a hill and, as they reached the brow, a magnificent house of pale stone loomed before them.

'We're staying here?' Mr Rawls asked, putting into words what they were all thinking. 'Looks like a stately home.'

'It is,' Drake said, heaving down on the steering wheel as the minibus careered around the stone fountain in the centre of the circular drive. Then he slammed on the brakes and the minibus skewed to a halt in the gravel.

In rapt silence, everyone clambered out, grateful to stretch their legs after so long on the road. The two Hunters, when Drake had finally managed to rouse them, couldn't get out of the vehicle quickly enough. They almost knocked him over as they bolted through the door and made straight for the grassy slopes, haring down towards the lake at full pelt, like two frolicking foals.

'This way,' Drake announced, with a wave of his hand at the house. He climbed the steps up to the main doors two at a time, and didn't stop to ring the bell, throwing them open as if he owned the place.

'Hello! We're here!' he called as he entered, his voice echoing through the interior.

Not knowing what to expect, Will and the others had followed him in. They now stepped hesitantly across the black-and-white marble floor, with a coat of arms set into the centre.

None of them spoke as they took in the dark wood panelling and the huge staircase that swept up to the first floor. Above them, the most elaborate chandelier hung from the ceiling, which itself was latticed with ornate plasterwork, and on the walls were a multitude of paintings.

'Those are amazing,' Will murmured. Before him was a large marble fireplace, flanked by a pair of identical suits of armour which were holding ornate-looking maces across their breastplates. Chester joined his friend in admiring them.

'Really cool, just like Marlinspike Hall!' he agreed. 'But who lives here? Some lord?'

Drake shook his head. 'No,' he exhaled, as if what Chester had suggested couldn't be further from the truth. He went to a closed door at the side of the hallway. 'These are the rules of the house. The study is on the other side of this,' he said, slapping the door with his palm so hard that it shook on its hinges. 'On no account are you to go in here, because you might see something that allows you to identify this location. Is that understood?'

He looked around the group, fixing each of them with a stare until they nodded their agreement.

'Everywhere else in the house is fine – go where you want – but don't stray off the estate or—'

'Estate?' Will interrupted. 'Just how big *is* this place?'

'Big enough,' Drake answered cryptically. 'In fact, it's probably better if none of you wanders out of sight of the house. There may be people staying in the workers' cottages, which are a mile away in that direction.' Drake stuck a thumb towards the back of the hall. 'If they are around at the moment, they'll keep themselves to themselves, anyway. They're not the sort of people who allow anyone to see them.'

'Sounds mysterious,' Mr Rawls piped up.

As he shook his head, Drake's expression was deadly serious. 'You really don't want to mess with them,' he said. Then he lightened up. 'However, you are likely to bump into Old Wilkie, the gardener, who lives in the groundsman's lodge. He's worked for the family for years, but if you get into a conversation with him, you're only to say you're staying here as guests of the owner. Nothing more, no names and *nothing* personal. Another thing – you are not to even touch the house phone. And you are not to use mobile phones or electronic equipment of any description, not for anything. I won't have us traced here.' He took a few steps to the back of the hallway, where he peered down a corridor. 'Where's he got to?' he asked, then yelled loudly again. 'Hello, we're here!'

'No need to shout,' a tetchy voice responded, and a man emerged from another corridor. 'I'm not deaf yet, and I knew perfectly well that you were here. I opened the main gate for you, didn't I?'

The man wore a tweed jacket over a light brown waistcoat, and his trousers had leather patches on both knees. Will couldn't work out if he was in his sixties or seventies, but he was light on his feet despite the fact he was carrying a walking cane. His face was craggy and he had a full, grey-tinged beard, and his hair was surprisingly long, although he was balding on top. His eyes were lively, and twinkled as he approached Drake. He stopped in front of him, looking him over. Releasing his breath through his lips, as if he was slightly exasperated, he then began to scrutinise the rest of them. There was something in the way he sized them up that spoke of hard-won experience, as if nothing in the world could surprise him. He lingered on Mrs Burrows, the only one in the group who didn't meet his gaze.

Noticing that Will kept glancing at the full-length portrait of a man in military uniform above the fireplace, he went over to join the boy. 'That was my father. Fine-looking figure of a man, wasn't he?' he said.

Will nodded, now looking at the tartan kilt and the beige beret the figure was wearing, and also the fact that – quite out of the norm for this type of portrait – the background wasn't a darkened room or the rolling English countryside, but a sun-baked desert, complete with an oasis ringed by a few palms. 'Is that a Land Rover?' Will asked, indicating the vehicle parked by the oasis.

'Yes – they were called Pink Panthers – long before the cartoon character existed. They were kitted out for long-range reconnaissance work in the desert. My father helped with the specs of the vehicles. He was one of David Stirling's first recruits from his old crew at No 8 Commando, when he first formed The Regiment in 1941.'

Will frowned. '*The* Regiment?'

The man nodded. 'Yes, and I bet I don't have to tell you what that winged dagger on my old man's beret means, do I, lad?' He pointed at the portrait with his cane.

'Er, the SAS?' Will answered.

'Yes, that's it – the Special Air Service. It was my regiment too. It's called *The* Regiment, because it's the best damned regiment in the world, even in these namby-pamby times.'

The old man wasn't looking at the portrait any longer, but staring absently at the clean-swept grate in the fireplace. 'Stirling used to bring the men up here to train in secrecy before they were dropped behind enemy lines, on sabotage missions.' He chuckled. 'To make the exercises more realistic, all the employees on the estate at the time had to play the part of Jerry soldiers. You'll find that Old Wilkie, the only member of staff I have left these days, is still remarkably proficient in German.' The man cleared his throat with a grunt, realising he was talking too much, then swiped his cane carelessly through the air. 'But I expect you all need something to eat and drink after your journey. If you'll go through to the dining room, I'll bring you some tea and sandwiches,' he said.

'Still doing all your own cooking and washing?' Drake asked, grinning. 'Why you don't get yourself a housekeeper, I don't kn—'

'Rubbish!' the man barked. 'Waste of bloody money. When the day comes that I need some old harpy round the place, poisoning me with her fodder, I hope I'll be toes up and long in the ground.' He turned away from Drake and addressed Will and the rest of the group. 'By the way, you can call me Parry, because that's my *real* name, unlike some around here.' He twisted back to Drake, hiking an eyebrow as if something absurd had just occurred to him. 'And what in Heaven's name possessed you to call yourself after a flipping duck?'

Before anyone knew it, he'd hunched like a boxer and swung at Drake, catching him in the stomach with a full-bodied punch. Will, Chester and Elliott moved towards Drake, in case they needed to come to his assistance, but went no further as the old man backed off.

Drake was almost bent double as he tried to get his breath. But, to everyone's surprise, when he straightened up again, he was both laughing and gasping.

'You hit like a girl, you geriatric bruiser!' he wheezed.

'Hey! Watch what you're saying!' Elliott exclaimed. 'Or I'll show you how hard *this* girl can hit!'

'Oh, please,' Drake said, holding out his hand as if to fend her off, still laughing. 'I can't take the two of you on at once.' He turned to Parry. 'What was that for, anyway?'

'That,' the man boomed, 'was for not sending me a single ruddy birthday card in five years, and then ringing me completely out of the blue yesterday to ask for help, you ungrateful little bastard. You know, when I didn't hear from you, I got some of my old crew to ask around and find out what you were up to.' Parry studied the hand he'd used to strike Drake, flexing his fingers. 'They told me they couldn't find any trace of you, and that you'd probably been killed,' he said.

Drake had got his breath back, and still didn't seem to be

taking it badly that he'd been punched. Far from it – he appeared to Will to be happier than he'd ever seen him before.

Drake shook his head. 'Sorry – what with one thing and another, I've been a bit busy,' he said. 'I'll make it up to you, Dad.'

Chapter Thirty-five

'Sunday lunch!' Chester exclaimed, looking over the table at his father. 'Never thought we'd be sitting down to Sunday lunch again.'

'I don't know what to expect any more,' Mr Rawls replied rather disconsolately.

There was a second's silence until Drake intervened. 'Yes – on that note, I want you all to raise your glasses with me.' He stood up, taking his wine glass from the table, as everyone else followed his example. 'We drink a toast to all those who aren't here with us today . . . the Doc, Mrs Rawls, Sarah Jerome, Tam Macaulay, Cal, Leatherman . . . to absent – and very brave – friends.'

Everyone drank with him, then took their seats again.

'And Chester, I have something for you,' Drake said. He reached beside his chair to pick up a package, which he passed over the table to the boy.

'What is it?' Chester asked, as he tore it open. 'A skate-board! Drake – you remembered I never got one for Christmas! That's awesome!'

Drake smiled. 'You can try it out on the tennis courts. The

surface isn't great, as nobody's used them in years, but it should be good enough for skateboarding. Look in the bottom of the bag – there are some pads. I don't want you injuring yourself.' As Will and Elliott admired the gaudily coloured skateboard, Drake glanced at his wristwatch. 'Where he's got to with the food? Stubborn old mule refused to let me help.'

In the kitchen, Parry propped his walking cane by the side of the range as he put on a pair of gloves and opened the oven door. Two joints of roast beef were sizzling on a tray, which he took out and inspected. 'Perfect,' he said.

All of a sudden, Bartleby and Colly appeared either side of him. They each lunged at the joints, seizing them in their jaws and then racing off through the open back door and over the fields with their prizes.

'Bloody scavengers!' Parry shouted, brandishing his walking cane at the retreating hindquarters of the two Hunters. 'Next time I'll use my shotgun on you!'

The assembled group at the dining room table hadn't heard anything, as the kitchen was several corridors away.

'I'm going to see what he's doing,' Drake decided. 'He's probably burnt the food or something.'

'I wouldn't bother,' Mrs Burrows had just said, as Parry swung into sight in the doorway, his expression furious. 'Our main course is currently heading away across the field behind the house, and at some speed too,' she added, before Parry had had a chance to speak.

'How do you do that?' Parry asked. 'How could you possibly know?'

Mrs Burrows tapped the side of her nose with her index finger. 'ESP,' she said, as if imparting some great secret to him.

'ESP?' Parry repeated, then sank into his chair at the head of the table and downed his glass of wine in one.

'Extra Smelling Power,' Mrs Burrows laughed, as she rose to her feet. 'Come along, Drake and Jeff – you can give me a hand to fix something else for lunch.'

'Um . . . can I say something?' Chester began, and Mrs Burrows took her seat again.

Drake nodded at Chester to continue.

'Well, it's what Mrs Burrows just said about her super-power – it gave me an idea. We're all here because of the Styx – and we've achieved some incredible things, haven't we?' He looked at Drake. 'We've wiped out the source of these viruses and destroyed their labs.' Then he looked at Will and Elliott. 'And we've also got hold of the vaccine for the Dominion virus. So we're good at what we do . . . we're a special team who, together, can take on the Styx, aren't we? Like those super-hero crime-fighting teams you see in comics and films. And if we're so good, shouldn't we have a name? A bit like the X-Men or the Fantastic Four?'

'Nice speech, Chester,' Drake congratulated him.

'What were you thinking of?' Mrs Burrows asked. 'Something along the lines of the Rebel Alliance, but snappier?'

'Teenage Mutant Ninja Topsoilers?' Will put in.

Mr Rawls quickly counted how many of them there were around the table. 'Or Drake's Seven?' he chuckled.

At this Drake rolled his eyes. 'Tell you what – you lot come up with a name while I raid the kitchen,' he said.

Mrs Rawls settled down to watch the evening news. She'd just finished a long phone conversation with her sister. It was one of those concerned-relative calls, where the other person has absolutely nothing to say but takes a long time to say it. Worse still, her sister was threatening to pay her a visit, to 'look after' her.

Her sister didn't like it that Mrs Rawls was all by herself in the house, and had been for some time since her husband, Jeff, had decided to take himself on an extended trip abroad.

Mrs Rawls didn't relish lying to her own family, or anyone else for that matter, but it had to be said that when she explained her husband's absence by telling people this, none of them seemed terribly surprised. They all knew how much stress she and Mr Rawls had been under since Chester had gone missing, and these well-wishers invariably muttered the usual 'He probably just needs time to himself,' and 'He'll be back soon, you'll see,' words of comfort.

Of course, Mrs Rawls knew differently. Or, to be accurate, she didn't know where he, or her son, currently were, but she was pretty sure neither of them had gone abroad.

She leant back in her chair, trying her best to concentrate on the television, but her mind insisted on wandering.

She'd told Drake she couldn't just stand by as her son, and then latterly her husband, did their bit in the fight against the Styx. On the mobile phone Drake had given her, which her husband didn't know she had, she'd talked long about her commitment, and how she was slowly going mad in the hotel, until Drake capitulated and came up with something she could do.

And the plan had been that she would act as if she was still under the grip of her Dark Light programming, and simply return to her home in Highfield. From there, she'd report any contact with the Styx or their agents to Drake using a dead letterbox procedure. This would entail leaving notes for him in the local newsagent's when she popped down there every morning to pick up the daily paper.

Of course, the plan wasn't infallible.

The Styx could simply 'disappear' her, as Drake put it. Or they might decide to give her a Dark Light booster, so she was really back under its control again.

But, on the other hand, if the Styx thought she was still fully programmed and could be useful to them, either as a link to Chester and hence to Drake, or if they chose to deploy her in some role, it was invaluable intel. And that, as Drake had explained to her, was hard to come by where the Styx were concerned.

As the news finished and the weather report began on the television, Mrs Rawls heard a noise behind her. The sound of someone moving across the carpet.

Her heart skipped a beat.

Is this it? she thought to herself. From where she was sitting, with her back to the door, she had no way of seeing who was there. Despite the urge to turn around, she didn't move a muscle. She tried to remain calm – she had to behave as if she was still Darklit.

A voice spoke in her ear – a low, breathy voice. It had an accent – maybe a touch of Cockney about it.

'We've got something we want you to d—' it rumbled.

The sentence was never completed as she heard a dull thud.

She wheeled around in time to see a hefty man crash to the floor, his dark glasses spinning off his face as he landed. He was wearing a coat with a waxy finish and he had a flat cap on his head. He'd been carrying a box, which now lay beside him.

And standing over him was another man of much slighter build – someone who looked like the Styx Drake had described. But this man was wearing a sports jacket and a pair of flannel trousers, and although his face was cadaverously thin and his eyes intense, the overall impression was that he wasn't some killer from the underground city she'd been told about.

'Mrs Rawls – Emily,' he said, offering her his hand, which was a little curious considering he'd just poleaxed a man in her sitting room.

'Yes,' she replied, shaking it.

He came around and sat on the arm of the sofa by her.

'Drake sent me. I don't know if you remember me, but I accompanied him here before.'

She frowned.

'It was when you and Mr Rawls were unable to recognise Chester, because you'd been Darklit. By the way, have you overcome the programming completely?'

He didn't wait for a response from her, uttering some words in a strange, rasping language that Mrs Rawls couldn't begin to understand. She gave him a small shrug.

'Seems as though you have,' the man concluded. He got to his feet. 'You need to come with me now. Drake's plan hasn't worked out.' He glanced down at the felled figure on the carpet. 'That's a Colonist, and he was sent to activate you.'

Mrs Rawls also rose to her feet, looking at the unconscious man. 'Activate me? What for? And what's in that box?' she asked, pointing at the grey box, which was around twenty centimetres square.

'I don't know what they were going to make you do, but the box probably has something harmful in it. Probably not a bio weapon, but it could be a bomb,' he said, picking it up and putting it under his arm. 'Either way, it's too dangerous for you to stay here any longer. You're to leave with me, Mrs Rawls.'

'Yes, er, Mr . . .' she said, frowning as she wondered how to address this man who had come into her house and saved her.

'How very rude of me. My name is Edward Green,' the man told her. 'But, please, call me Eddie. Everyone does.'

Chapter Thirty-six

Will, Chester and Elliott were down by the edge of the lake when Will heard his name being called.

'I think Drake wants you,' Elliott said, spotting how he was beckoning Will over.

Will climbed the slope up to the house, joining Drake by the table and chairs on the terrace.

'Have you just got back?' Will said. Drake had been going off for two or three days at a time, but would never tell anyone what he'd been doing.

Drake nodded.

Will saw he still had his holdall slung over his shoulder. For some reason Will assumed that Drake had brought him a present, just as he'd done when he'd given Chester the skateboard.

'Is that something for me?' Will asked expectantly, pointing at the holdall.

But Drake didn't answer, and as Will saw the man was being uncharacteristically hesitant, he realised that this wasn't the case, and became quite alarmed. 'What's wrong?' he said, but again Drake didn't answer, taking the holdall from his shoulder and placing it on the table. He unzipped the top and opened it up to delve inside.

'I don't know quite how to tell you this, Will,' Drake said, as he took out a white carrier bag, but kept it in his hand. 'Let's sit down, shall we?'

Will pulled one of the chairs from under the table and sat in it, waiting for Drake to continue.

'You know you asked me to deliver your father's journal to the British Museum. You wanted to get it into the hands of someone qualified to understand it, someone who could present your father's incredible discoveries to the world.'

'Yes,' Will murmured, not liking the sound of this at all.

'I don't have to tell you, the big problem is that there's no physical proof to go alongside the journal. I mean, it wasn't as if you could have brought any artefacts or specimens back with you, to support all the claims your father made in it.'

By this stage, Will felt fit to burst. He had to know what had happened. 'Drake, just tell me – I don't care if it's bad news. I'm ready for it.' He glanced at the white carrier bag. 'What's in there?'

Drake held his hand up. 'Please, let me finish.'

'Okay,' Will grimaced.

'Apparently your father's journal was examined by several specialists in the various departments of antiquities at the museum, then somehow it found its way to a Professor White at London University.'

'Professor White,' Will mumbled several times, then suddenly leapt to his feet. 'I know that name!' he exclaimed. 'No! He's the creep who took all the credit for the Roman villa Dad found in Highfield. He nicked it from my dad. No, not him!'

'Sit down, Will,' Drake said firmly. 'I haven't finished yet.'

Will's face was flushed red and he was breathless with indignation. Nevertheless he took his seat again as Drake resumed. 'Turns out Professor White rather liked what he read, and turned it over to two of his students. And they wrote a book.'

'What sort of book?' Will demanded.

Drake opened the carrier bag and glanced inside. 'It's the first novel this pair have had published. You know better than anyone that what survived of the Doc's first journal is probably still in Martha's shack, where you left it. And at the beginning of his second journal – the one you brought back with you – the Doc tried to recreate a day-by-day record of the events building up to the discovery of the Colony, and everything that came afterwards.' Drake took a breath. 'Anyway, these two students were so inspired by what they read, they came up with a whole story based on it.'

'They did what?' Will said, although he could barely speak, he was so tense. 'So it's an academic book, then?'

'Um . . . not quite,' Drake replied, as he took the book from the bag and passed it to Will, who grabbed it and studied the cover.

'*The Highfield Mole*,' Will read. '*The Highfield Mole?*' he repeated several times. He flipped the book over to look at what was written on the back.

'You see – it's a children's book,' Drake told him. 'They turned your father's journal into an adventure story, for younger readers.'

Even though they were still by the lake, Chester and Elliott heard Will's scream from the top of the slope.

'NOOOOOOOOOO!'

Epilogue

Parry's voice echoed through the house as he summoned everyone. It sounded urgent.

'What's all the panic?' Will said, as Chester met him in the corridor outside their bedrooms.

'Don't know,' Chester shrugged, as he spotted that his friend had his new book with him. 'You're actually reading it – can I borrow it after you? Is it any good?' he asked.

Will pulled a face in response. 'It's like some weird dream. You're welcome to it when I've finished,' he said.

As the boys reached the top of the main stairs, Elliott flew out of her bedroom. She was wearing a bathrobe and a towel was wound around her head – after a life of only the most basic of facilities, she'd decided the bathroom was her favourite place. Much like any teenage girl, she would spend hours locked away in there, relaxing in the bath, or doing her hair in the mirror.

Now, as they trooped into the drawing room, they saw that Drake and Parry were standing in front of the television, transfixed by what they were watching. Chester peered into the hallway to see if his father was coming, but there was no sign of him. At that point Mrs Burrows tore in.

'Why all the commotion?' she asked, as she stopped beside Will.

'My father just had a tip-off from a contact in the security services. Something's going down in London,' Drake replied, turning up the volume with the remote. 'Something big.'

'. . . among these initiatives was the order for the immediate closure of the three infection response departments, and the transfer of their key staff to a single "super unit" at University College Hospital,' the news presenter was saying. 'This order came straight from the top, from the Prime Minister himself, according to sources close to Number Ten.'

The Prime Minister was then shown at a packed press conference. 'We're all aware, in these times of severe economic hardship, of the pressing need to trim public spending,' he said. 'As a result of our in-depth review of the health budget, we have identified a number of areas in our hospitals that will benefit from centralisation and rationalisation. These will produce substantial savings for the country, with no reduction in the very high standards of patient care and treatment we have set ourselves.'

The news presenter's voice resumed over a clip of the Prime Minister, his face tired and drawn, as he slid into his chauffeur-driven car. 'Today's announcement that such important facilities have been earmarked for closure came as a complete surprise, even to many junior health ministers. A formal protest was lodged this morning by the British Medical Association at the lack of consultation on the Government's decision to shut, in particular, the infection response units . . .' There followed scenes of men carrying sealed containers from a hospital building and loading them into a lorry. '. . . and the speed at which the closures are already taking place.'

'I don't believe it. That's St. Edmund's,' Drake realised. Then a further two hospitals were shown, their main entrances flashing up on the screen in quick succession. 'Well, what do you know – there are St Thomas' and the London. What a coincidence!' he added, then turned to Elliott and the boys. 'Why, at a time when the outbreak of a serious epidemic is so widely feared, would the Government take it upon themselves to hamstring the country's ability to deal with one? Why would they do that?'

'But what exactly does all this mean?' Chester asked.

'It means the Styx,' Will answered.

'Has to be,' Drake agreed. 'It's too much of a coincidence that this has happened to precisely the three hospitals I provided with samples of Elliott's blood, for safekeeping in their vaccine banks. The Styx are making their move and snatching back the Dominion vaccine – you just see, no doubt those specimens will mysteriously disappear en route to the new "super unit".'

'But we've still got our specimen here, haven't we?' Will said, patting Elliott's shoulder.

'That makes you a very important person,' Chester added, looking at Elliott in her bathrobe.

'Thought I was, anyway,' she complained.

Drake wasn't listening to the three of them as he considered the implications. 'Of course, by crippling our Topsoil facilities, the board will be cleared for the Styx. You can bet they've got more surprises up their sleeves – some more nasty diseases to spread – because that's exactly what they've been doing to us for centuries.'

'But if the Prime Minister really pushed this decision through, do you think he himself has been Darklit?' Mrs

Burrows posed. Her question was never answered as Parry waved his cane at the television.

'Here we are,' he announced, as the report on the hospitals was interrupted, and BREAKING NEWS appeared at the top of the screen.

Will frowned. 'You mean the thing about the hospitals wasn't why you called us in here?' he asked.

Drake shook his head. 'That was the first we'd heard of it.'

'Quiet everybody!' Parry barked. 'Here it comes.'

Will and Chester gave each other baffled looks, then watched the television screen as the picture broke up for a second before a reporter appeared. It was evident that she wasn't in the studio, and that the incident was being covered by a hastily-arranged outside broadcast.

The reporter was in a street lined with tall glass buildings, while behind her frightened-looking people were running in all directions. Most of them were office workers, but there was also a handful of armed policemen. The reporter seemed flustered and unprepared as she spoke. 'I'm . . . I'm here in the City of London – at the heart of the financial district – and no more than half a kilometre away, at the Bank of England itself, it appears that a gun battle is under way.' Somebody off-screen spoke to her. 'And I've just been told we've obtained a film taken by a member of the public on their mobile phone.'

A jerky and rather poor quality clip began which showed a street blocked by police cars. With the sound of automatic gunfire, policemen hastily took shelter behind their vehicles.

Then the camera zoomed beyond these vehicles, to the normally busy intersection right in the very centre of the City, where the Bank of England was based in a building called the Royal Mint. All of a sudden, there was a massive explosion, and windows were blown out of the building, accompanied by the sound of more gunfire. The reporter began to speak over the remainder of the clip, which showed smoke billowing across the deserted street. 'This film, taken less than twenty minutes ago, appears to show an attack on the Bank of England by a gang of armed gunmen.'

The reporter was back on the screen again. 'We are also hearing that fighting has broken out in several other locations in the City, and that—'

There was another explosion and the reporter ducked. Then the screen was filled with static until it went blank. A second later, the news presenter in the studio came on again.

'We seem to have lost the link with our OB van. I hope Jenny is okay,' he said, frowning. Clearing his throat, he pretended to glance at his papers as he collected himself, then looked up. 'So for any viewers that have just joined us, we are receiving numerous reports of armed attacks on the Bank of England and in several nearby locations, and of at least two major explosions.' He held his hand to his earpiece. 'I've just been informed that a meeting of the Governor of the Bank of England and his senior advisory committee was sitting in the Bank at the time the attack began . . . and that numerous casualties are expected, which may include the Governor himself. Although I should point out that this is unconfirmed at the present time.'

Drake shook his head. 'So this is the start of it all. The Styx are attempting to destabilise the country by attacking its major City institutions,' he said quietly. 'This could tip us into another doozy of a recession, like nothing we've ever seen before.'

The news presenter continued. 'These are some enhanced

CCTV stills just sent to us by the police. They show the occupants of two separate vehicles who entered the City just prior to the incidents. The police are asking for anyone with information about these men to come . . .'

'Colonel Bismarck!' Elliott burst out. 'Will, look, it's the Colonel!'

Stepping forward, Will stared at the slightly fuzzy images of two faces taken through vehicle windscreens. One of the men meant nothing to him, although with his light-coloured hair and square jaw he certainly could have been a New Germanian soldier. However, the other face was familiar – the man was older than the first, and he had a very distinctive moustache. 'It could be him,' Will said. 'But it's not that clear, and I wasn't taking much in after Dad died.'

'It's him,' Elliott insisted. 'I know it.'

'So they're using soldiers from the inner world to do their dirty work now,' Mrs Burrows suggested.

'Which means they might have the whole New Germanian war machine at their disposal,' Drake said. 'The whole damned army.'

'And the Rebecca twins could be back in town,' Will added grimly.

But everybody in the room was shocked into silence by the photograph that flashed up next.

'Drake! It's you!' Elliott gasped.

Drake took a step back from the television.

'This individual,' the news presenter said, 'is believed to be behind the group mounting the attacks, and the police have gone as far to say that he's the "brains" of the organisation. Going under the assumed name of Drake, he's thought to still be in the country, and a national manhunt to find him has been initiated by regional police forces.'

'Classic manoeuvre – only to be expected,' Parry said gruffly. 'The Styx are making it difficult for you to move around.'

Drake nodded. 'Guess I won't be the one going down to the shops from now on.'

A bleary-eyed Mr Rawls chose that moment to make his entrance. He stifled a yawn, as if he'd just woken from a nap. 'Got the cricket on?' he asked, scratching his head. 'What's the latest score?'

'I'm not sure, Dad,' Chester replied, 'but it looks like the Styx are having a good run.'

Acknowledgements

I am indebted to . . .

The great Barry Cunningham, publisher and editor, who started this whole thing. While there may not be any acts of magic in the stories, he sure as hell performs them in the real world.

The team at Chicken House: Rachel Hickman, Elinor Bagenal, Imogen Cooper, Mary Byrne, Claire Skuse, Nicki Marshall, and Steve Wells for his fantastic design work on the books. And Siobhan McGowan of Scholastic Inc.

Friend and agent, Catherine Pellegrino of Rogers, Coleridge & White.

Simon Wilkie, Karen Everitt, Craig Turner and Charles Landau, who make it all possible.

Sophie, George and Frankie, for putting up with me.

And to Hanif, who told me that it should never be easy. He was right. And it isn't.

st, 'The Secret Sits' from *Quantula* in *Robert Frost: Poems* (The Penguin Poets, 1955); Andy McCluskey ul Humphries, lyrics from *I Betray My Friends* by chestral Manoeuvres in the Dark (1980), which appears on *Navigations: The OMD B-Sides Compilation* (2001); Johann Beuys & Andras Warhola, retelling of the seventeenth-century 'German Book of Catastrophes' from *Folk Traditions of Old Germany, Volume 6* (Lehmbruck & Ernst, 1909).

Every effort has been made to trace or contact all copyright holders. The publishers would be pleased to rectify any errors or omissions brought to their notice, at the earliest opportunity.